W9-AHR-891

Mr. Big

DANIEL FORBES

Coward, McCann & Geoghegan, Inc.
New York

SBN: 698-10656-3
Library of Congress Catalog Card Number: 74-30600

Printed in the United States of America

Mr. Big

one

"Mr. Charles Taylor."

Mr. Charles Taylor, dry of mouth, walked forward. The voice that cued him was not a toastmaster's or the bawled cockney of a master of ceremonies at a title fight. It was nasal and polite, conversational even, a voice that had never raised itself; not at any rate since the playing fields of Eton or subsequently perhaps, once or twice, in fraught moments astride a polo pony.

Which of the functionaries the summons came from Taylor was not sure. He did not hesitate but walked from the turquoise and gold of the south gallery through the gold and white of open glass doors and into the ballroom. He kept on walking, silently counting, across the crimson. *Three, four, five. . . .* Everywhere was crimson and white and gold. Above his head hung chandeliers like porcelain bombs. The smell was of marble, sunbursts of spring flowers and furniture polish. In the musicians' gallery the band of the Royal Marines played a Strauss waltz, and in the momentary pauses between phrases, from the white chairs on his right, from the triple-decker crimson benches against three walls, came rustlings and coughings as from a theater audience. He strode stiff-legged, interminably, with soundless footfalls.

Eight, nine, ten.

Suddenly Taylor was shivering. Twelve he'd been aiming for, the nasal bugger with the braid had said twelve paces approximately, but already he was level with the blurred dais; if he kept on, he'd be through the doors opposite, a historic case, written up for laughs in gossip paragraphs, if he wasn't stoned to death for the insolence. He turned, stepped toward the dais, and bowed the practiced bow.

In hacking jacket, smoking jacket, brushed topper, Kew house, the slate bathroom of his flat in Grosvenor Square, wherever and however in the past weeks he had found himself alone, he had caught himself bowing to mirrors. Formal bowing, nonchalant bowing, bowing-in-depth, arse jaunty as a mooring buoy, the bow that cringed, the bow Prussian, and on occasion, when all this had become too ridiculous, the Ali Baba bow, fingers sweeping downward from declining forehead, and the camp cavalier bow, left leg forward, right knee flexed, arms circling, wrists fluttering. Once, naked in the slate bathroom, the door bolted against the unlikely entry of Phoebe or Mrs. Barnett, he had knelt for the knighthood that was not to be his, or not yet. Sliding a towel down the steamed mirror, he had scowled at the man sliding a towel downward, kneeling on one knee, on two knees, not knowing how the kneeling was performed, and tossing the towel aside in disgust.

Now, bowing, averting his eyes from the shins and ankles in front, he glimpsed the tip of the tail of his morning coat. He straightened up. There came a light handshake, and she was smiling, speaking of charities.

Behind her were twin thrones, equerries in morning suits, and a remote red-and-black blaze of Beefeaters. Behind and above, too high above for him to allow his eyes to lift, was a velvet canopy, crimson and gold-embroidered. Taylor heard himself saying, "It's a question of doing what one can, Your Majesty," and she was hanging the medal on the hook which had been pinned to his lapel by the braided ponce in the south gallery. Before his eyes the glint on the bodice of the woolen day dress was from a square diamond—Taylor had never seen such a diamond—and hanging from it a second, heavier diamond, a giant's teardrop, big as a baby pear.

But it was accomplished, because she had stepped back, and an equerry was studying foolscap for the next name.

Taylor took a pace back and bowed. He right-turned and walked over the crimson, past audience rustlings, through the gold and white of doors, into the north gallery.

"This way, sir."

"Thank you," Taylor said, gracious as royalty.

He craved a cigarette, but at the end of the gallery a second flunky in knee breeches and a black jacket with gold trim ushered him back into the ballroom, to a white chair with red satin cover among the rustling spectators. Ahead, beyond the backs of bare male heads and female hats, a stout woman, a defeated Member of Parliament whom Taylor had met at fund-raising parties, was curtsying before the Queen.

The rustlings had ceased; the Royal Marines were silent between tunes. All that was audible was a tension as with courageous deliberation the matron sank on protesting knees and spread her skirts. More quickly, and listing, she rose up again. Coughing and sighing signaled an end to suspense. "If I Were a Rich Man" played the band. Taylor looked toward the upper gallery for a sight of Phoebe and Ann. Fingernails were scraping at his wrist; a voice was whispering rowdily in his ear.

"Time, old boy, d'you know the time?"

Taylor tucked back his cuff and lifted his wrist to his neighbor. The man blinked watery eyes, muttered, and twisted about in his chair as though in search of confirmation from some palace clock. The space between stringy neck and starched Edwardian collar was wide enough to have dropped a golfball down. Suspended from a red ribbon the newly hooked medal was a star with lions and wreath. Order of the Bath, thought Taylor, guessing: he's a bloody general, or earl, must be, he'll have seen fifty investitures. Taylor resented and envied the man's detachment.

"Train's the one fifteen," came the shouted whisper. The earl had taken Taylor into his confidence. "Waterloo. If I miss it, the next one's four o'clock. What?"

"You'll catch it all right," whispered Taylor.

He spotted Ann first. She was nudging her mother and flapping furtive fingers at him, mouth open in a grin which revealed the brace she detested. Phoebe raised her eyebrows in his direction and smiled. Not only was she getting away with the cloche hat she had bought for tenpence at the St. Winefride's jumble sale, but if the press photographers outside got their lenses on it, she'd be launching a cloche revival. For looks there was not a bird in the ballroom, not in fifty miles, to hold a candle to her. She looked in the jumble sale hat like Lady Diana Cooper, and the Astor girls, and Gertrude Lawrence, and all the drawing-room beauties in the twenties biographies on his library shelves. If only, Taylor thought, looks were all. His wife was no longer regarding him, but his daughter was, grinning with white wired teeth. He lifted his hand six inches in salutation.

Ten years' time, Taylor promised himself, he'd be back. Eating off gold plate with the top geezers. Sir Charles Taylor. The ballroom, Buckingham Palace, it was right here they had the banquets. He'd be sixty. Sir Charles. Lord Taylor, maybe. Your lordship.

A chair creaked as his acquaintance, the stout woman, sat. Beside him the earl had put on glasses and was holding against them a British Rail timetable, turning pages and talking to himself. Ahead, a woman in a forgettable hat was curtsying and departing, bemedaled. A new name was called. Through the glass doors strode a robed African: gleaming black, sandaled, grave as a judge. A half dozen medals and handshakes later, shortly before noon, the ceremony ended. In the musicians' gallery the band played "God Save the Queen."

Taylor moved with the slow throng down a staircase flanked by cuirassed Household Cavalry. In his folded palm he held a cigarette, which he lit the instant he stepped into the sharp March air. In the quadrangle newspaper photographers and television crews were priming their cameras. Through the quadrangle, in the palace forecourt, more cameras waited. The guard mounting was over and many of the sightseers had drifted away along the Mall and into the daffodils in Green Park. But several score with nothing better to do, aware that an investiture had taken place, remained outside the railings, peering in. They badgered the police constables for names and unslung their own Pentaxes and Yashicas.

The accredited cameramen captured the posed smiles of two national heroes: a solicitor's clerk from Edinburgh, a diabetic, who had rowed a rubber life raft single-handed around the world; and a British golfer who had been minting money for himself on the American circuit. There was further mileage from two new knights, a carefully uncombed poet, a Scotland Yard detective decorated for bravery, and the routine flurry of civil servants, trade union leaders, Commonwealth diplomats, and frail photogenic postmistresses from the Hebrides. As a boring rich man, an unexceptional property developer, Taylor was neglected and satisfied to be so. Only the *Times,* a newspaper of record, called to him.

"Would you hold it there, Mr. Taylor? In a bit please, Mrs. Taylor. Bit more. Yes, and the little girl, good, in just a bit. That's it."

Click.

The cameraman whipped out pencil and pad. Certainly, he agreed, scribbling, he'd send a print. "Ch Taylor OBE. Mrs. Phoebe. Ann 10 daught." The cameraman moved off fast. A photographer from the *Evening Standard* had drawn Phoebe aside and was snapping her from urgently assorted angles. *Click click click click.*

He doesn't know who she is, yet, Taylor thought, but he knows what he's doing. Close to, in the thin sunlight, she looked less like Gertrude Lawrence. At least she was sober. Ann was on tiptoe, leaning against him and turning the medal over.

"Does it have a box? Who are the pictures? Is that King Philip? Not Philip, *you* know, who was it? Can I have the box?" She read aloud the inscription. "'For God and the Empire.'"

"Let's get home, sweetheart. Tell Mummy."

An agency photographer had appeared beside the man from the *Evening Standard* and was eyeing Phoebe with a worried look, uncertain whether she was front page or a waste of film. Laughter clanged from a lionized group, the poet and his family, assaulted by cameras. The agency photographer posed Phoebe and Ann. Taylor had made a half dozen paces toward the cars parked beyond the Privy Seal entrance when a voice said, "You're looking old, Charlie. You can still give yourself up."

Taylor halted. The man carried his gray topper in one hand and with the other was unpinning the medal from his lapel. He had bony cheeks, a jutting arc of a nose, and sparse sandy hair in need of advice and something revivifying from a barber's. His complexion was colorless, undernourished, as though he might have been living in a submarine, refusing food. But he was not stunted. Even over Taylor, who was six feet tall, he had a height advantage of several inches. Taylor had to look up. Before entering the submarine the man might have been a guardsman or wrestler.

"Do I know you?" Taylor said.

"I think about you often, Charlie. I owe you an apology." The man placed the medal in its box and the box in a pocket of his hired morning suit. "It's a laugh"—he did not laugh—"but I honestly used to think you were our Mr. Brains behind that spot of bother. Truth is you were past it, Charlie, even then. Twelve years, isn't it?"

"I can bust you, Poole."

"What are you now—fifty? Maybe you had the brains, Charlie, but you were past it. Villains like you, I see it all the time, you age fast. By forty your judgment's gone, by fifty your nerve."

"No pension, Poole. I can crack you in two. Think about it. Just your tin medal and memories."

"Course, if I'm wrong, if it *was* you—and we both know it was, don't we, Charlie?—it's not too late. Make restitution. One signature on a check, Charlie, another on the confession, you'll be surprised. We've one or two soft judges since your day, happen you'll get off with seven. No more strain."

"The only strain is you, copper."

The voices of both men were without expression. Their faces competed in impassivity. Nothing was given away except contempt. Taylor noticed Phoebe and Ann approaching. He turned away from the policeman.

"Slicker gets out today," Poole said.

Taylor looked back, which was an error. The only technique for Poole and his remarks was to ignore them. Could it be, Taylor wondered, the copper was right, that nerve and judgment were falling away? Ten years ago he'd not have looked back.

"Today or tomorrow, isn't it?" Poole said. "Expect you'll be having a bit of a reunion."

"Who will?" said Phoebe. "Hullo. I remember you, don't I? Congratulations. We've been reading all about you, haven't we, Charles? Such a very painful experience. I mean yours—those ghastly hoodlums."

"Ma'am?"

"You used to call round, years ago, when we first moved in at Kew. Security and burglars and things. Sergeant, ah, um—"

"Inspector Poole," Taylor said, and took his wife's arm.

"Chief inspector," murmured Poole.

"I'm afraid I'm always going to think of you as sergeant, Sergeant. Like first love, remembering the beloved as he was, all dewy and magical, never as he became." Confused, Phoebe grimaced. "That's really a kind of compliment if you can figure it out. Congratulations on the gallantry. Where's the medal? Hiding its blushes?"

"Darling, Mr. Poole's in a hurry to get back to the Yard or somewhere."

"Good-bye, Mrs. Taylor. Charlie—"

Taylor was already walking away. Ann caught up and loped alongside. Who was that man? Did she *have* to go to school this afternoon? Honestly, there was a record she needed *desperately;* she could do that instead, if she had the money. Taylor, half listening, took out his wallet. They crunched across gravel to the parked cars.

"Grosvenor Square," he told Martin. "Then take my wife on to Kew."

"We could have lunch," Phoebe said.

"Thought you had a St. Winefride's meeting."

"Not till three. Take us somewhere you can wear your medal. Let's all go to the Savoy. I want to be seen."

"I'm sorry, I've a business lunch," Taylor lied.

Martin, peak-capped, chauffeured the Rolls Corniche through the gates and turned left for Constitution Hill. Beside him sat Ann. She had snapped her seat belt shut and was bending forward, twiddling the stereo for pop music. There were lambswool rugs, fridge, and radiotelephone. Taylor looked back through the rear window.

"Don't tell me he's spoiled your day," Phoebe said.

"Who?"

"That cop. Why so cross all of a sudden?"

"What're you talking about?"

"Hardly the urbane Mr. Taylor we all know and love. You haven't been embezzling fivers from Charles Taylor Limited?"

"They're my fivers." He turned his head away from her and put a cigarette between his lips. "I don't follow you."

"You were pretty brusque with him, poor man. Thought maybe you had a guilty conscience."

"You're not making any sense. I'll telephone you about six." He wanted to know, but without touching his temples, if he were sweating. He kept his head turned aside so that she would not see how her prattle had struck home. "We can take in a movie."

He blew smoke against the window. They had entered Hyde Park Corner at a moment when the traffic was hesitant and disorderly, only taxis and the red double-decker buses seeming sure of their direction. From the

Corniche's stereo a man suffering from thrombosis was exclaiming rhythmically. Martin insinuated between and past dithering cars and into Park Lane.

"Ann, turn that noise down," Taylor said.

"I can't, it's number three on the hit parade."

"Martin, turn it off please."

"Charming," Ann said, lowering the volume.

"So do we go ahead with your birthday supper," Phoebe said, "or will it be business with the board of directors?"

"Don't be like that."

In Grosvenor Square he kissed the high rounded cheekbone, then leaned forward to kiss the crown of Ann's head. So that she would miss none of the pullulating bedlam from the stereo, should her father choose this moment to speak to her, Ann leaned forward too, away from him. The moment Martin opened the rear door from outside she raised the volume.

Taylor threw his cigarette on the pavement and watched the Corniche glide away.

"Mornin', Mr. Taylor." The porter, onetime steeplechase jockey, four times married, opened the lift door. "And 'eartiest congratulations, if you don't mind me sayin' so. Very well deserved indeed, sir."

"Thanks, Harry."

"And 'ow is 'Er Majesty?"

"Fine. We talked a bit." The tremor in his hands was barely perceptible when, in the lift, he lit a fresh cigarette. But there should have been no tremor at all. There'd been none half an hour ago, before Poole; not even a couple of hours ago, poised in the south gallery, dry-mouthed, while the ponce with the braid and stuffed-up nose had lectured about steps forward, steps backward, and the protocol of "Yes, Ma'am, no, Ma'am."

But it wasn't every day you walked into the copper who'd driven himself halfway around the bend, and most of the way around the world, trying to put you away for the biggest and brightest tickle in the history of British crime, which was how one of the newspapers had described the Great Train Robbery.

Which newspaper? Taylor tried to remember. For a time, riskily, he had hoarded newspaper cuttings, even though none had mentioned his name, or known it, and they'd had to make do with Mr. Big.

He frowned at his hand, jiggling the key into the lock of his penthouse flat.

Urbane, she'd said. Bored would have been nearer the mark. Bored rancid. If only she knew.

Poole knew nothing either, or rather he knew, but he could do nothing about it, never had been able to and never would, because there was no evidence and nothing to be done. While the rest of the team had scarpered to the four winds, and much good it had done them, Charles Taylor was the one who had stayed put, anonymous, protected by brains and class and loot. Did Poole really believe that suddenly, at fifty, he'd become vulnerable? That his nerve had gone? That he couldn't do it all again if he chose? That at a whiff of a copper's breath he'd be off, wetting himself, escaping in dark glasses with a rug around his legs on the promenade deck of an ocean cruise?

The only reason he'd ever budge further from the West End than Kew, or Cheltenham races, would be precisely to have Poole and his Heavy Mob floundering after and so enjoy again the pleasure of eluding them. A touch of edge and pace to life. A sprinkle of spice into the big yawn.

Out of the question. The hell with Poole.

Taylor hung up the morning suit, sweated for ten minutes on the rowing machine in the gymnasium, then bathed in the slate and mosaic bathroom that remained his pride, though there'd been well-bred creeps who'd chanced their arms by hinting with smiles and jokey enthusiasm that they'd thought it vulgar. The most fashionable young man of the house-beautiful magazines had designed it for a fee higher than the cost of building it. At least, he'd been the most fashionable at the time. Probably retired by now, living in Tangier off the fee from the Charles Taylor bathroom. Taylor selected slacks and a check shirt that would have aroused winces among the true blues at Booker's Club, and in the kitchen plugged in the kettle for tea.

Cups had accumulated in both sinks, but that was what cups did when you chose privacy in preference to staff and you restricted Mrs. Barnett's moppings and dustings to a couple of sessions per week. A month after moving in he had handed the resident staff three months' wages and sacked them, because if Phoebe wasn't going to use the place he certainly wasn't having strangers cluttering it. Some people knew what to do with servants because they were born to it, but he hadn't been, and apart from Martin he wasn't interested. At the same time he needed Grosvenor Square because when life meant keeping up a glossy spectrum of fronts, Grosvenor Square was one glossy front he needed. If Phoebe was so deep into committees and quiet gins and church shenanigans in Kew that she couldn't live anywhere else, that was that. They talked on the telephone, and when they were available to each other he commuted, and they managed. No denying Kew was better for Ann. So he'd had the staff quarters in Grosvenor Square converted into a gymnasium, and if he invited to dinner and bridge a few useful lordships from Booker's Club, staff could be hired; as he'd hired Alain from Claridge's in those long-ago days of the Sussex country house, before he'd realized with amazement and relief that he hated the country and loathed the house and that Phoebe was much of the same mind, and they had abandoned the beamed chintzy horror and its wandering extensions and stabling and verdant landscape to field mice and trainee burglars.

Meanwhile, Mrs. Barnett had learned to leave the Orange Pekoe and Lapsang Souchong and stale coffee beans at the back of the cupboard and keep the India teabags by the kettle. He could make tea, which was probably more than could be said of some of their lordships, and now he did so; a pint of rust-colored transport café brew which he carried to the green drawing room.

The carpet was cucumber green, the walls a beige hessian almost totally hidden under William Roberts paintings worth at the last valuation seventy thousand pounds. In a far corner stood a boudoir grand piano in shiny rosewood, recommended by the salesman on the telephone and delivered unseen in the Harrods van. Taylor sat by a window from where he could look down through the leafless sycamores onto President Roosevelt and the shaved lawns. He put the tea and his medal on the table.

Deliberately all this had taken time. Bathing, pottering, teamaking. Now, instead of looking down on Grosvenor Square, he spread his hands and studied them. The tremor had gone.

Just the same, brooded Taylor. The hell with Poole and his Heavies. The hell with medal winners, lordships, everyone. Except Ann, and Phoebe. And his Mum.

The digs about his age and nerve had got to him; so, he reasoned, he was vulnerable after all. Of course he was. Everyone was. The Queen was vulnerable, and army generals, and adoring Oscar winners, and directors of Shell, and Arab sheikhs, and the Pope. The Yank Presidents like the one below with the pigeon streaks on his skull and cape, they were more vulnerable than anyone. The higher, the more vulnerable, it was an inflexible rule, until you got to the top branch, a sitting squirrel against a blank sky and exposed to everyone with a rock to throw. So why did he keep climbing?

To increase the insurance against sleuths like Poole? To build the ramparts higher? He was long beyond discovery. To escape the yawning boredom of gentility and the apologies that sorry, no, but he didn't shoot or ride to hounds? The higher he climbed the more balls-achingly genteel and boring it all became.

He surveyed his steady hands. The strain was less now than in the first years after the train coup. Then the danger had been the yearning to win applause by dropping hints, even by openly bragging, and often enough on the bad days, after a session with the copper Vibart and that pup Poole, the urge to cut and run and join the remnants of the team in Mexico City or Montreal. But he'd rooted himself at home in Fulham, then in Kew, a married man, and forced on himself a monk's silence. Discipline plus nerve plus brains, these were the impregnable combination. He'd been patient with the law, faked outrage with the Sunday newspaper reporter who'd thought he was on to something, and concentrated what was left of his energies on acquiring respectability, a patina of manners and education, and doubling, trebling, quadrupling his half million of train loot. That had been the easiest bit of the whole ludicrous business, swelling the bank balance. You shoveled the money into where it would grow, like land and property, and it grew like weeds in a hothouse. You became a citizen of substance and standing. The upper crust came to you for a loan. They opened their doors. The strain diminished.

But still after a dozen years there was strain. What'd Poole said? Give yourself up, no more strain? The bugger had insight.

There was strain and isolation and of all things a nostalgia which at times became an ache. Trouble was, you grew up lower middle class, as the sociologists called it, which meant Walls' frozen steak-and-kidney for tea, and bloodying the noses of the Liverpool yobs who came howling down for the Chelsea match, but when suddenly you had the loot and began to educate yourself and to jump the ladder two rungs at a time, you no longer knew who you were. You knew you'd never go back to the gungy streets, but you despised the world you'd hauled yourself into, and when you played along with it, aped its attitudes, drank Montrachet and ordered your pies by telephone, you came close to despising yourself or at best losing yourself. The gungy streets semaphored a weird appeal across the years.

Taylor got up and went to the record cabinet. He picked through a yard of seventy-eights: Jessie Matthews singing "Gangway," the Casa Loma Orchestra's "Malady in F," Ambrose and vocal crooning "Love Is the Sweetest Thing" and "Auf Wiedersehen, My Dear."

A tough study all right for the professors, he thought; a case history of climbing from lower to upper, skipping out the middle. Poole was right for the wrong reasons. There was strain but not from fear, or not chiefly. The trouble was in dumping the patched and smelling coat which had fitted and trying on the new hand-stitched Harris which itched at the back of the neck and cut into the armpits.

Or to be specific the suits of black, blue, or dark gray which were the only colors, he'd learned early on, that could be worn by a gentleman. With matching socks and handmade shoes. Brown of any shade being social death. And Taylor admitted to himself that he'd not venture into St. James's or the City in this present gear of slacks and check shirt.

Sport he'd not compromised on because there were limits, and his childhood passions of football and cricket remained his passions. He'd played them at school, and as an army private in wartime France, and as a sergeant in peacetime Germany, and demobbed in the early tearaway days in Fulham, and his only concession to the true blues was to keep his mouth shut about them. As he kept it shut about the true blues huntin' and shootin' which he detested.

He chose a long-player of Carroll Gibbons and his Savoy Orphans: "Room 504," "A Nightingale Sang in Berkeley Square," "When Day Is Done." From his chair he watched through the window a boy policeman in helmet and heavy blue coat on the curb by the American Embassy, standing, punching a gloved fist into his palm, waiting to be relieved at two o'clock by the bigger one who was equally young and looked like a schoolboy Burt Lancaster. Most of the coppers these days seemed to be twenty years old with complexions like cream.

He picked up the tea, sipped, and stared ahead at a William Roberts without noticing it, as he noticed none of them anymore, though he continued to collect, and had tried to enjoy them just as he'd tried to enjoy the stuff in the Tate and National Gallery and antique furniture and concerts and the theater and all the cultural scramble you needed to be in on if you weren't to be written off as a clod.

Not that he wasn't acquainted with lordships who'd never stepped inside a gallery or theater or opened a book. But they didn't need to. If you were where you were satisfied to be, you could be yourself. If you were climbing, you juggled with assorted hats: a cultural hat, a political hat, a church hat, a racecourse hat, the appropriate hat to be caught and doffed to whoever was assisting with the next leg up the ladder. The one vital all-purpose hat, without which the rest might as well be junked, being the financial hat. Taylor swallowed tea and permitted himself to smile. He'd owned the financial hat since 1963, the morning of August 8, when they'd fixed the signal at Sears Crossing, and the royal mail train from Glasgow to Euston had braked and halted.

Putting down the tea, he picked up the medal. Ought to get it engraved, he thought, and breathed on it, then shone it on his shirtfront. "For God and the Empire. Sears Crossing. 1963." Ought to bequeath it, he mused, to the British Museum.

Once Leatherslade Farm had been found by the rozzers, and the mess of prints there, and the thing was blown, they'd all scarpered, or tried to, like mice from a slammed door. All except himself, and he was in the clear because he hadn't been at Sears Crossing or the farm, he'd been home in Fulham with his mother, technically he'd done nothing, he'd been nowhere, and before you could say "Flying Squad" his half million was away, flown, air-freighted to Malta in thirty-four separate packages, and from Malta to Zurich. No one grassed, only three of the gang knew his identity, and that the planning had been wholly his, and so long as he refrained from strutting along Piccadilly, bragging, or taking off around the world on a lunatic binge, he was safe.

He substituted tea for the medal, swallowed, and reached for cigarettes. Brooding was giving way to reminiscence, which he recognized as an indulgence. But the morning had been exhausting, and Poole had shaken him. One way of flushing turds like Poole from the system was to indulge, to spell out in memories your own incomparable achievement.

"The moon that lingered over London town," sang Mr. Gibbons.

The climbing had been insurance. It was as simple as that. He hadn't planned it, not at first. He hadn't even grasped the degree of protection well-placed friends could provide. Awareness began the day he'd lunched the circulation manager of the muckraking Sunday newspaper, which had led to his buying advertising space for the Bognor shopping precinct, which had resulted in an end to the paper's innuendoes about Charles Taylor.

In the years in Fulham Broadway and Hammersmith and the council estates off the New Kings Road, protection had been an activity involving putting the boot in. After Sears Crossing, protection become a matter of putting a word in; normally with an accompanying check, and in the case of one invaluable police superintendent, a cash donation to the Police Widows' and Orphans' Fund handed over in the gents of a pub at Parson's Green. Checks, lunches, favors, the doffing of freshly acquired hats at the right moment in the right place—with such initiatives the circle of friends had widened. Many probably would serve no useful purpose, but you never knew. The fact they existed was an insurance and a reassurance. And the higher you climbed, the more influential the friends. From a bridge partner and member of Booker's who happened also to be high in the Home Office, he'd learned that Heavy Mob detectives were merging with the Regional boys in a blitz on the gangs that were investing in legit businesses. That'd been six months before the commissioner had announced the crackdown in his annual report. The prior knowledge had made no practical difference because he, Charles Taylor, had become as legit as an archdeacon. But it had been nice to know. Knowledge was one sort of protection climbing brought you. It was comforting to be a jump ahead.

The moneymaking had been simple. The grind had been getting the gentility. You could move from Fulham to Grosvenor Square on the strength of loot alone, but you couldn't walk into Booker's or the Royal Enclosure at Ascot or the country houses and boardrooms and bridge parties where influence and true protection lay. The private tutors, evening classes, and interminable study and efforts, that'd been the real grind. Attendance four and five evenings a week in chalk-dusty schoolrooms that he'd thought, at fifteen, he'd quit forever; being civil with instructors and fellow students, but not so civil you'd be caught up in after-class coffee sessions; and once or twice coming perilously close to forgetting which false name he'd assumed for which study group. English, Liberal Studies, Art Appreciation, World Affairs, Romance Linguistics (abandoned after two hours), Sociology, Economic Theory, History of Drama. Goldsmith's College had offered a Railways Study Group (Amateur) which had been tempting, but he'd resisted and in any case, so far as railway studies went, he was a pro. The Criminology, he'd steered clear of that too. In place of railways and criminology he'd persevered, for three years, with private elocution lessons.

"We must first unlearn all those little telltale habits which in our case are quite marked, Mr. Telford, wouldn't you agree?"

By telltale she'd meant cockney. He could hear her still, a beefy girl with mottled arms and a chest like the continental shelf, enunciating too precisely, opening her jaws as though for a medical inspection. Four days after the introductory lesson she'd been killed in a car crash on the South Circular, and he'd found as replacement a Mrs. Haldane, a speech therapist with a queue of letters after her name who'd insisted that correct speech being a matter of breath control, for six months he would simply have to learn to breathe. He was having none of that, he needed results, and he'd jettisoned Mrs. Haldane and turned to an aging actress who had studied under Elsie Fogarty and to whom he went for more than two years, heeding her every rounded word, molding his lips into slow contortions, watching them in a mirror, uttering desperate vowel sounds, and detonating his consonants with rare acrobatics of tongue and teeth. If a correct accent had not been vital, if he'd been anything but realistic, he'd have laughed. As it was, he'd given his name as Larry Scofield. When the actress instructed, teaching him as she taught children, that he should compose his own jingles as practice for specific vowels, he'd mouthed, "It's plain the train's a gravy train, the bread is baked with grain aboard the train." One morning in the third year of lessons, when at the end of a session she'd revealed she was entering his name for an amateur poetry-reading contest, he had realized he'd progressed far enough to quit, before he found himself standing up reciting poetry at the Albert Hall. Now, six years later, so long as he didn't become excited or angry, forgetting the hard-won vowels and reverting to telltale habits, his accent was as near old-school BBC as dammit, and a sight more euphonious than the honkings that issued from some of their lordships in Booker's and the royal Enclosure.

Young Burt Lancaster, Taylor noted, had taken over. Fifteen minutes early. The window commanded a view over the entire square, or those patches of it not screened by trees, and there'd been a recent occasion when he'd been able to watch Burt patrolling the south side while here on the north, immediately below, two chalk-striped heisters had been trying the handles of parked cars. Neither law nor heisters had spotted the other. Taylor had looked on in delight, a silent supporter first of the heisters, then of the law, in which his own determined respectability had given him a stake. The heisters had won, as he'd suspected they would, forcing the door of a blue Porsche and gliding away while Burt had plodded along the farther side of the square, unseeing and unseen. Taylor had been amused but contemptuous. Luck had been with the heisters. In spite of their chalk-stripes they'd had little finesse and no lookout. Sooner or later they'd be nicked.

He blew a jet of smoke and watched the random figures ascending and descending the steps of the embassy. Not, he reflected, that he was a member of Booker's yet. His name was to go before the committee tomorrow. With droopy Dick Moreton proposing him, Lord Moreton of Harrowby, one of the honkers, there was no problem.

Success generated success. As with cash, so with the visible and tangible marks of social achievement. Once aboard you had only to hold on. Today the OBE; tomorrow, on his birthday, membership of Booker's. And with Booker's the opening of a score more doors; to more directorships, to weekend invitations, to possibilities of a parliamentary seat which he'd toy with, keeping them guessing, before refusing. At this rate the knighthood might be only a couple of summers ahead. Twelve years and close on a million quid it had taken, but now it was rolling.

Rolling and boring. He was trapped for the rest of his life. No wonder there were occasions his hands sweated. Anyone of less steel would have become paranoiac and schizophrenic and God knew what, and probably gone back to the old gangland games simply to get his feet into reality again.

Taylor swallowed the last of the navvy's tea. The medal he bedded down on the gray pad of its black leatherette box. He was hungry, but this was a lunchless week because he needed to lose three pounds, and he wasn't giving in. As well he hadn't been in a mood for lunch out with Phoebe. Come the evening she'd not be in the mood for a movie because she'd be cocktailing at the Hurlingham Club, so he'd take his seat in the directors' box at Stamford Bridge for the floodlit game against 'Spurs. But the afternoon was his own. He'd call with the medal on his Mum, housebound since her fall, and tell her about the Queen. He might call Suzy and in her skinny expert embraces release what remained of the morning's tension, or look in at Crockford's for bridge, or see the Barbra Streisand at the Carlton or call unannounced at Charles Taylor Ltd. and be matey with the competing sycophants, or do none of these but remain in the green drawing room and be plain idle.

Whichever way it was looked at, the prospect failed to please. Carroll Gibbons, side one, fell silent. When the telephone rang, Taylor thought: Slicker. He flexed his fingers, curling then straightening them, allowing the shrilling to continue. Slicker could piss off, the faster and farther the better.

It could not be Slicker because coincidences like that were for storybooks; having the name lobbed at you by John Law, first time he'd heard it spoken in years, and a couple of hours later the man himself telephoning. Also, he had a new unlisted number and Slicker had been away eight years.

Ann maybe, soliciting for something Phoebe was implacably against? Howard with congratulations plus a new crisis at Charles Taylor Ltd. or to say their Mum had fallen again? Taylor walked to the ringing telephone and put the handset to his ear.

A voice said, “Charlie boy?”

“Who is it?” said Taylor.

“Choo-choo. Choo-choo-choo. *Whoooo-eeeee!*”

The mimicked whistle of a train was overtaken by laughter, a creepy merriment crackling through the telephone. It was Slicker.

“Where are you?” Taylor said.

He did not want to know. He would have liked to have known how Slicker had found his number, but to have asked would have been to concede credit and an immediate advantage.

“Lookin’ up me mates, Charlie boy. All right if I drop round?”

“No. You in town?”

“Told yer, I’m circulatin’. I’m goin’ to buy yer a steak.”

“Make it Number Seven.”

“Number seven, legs eleven. That’s goin’ back a bit, gives me the nostalgias, that does. ’Alf an hour?”

“Tomorrow. Ten o’clock.”

“Yes, well, I’m a bit tied up meself. Couple of pressing swindles, I mean deals. Tea with the Queen Mum. That sort of thing, don’t you know, what?”

At the other end of the line Slicker was laughing again. Taylor replaced the receiver.

He walked back to his chair and fumbled a cigarette from its pack. He could not find his lighter and had to go to the kitchen for matches. His hands were so unsteady that he snapped two matches before succeeding in striking the third.

three

He traveled to Putney Bridge by his preferred means of transport, the tube. Taylor had an affection for every kind of train, and the underground was quick, anonymous, and evocative of the workaday world he had once inhabited. At the start of the journey the station names were those of his acquired world and seemed each to echo its own music. Green Park was cellos; Hyde Park Corner, trumpets; Knightsbridge, the kettledrum; South Kensington, a thirties dance band, Jack Payne or Guy Lombardo and "Just the Way You Look Tonight"; Gloucester Road, probably a military band, something with horses and sabers. Beside him sat a man in dungarees nursing an open bag of carpentry tools; opposite, a youth with a wispy beard, a black railway porter, and an Indian woman wearing a sari, earrings, and a caste mark which gave her the appearance of having been shot between the eyes. Taylor smoked a cigarette and read in the *Express,* then the *Times*, accounts of his team's one-nothing home defeat by 'Spurs. At Earl's Court he changed to a silver tube, at midmorning almost empty, which surfaced into daylight. West Brompton, Fulham Broadway, Parson's Green, Putney Bridge. He crossed the road at the lights and stood at the north end of the bridge, looking down over the parapet. The morning was cold and cheerless. A wind pestered the crocuses in Bishop's Park and made the daffodils bend over. Sole tenant of the garden was Slicker, filing his nails on a bench facing the river.

Taylor walked down the steps, along the path, and sat on the bench. Slicker glanced sideways, then returned to his nails.

"Where's the medal then?" His laugh was too pat, not a reflex but a habit. "Don't yer wear it weekdays?"

"Good to see you, Slicker,"

"Good to see you, Charlie." Slicker gazed ahead, not at Taylor but at the brown river and the massed red-brick buildings on the far embankment. "Good to see a lot of things, come to that." He returned to his nails. "Too bad about Chelsea. Heard you was a director."

"We're all right, we'll finish around the halfway mark."

"So I should 'ope." He looked behind him, then up toward the bridge. "Bit public, innit?"

"What is?"

"'Ere, Number Seven."

"Why? What're we doing wrong?"

Slicker shrugged.

Taylor said, "What can I do for you?"

"What can I do for you, sir? Nice line in velvet trimmin's? Our latest platinum hairpiece? Tiger-skin jockstrap? Where'd yer pick up the posh talk, Charlie? Been takin' lessons?"

"Is it money?"

"Way I saw it, Charlie, the question was goin' to be, what can I do for you?"

"I've my own company and nine outside directorships, Slicker. I wear this bowler and hail taxis with the umbrella. Yesterday I shook hands with the Queen. Don't tell me you didn't know."

"Everyone knows. But you must 'ave somethin' goin'."

"Nothing I don't pay tax on."

"Prospects?"

"No chance. I don't need it."

"No, suppose yer don't." Slicker laughed without mirth. He wiped the file on the cuff of his overcoat, removing nail dust, and continued filing. "That's it then, innit?"

"You on parole?"

"What's parole? I'm a free man."

"Go to South Africa." Or to the birds and sunshine of Brazil, where Biggs had done not too badly. Anywhere so long as it was out, the other side of the world from London town. "Or New Zealand. I'll pay the fare. I can set you up."

"Thanks."

"Ever thought of farming?"

" 'Ave you?"

"I can fix it for you in Natal."

"Fantastic."

"Think about it."

"I'm like you, Charlie boy. I like London."

Taylor turned his head and studied Slicker for the first time. First time, that was, for a decade. He'd put on weight in prison. His ill-cut hair was turning gray, though he was still somewhere in his mid-thirties. In the twenty-four hours since his release he'd acquired a camel-hair coat, suede shoes, gloves and a snap-brim hat in bottle-green leather. He looked like an advertisement for the fast life. Taylor braced himself against feelings of sympathy which could lead only to trouble. Slicker had scarpered like the rest and in two years had run through a hundred thousand pounds. But he'd worn gloves at Leatherslade Farm, and there'd been no evidence against him, any more than there'd been against Mr. Big. He'd come back to London, got a cold shoulder from Taylor, and embarked on a flurry of security truck hijackings, which had ended up the stairs at the Old Bailey and the judge chuntering on about men who'd had every chance. Slicker lacked imagination. What he had, given someone behind him to set a job up, was cheek and a dozen kinds of expertise. Or had had.

He was drawing from the patch pocket of the camel hair a copy of yesterday's *Evening Standard.* He unfolded it at the picture of Phoebe in the cloche hat and offered it to Taylor.

"You done all right, Charlie boy."

"I saw it."

"Met 'er once, didn't I? Yankee bird. Fair stunner."

Taylor remembered the first occasion on which Slicker had returned to London in search of a fresh train coup, and Phoebe had just had Ann. He himself had met Phoebe only a year earlier, not long after Sears Crossing, and had married her because suddenly, after years of assorted women and steadfastness in avoiding marriage, the right wife was going to be handy. Phoebe had style, Daddy ran New Jersey Petroleum, and she was available, fresh out of college and doing Europe. Would the drinking have started if he'd revealed to her who he was, what he had done? He had communicated strain and tension without explaining why, and probably he'd communicated not much else. Her encounter with Slicker he remembered because she'd been very merry, hamming up her Scarlett O'Hara act, and Slicker's reputation as a hotshot for anything in skirts had made him wary. Needlessly so because Slicker's energies were being directed into the mindless hijackings. He heard Slicker say, "I'll buy yer both a steak, you and the missus. Name me an evenin'. Then that's it. I won't embarrass you no more."

"I'll call you. What's your number?"

"Charing Cross 'Otel. With bath, telly, and maid service." Slicker giggled. "Thought I'd pick up the threads in the manner in which I 'ope to become accustomed to."

Small hope, Taylor thought. He tried to imagine what he knew he never would experience: the effects of eight years inside. It would be stultifying. It had to be. However cockily you started a stretch of that kind, you'd end it dim, surely, your wits as turgid as the Thames, and fatally out of touch. Whatever else, a villain had to keep up to date; he had to be contemporary. Taylor clenched and unclenched his fist in his coat pocket, aching to ask about old colleagues inside: Goody, Wilson, Buster Edwards, Reynolds. He refrained. He took a cigarette and offered the pack to Slicker.

"Gave 'em up," Slicker said.

Wind rocked the launches and pleasure craft moored upstream. High above them in shouting letters across the fifth floor of a red-brick mansion block was the statement STAR AND GARTER. Beyond the south end of the bridge jutted the gray stone of the parish church, and distantly beyond, stark against the sky, rose the International Computer Tower. Four buses grumbled in convoy over the arched bridge, only their red roofs and a sliver of top-deck windows visible. Slicker had stuffed the newspaper back into the camel hair and was tapping his front teeth with the nail file.

Taylor stood up and walked back through the tidy garden toward the steps, past lawns and concrete sculptures which had grown so familiar in the months of planning and covert meetings preceding the train robbery.

There might be a couple of telephone calls or so, but he would never see Slicker again, any more than he would do a tickle again. The sculptures bore titles which he could have recited even now: "Adoration," "Affection," "Protection," "Leda," writhing with her swan, and the huddled man, woman and baby which was "Grief."

"For reading, for signing," Miss Widdicombe said, and moved two heaps of letters, papers, and checks half an inch in a southerly direction across the shine of the Georgian pedestal desk. "The surveyors' meeting is number two conference room in nine minutes. Mr. Howard telephoned from the airport—he'll be in later. The coffee's tepid."

"Sugar?"

"You should learn to do without."

"For God's sake I only have one small one. Sixteen calories."

"You'll not work off sixteen calories sitting in the surveyors' meeting."

"Don't be so sure. I might thump the table." Taylor reached for the sugar bowl. His secretary's solicitude irritated. Last week she had left on his desk a newspaper clipping giving the latest figures on smoking and lung cancer. Next week, at this rate, it'd be a report on coronaries and the middle-aged executive. His eyes lighted on papers contained by an elastic band. "What's that?"

"Clutter."

"Clutter?"

"For throwing out. Mainly the Croydon scheme. I'll have more for you tomorrow."

"Do I have to look at them?"

"It's the spring clean. They'll take you forty seconds."

Taylor grunted. He rolled the rubber band off the clutter. The coffee was not tepid; it was cold. Miss Widdicombe had vanished. Once she had been silently in love with him, then silently hostile. These days she was neutral inclining toward motherliness. She lived with the purser of an ocean cruise liner whom she saw for only eight to ten weeks in the year.

Reports and minutes on the abortive Croydon development scheme. Superseded financial statements. Departmental memoranda. All old history. Miss Widdicombe was compulsively anticlutter. Taylor frowned at a forgotten folder of names which had approached Charles Taylor Ltd. for a loan and been turned down by his brother, Howard, who adored and had appropriated the interviewing role. "E. Montgomery, racing motorist, car salesman. Alternatively £75,000 investment in projected new V12-cyl. racing engine and/or negotiation sale of lease, Europa Sports Cars Ltd., Hackney Road. Nil security. Application rejected." Power-happy Howard would listen intently to the motley cadgers and con men who came cap in hand. He would nod, question, jot down figures, show interest, and finally say no, with regrets and a lecture on the economic health of the nation. Taylor dropped the clutter in the wastebasket.

He found himself looking at but not registering the glass tank of luridly striped and speckled tropical fish. A gloomy Paul Klee, "Girl with Flowers," brown gouache on brown wrapping paper, hung on one wall; on the wall opposite, a Klee pen drawing of a puppet show. There was a Queen Anne walnut settee. The carpet was a twenty-foot square of obligatory Persian. The view from the windows, a far drop below, was of bowler hats and car roofs in Leadenhall Street. Taylor closed his mind to the imminent gnawing boredom of the surveyors' meeting. He would have signed a three-figure check for a magician who might have spirited him out of Charles Taylor Ltd. and deposited him, hey presto, in the anonymous dark of a cinema.

He slid toward him the check and letters for signing and picked up a pen.

"Stay Straight, old boy," Dick Moreton said. "So long as the going's firm. Take my word."

"He fell at Haydock," said Taylor. "If I were on anything, it'd be Jacobin."

"Jacobin? Too temperamental, old man. Overbred. Hasn't the legs, wouldn't wonder."

"He might surprise you."

"Take my word, old boy. You'll get seven to two on Stay Straight."

"Not enough, Dick. It's far too open. It's one for leaving alone."

The subject was Cheltenham Week, the debating chamber the bar at Booker's Club. Taylor eyed an oil painting of a periwigged gouty bully that hung between two Georgian windows. In spite of the depressing meeting with Slicker, and now the honking of Lord Moreton, he was in passably fair spirits. Tomorrow he would stand here unchaperoned, a member, no longer obliged to be signed in like laundry or to heed the honkings of the signatory. At his elbow, swilling champagne, leaned Lord Moreton: member of Booker's and the Turf, Master of Hounds, a Steward of the Jockey Club. He was also an ineffectual businessman who owed Taylor sixty-five thousand pounds, a sum which by tacit agreement was now on permanent interest-free loan. But he knew about steeple-chasing and was unaccustomed to having his tips questioned.

"Please yourself, old boy."

I will, thought Taylor.

"Not like you to be windy," Lord Moreton said in his megaphone voice, and farther along the bar three members looked around. "What's the problem? Took a hidin' on the Mackeson's, what?"

"Wouldn't have called it that."

The candidate for membership wanted to spit "old boy" back in his lordship's empty face. But there was a time for everything. Like tomorrow, after his election.

"You weren't the only one, old boy," prattled Lord Moreton. "Now's the time to hang on, shorten the rein. Sorts the sheep from the goats, what? Question of nerve, old man. Nerve."

The gouty bully in the frame leered at Taylor as though about to float from the wall and ask to borrow money.

Taylor sipped champagne. Nerve. The same word Poole had used. He thought he should leave before he answered Lord Moreton with a sarcasm that would accomplish nothing. His last efforts at equanimity were draining from him as though through surgical tubes.

Smiling, skeptical whether the clubland game could ever be worth the candle, Taylor swallowed the last of his champagne, offered pleasantries and excuses, and left.

Poole swallowed milk. He sat at the kitchen table in his semidetached house in North London, hand on his flat stomach, and thought about Taylor. On the drainboard by the sink stood the goldfish bowl with its solitary orange occupant. Tony had been supposed to change the water, but he had not been able to find his football boots or his chemistry homework, naturally. He had been late for school even before bringing the goldfish to the sink. So Dad would change the water. Again. Through the window Poole could see the near corner of the vegetable garden. The spinach, lettuce, leeks, and broad beans were in, but there were still the shallots and celery, and now he was off the sick list and back at the factory he'd probably be doing those at four in the morning, by flashlight.

As sure as taxes and the rising price of everything, Charlie Taylor had engineered the train robbery. He'd not been present but it had been all his. This copper knew it, Taylor knew he knew it, and there was nothing that could be done about it. That was the private humiliation this copper had carried in his belly for what ought to have been the prime dozen years of his career. There'd been times, in recent years even months at a time, when Taylor had not entered his thoughts. At other, darker times, he'd attempted to exorcise Taylor by telling himself the man hadn't lied, that he was innocent. But that exercise had been pathetic. You didn't attend a score of interrogations of anyone, particularly a prepared liar like Taylor, without sensing the truth behind the lies. To see the truth, you didn't need spoken admissions and sworn statements. There'd been one certain occasion—he remembered it as vividly as if he had a photograph—when Taylor, the sweat dribbling down his temples, had been on the point of blurting out the truth, both to be free at last of the pressure and to boast. But he'd blurted out nothing. Only the sweating pause, Vibart and himself holding their breath, then once more the dancing lies, one after the other, controlled, consistent without a flaw. In the truth there were always inconsistencies, faltering contradictions, wayward trivial flaws.

A year after the train robbery he'd even been given the name. "Why don't yer ask Charlie Taylor?" Told it in the visiting room in a top security wing by one of the robbers who'd been put away for a thirty-year stretch and who spelled the name out in a moment of grinning mockery, defiant, knowing he could deny it and make a monkey of the poor sod of a policeman into the bargain if the policeman so much as tried to claim a name had been spoken. If only electronics had been part of a copper's lawful kit, tapes and bugging equipment, and he could have had the name on record.

But even if he had, it would not have been evidence which could have got Taylor even halfway to the Old Bailey.

Poole watched Janet walk past the vegetable garden. She carried the shopping basket in which would be, he supposed, the prescribed tablets. Instead of turning left for the kitchen door, she continued past the vegetable garden and halted in front of the cherry tree. She put down the basket and reached for the nearest branch, bending it toward her and examining it.

Poole pressed his hand to his stomach and inclined forward over the table until the pain had passed. Funny about the ulcer, though funny wasn't the word. This was the second, and it had flared up at a time when once more he was obsessed with Charlie Big. The first ulcer had followed the train robbery, when he'd been on to Taylor, working around the clock, achieving nothing.

Not that there was any connection, apart from in those moments of fancy which your rational copper wasn't supposed to indulge in. For one thing peptic ulcers didn't arrive overnight, and until the investiture and Slicker's being released, Taylor couldn't have been further from his mind. Funny all the same. Ulcers had psychosomatic origins, so the doctor said. Excessive acid secretion brought on by anxiety, overwork, driving yourself.

The frustration of Charlie Taylor being everlastingly a free man?

"I'm going to prune the cherry," Janet said, coming into the kitchen in her head scarf and robust shoes which doubled for shopping and gardening.

She was plump and pink, a cartoonist's rustic contrast with her pale urban husband. With hands roughened by daily sessions in the garden, she began transferring groceries from the basket into cupboards.

"Do the celery and shallots, would you?" Poole said. "If you can get round to them. I don't know when I'm going to have the time."

"You should make time, else you're going to find yourself back in hospital. Or the cemetery."

"Any luck at all I'll be having the weekend after next off and we'll be down at the cottage. All of us."

With two thousand pounds left to Janet in her father's will the Pooles had made the down payment on a cottage with an acre of land. For the two boys it was already a dull and spartan place, far from London, football, and their friends. For the parents it was a haven, the paradise to which one day they were going to escape permanently.

"There you are then, directions on the tube," Janet said, and placed on the table a stapled white paper bag. "You're a mess these days."

"I'm sorry."

"I'm sorry, love." And she stooped and kissed him. "What is it for the shallots then? Nine inches?"

"Nine or ten. About a foot between rows."

Janet went out into the garden. Poole took the tin cylinder of antacid tablets from the paper bag and the top from the cylinder. These days, he reflected, a little bit of a mess. The male mid-life copper's crisis. He'd have done better on the other side of the fence, with the villains. Then again, perhaps not. Perhaps he'd have made a fifth-rate villain, all nerves and obstinacy and spilling his pills on a job. At least he was a second-rate copper. He'd have been first-rate if they'd backed him at the factory instead of pretending there was no Mr. Big.

The tablets were spherical, beige, and inscribed with a squiggle resembling a coat of arms.

"Posh," Poole murmured, and he thought back to the palace and the gong he had been awarded for bravery on the field of battle. The gong had delighted Janet, compensating her in some small degree for having married a policeman.

The field of battle had been half a mile of Leytonstone High Road. More exactly the hood of the Coope brothers' getaway car along half a mile of Leytonstone High Road. The older brother had tried to shoot him off the hood and had succeeded in shooting him in the arse before he had fallen off and the younger brother had buried the car in a wall. If he'd fallen off the car without being shot in the arse, he'd probably never have got the gong, which would have been all right with him, it would have saved the tedium of all the funny remarks. But it would have been a disappointment for Janet. He had not felt the bullet. He'd not known he'd been shot until the crowd pointed out to him, in the middle of Leytonstone High Road, the blood he was sitting in. He'd lost the merest thimbleful of flesh. Four days in dock and ten days' sick leave. The comedians at the factory and some of the cheekier newspapers had got a good deal of mileage out of the wound. But he knew which he'd choose, given a choice between being shot in the arse and this bloody ulcer.

He stalked to the sitting room to answer the telephone. It was Detective Sergeant Fothergill wondering if and when he might be coming in because there was a possible lead in the Brixton wages snatch, and the super had been asking for him, and Ginger Cobbett had been in the corridor since eight and wouldn't speak to anyone else.

"I've understood about two words of all that," Poole said. "What the hell are you eating?"

"Cox's Orange Pippin. Bit on the soft side. Cost sixpence."

Another second-rater, Fothergill. Poole, frowning, tried to think of anyone at the Yard he would class as a first-rater. Fothergill was an unusual combination for a copper: youngish but lazy.

"I'll be in in an hour," Poole said. "What've you got on today?"

"Glad you asked that, sir. I've a list here with sixty-one items. If you—"

"Add Slicker to your list. Nice and discreet. Just a friendly eye. You can put him at the top."

"The super won't care for that."

"Discreet, I said. You could always shave off those gruesome sideburns."

Poole put on his tie, watching through the bedroom window the No. 16 bus move away from the request stop in the road below. He was tempted to take a taxi. But he was often tempted to take a taxi. He always took either the bus or tube.

The taxi bore Taylor up St. James's, waited with engine running while he called at Fortnum and Mason, then drove through Belgravia and Chelsea to Fulham. In the Wandsworth Bridge Road he paid off the driver and set out on foot along identical streets of terraced Victorian villas. To alight a hundred yards from his destination and look about him before walking on had once been a habit. Occasionally in Fulham he still proceeded thus, not because old habits died hard, but partly because in memories alone, these days, lived the sense of risk that gave salt to life and partly for the exercise. He pushed open a low iron gate. There was a movement behind the lace curtains.

Howard answered the bell.

"Hullo. I just got in. She's in good shape. Wants to ship the whole Chelsea team down the Thames, sink them, and play the reserves instead."

"I've had the same thought," Taylor said, stepping inside.

Though recently redecorated the hall remained gloomy. From a peg hung the fur from Debenham and Freebody which he had given his mother two Christmases ago. For fear she never otherwise would have worn it he'd had the store remove the label and told his mother that he'd bought it at a sale in Fulham Broadway. A smell of cats and fried liver crept along the hall.

"Paris is murder," Howard said. "Happy birthday. How long can you stay?"

"Long as she likes."

"I have to go. The Paris development's in real trouble. I've a meeting with Fresnais and his frog bandits at three."

"Zut. Do not offair more zan zeven."

"Seven and a half."

Taylor opened his mouth to command seven but closed it without speaking. Juggling with figures was as much his younger brother's niche as interviewing the con men. Their father had died at his fruit stall in the North End Road, grading apples. Howard had become the first of the family to receive a professional training; but the father was dead, and the apprenticeship in accountancy had been paid for by Charles out of his erratic and shady profits as a general dealer, salesman, and speculator in the years before the Heathrow wages snatch and Sears Crossing. The career as tax consultant had toppled when the Inland Revenue passed a folder of comment to the Fraud Squad, and Howard Taylor, accountant, had been struck off. Now an enthusiastic director in his brother's company, curious about where the initial capital had come from but asking no questions, Howard lived in a six-bedroomed house in Surrey and sent his sons to private schools.

Sometimes Taylor wondered if emotional Howard had conveyed his suspicions to their mother. If he had, she'd never faced him with it. But she was capable of double-edged comments.

"You're fed up," Howard said. "Why? -

"Nothing." Taylor hung up his black coat, bowler, and umbrella. "I'll take her to Brighton at the weekend if she'd like."

"She'd love it. Just don't ask her to sell this place."

"Charles!" the mother called from the sitting room.

She sat with one stockinged leg horizontally on a pile of cushions and in her lap a Bible, rosary, and a tin of humbugs. A plump old body with her wits about her.

"Push 'em overboard, splish splash splosh, that's what I'd do. Laughingstock they are, and they'll make you one too, see if they don't. Many 'appy returns. It's on the sideboard."

There were two sideboards. There were four tables, too many chairs, various cabinets, filled cupboards, a trolley, cake stand, coal scuttle, sewing basket, cat basket, boxes of papers and nonsense and trinkets, all worthless. Mrs. Taylor sat besieged by possessions, happy in her mockery of the Chelsea team. Bric-a-brac obliterated every flat surface, including areas of carpet: china horses, pots of plastic flowers, framed verses about gardens and happiness. The framed bleeding heart over the fireplace, its colors imperishably pyrotechnic, was older than Taylor himself. He kissed her and handed her the jar of spiced plums from Fortnum's. His own wrapped present, when he spotted it, was too square to be a crucifix. It might be a vase or something china to hang on the wall.

"Splish splash splosh. And don't think I don't blame the

directors. Time you made way for younger fellers, all of you." She had put the humbugs on the floor and was wrestling with the lid of the spiced plums. "Past fifty a man's 'ad it, it's a natural process, nothin' to be ashamed of."

"For heaven's sake, Mum."

"You'll see. Fifty's fifty. No use pretendin' you're a sprig."

"I'm not Methuselah."

"Fifty and twenty-nine days your Dad was when 'e was taken. 'Alf past ten, Saturday mornin'. 'Ope you're goin' regular."

She meant going to confession. For God's sake, Taylor thought.

"'E washes away our sins," Mrs. Taylor said, and sponged plum juice from her chin. "We've all got sins, some of us more than others. Not that you can believe 'alf what you 'ear. You was clever all right, but you was never that clever."

"What d'you mean, Mum?"

"Mean what I says. Go on, open it then, it's for flowers." Mrs. Taylor munched: a faint and rhythmic squelching sound like treading through sea wrack at ebb tide. "These plums 'ave been done something to."

"Mum, I'm sorry, I'm not with you. What're you trying to say, you can't believe half what you hear?"

"'Ear no evil, see no evil," announced Mrs. Taylor, closing the subject.

It's a conspiracy, Taylor thought. I can't take anymore. I'm canceling the birthday dinner.

Poole, Dick Moreton, Miss Widdicombe critical of his calorie intake, now his mother, all of them putting him down, hinting he must suddenly be decrepit, a has-been. Even a never-was. Was it happening? He was in his prime. He was Charles Taylor, millionaire, donor to threescore charities, honored by the Queen herself. His head had grown heavy with frustration and anger; it was buzzing and alien, as though some celestial handicapper had gone mad, festooning his brain with chunks of lead to reduce him to the level of ordinary people.

Why were they suddenly getting at him, these murky fifth-rate conspirators? Did he have to do another job to convince them? Something that would sink the train coup into the category of a pickpocket's day at the races?

He picked at the wrappings of his present with carefully controlled hands. Paranoia, that was delusions of power or persecution, wasn't it? Schizophrenia was the multiple personality. He'd have to hold onto himself. It was all too ridiculous. Another job? No way.

But he could indulge in the daydream. There was more pleasure in the daydream than life as he lived it now. The post office cage? A jet plane of bullion? The crown jewels?

"Queen Elizabeth II," by Pietro Annigoni, geometrically hung and impressively boring?

Now there's something might take a bit of disposing of, Taylor reflected, amused.

He eyed the portrait. It watched over the bald heads and flowered hats, the chatter and checkbooks and circulating champagne, at a fund-raising reception at Fishmongers' Hall. Already, after only twenty years, the painting was historic. Someone, mused Taylor, someday, might nick it as a joke or a protest. But for cash? For sale, or a sack of ransom?

The moment of amusement passed. He looked through the window at the Thames. His glass was empty, but he wanted whisky, not champagne. He could not decently leave yet. With the lord mayor holding forth at his elbow, and dead ahead, twelve inches away, Thea, Countess of

Kirkaig, massaging her necklace, he could not even glance at his watch. The evening reached interminably ahead. After the reception, a drink with his stockbroker at the Berkeley. After the Berkeley, the birthday dinner.

". . . balance of payments sorted out, don't you agree?"

"No question," Taylor agreed.

He had missed the question, but clearly the answer was to be agreement, and he reinforced his agreement by nodding and looking sage. It was when the question was a blunt "What's your opinion?" and the tone and expression were blank, not smiling or frowning or yielding a clue of any kind, that there could be a problem. Then the safest solution was to be so long silent, looking sage while you pondered your opinion, that the questioner, or someone else, would become impatient and answer for you.

Of course, if you looked too sage, they might become interested in what the opinion was going to be and not interrupt, but wait, with gathering expectancy.

The lord mayor was not wearing his regalia but his banker's black. Thea, Countess of Kirkaig, said, "It depends on the rainy season. Porgy prefers the Seychelles. Do visit us."

The chandeliers sparkled. The window hangings were old gold; the carpet was Wilton. The Regency tables and gilt, saber-leg armchairs had been placed against the walls. Cigar smoke writhed between the superior talk and restrained jewelry and fizzing glasses.

It's the life, Taylor told himself.

five

"Evening, Tommy."

"Good evening, Mr. Taylor. And may I wish you a happy birthday, and all the best."

"You may, thanks, and what happens to what's left of it is going to be up to you. Can I smell that trout, the one you do stuffed, or do I just hope I can?"

"One trout *soufflé au Riesling?*"

"Lead on."

And a shame this dinner's not just you and me, talking soccer and harmonizing some of the old ones, Taylor thought. Dinner? The big birthday yawn.

Smiling, murmuring compliments and urbanities, Taylor stood aside, allowing the evening gowns and dinner jackets into the restaurant in Tommy's wake. To have canceled the dinner would have been the act of a neurotic. Now, after the Berkeley, and opening a new bottle at his flat before the dozen guests had started to arrive, several calculated scotch whiskies warmed him. He smiled and bowed. To be daunted by hints and jibes was halfway to justifying them. At one time he'd had twice the ability of all of them, everywhere, lordships, coppers, mates, and in August, 1963, he'd proved it. Now, he suspected, he had ten times the ability. And he didn't have to prove anything. He didn't have to prove himself to himself or to anyone. To try to prove it, and overreach himself, that was what cruds like Poole were waiting for. So let them wait. Till kingdom come and the last whimpering men. And the hell with them.

"Phoebe darling, would you take that end? Arthur and Reg, either side, all right? Janice, here by me where I can keep an eye on you. The Lady Rose, madame, you too please. Howard where you are." Howard, he noticed, was alone among the men in not wearing a black tie. Striving for something different, his brother wore under his dinner jacket a frilled lemon shirt with a blossoming Byronic cravat and had succeeded only in looking like a shopwindow in time-expired Carnaby Street. "Everyone, spread yourselves. Tommy, how'm I doing?"

He was doing impeccably. How to break free from the falseness and skull-cracking monotony, that was something else. Take up clay modeling? Learn a language? Cultivate another peer?

For the present he was affably drunk on a stomach as empty as a drum and bent on conviviality, as a birthday occasion demanded. Phoebe was not sober, and Taylor had not expected her to be, but she was predictably beautiful in a Jean Muir kaftan which at first he thought he could see through but decided he could not. He guessed she would grow progressively quieter as the evening stretched itself out, but for the moment she was garrulous, and his glances kept returning to her. She was a beauty, and maybe it would stir the party up a little if he begged the guests' pardon and cleared the table and made love to her right now, here on the grill room table.

"Mean if she wants to breed like a guinea pig, well, fine." The New Jersey vowels, only a step from Brooklyn, had become more pronounced with the gin. "But let her at least do it some place where we don't all have to hear the details, like at sea."

Four tables had been grouped together in the Connaught grill room. Taylor sat with his back to drawn red-and-gold damask curtains. He lit a cigarette. Reg would think him a peasant because Reg was a wine lunatic, but Reg would keep his opinion to himself because Reg needed premises for a lengthening chain of estate agencies. Taylor blew smoke and looked beyond Reg at a gaunt man fiddling with a spoon. Had he been wholly wise, he wondered, in inviting Lord Pollard, who needed nothing? A shy and gentle lordship, not the lordship stereotype and no fool, and on the board of the Panco Group. Charles Taylor Ltd. was beginning to have stirrings of thoughts of a deal with the Panco Group. But mixing business with relations and friends was like mixing drinks with the lights out.

Friends?

"Charles won't go," Phoebe was saying, "he won't go anywhere, so I'll be joining with Marion in Nassau, then on to Daddy."

Reg was saying, "They've clamped down on food exports. If they don't get concessions from the Japs, we're all going to feel it."

"Where's the sense in delphiniums," Janice asked Lady Rose, inclining away from tobacco smoke, "when they hate London and you only have them a fortnight?"

"It was a box number advertising used chair lifts," said Phoebe.

"So I ruffed a heart in dummy, established the clubs,

and there they were, high and dry with their ace, queen, and knave," Sir Arthur Jacob said.

"Thank you," said Taylor, his head humming. He accepted the wine list from the sommelier but did not open it. "D'you have the sixty-one Lafite-Rothschild?"

"Never seen Charles so abrupt," said Phoebe, "and this poor policeman freshly decorated for bravery in the face of withering fire or something. I mean how many wives really know? Charles is probably a parking meter raider. They skate off to their offices—"

Taylor fixed Phoebe with a smile that was interpreted only by her and Howard. The smile cut off her monologue as with a sword. She turned her head and regarded an illuminated painting of a hunt.

"I'd a singleton spade, all the top hearts, and my partner's response is this shutout, I ask you," asked Sir Arthur.

"If the Japs sneeze, we'll all catch a cold," said Reg.

Because Howard was an emotion seeker, eager for drama, and would now be poised for the shared glance from his brother, Taylor refused to look in his direction but conversed with the sommelier. The sommelier pointed here at a name on the wine list, then there, and spoke of vintages. When he departed, Taylor looked across the tables and said, "Phoebe, tell Rose about Ann's trip to Amsterdam—the bookings."

The tautness in Phoebe's features fell away. Ann and her class from school were to spend Easter Week at a convent in Amsterdam but owing to clerical errors the travel agent had sent to each child particulars of a Hotel Willem in the red-light district. Phoebe, forgiven, told the story in a rush of half-finished sentences which left Lady Rose groping after its point and continuing to nod, expectant, after Phoebe had repeated the point and finished the telling.

"Nothing from my partner, three no-trumps on my right, so what could I do but show my diamonds?" resumed Sir Arthur, and Lord Pollard, his victim, shook his head as though to say, What indeed?

A headwaiter in tails and black tie, a chef waiter in white tie, and a commis waiter in white jacket made recommendations and took orders. The carver in white apron wheeled his trolley across the carpet and parked it beside a German couple dining at the farther end of the grill room.

"He said it was Caravaggio's obscene period," Reg told Mrs. Hartley-Rumbold.

"So I led the club and crossruffed," Sir Arthur said.

Who the hell are all these people? Taylor asked himself. His mind wandered. Phoebe, silent, took only a token sip from her glass. Her husband stubbed out his cigarette and smiled at her across the tables; a changed smile from the one of minutes ago, prompting a return smile from Phoebe. I'll go to Kew tonight, he decided.

Howard observed the reconciliation and looked away. Deprived of a scene, disregarded, he disregarded his neighbors. He scowled at his cutlery, playing his fingertips along its cold brightness, chinking the knife against the spoon. His brother's forgiveness of Phoebe's drunken indiscretions had always been incomprehensible to him.

"To Charles, and a happy birthday," said Henrietta, glass lifted.

"Hear, hear," said Janice.

"What?" Sir Arthur said. "Rather." He stood and lifted his glass, which was empty, and looked this way and that, blinking and beaming as though he had proposed the toast himself. Without his noticing, a waiter materialized, tilted a bottle, refilled the raised glass.

Smells of fish, garlic, and soup steamed from plates and mingled with meat smells from the passing trolley. Sir Arthur spilled a gobbet of duck pâté onto his lap. Phoebe remained withdrawn. Her husband made an effort and flirted alternately with Janice and Lady Rose, though his mind was elsewhere. He drank wine like an Italian farmhand. He was cutting into Scotch beef when Tommy stooped and whispered in his ear.

"There's a Lord Moreton on the phone. Shall I tell him you'll ring back?"

"No."

Taylor apologized to Lady Rose and Janice and followed Tommy from the grill room. The white telephone's handset rested on its side. He picked it up and said, "Dick?"

For a moment there was nothing. Then came the honking.

"Hullo, old boy. That you? I'm at Booker's. Afraid you've been blackballed."

The voice from Booker's talked on. Taylor's free hand delved mechanically for cigarettes. Whatever he might have answered, Lord Moreton would not have been interested.

"Quite a stunner, old man. I'll have to resign. Nothing for it. Peter's writing his out now. He's fairly cut up, don't advise you to see him for a bit, not really. No odds to me. Tiresome place, Booker's. Too many damn foreigners, that's the top and bottom of it. Still, bit of a stunner. Great-great-grandfather a founder-member, so I'm told. Hullo? You there?"

"Yes," Taylor's hand was clammy around the phone. "I'm sorry."

"Quite so, well, thought you ought to know."

"Sorry you have to resign." Taylor tried to sound concerned. Momentarily he pressed the cold earpiece against his forehead.

"That's the form, old boy. No choice. Question of loyalty to you, honor, all that. They've let too many Scots in if you ask me. Bloody bagpipe blowers. Place is like the Highland Games."

"Will it get in the papers?"

"Papers?"

"The press?" He switched the handset to this other hand, but that too was damp. He must have left his cigarettes in the grill room. On the wall was an old lithograph with the caption "A Little Mortgage."

"No idea, old boy. Not headlines exactly, what? Suppose it might. Lord Moreton resigns from Booker's, eh?"

Sod Lord Moreton. Taylor said, "Tait, was it?"

"Tait?"

"Colonel Tait. Your chairman. Who did the blackballing."

"Wouldn't have thought so. Old friend, Taity. So are Maurice and Frank, come to that. At Harrow with Frank. Still, must've been one of them. Or all of 'em. You've put someone's back up, old boy. Thinkin' I might join White's. Useful grub. All very tiresome."

"Thanks anyway. Thanks for telephoning."

He wanted to continue along the corridor and out into the night, but he rejoined the birthday party. His plate had been removed. The carver was waiting to carve anew. Taylor shook his head.

"We take the M Four and branch off at Newbury," Mrs. Hartley-Rumbold was saying.

"Clobber them and clobber them hard, it's what they understand, they appreciate it," Sir Arthur said.

Taylor grew aware of Phoebe smiling at him across the tables and raising her eyebrows, seeking reassurance. He smiled back and motioned dismissively with a small gesture of his hand. Then he put his hands on his knees, under the table. He could not trust them to hold cutlery or light a cigarette.

"The stock market," teased Lady Rose, "or a girlfriend?"

"Beg your pardon?" Taylor sensed that Lady Rose had asked the question a moment earlier and now was repeating it. "Some people'd call them eleven girlfriends, way they've been playing." His voice sounded remote and unfamiliar to him, as though someone else were speaking from some other table. "The Blues—Chelsea. Birthday greetings."

"But that's enchanting!"

"And her shoes," Janice told Reg. "We know she's tea on the lawn and horse trials and all that, but for heaven's sake this is the twentieth century."

"Kilos, liters, load of tommyrot, they'll have us driving on the right yet, mark my words," Sir Arthur said.

The prattle passed Taylor by. His thoughts did not wander anymore; they were lucid and concentrated, but not on his dinner party. When he noticed Janice regarding him with intent eyes, he supposed she had been speaking to him and gave her his smiling attention.

Before him was a bowl of green salad which he remembered neither ordering nor being served. He slid his hand under his jacket and felt his soaking shirt.

Lord Pollard was saying, "She may or may not be the wealthiest woman in the world, probably she is, I've never made a precise study of it. My point is that the penny-pinching monarchies incline to be the autocratic monarchies as a matter of historical fact."

Taylor murmured further apologies to Lady Rose and Janice. "Chelsea. They're good lads, deserve a reply." He put his napkin beside the green salad, pushed back his chair, and walked from the table.

He sought through the directory, picked up the white telephone and dialed the Charing Cross Hotel. He was pessimistic about finding Slicker in. Slicker would be renewing acquaintances in Soho, doing the strip clubs, but he was put through promptly.

"Well, 'ullo, don't tell me I've come into a farm up the Zambesi?"

In the background was blurred pop music from radio or television. He's got a bird with him, Taylor thought. He had walked only from the grill room, and he was fit, but he was breathing as hard and fast as if he had run a mile.

"Something closer to home," Taylor said. "Make it Number Six. Tomorrow. No—wait." Steady. Slow. No rush. Crime was like whisky, the better for being allowed to mature, in the cask, undisturbed. And looked at and considered, in the glass, before being savored.

"Monday," Taylor said. "Eleven o'clock."

six

Number Six was an East End pub, the Town of Ramsgate. At least, Slicker hoped it was. By eleven ten, still with no sign of Mr. Boss Man, he was beginning to grow anxious.

If the Town of Ramsgate had not been Number Six, where the hell had? Catford dogs had been One. Two had been the Long Pond on Clapham Common, and real brass monkey weather it'd been the times he'd met there. In this boozer he'd only had one meeting. With Biggs and one of the laborers. Since then it'd been done up so's he'd never have known it. Slicker sipped his beer and looked around.

So soon after opening time there was only one other customer, a lined, scrubbed sage who might have been a docker or a driver, sitting with a glass of Guinness. Slicker was ninety percent sure this was the right place. But nothing except a hundred percent, he reflected, had ever been good enough for the guv'nor. That was why the guv'nor stayed outside always, while the rest were inside, nicked, or else running, or by this time out again and pretending to go straight, or even trying to go straight, while every copper with a spare minute shambled after them, just to make sure.

One hundred percent effort and accuracy for himself too, the guv'nor, as well as for the team. He'd permitted no margin for error from anyone, ever. So if this was the place, and today was Monday, where, ten minutes late, was Mr. OBE? Mr. I-Say-What's-New-at-the-Palace-Your-Majesty? Ten minutes wasn't late for most geezers, not in London traffic, but it was late for Charlie boy.

Slicker carried his pint glass past the silent jukebox, opened the door, and looked along Wapping High Street. Except for two leisurely youths loading crates into a van, the street was empty. A winding canyon of warehouses.

"In or out, dear, would y' mind? You'll be letting the snow in."

There was no snow, but an east wind whipped along the street, trundling empty cigarette packs and scraps of newspaper in its wake. The barmaid was sliding slices of liverwurst into bread rolls. Her arms were meaty enough to have withstood polar temperatures, or might have been had they not been so starkly nude. She wore a sleeveless satin blouse and topped up Slicker's glass with the extra half, pulling on the pump with a muscular white arm in which the biceps stood up like an Edam.

Slicker sauntered with his glass to the farther end of the long bar and out of a door into the east wind, closing the door behind him. He turned up the collar of the camel-hair coat and walked along a walled projection that was part jetty, part terrace, and in summer, he supposed, would be jammed with customers. Sea gulls hung and tilted above the stern of a motor cruiser. The river was busy with detritus, marker buoys, anonymous craft. Tugs were pulling a barge, and beyond the barge, on the far bank, crowded the cranes and wharves of Rotherhithe. Immediately below, where the Thames buffeted the jetty, and throttling back to slow ahead as it came abeam, chugged a cream and orange powerboat. Slicker was able to read on the hull the name Crestliner. The solitary figure at the wheel, looking up at Slicker but giving no sign of recognition, wore black oilskins.

It's Charlie boy, realized Slicker. 'E's joined the bleedin' navy. Staring, he did not hail Taylor but took a long swallow of beer.

The boat crawled on in search of a mooring, passing beyond the jutting stone of a warehouse and out of sight. Slicker put his glass on the parapet and walked up and down, hunching his shoulders against the cold. When finally the door from the bar opened, he tucked back his glove and looked at his watch. Eleven twenty-five.

"Thought I'd give her an airing," Taylor said. "First time this year."

He carried the *Financial Times* and a small whisky and had changed out of oilskins into a dark overcoat. One shoe and the cuff of the trouser leg above it were sodden from stepping ashore.

"Good luck," he said.

"Right," Slicker said, recovering his beer.

Taylor gazed up the river, then down in the direction of Limehouse and dockland. "Magnificent," he said, and tipping back his head, he inhaled the wind from the river.

"Think so?"

"You were here before. I remember." Taylor's manner was cheerful, even jaunty. He watched the distant barge, a black slab on the brown river. "We'll not use it again. Forget the old code. We'll use the underground. If we use anything."

"What d'yer mean—if? Thought there was goin' to be a job."

"You've been out of circulation. You've put on weight. Listen, there's the Victoria line since your day, supposing I said we take every second station from Brixton, alphabetically, and Brixton is C. Where's F?"

"Oxford Circus."

Taylor's head snapped back, and he laughed.

"And G's Euston and haitch 'as to be 'Ighbury and Islington," Slicker said. "Trouble with you, Charlie boy, you've got areas of inexperience. Like you've never done time. Anyone ever tell you the nick's not outer space? There's a supermarket goin' up in the Portobello Road, Billingsgate's scheduled for redevelopment and Christmas is December twenty-fifth. Next question?"

"Inside, it's warmer." Taylor led the way. He was still laughing. "Why don't you fill me in on my areas of inexperience?"

They sat in an untenanted region by the terrace door. The jukebox was erupting like lava; no corner of the bar was immune. The sage with the Guinness had gone, but at the bar leaned half a dozen men. Behind the bar the barmaid drew beer with her shot-putter's arm.

Slicker let Taylor pay for the drinks. He was careful to ask for only a half and to show little interest in it. Though he could no longer remember the names, there had been candidates for the mail train team whom the guv'nor had rejected because of rumors of their drinking. Taylor, chain-smoking, asked question after question about prison and the handful of high-security-risk prisoners, scattered through a dozen prisons, whom he had once organized and directed. In turn he was sympathetic, contemptuous, jocular, and inquisitive. He wanted to know why Slicker had been moved around three different prisons during his stretch, and the friends he'd made, the enemies, how he'd filled his time, what he'd learned. He handed over a ten-pound note for cheese rolls, declined a share of the rolls when Slicker brought them, and told him to eat up and keep the change. But Slicker felt under scrutiny. Taylor, he guessed, was interested more in how he answered than in the answers, more in how he'd coped with prison than in a critical analysis of the penal system. The folded *Financial Times* on the table beside the whisky lay like a statement of the gulf between their two lives.

"Do I pass?"

"Probably."

"What's the job then?"

"There's a man called Tait." Taylor revolved his cigarette lighter in the palm of his hand. "Colonel Graham Athelney Tait. Life Guards, member of the Queen's Household. Silver Stick Adjutant in Waiting."

"Don't think we've met."

"You're not going to. He's the opposition."

"Loaded?"

"Comfortable. Shipping broker. House in Gordon Square, estate in Hampshire."

"We're going to nick his stick?"

"If it excites you."

"Probably plastic." Slicker, frowning, munched cheese roll. " 'Ow comfortable is comfortable?"

"You'll do all right. Five grand suit you?"

Slicker bit into the roll, watched the gold lighter's slow somersaulting in Taylor's palm.

"Who else?"

"Who else d'you want?"

Slicker raised baffled eyes to Taylor's face but saw no sign of comedy. "Sorry, I'm slow today. It's this Mr. Stick, it's all too excitin'. Like what you're sayin' is, correct me if I'm wrong, but what I do is I find me own mob?"

"The nick's not outer space. Billingsgate's scheduled for

redevelopment. You know who's in circulation. Don't you?"

Slicker said nothing. And then, "Do you?"

"You for one."

"And the Zambezi, it'll be an ostrich farm, right? These fifteen 'undred ostriches, but none of 'em can get their 'eads out of the sand. You've become the real joker, Charlie boy. I'll admit it, I thought you was serious."

"Go and pee," said Taylor. "Take the paper."

Slicker eyed Taylor. The man who had risen from the warrens of West London to riches, honors, and an accent like a Tory chancellor sat flicking his lighter on and off. Slicker pushed back his chair, picked up the *Financial Times,* and walked to the door marked Gents. No one was inside. He opened the lavatory door, locked it behind him, and unfolded the newspaper. Within was a bulky envelope, unsealed and unaddressed. After counting the first score of twenty-pound notes, he wondered how many more he would count before he gave up. They were twenties, a faded purple in a wad three inches thick.

In the bar Taylor smoked and remembered 1963, year of Profumo, and the Great Train Robbery. Slicker's company excited him and took him back, and he found himself smiling at the self-indulgence of the scamper down memory lane, then expunging the smile in case the youths at the jukebox might imagine they were being solicited. The Great Train Robbery, and Manchester United won the Cup. Jack Nicklaus had won most of the golf presumably. Sonny Liston heavyweight champ. Kennedy shot. Churchill had been alive and an MP—hadn't he? Philby had scarpered to Russia, and that Russian bird, Valentina Howsyerfather, the first female in orbit. Bloody murder in the Congo, Pete Seeger singing "We Shall Overcome" in the States. Relko, the Derby, Yves Saint-Martin up. What else? Coldest sodding winter for two centuries. Taylor frowned toward the street door, momentarily open while a departing customer buttoned his coat. The March wind reached him even at this farther end of the bar.

Macmillan resigned, and Adenauer, and that Israeli bloke. Ben Gurion. Pope John dead, Nehru dead, Beaverbrook dead, Gaitskell dead. Kennedy. *Fanny Hill* prosecuted, that'd been a gas. What the hell had they been singing? Had the Beatles arrived? They must have. Hadn't Slicker swanned around singing "She loves you, yea, yea, yea"?

In the Gents, Slicker folded down the flap of the envelope, replaced it in the newspaper and returned to the bar. The youths were tapping their feet and bobbing their heads round the squalling jukebox. The muscled barmaid pulled pints. Taylor had not moved except to light a fresh cigarette. Slicker sat and placed the newspaper on the table between them.

"All right, you're serious." He picked up his bottle-green hat and stroked a finger around the brim. "Pity."

"Why pity?"

"Why? I could've used those twenties."

"Well?"

"I just done an eight-stretch, Charlie boy. I'm not yearnin' for another, not just yet."

"What's your problem?"

"No offense, but you are. Find me own mob? I'm lost, Charlie boy. Out of me depth. Like the way I saw it, I'll be honest, you sets up the tickle, you bein' the one and only true fount of wisdom and lolly, you 'ands out the orders, and you picks the team. Like before."

"It isn't like before. It's a routine screwing."

"I believe you. So what're you up to with routine screwin'? You." Slicker settled the hat on his head. "You said it, everythin' changes. You've changed all right. You scare me stiff. Or does this Silver Stick 'ave the keys to the Bank of England in 'is safe?"

"I don't know that he has a safe."

The door at the far end of the bar opened to admit two lorry drivers and a blast of wind. The barmaid glanced around from the cash register, but before she could voice her opinion, the door had slammed shut. From the jukebox a voice bewailed its lot: girlfriend gone, no friends of any kind, far from home. The youths bobbed and jigged. Slicker took off his hat and placed it beside the *Financial Times.*

"And if there is a safe, you don't know if there's anythin' in it."

"No idea."

"But if I get a mob together and turn the place over, it's five grand."

"Right. But I can help with the team."

"And when we've done Silver Stick, we've got a team, because the team's what you're after." A slow smile stretched Slicker's mouth. "Then comes the big one. Like 'Eathrow was the run-up on the train job because we needed the capital, Silver Stick's the run-up to the big one because we're after a team."

"There's no big one, Slicker."

"Thousands would believe you. Tell you what I'll do."

"Surprise me."

"Buy you a drink." And hurriedly: "Small one."

At the bar Slicker substituted a cold gravity for the grin and turned his head into casual profile so that Big Boss Man might see and know that he had chosen well, that Slicker was as foursquare and dependable as in the old days. He limited his own to a half of bitter and returned with the drinks to Taylor.

"No use askin' for just a hint, I suppose." Slicker lifted the lid of a cheese roll and regarded its interior. "About the big one."

Taylor blew impassive smoke.

"Thought as much. So all I know for sure is it's goin' to be breakin' and enterin'. Same as for this Mr. Stick."

"You assume."

"No 'arm assumin'. I like to dream of the big one these cold nights." He bit into a roll. "Tell you who you want for the peter, that's Blinky Johnson."

Taylor winced. Not at Blinky Jonhson but at the word "peter." He had grown up with this underworld expression for a safe, never knowing until Phoebe had lifted uncomprehending eyebrows, then laughed him almost out of the house, that in New Jersey it was childhood slang for penis, equivalent to willie and john thomas.

"You'll do the peter," Taylor said.

"Me?"

"Your trade, isn't it?"

"It's just that inside you don't get much scope with the practical aspect. Blinky's the best there is. 'E done the National Westminster—"

"Try forgetting Blinky. If you can't do it, say so."

"I can do it." Slicker munched cheese roll. "I'll 'ave old Dicer as wireman if I can prise 'im out of Birmingham."

"No wireman."

"What?"

"You go in alone. You'll want one driver."

"One driver. Thanks. Very generous, that is. Me and a driver." Slicker pondered. "I'll try Mossie Banks, but I warn you, 'is askin' price is two grand."

"There's a boy called Montgomery, runs a showroom in Hackney Road. Offer him two, or what you think, out of this." Taylor rested his hand on the *Financial Times.* "I'll square with you later."

"Montgomery."
"See him. Use your judgment."
Slicker meditated. "That the team then?"
"That's it."
"No lookout?"
"The driver's your lookout."
Slicker swallowed beer. Eight of 'em there'd been on the Heathrow Job, fourteen on the mail train plus a half dozen faceless odds and sods in the lawyers' offices and house agents' offices. Now there were to be two. Three if you counted Charlie boy. Slicker hoped Charlie boy knew what he was about. One way of looking at it, a carve-up for only himself and a driver, after the guv'nor had taken his cut, that ought to pay for a few weekends in Majorca.

He said, "So which do we do, Gordon Square or the landed estate?"

"Both."

"Both. Of course." Slicker nodded gravely. "At the same time."

"It's all practice," Taylor said, and told Slicker the addresses.

Colonel Tait and his wife, Taylor said, usually drove to their country house on Friday evenings and returned to London on Monday morning. Gordon Square had a living-in Portuguese couple who usually went out to bingo on weekend evenings. The country house had a cook-housekeeper and gardener, married. There was a dog, sometimes ferried between London and Hampshire, sometimes not. Slicker would have to check. Casing the houses, choosing the time, recruiting the driver, all details, everything, it was up to Slicker. Straightforward screwing, up his street. Gordon Square could be done on a Sunday night, the country house on the Monday night after Tait and his wife had screamed back to London with police escort to tot up the damage. Only the exaggerated care of

Taylor's speech, like an inebriate's, betrayed his excitement.

"I don't need to say this, but I'm saying it for the record, the least whisper of my name, anywhere, I'll know about it."

"You didn't need say it, I'll forget you did." Slicker finished his half pint. "Want an ax job on the grand piano?"

The pair regarded each other, Slicker mocking, Taylor without expression. Slicker had wondered, and known that Taylor knew he wondered, why Tait? A shipbroker and Silver Stick would not be short of a bob or two, but as the job clearly was not for cash, what other motive had prompted the choice of Tait? Deduction: personal reasons and none of Slicker's business.

"None of my business, Charlie boy, but aren't the rozzers goin' to ask themselves who's got it in for Silver Stick?"

"All right, who has?"

"Couldn't tell yer. Likely Silver Stick might 'ave a fair idea. It was only a thought."

"But I do the thinking."

"Course yer do. But if yer fixed another couple of jobs in Gordon Square, or in 'Ampshire, nothin' to do with Silver Stick, might be a little less obvious."

"Up to you. I don't want to know. More places you turn over, greater your chance of being nicked."

Taylor had considered the risk. Burglaries at both of Tait's places were going to be too much of a coincidence for the coppers to swallow. To do Tait's homes alone, or to throw in others, either way there were risks. He wanted to laugh aloud. Wasn't that what it was about?

"What d'you think of the barmaid, Slicker?" he said.

"Me?"

"Your style?"

"She can 'andle a pump, what yer might call a firm grip on the pump." Slicker grinned and craned his neck. "Goin' into the procurin' business, are yer?"

"For you I just might. I like to keep the team happy."

"Don't worry about me."

"I'll try not to. And you try not to splash that salary, please."

Slicker stowed the folded *Financial Times* into an inner pocket of his camel-hair coat and picked up his hat. "When do I see yer then?"

How long will you need?"

"Might depend a bit on the Montgomery bloke, mightn't it? Maybe two weeks to set it up—"

"I don't want to see you till afterwards. Three weeks from today?"

"Should be all right."

"Noon at—F?"

"Effing Oxford Circus. Bit of a circus this one sounds like if yer ask me."

"I'm not asking you."

The jukebox youths were chatting up the barmaid. Taylor walked ahead through the long bar. Behind, Slicker turned his head toward the barmaid to utter a ta-for-now, but she was in witty conversation with a party in a safari jacket. Slicker followed Taylor into the street.

"Givin' me a lift in the good ship *Venus* then? Shiver me timbers?"

"Best way to Hackney Road is the tube to Bethnal Green. Change at Whitechapel and Mile End. If you want to get started. Don't know the buses."

"What're you on about? I'm a man of means, aren't I? What's wrong with taxis?"

seven

In a private suite high in a leading West End hotel, as the press, finding no reason to provide free publicity, might have called it, the hothouse roses in the Finnish glass stirred and rearranged themselves, pointlessly, under Taylor's fingers.

Through the window and across Park Lane, in the park, the trees were coming into leaf. The sky was blue; the remorseless daffodils blew their trumpets. April had come in like a lamb, and everywhere, Taylor supposed, friends, neighbors, and perfect strangers would be telling one another they'd suffer for it later. Shirt-sleeved, he roamed the sitting room, and at the table of drinks moved the vodka and martini bottles to one side, the whisky farther forward, and the champagne bucket with its protruding gold foil into a position of nonchalance toward the rear.

He poured whisky but left it on the table and wandered away so that he would not drink it. Already he had drunk two and twice cleaned his teeth. The stereo played, serenely, *Best of Bing,* which he'd bought in the foyer. Why, he wanted to know, finding himself rearranging the rearranged roses, did waiting for her put him on edge? She was a perquisite of wealth like the others. He was not certain they even liked each other. She was twenty-five minutes late and had not phoned. When the doorbell buzzed, he counted to ten, gazing out at traffic and daffodils, then sauntered to the door.

She wore a knitted wool dress and a complicated necklace from some Asian boutique: metallic disks, chain, dangling extensions.

"Mr. Leo Scofield's suite?" she asked, deadpan.

"No puns please," he said.

She sat back in an armchair, handbag tidily on the carpet beside her feet. Bing sang:

Once I built a railroad.
Made it run . . .

Taylor summoned a smile. The first grimy moments were none the less grimy for being passed amid roses and stereo.

"Had lunch?" he said.

"Ages ago."

"What did you have?"

"An apple, a carrot, and two yogurts."

"Two?"

"Hazelnut and cherry."

"No wonder you're fat, you should watch the yogurts." He regarded Suzy, her body bamboo-thin under the wool dress. She had hips like coat hangers and shoulders, when naked, as white and hard as billiard balls.

Once I built a tower
To the sun. . . .

"Champagne?" he said.

"The obligatory champagne. It'll make me randy."

Taylor picked in silence at the gold foil, disapproving the bluntness and Americanisms. Where was there a bird with Suzy's looks and brightness and sense of fun who did not have to be outspoken, who not only was *nice,* or as nice as a high-class call girl was allowed to be, but who was not frightened of showing herself to be nice?

In opposite armchairs they drank and skirmished with words while Bing sang "Thanks," then "Just One More Chance." They went into the bedroom, and after they had made love, Suzy lay open-eyed, tracing letters on Taylor's chest.

"Leo the Lion," she said, tracing the words with a fingernail. "I am totally out of my mind, but I could almost get fond of you."

"They all do. Besotted."

"You're foul. And look at this hair, it's gray." She tweaked the hair. "It's not even gray, it's white. How many times have we met?"

"Are you going to say, 'We can't go on meeting like this'?"

"Go on, how many?"

"Six?"

"Four. What color are my eyes?" She had shut her eyes.

"Hazelnut?"

She opened them. They were green.

"See?" she said.

"Not really, but I'd like to," and he drew down the sheet and blanket which she had pulled over her for warmth and gazed on the young skinny body. "So what goes on in that mind you're totally out of?"

"You'd be furious."

"Don't tell me then," he said, though he suspected she would. "Tell me"—and his voice was husky—" 'let's go away together, darling, far away, let's leave all this behind.' "

"I've been thinking, what it is, I think you bring out the the mother in me."

After a moment, Taylor said, "Really."

"Knew you'd be angry. But it's true, isn't it, you're in need of mothering. You won't talk about your family or friends; you never tell me anything. Most of them never stop yacking. I just might almost get besotted, could be, but the thing is you don't believe it. You worry, and you're insecure. You'd like to be besotting, but you don't think you are. You're too intelligent."

"It's analysis time."

"You're cross."

"I'm not cross. Incestuous, obviously"—and he gathered Suzy in his arms—"but cross, never."

They made love once more, and later, while Suzy bathed and dressed, he counted out ten ten-pound notes, added another because of the increase in the price of yogurt, and put them in her handbag. After she had left, he swallowed flat champagne, returned Bing to his sleeve, and scooped the roses from the vase. In the foyer he bought the *Evening Standard* and the *Evening News,* the third edition of each which he had bought that day, and was buying, edition upon edition, every day. With newspapers, flowers, and record he waited while the doorman hailed a taxi.

"Hackney Road," he told the driver.

A letter bomb at the El Al office in Regent Street. Soaring steel prices. Two dead in pileup on the A21 at Sevenoaks. All old stuff. Hours old.

Still not a mention of Colonel G. A. Tait, Silver Stick Adjutant in Waiting. Agreed, only two weeks had passed since the five thousand had changed hands, but a man could become impatient.

The plate-glass window of Europa Sports Cars Ltd. extended for almost half a block. For the second time in two weeks Taylor peered in at the overpowered cars and the big-shouldered boy in the inner glass-walled office. Two weeks earlier, before glancing through old reports and memoranda amassed by Miss Widdicombe as clutter, he had not even been aware that Charles Taylor Ltd. owned the leases of property in this corner of the East End, let alone that from here came cadging car salesmen with ambition and hopes of loans.

The older, ill-looking salesman with warts on his hands was talking with a customer seated in a secondhand Panther J72 as lividly gleaming as if it had come straight from the paint shop. Taylor walked to the glass-walled office where Montgomery, a cigar between his fingers, was stooping over the shoulder of a girl typist, inspecting a letter in progress.

"Excuse me, would you mind?" Taylor's voice was apologetic, low-pitched, clear as water. Competing with the apology was an absolute assurance and a ring of sufficient money to fill the vaults of several banks. "I'm considering, not buying, for the moment, but the Ferrari's a beauty. D'you have any literature on it, something I could take away?"

No sooner had he spoken than the possibility occurred to him that the green vehicle he had in mind was not a Ferrari, that there was not a Ferrari in the showroom. Since entering the chauffeured Rolls bracket, he was no longer infallible because he was no longer interested. He avoided the Motor Show, and though he would watch on television the racing at Silverstone and Brands Hatch, he would not make the journey there. In profile the green Ferrari, the Berlinetta Boxer, if that was what it was, looked like the cockpit of Concorde.

But so did the Lamborghini. Didn't it? John Pollard owned a Lamborghini.

"She's a beauty, only eight hundred on the clock," said Montgomery, and to the girl, "Dig out everything on the Boxer, will you?"

Montgomery knew cars. After thirty seconds of aerofoil spoilers, rotary pistons, kick-down and added torque, Taylor stopped listening. Hearing the enthusiasm but not the words, he followed Montgomery around the glittering nose cone of steel and glass, and around again. He was not even certain Montgomery was speaking exclusively of the Ferrari. Pointing and caressing, the athletic young zealot had sidestepped to a Maserati. Taylor observed and was silent, like an old sweat from the Yard's Heavy Mob, while Montgomery voiced figures and mechanics: twelve hundred, transverse four camshaft, servo assistance, viscous fan coupling, one-four-eight, overhead camshaft.

That made two camshafts, surely, overhead and transverse four; the big-chested enthusiast could not have been talking about one car. Taylor caught the word Alfa, then Opel. He repressed an urge to laugh and offered a cigarette, which Montgomery ignored, showing the cigar. He reflected he'd be fortunate to escape without signing checks for three cars at least.

Not only was Montgomery big in the chest and shoulders, unless that was the cut of the jacket, but he stood three or four inches over six feet, and when he sat, demonstrating the Ferrari's console, cigar stylishly between fingers as though for an advertisement, he had to slide the driving seat back to its limit before straightening his knees. He wore two hundred pounds' worth, in Taylor's estimate, of new jersey-knit suit in a brown and beige plaid. Taylor wondered if business was booming or if Slicker already had recruited with banknotes the team's wheelman. The red sports shirt was carefully open at the collar, and lapping the back of the collar the combed hair was as glossy as the publicity pamphlets now being brought from the office by the typist. Montgomery took the superfluous paper without a glance at the girl.

He talked grammatically and without humor, like a political aspirant in front of the constituency committee. Taylor placed him as an able, ambitious bore. He'll do, he thought; he'll do very nicely.

"How much?" Taylor said, and for the first time the younger man hesitated in his sales pitch.

Now he's summing me up; if there's something grabs him as much as cars, it's a profit; he's right for the job, Taylor thought.

A sum was tossed in the air, fifteen thousand four hundred pounds, and a trial run offered. Taylor accepted the publicity material and Montgomery's card: "E. Montgomery, Consultant, Europa Sports Cars." Consultant pleased Taylor. The boy had hopes, a foot already on the ladder. He was speaking with urgency about antirust warranties.

"I'll be in touch, many thanks," Taylor said. Before he was halfway to the street door, Montgomery had reached the glass office, putting the departing customer out of his mind, glossy locks afloat over the red and plaid.

Taylor thought: Next time we meet could be for the final briefing, or on the day, he'll not even remember me.

"Kew," he told the taxi driver, and stuffed the pamphlets into the evening newspapers for disposal. The roses and record he gathered onto his lap.

"Charles, they're beautiful!"

Phoebe sank her face into the roses. She carried them

into the kitchen, lopped three inches off the stems, and arranged them in a teapot. Her arrangement technique was to shake the teapot. Action arranging, she called it. How the flowers came to rest, so were they arranged. Taylor plugged in the kettle for tea.

"Where's Ann?"

"Your study, doing homework."

"Homework?" He reached for cups. "She doesn't have any homework."

"It's voluntary. A project on Africa."

"What happens to her TV?"

"Says she's going to be a selective viewer."

"Forgoing *Weather for Farmers* and the news in Welsh. Good. You're dressed up."

"Rachel phoned, I'm going to the club. Why don't you come along?"

"First time you've suggested that in about two years."

"First time in two years I thought you just might say yes. What goes on anyway? I've never known you so merry."

"Merry?"

"Not merry, more fizzy, kind of suppressed manic, for days. Pleased with yourself. I almost might have figured it was the OBE except the Booker's debacle canceled that out."

"The Booker's debacle has canceled a lot of things out. I've had my bellyful of aristocrats and pedigrees for one thing. Right up to the top royals."

"Well, that's news. So what's the exhilaration? Charles Taylor Limited up five points?"

"It's the weather. Spring and the rising sap."

Phoebe looked at him warily. She said, "Sure," then lifted the teapot of roses to her nose, inhaled, and carried them from the kitchen.

Taylor, carrying tea, glanced into the study. "Hullo. Don't stop. Everything all right?"

"Come here," Ann said. "Where's the Zambezi?"

Taylor wanted to smile. Coincidences could be funny. He belived in them. You could go five years without seeing a particular acquaintance, then twice, three times, on consecutive days, you'd spot him across the street. Or her.

"Here, somewhere," he said, studying the open atlas on the desk. Adjacent to the atlas, on cartridge paper, Ann had drawn a painstaking outline of Africa with the "Nile," "Niger," "Sahara Dessert," and clustered around the Nile a huddle of triangles and whiskered faces labeled "Pyramids," "Sphynxs."

Slicker, he thought, will do the Tait job. He might waltz it, and he might be nicked. What he will not do is walk out with the five grand.

"There," he said. "*Sanders of the River*. Paul Robeson."

Clearly she had never heard of Paul Robeson. He opened his mouth to sing the boat song from *Sanders of the River,* but Ann uttered first.

"This room *stinks*."

"You're the one who's been here."

"*Charming*. It's all your disgusting cigarettes. Look at that, they've been there *days*."

"Greta should've emptied it."

"Greta's got flu."

"The daily then, what's her name, the lovely Mrs. Sullivan."

Ann giggled. "She left. Don't you know *anything?*"

"Who found the Zambezi? Tell me that."

Upstairs he changed into a polo-neck sweater and the trousers of a Donegal suit. From the dressing-room window he could see through the trees the Crestliner aslant on the mud. To the left the view was blocked by the brick of the Commonwealth Mycological Institute, but to the right, beyond the garden and swath of wasteland and towpath, the Thames trudged toward Kew Bridge. Above the chestnuts and willows on the island prodded the faraway tops of tower blocks, and between the end of the island and the bridge, on the mud and pebbles of the north bank, lay abandoned barges and a shabby houseboat.

Descending the stairs, he paused to glance through the bay window looking out over parked cars, the Green, and the gates of Kew Gardens, where at the turnstile leaned the red-necked copper, impatient for closing time. At this late-afternoon hour, before the season of visitors and cricket, few people were about apart from the copper and a woman walking her dog across the Green. Taylor could understand why his wife refused to give up the house.

She was at her writing desk in the drawing room, a gin and tonic at her elbow. He lay back in an easy chair with a second cup of tea. "Thought you were off to Hurlingham."

"Seven o'clock," Phoebe said. "Is July all right?"

"All right for what?"

"Me going off."

"Going off where?"

"For heaven's sake, I'm going to see Daddy. I meet Marion in Nassau; then we fly on to New York. We discussed it all."

"Ten seconds ago we were discussing Hurlingham."

"Please, I'm writing to Marion. Is July third all right with you or isn't it? For about two weeks."

"Fine."

"I don't have to be with you to watch a cup final or collect a knighthood or anything?"

"July is fine."

Phoebe bent over her writing paper and wrote: lurching wind-tossed writing which bore traces, but traces only, of the private school calligraphy at which she had once excelled. She turned around.

"Look, you're not doing anything, why don't you come?"

He preferred the Hurlingham Club on summer

afternoons, on the terrace, the Cadena Café trio playing their selection from *The Arcadians* and on the lawn ferocious croquet. The men in white blazers, the women re-creating Simla. Darjeeling tea. Mr. Kipling. Old ladies with stern faces, and the captains and the kings.

"Come?"

"C-o-m-e," spelled Phoebe, "come."

"Got it."

"So hell, sorry I spoke, forget it."

"This the States we're discussing now or the Hurlingham Club?"

"Well, it isn't our sex life."

"For God's sake can't we discuss this in bed?"

After a moment of startled silence the laughter broke: a crescendo of mutual juvenile laughter with Phoebe attempting shushing sounds for fear the racket might bring Ann into the room. Taylor stood up, kissed the back of his wife's neck, reached down for her glass, and tasted the colorless liquid.

"You forgot the tonic."

"I did not either, smart ass. What d'you think those bubbles are—soap?"

"C'mon then."

She stared up. "You're not serious."

"Don't waste time. We've only two hours."

"I've told you, I'm going to the club."

"I'm going to see the Lee Marvin Western, but I don't keep boasting about it."

"You're insane. What about Ann?"

"Ann's up the Zambezi. We'll use the top guest room and make noises like guests."

"There's Greta."

"Greta's got flu, don't you know anything?"

"No," said Phoebe with finality, and sipped from her glass.

Taylor took the glass in one hand, Phoebe's arm in the other, and ushered her from the drawing room. He glanced into the study, but it was empty. Abandoned on the desk were the paper and open atlas. From the sitting room issued sounds of pop music. Carrying the glass, he followed up the stairs.

In bed in the attic bedroom Phoebe said, "The gin didn't spoil the performance, would you say?"

"I didn't have any gin."

"Maybe I wouldn't either if your enthusiasm was a bit more frequent."

"Phoebe, love."

"This is crazy," she said, and scrambled out of bed. She snatched up her clothes, unlocked the door, opened it a fraction, and peered down. Leaving the door defiantly wide open, she hastened nude down the stairs.

eight

Janet Poole in T-shirt and unsuitably tight shorts halted a trowel on its journey earthward. From the cottage had started a commotion of ringing and banging. Her husband was digging on the far side of the rubble heap, except that now he would have stopped digging and be watching the cottage. Janet refused to look up. The trowel dug at a buried brick.

"For you, Dad!" Tony bawled from the cottage door, and leaving the telephone dangling on its plastic spiral, he hurtled back through the cottage and out of the rear door to his brother and a resumption of goal-kicking practice.

Poole stabbed his gardening fork into the earth and walked toward the cottage. The telephone had been the first item of electronic equipment he had had installed. He had hoped installing it might take six months, or eighteen, but being a policeman, and more impressively a policeman from Scotland Yard, he had been given priority, and three days after he had filled in the forms the telephone had been in and functioning. It would be the first item to go, he had assured Janet, once he was retired and they were living here permanently.

Except that once he was retired the factory would no longer be calling him.

Janet watched her husband striding across dug soil. She was kneeling, prizing stones from earth which one day would be a lawn. Possibly an oblong lawn, possibly L-shaped. They hadn't decided yet. She watched the long, stooping back, the legs stamping soil from gumboots at the cottage door. If he has to go back to London, I shall cry, I shall cry all night, I don't care, she thought.

"Yes?"

"Fothergill. Sorry to bother you, sir. How's the countryside?"

"Pleasant up to now, thanks for asking. It was to have been the weekend off. Two days. Remember?"

Still might be two days, Poole thought. If he were being summoned back to London, or something had come up making it advisable to get back, the sergeant would not be the one to tell him. Probably.

"Have you got the radishes in, sir?"

"As a matter of fact, we haven't got anything in. We get interruptions from people asking tomfool questions. What is it?"

"Hate to say it, but probably nothing. You may even know, in which case I'm covered with shame. I just heard Taylor's been blackballed from Booker's Club. Two weeks ago. You're the Taylor enthusiast. Thought I'd pass it on."

"Booker's—in St. James's?"

"That's it. Very patrician."

"Where did you hear?"

"Hate to say this too, but in the canteen. Inspector Forge with his ear to the social whirl. With respect, but he ought to be editing the gossip page in something glossy."

"Bit slow off the mark, isn't he—two weeks ago?"

"Quicker than the gossip columns. They haven't had it at all yet."

"Phone them. Earn yourself a tenner."

"You mean that?"

"No. I don't know. I don't think so. I'll think about it. Why was he blackballed?"

"No one ever knows; it wouldn't be gentlemanly."

"No, suppose not." Poole could hear the boys creating uproar in the long grass at the back of the cottage. "Anyway, thanks. What about Slicker?"

"Two nights ago he was at Wimbledon dogs. Haven't seen him since then. Far as I know he's not been with Taylor since that pub in Wapping."

"Far as you know."

"Bit tricky keeping unofficial tabs on a bloke when I've enough paperwork to last till Christmas."

"You're idle, Sergeant. We're going to keep unofficial tabs on both of them. A man who's gone to the top of the heap like Taylor doesn't pick up again with a rogue like Slicker unless he's got something on the boil."

Does he? Might it not be mere innocent nostalgia, like army sweats at reunions, reliving North Africa and the Normandy beaches? Poole postponed a little longer the moment when he would hang up and walk through the cottage to investigate whether the bedlam was the boys laughing or the boys fighting. The longer he left Janet in the dark, the greater would be her relief when he told her they still had another thirty-six hours or so for digging, clearing and being together.

"Who else are they seeing?" he said. "Where's Slicker spend his time? Are any of the train lot due for release? What about girlfriends? Taylor's fifty, he'll be biting his nails, wondering about his manhood; he'll have girlfriends like a dog has fleas."

* * *

Suzy sat in the Rivoli Bar at the Ritz, waiting. She sipped infrequently from a glass of white wine, helped herself more frequently to the unnecessary bowl of little square biscuits, and turned the pages of *Horse and Hound.* She was aware of being a distracting influence on the important conversation between the two City gents who kept glancing her way from a table against the opposite wall. On the other hand, disappointingly, she was clearly no distraction to the granddad in tweed who sat with scotch and soda, his knobby red hands folded in his lap. He looked very sweet. Probably a duke up from the country to buy a saddle. There were only half a dozen customers in the bar. She'd give it another twenty minutes, then move to the Carlton Tower.

She did not know whom she was waiting for, or whether he would turn up, and she did not mind. She rarely picked up a client in a bar because once you started frequenting the quality bars, a lone lass turning the pages of *Horse and Hound,* the barmen got to know you, and most of them were uptight snobs. Once one had asked her for fifty quid or he'd call the hotel detective, cheeky bugger. This one was all right though, voice like the male lead in a Noel Coward comedy, and it wasn't as if she were lowering the tone. High neck, hem well down over the knees, knitted jacket. Cost a bomb. Anyway, she liked the Rivoli Bar. It was calm and rather faded. No glitter. She wouldn't have been here at all if Leo Scofield hadn't let her down.

Or whatever his name was, because it wouldn't be Leo Scofield. Ah, well, they came in all sizes. Five more years at this rate she'd be worth—what? Forty thousand? And the house. Alex would be nine, time for boarding school, if she could bear to let him go. Eton?

Suzy clamped her pink lips on the giggle which tried to squeeze through at the thought of Alex entering Eton. She got up, exchanged *Horse and Hound* for *Country Life,* and returned to the sofa. She enjoyed the house advertisements in *Country Life.* Gloomy photogenic residences on 17,000 acres in Argyllshire. Nineteen miles of salmon river. Trout. Stags. Gillies. Coats of arms. Stabling for 124 horses. Some modernization required.

Here came a possibility, through the door, across the carpet, looking twice at her on his swagger to the bar. Unlit uptilted cigarette between his teeth—good teeth, they looked. Good hard features, plum-colored shirt, handmade shoes. Something in television? Probably queer. She'd met people who said you could always tell, but she never could. Suzy looked down at a half-timbered house, conservatory, paddock, 2m Bishop's Candle, Somerset.

Sorry, going boxing, we'll make it tomorrow instead, Leo the Lion had said. Going to another girl, more likely. Or home to wifey. He had to have a wife, probably six children. He was a puzzle. Wouldn't talk about himself. Smallest question, down would come the blinds. Still, what did it matter; sooner or later he'd call it a day, vanish like all of them. Probably wasn't with another girl either, he wasn't especially avid. Not what you'd call a rocket. Not like that Yankee professor at the weekend. Or the Arab who'd called her to Claridge's! Pow! Would you just mind where you're laying your pipeline, mister! He hadn't been all that free with his dinars, though. Wouldn't have gone if she'd known, but on the phone he'd been Mr. Brown, and once you were there you went through with it or you were as racist as the rest of them, and anyway they were all blokes under their burnouses. Second time he'd called, "Shalom," she'd said, and hung up.

Suzy sipped and looked at the Victorian scenes painted on the walls and pillars: hansom cabs, guardsmen strutting, crinolines, stovepipe hats. Swaggerman at the bar was watching her. She looked directly into his eyes.

Come on then if you're coming. Don't be shy, dearie.
Still, I'd have preferred old Leo, Suzy thought, as the man started threading between tables toward her, showing his white teeth. Enjoy your boxing, Leo.

Both boxers were colored. Chicho Varas, the Puerto Rican, a tornado with a beard, lashed a fist through empty air where an instant ago the head of Brian Tucker had been. Tucker stepped in, hit the Puerto Rican in the ribs and belly, and stepped out again.

"Pace it, Brian!"

"Use the ring!"

"Nicely, Brian!"

Being the elite of fight audiences, the spectators did not bay and whistle as did the rabble in the back seats at the Empire Pool or York Hall; or not anyway until the main bout, or the arrival of the heavyweights, by which time further brandies would have been drunk, and the private betting would have grown serious, and over the loudspeaker the master of ceremonies would be requesting that gentlemen remember, please, the club's rule of silence. Advice in this middleweight bout was offered in barely raised voices, and Taylor offered none, though his interest was larger than that of the majority of members sipping and cigar smoking around the ring, under the chandeliers of the Café Royal's Napoleon Room. Tucker, a Jamaican cockney, was a promising prospect. Taylor, having contributed a check to his training and living expenses, owned one-ninth of him.

"Watch their feet," he said. "Tucker's up on his toes. Now—look at Varas."

"Flat-footed," Lord Pollard said, enthusiastic. "He doesn't look finished yet."

"It'll go the distance," said Taylor.

He blew cigarette smoke, fingered the stem of his glass. The evening was a success. John Pollard was worth cultivating for more purposes than he, John Pollard, suspected. Though uninvolved in sport of any form, his shy lordship had surprised Taylor by accepting, out of curiosity, the invitation to be his guest at the National Sporting Club. Two floors up, in the Dubarry Room, they had dined and discussed the steel shortage, land development, and politics. Now, at their knees a low table bearing the port and brandy bottles labeled with Taylor's name, Lord Pollard enthused and questioned.

"How can anyone *tell* who's winning? They both—ugh!" Lord Pollard winced as simultaneously both fighters hit and were hit, hard, a concurrent thud-thud of leather on flesh and bone. "Horrible. How'd they keep it up? How many more rounds?"

When the round ended, a roly-poly member with a Punch cigar between thumb and three fingers, little finger lifted, turned in his seat. "Tenner on your boy to win, Charles? Loyalty'll get you nowhere. Give you three to one."

Whorls of slow tobacco smoke spiraled toward the lights over the ring. Tucker won on points, and when the next bout started, two bantamweights who fell on each other with a flurry of punching, Taylor's thoughts began to stray. He was fairly sure he had established himself with John Pollard as an agreeable, useful friend, and now he would have liked to say good-night. Small hope of locating Suzy at this hour, though that would have been the ideal. He'd not seen her for four days. Or Phoebe either, come to that.

The thinner, more meager of the two bantamweights shocked himself, his dinner-jacketed audience, and his opponent by knocking him out. Applause clattered in the Napoleon Room, and fiftypence pieces and banknotes curved into the ring. The roly-poly man wobbled to his feet and tossed a folded banknote, like a bun at the zoo. Lord Pollard sat on the edge of his seat, delighted and horrified. Taylor topped up the glasses.

Good company or not, he mistrusted his guest. The arrogance was not obtrusive, but it was there. Come the crunch, Lord Pollard too would place a blackball in the box. He had the family crest, the centuries of ancestors, the columns in *Debrett's* and *Burke's,* the remote but undisputed kinship with the Queen herself, all of which his host had read and studied before telephoning the invitation. Charles Taylor, host, had only money. Though he might consort with the sporting lordships here at the National Sporting Club, he was forbidden, he now knew, to follow them into the clubs along St. James's Street and Pall Mall. You still had to be born to it. He had the trappings, but he was not a gentleman. It was as if he exuded a smell which demonstrated that he was not a gentleman; even though he'd learned to say telephone, not phone, and lavatory, not toilet, and to know duchesses, and never to wear brown or own a two-tone car. Whatever anyone said, the class thing remained, a pernicious burrowing grub that left its slime on you and could never be escaped.

Three cheers for blackballing anyway. A dozen tedious years acquiring position and resisting the pull back into gangland games. Now the blackballing had tipped it. All these years had he merely been waiting, unaware, for an excuse?

"You've a bastion of male chauvinist piggery here, Charles," Lord Pollard said, enjoying himself, looking about at the ubiquitous black ties. "Do I know anyone? Wasn't Oscar Wilde a member?"

A bell sounded. Taylor explained that the elegant letter *N* adorning the walls did not stand for Napoleon but for

Napoleon's chef, Nicol, who'd saved his francs, probably cut a few corners on the truffles and venison, and bought the place. In the ring's glare two youths with white tense bodies stalked each other, darting out tentative fists, but as yet too apprehensive to attempt more.

Taylor watched with an appearance of interest. Four cheers for blackballing. The belief that cash and the long flogging years which had brought the mask of gentility would also bring acceptance had been a delusion. He'd seemed to be accepted. But the Booker's Club humiliation had poked home the reality. Well, thank you, Booker's. At last, to know his place.

He realized he was smiling and wanting to laugh aloud, wondering whether he should send an anonymous donation to Booker's.

"Keep off the ropes, lad!"

"Watch his left!"

"Stay with him, Terry!"

Suddenly the bout was alive, the white-limbed red-headed Scot crowding his opponent in a corner with a whirl of punches, the equally white Londoner covering up, sagging, then unleashing hooks which pushed the Scot backward across the ring.

Taylor shielded his smiling mouth behind his hand, a schoolboy again, concealing mirth from the teacher. He groped for a cigarette.

"Keep at him, Terry!"

"Box him!"

To thine own self be true, in a nutshell. Being back in business, the business he knew, there lay true satisfaction.

"He's on his heels, the redhead, Cameron," Lord Pollard said, forward on the edge of his red velvet chair.

"He's got the punch if he can land it," Taylor said.

The taylor should stick to his last, Taylor mused.

Sipping port, he sat back in his chair, stretching his legs under the chair of the roly-poly member in front, approving with his eyes the fight to which his mind paid little attention. Cigarette ash flecked his white shirt and black lapels.

Between rounds he debated with John Pollard whether the International Monetary Fund was on a losing wicket in trying to allot gold a weaker role in world finance. They disagreed over the potential of Sardinia for property development. They agreed that the latest proposals for redeveloping Piccadilly Circus were nonstarters. Above them in the ring the bout ended with the boxers leaning against each other for support. Taylor poured port.

"Heard Graham Tait's been burgled," Lord Pollard said. "Twice in two days. First his London house, then down in Hampshire."

"Tait?"

"Being with you made me think of him. Sorry, bit tactless." John Pollard held his port up to the light, what light there was. He sniffed it. "That Booker's business was unforgivable. They're dinosaurs at Booker's. I'd say you were well out of it. These the heavyweights?"

"Light-heavy. Watch Hudson, in the blue trunks, watch his right hand." Taylor stubbed out his cigarette in the ashtray. "In the papers?"

"What? Don't know, expect so. Bertie May told me. He and Jill were down at the Taits' for the weekend."

There had been nothing in the papers. Taylor had skimmed them all, mornings and evenings. But he'd had to say something. He longed to stay with the subject.

"Bertie couldn't talk about anything else," said Lord Pollard. "I ask you. What I'd call a morbid interest. Know what Auden said?"

"What?"

"'Wicked deeds have their glamor but those who commit them are always bores.' Something like that."

Taylor nodded. You too, your lordship. By definition. Hunted any good foxes lately?

Tonight was fight night, Monday. So Slicker must have done Gordon Square Friday or Saturday and Hampshire last night. He couldn't have done Hampshire first. Could he?

Taylor leaned back and watched with feigned interest the bobbing right hand of Hudson. Professionalism, now he had accomplished this foray back into the crime business, was keeping your trap shut.

nine

The budding chestnut trees obscured three-quarters of the Roosevelt statue. Taylor switched on the kettle. From the mat outside the door, set down there with geometrical precision by Harry, he gathered up the morning newspapers. With papers, tea, and a fresh pack of cigarettes he returned to bed.

The *Times* reported:

Thieves broke into both the town and country residences of Col. G. A. Tait at the weekend and stole jewellery and antiques to the value of £7,000.

Col. Tait, member of the Royal Household and a former polo colleague of the Duke of Edinburgh, discovered that his house in Gordon Square had been ransacked when he returned to London with his wife from Hampshire on Sunday. On Sunday evening their home at Alton, Hants., was entered and robbed.

A police spokesman said there was no evidence directly connecting the two crimes. "It looks like plain bad luck. There has been a spate of breaking-and-entering in the Gordon Square neighbourhood recently. We are watching the area."

Inspector Peter Church of the Hampshire police described the burglary at the six-bedroom country house as "obviously the work of professionals."

Col. Tait, a director of the City shipbrokers Hollis and Ledbury, accompanied the Queen and Prince Philip on their recent visit to Italy. He was appointed Silver Stick Adjutant in Waiting in 1966.

The *Financial Times* carried one sentence.

The *Express* used one paragraph headed "Lost Weekend," and Taylor guessed that what had started as a half column had become truncated, edition by edition, as news of the late Commons debate on prices had expanded.

He picked up the telephone and dialed. "Harry? Would you mind slipping out for a *Sporting Life* when you've a moment? I'm going through the card today. Might as well pick up the rest of the dailies while you're about it. *Mail, Mirror, Sun, Telegraph, Guardian.*"

Waiting, he read the business pages, then the sports. Within ten minutes Harry had arrived with an armful of newspapers.

The *Telegraph* carried an untruncated third of a column. Entry at the Gordon Square house in Bloomsbury had been made through a rear lavatory window. The safe had been blown. Chief Inspector Salmon, CID, was conducting the investigation. The gang responsible for the break-in at the Alton house had chosen the two hours when the resident help, Mr. Robert Philipson and his wife, Edna, had been visiting friends.

The *Guardian* printed a solitary paragraph on page six, the *Mail* a caption under a picture of Tait stepping from his Daimler. The *Sun* and *Mirror* competed with photographs of a hearty daughter and quotes. "They were lucky Daddy wasn't at home. He has his old polo sticks in the hall cupboard, and believe me, he'd have used them. He'd have biffed those brutes in a way they'd not have forgotten in a hurry."

Taylor leaned back against the pillows, smoking, smiling, two or three times laughing out loud. He was not certain that sweet was the word for revenge because in an ideal world, for true sweetness, the victim would have to be aware who had put the boot in, and why. But there was satisfaction and comedy. Pity Slicker hadn't snapped those polo sticks in two.

He shaved, showered, telephoned Phoebe, but was answered by Greta: his wife had gone for shoppings, okay.

He telephoned Miss Widdicombe at Charles Taylor Ltd. and heard the pertinent parts of the mail read out. A moment after he had replaced the telephone it rang: John Pollard thanking him for the evening, suggesting a day for meeting the surveyor and architect for the Eastbourne shopping precinct. Taylor refrained from mentioning the Tait burglaries.

He telephoned Martin and asked for the Rover. Dressing, he consulted *Sporting Life,* folded open at the table of correspondents' selections and balanced atop a radiator, against the window. Young Burt patrolled in a northerly direction toward the American Embassy. This week he had the 6 A.M. to 2 P.M. shift. Where was the creamy kid Law whose shift this normally was? Sick? Promoted to plain clothes?

He dialed a stables in Lambourne, and afterward a trainer in Kildare. He talked with his bookmaker. After checking that all lights were out, the taps in the bathroom off and the kettle unplugged, he locked up and took the lift down.

"Feeling's not so strong as it was, Harry. Pinkerton could be the best, four o'clock, but keep it each way." He passed Harry a five-pound note. "That's a measure of my doubts. Don't spend your own. It's a strong field."

Cover your tracks, Taylor reflected, and leaned back in a corner of the accelerating Rover. Leave nothing to chance. The world's truths lay in a handful of clichés.

"Furthermore, Harry, if I may call you Harry" —prosecuting counsel, smooth as syllabub—"on the morning when news of the burglaries was published, the accused requested you to bring him every newspaper." "'E was goin' through the card, sir." "Going through the card, an expression of the turf, I believe. That is what he told you." "That's right, sir." "But, Harry"—pouncing, vinegar in the syllabub—"you then left immediately, did you see the accused so much as glance at the racing pages? Was not this mention of racing the merest pretext—" "Give me Pinkerton at eight to one, didn't 'e? Won me fifty quid?"

Hyde Park Corner. Knightsbridge. Sloane Street. Martin parked on a yellow line and crossed the road to Partridge's for brown sherry, Turkish delight and alcoholic cherries. Taylor, smoking, watched a poodle relieve itself against a pillar box. The animal's mistress posted letters. Claret gabardine coat with a leather trim, crochet hat, pigskin shoulder bag, she was an actress in work, or model, or buyer for a fashion house, or someone's mistress beside the dog's. Taylor wanted her to look his way so that he might offer the long stare and discover the category to which she belonged, but she gave a tug on the leash and swayed away.

Martin negotiated the Rover through clogging traffic. Kings Road. New Kings Road. He parked in a turning off Parson's Green. Taylor walked through the streets of terraced houses, delighting in the cloudy day, the solitary whistling postman on his second delivery, the variegated parked cars, the absence of commotion, the builders' skips outside the houses which were coming up in the world, as he had, though God knew they'd plenty of mileage to go before they'd reach within hailing distance of him. In his head, silently, he sang "Among My Souvenirs."

"How are you, how's the leg?" He kissed her and took the broom from her hands. "Why can't you leave all that to Mrs. Thing?"

"All she does is talk. Talk talk talk. Says she's got a bad back. What's that you've brought?"

"Go and sit down. We're having sherry, Turkish delight and—" He unwrapped the glass jar and read aloud from the label. "'Fruitignac, candied morello cherries in fine cognac.'"

"Tee-hee-hee," tittered Mrs. Taylor, hobbling in carpet slippers into the sitting room. "Early, isn't it? Usually 'ave me cuppa now."

She shooed a cat from her armchair. Taylor brought glasses from the kitchen. He stepped over the cat basket, past a tea trolley piled with ornaments, playing cards, sewing, a Bible, and circuitously between the cake stand, a carton of apples, spare tables, electric fire, and propped folded deck chair.

"You're a caution these days. What're you up to?"

"Up to? Everything's lovely, Mum. When did the doctor last call?"

"Doctor! What does 'e know!" She shooed a cat from her armchair. "'Oward phoned, said if you called 'ere, would you phone 'im back. Look, d'yer mind? There's the ashtray, don't be drippin' it all over."

Taylor carried the Edward VIII coronation ashtray out to the gloomy corridor and telephoned the office. His brother was put through, needing to confirm that Charles would be free tomorrow for the accountants' meeting.

"Eleven thirty," Howard said. "I'm off to Paris again at three."

"Mon Dieu. Au revoir."

"Charlie, please. Eleven thirty all right?"

"No. I've an appointment at noon. Bring it forward. Or the afternoon."

"You're clear all morning. I checked with Miss Widdicombe. She showed me your appointments book."

Howard, don't argue, Taylor wanted to say. Life was too good, and he was too cheerful for arguing. Fizzy, Phoebe had called it. It was springtime in London, and Tait had been screwed good.

He said, "I'll have a word with them. But noon is out."

At three minutes before noon Slicker surfaced up the steps from Oxford Circus underground. He spotted Taylor among an army of shoppers at the corner of Oxford Street and Regent Street, waiting for the traffic to pass.

Slicker stood aside from the humanity crowding the entrance to the tube and looked up at the sky. He had grown a mustache. He had grown and newly shampooed his hair, which protruded from under the back of a new velvet hat. He wore a new cocoa-colored raincoat and a tie from the Burlington Arcade but had skimped on the suede shoes, which were new but cheap. He had treated his complexion either with lotions or sun-ray lamps. He looked like a theatrical agent back from an Alpine holiday.

"Cross over, keep walking, I'll follow," Taylor said.

They did not look at each other. After Slicker had

walked away, Taylor sorted change for the news vendor outside the underground. He opened his newspaper and looked at a display advertisement for Augustus Barnett: Hundreds More Booze Bargains. Then he folded the newspaper and started walking. Past the BBC he caught up with Slicker.

"The law, the thin one with the sideburns," he said, "would you believe it?"

"He's after the pickpockets," said Slicker. "I've seen 'im before."

"When?"

"Don't get anxious." Slicker grinned. "Seen 'im at Wimbledon dogs. 'Eard 'im comin', didn't I? 'E's so thin 'e rattles when 'e walks. Don't worry, Charlie boy, 'e doesn't know me from Adam."

Probably not, Taylor thought, but Slicker's nonchalance wasn't good enough, and he tried hard to remember whether he too might have seen the thin face before, long ago. A minion of Vibart, walking three paces behind, running errands? A mate of Poole in the train days, in uniform perhaps, swift as an arrow with a notebook and pencil stub? He thought not. The thin copper was too young.

"You never learn," said Taylor, regarding Slicker's coat and hat. "I told you not to splash. How many cars have you bought?"

"Funny."

"Let's see your wrist."

Slicker did better, reaching with both wrists as though cooperating for handcuffs. The left wrist he lifted to Taylor's eyes, hiking back the cuff of the gabardine. The watch was an old Longines. Even the strap was worn.

"Now that's out of the way," Slicker said, "aren't yer goin' to congratulate me?"

"I gave you two jobs. Two. Tait's places. Those other

two in Gordon Square, if this were the army, you'd be tied to a cannon and shot in half, and I for one would be cheering."

"Nasty. 'Please yourself' is what you said. Initiative beyond the call of duty."

"Your initiative's going to shop you one day."

"They was easy, all we did was walk in. Spur of the moment. I was thinkin' of you, Charlie boy."

"Thanks, but I've told you, I'll do the thinking."

"Seen the papers? 'No obvious connection,' Scotland Yard sweatin' along various lines of inquiry, all of 'em useless."

"You hope."

"All practice, innit? Tell yer somethin' else. We got a cashbox worth more'n all Silver Stick's rubbish put together."

"I ought to finish with you right now."

"Not goin' to though, are yer? You'll be needin' me. Like old times—right? We're a team, Charlie boy. You with your lolly and posh chat, me with my beautiful eyes."

ten

Taylor looked around but saw no one. Slicker's step was springy in the crepe-soled suede.

They walked along the valley of Portland Place, past the Swedish and Polish embassies, the impregnable Chinese Embassy. Taylor remembered: Wicked deeds have their glamor, but those who commit them are always bores. Was that it? He pondered and composed.

For the cock of the dung heap, envy and pretense;
No one likes the champion
Except himself.

I'm a poet, Taylor thought. And why not? Lord Pollard or Auden or whoever, they had no monopoly on the penetrating insights.

He said, "Just soft pedal the flashy gear, will you?"
"Flashy gear?" echoed Slicker.
"You don't exactly blend with the background."
The pavements were virtually bare of pedestrians. Across the zebra, wheeling a pram that shone like a quizmaster's smile, strode a uniformed nanny. Slicker glanced behind him. He was grinning again.
"Takin' a risk, aren't yer, Charlie boy? Bein' seen with a villain like me?"
"We shan't be making a habit of it." Taylor looked back along the empty pavement. Risk played a large part in it. The risk challenged and invigorated. "The way you're messing about, this could be good-bye. It's just possible you're getting on my wick."
"Don't be like that. I'll not say another dickie-bird."
They waited for a gap in the wall of traffic along Marylebone Road. Exhaust fumes vibrated in the air.
"So was it Montgomery?" Taylor said.
"Yes. Two grand."
"You'll get it back. How did he do?"
"Knows where the steerin' wheel is."
To say nothing of the transverse four camshaft and aerofoil spoilers and viscous fan coupling, Taylor thought. He said, "No panic?"
"Not once he'd made up his mind. Took some coaxin', though. You never told me 'e was clean."
"What about the car?"
"A Jag, borrowed and disposed of, no problem. You never said he'd raced at Brands Hatch either. That where you found 'im, on the telly?"
They walked together toward Regents Park. Taylor, eliciting only sparks from his lighter, paused and cupped a hand around it.
"How do you feel about him?"
Slicker shrugged.
"He'll come in again?" Taylor said.

"For the big one?"

"I've nothing else in mind."

"Suppose you realize this is a boy who doesn't know nothin' except cars? 'E's twenty-two, looks about twelve, except 'e's nine feet 'igh, and lives with Mummy and Daddy."

"I like that. And he has the nerve?"

"Pro racin' driver, ain't he? Or tryin' to be."

"So what's the problem?"

"I'd be 'appier with Mossie, that's all. Mossie knows the game."

"And the Law knows Mossie."

In the park, Taylor turned off the Broad Walk onto the grass and sat on a bench. Slicker sat beside him, hands in the pockets of the gabardine. The sky was overcast. Above their heads the obliterating branches of a sycamore added to the gloom. Except for a pensioner walking a Labrador around the stone fountain they had this acre of parkland to themselves.

"So go on, tell me," Taylor said.

"But keep it short."

"What d'you mean?"

"From the sound of it you don't want to know. You don't either, do you? You've got your team, a driver with no record, and reliable old Slicker, so long as 'e does as 'e's told and gets 'is gear from jumble sales."

"If you want congratulations, fine. Congratulations. I picked you because we've worked together and you used to be among the best. The way you seem to have done these four in a row, perhaps you still are. So don't be so damn touchy."

"And you've been waitin' all these years for Slicker to get out of the nick?"

"No," Taylor admitted. "You happened to appear more or less at the right time."

"So I'm lucky."

"We're going to be lucky together."

They walked again while Slicker narrated the screwing of three residences in Gordon Square and a country house in Hampshire. The loose stones at the edge of the path grated under his crepe soles.

The most frustrating had been Hampshire because of the couple living there. Watching, waiting, hiding, driving around until the couple had quit house and garden in an old Austin.

The dodgiest had been Silver Stick's safe in Gordon Square, a bastard of a model, up-to-date, welded and laminated with copper. The burners were a waste of time, and it wouldn't cut, or not this side of summer. He'd put the gelly in, and because he'd been on the nervous side about the bang, the first go he hadn't put in enough. The whole nonsense had taken the best part of an hour while Monty had been wetting himself in the square outside.

The only scare had been the previous night, four doors along at the corner house. In three minutes he'd scooped up cashbox, a fancy casket of jewelry and some kind of gold clock, and he'd been taking a fast inventory of a wardrobe, wishing he knew more about furs, when the blower rang and out of nowhere appeared, like it'd been waiting to answer it, this snarling hairy rat which turned out to be a Pekinese, its squashed face yapping and snapping and its hair a-shimmer as though scented and combed for Cruft's. If it'd been a police dog, all right; you knew where you stood with police dogs, they always came at you the same way and you knew how to cope, or you didn't know. But this scuttling beast? He'd caught it a glancing blow with his shoe, which caused it to yap louder. So he'd held his breath and tried love, stretching out his hand, which the beast bit. He'd wanted to throw the cashbox or brain it with the clock, but he'd preferred keeping the tickle intact so far as possible, and the truth was he'd never brained anything, he was just a shade squeamish, or thought he likely might be, when it came to dog blood and crunched skull. He'd thought of trying to trap the thing under the eiderdown or one of the fur coats and stuffing it, coat and dog, under the mattresss, where its yowling would be muffled, only it might have squirmed free or suffocated, and what was the law on suffocating a Pekinese? Probably thirty years from some judges, those who were Pekinese breeders. So then he'd thought of trapping it in the coat and throwing it out of the window. That way he'd have seen or heard nothing of what became of it, so long as he threw, then shut his eyes, and the window, quickly enough. But what if it survived, wrapped in fur, to carry on its yapping in the square, and attack Monty? Monty might not have been so squeamish; he might have reversed the Jag over it. All this while the horrible thing had kept up its barkings and dartings, and he'd taken a fur coat and fallen on it like one of those Roman gladiators with a net and lugged it muffled and squirming into the kitchen, where he'd shut it in, still snapping, with a load of liverwurst, lettuce, eggs, and treacle tart, swept out of the fridge and onto the floor.

"See that, ought to 'ave 'ad a tetanus shot for that, might've bloody died," Slicker said, showing an almost invisible pinkish indentation between two knuckles. " 'Adn't been for me gloves, it'd 'ave 'ad me finger off."

They walked past a football pitch, deserted except for pigeons pecking in the goal area.

"So you'd say he passes," Taylor said.

"Told yer, he doesn't know anythin', only 'ow to drive."

"But he didn't in fact wet his pants."

"All right then, no, he didn't. Neither would Goldilocks if she got two thou for drivin' a car. Can't yer think of anythin' else? Like when do we start on the one as counts?"

"Where'd you leave it?"

"Flat in Gower Street. Four suitcases and a knapsack."

"I'll have it picked up tonight," Taylor said, and held out his hand for the key.

On the lake a middle-aged couple, robed and scarved as though expecting snow, were changing places in a rowboat, murmuring encouragement as they held to each other. The tourists are starting, Taylor thought. He put the key in his pocket.

I'm at risk, I'm in possession of material evidence, he told himself, and pleasure crawled in his stomach. If I was hit by a runaway horse, and the fuzz found the key, and they were looking for a key to a Gower Street flat. . . . It was old times again. "Key—what key? Oh, that key. Found it, Inspector. Straight up. Fell off the back of a lorry."

He'd see to the fencing of the suitcases and knapsack himself. He didn't need to, it was an additional risk, he knew dependable names from the past who would take the stuff off his hands with no questions asked, if they were still in business. But the crawling sensation was like wine in his empty belly, he wanted more, and the risk was both negligible and the point.

"You'll be lucky if Silver Stick's rubbish covers the rent," Slicker said. "Month in advance I paid for that flat, near on two 'undred quid, and it's only a couple of rooms. Bloody diabolical. I'll tell yer, Charlie boy, the geezers inside are dead straight compared with some yer meet out 'ere. See what Silver Stick said 'is load of old scrap was worth?"

Taylor laughed. He looked behind him, over his shoulder.

"Glad yer find it funny," Slicker said. "Stinkin' criminal, I call it. To 'im what already 'as shall be added a 'undredfold. Bet yer anythin' he's claimin' for two dozen silver sticks, guaranteed antique, 'allmarked, the lot." There was outrage in Slicker's voice. "Honest, I've 'alf a mind to write to 'is insurance company."

He glanced back and said, "Company," but Taylor was already strolling over the grass toward a bench.

The policeman on the Triumph motorcycle approached along the path at fifteen miles an hour. His gauntlets reached to his elbow, his goggles were pushed up onto the brim of the white helmet. He drew level, VHF radio crackling on channel six. As he rode past, he looked at the pair on the bench. The one with the hat and mustache was watching the rowboat on the lake. The man beside him had bent forward to pick grass from his shoe.

Taylor turned his head in the direction of the receding cop. The plate over the rear mudguard read "Royal Parks." The engine note faded. Copper and motorcycle followed the curving path beyond trees and shrubbery and out of sight.

Slicker grinned and said, "Excitin' enough for yer?"

Taylor sought for cigarettes and lighter. Slicker's mockery was tiresome, but there were times when it was on target. No two ways, it was exciting. Exciting and easy and sweet. He was frightened to admit it to himself, but in the past few weeks he had felt lifted as he had not felt lifted in a dozen years. He lit the cigarette with steady, deliberate hands.

"So much for Silver Stick," Slicker said. "So what now?"

"Take a holiday."

"C'mon, Charlie boy, what's the mystery? I want in on the big one. What's it goin' to be? Hey—Charlie!"

But Taylor was striding away along the path.

eleven

"They've just, um, split," Sergeant Fothergill said indistinctly. "Might be able to get after Slicker if I'm sharp, but, um, Taylor's probably in a cab by now."

An empty beer can and splinters of glass littered the floor of the telephone booth. Poole had answered almost immediately, catching Sergeant Fothergill with half an imported Common Market pear in his hand and the other half in his mouth. The sergeant twisted his head and opened his mouth. Masticated pear dropped beside the pear in his hand.

"Where are you?" Poole said.

"Regent's Park—just along from York Gate."

"Get back here. Something's come up."

"New?" Like a trip somewhere, Fothergill hoped. Or a

bomb in an embassy. Or a cat stuck up a tree. Anything, so long as it wasn't this hopeless goose chase.

"New angle—old subject. You know those two houses that were done at Easter, belonged to a shipbroker named Tait?"

"I read the report. Inspector Rudd's pigeon. He doesn't want me on it, does he?"

"You're on it. With me. Know what else Tait is?"

"Silver Stick Rampant, or something. Two stars and a fork from the Good Food Guide."

"He's chairman of Booker's Club."

"Oh?"

"That's what I like about you, Sergeant. The unbridled enthusiasm."

"Tait's chairman of Booker's, and Booker's blackballed Taylor," Fothergill said. "And Taylor's keeping company with a burglar. Why?"

"Why what?"

"Tait's pretty small beer, isn't he? I mean he's not exactly an oil sheikh. If Taylor's such a big man, what's he doing knocking off credit cards from someone like Tait?"

"Getting his hand in?"

"Getting his hand in for what?"

"Heaven's sake, Sergeant, watch it. You almost sound concerned."

And you sound like a one-man crusade, Fothergill thought. The half pear was cold in his palm. The masticated portion seemed to be turning a khaki color.

"I want Slicker's mug to go the rounds," Poole was saying. "House to house, taxi drivers, garages, pubs, shops, banks, the lot. Gordon Square and Hampshire. I'll fix it with Hampshire."

"Hope you'll fix it with Inspector Rudd, sir. Sounds like trespass."

"It's fixed. He was glad to get shut of it. Hurry up back."

Outside the phone book Fothergill threw the masticated portion of pear into the hedge and bit into the remaining half. Poole was obsessed. Obsessed and possessed. If he didn't tread carefully, they'd pension him off.

All the same, the old hulk had uncovered a bit of a pattern. Slicker out of the nick. Taylor spurned by this Booker's Club. The Booker's Club chairman turned over twice in two days, like it was the wrath of God.

Sergeant Fothergill, chewing, stepped out for the Baker Street Tube.

Taylor telephoned Jacko's Club and asked to speak to Jacko. Jacko would be effusive and demand to see him for old times' sake, or he would be suspicious and demand to see him for identification's sake. Either way, Taylor believed he would be lucky if he got away with only the telephone call.

Did he want to get away with only the telephone call? Now he was in this far, the wine prickling his belly, he wanted to be in deeper. But this side of recklessness. A safe, sober way this side of recklessness. He would play it by ear and instinct.

The foreign voice at the other end of the line denied knowledge of a Jacko's Club or a Jacko and had to be cajoled, then made anxious by name dropping, before agreeing to see what might be done.

Taylor carried the telephone to the window. A speckled cloud of starlings was wheeling above the trees, undecided where to descend. By leaning back against the wall and tucking the curtain aside, he could see the rooftop television cameras that watched the entrances to the American Embassy. Jacko, when the familiar whisper grated down the line, was effusive and suspicious. Taylor agreed to drop by.

"Drop by where, Charlie? Got a new address since your day."

"You've had four or five new addresses since my day, Jacko. How about Shepherd Street, behind the Playboy Club?"

"I'll be there," Jacko said, and chuckled, a throaty sound like the rustling of paper bags.

Taylor poured a second cup of tea and sat with it, considering and smoking, before making a second call.

"John, this share transfer, I'm not about to give up. In fact, I've a new set of figures might interest you. Lunch next week?"

Silence fell while Lord Pollard and his secretary consulted. A date was agreed. Taylor and Lord Pollard swapped brusque opinions on the latest rise in bank rate.

"And, John, a small favor, don't know whether you can help, but Phoebe said she'd quite like to go to a palace garden party. She gets these whims. Is there any way an invitation can be arranged?"

Not his province, Lord Pollard said, but Emma, his niece, she was a lady-in-waiting, she'd probably fix it easily enough; he'd have a word with her.

"Thanks, John. Phoebe'd be delighted."

"I imagine the invitation would be for the two of you. July, aren't they, Thursday afternoons? Does that sound all right?"

"Fine, John. Fine, fine."

Fine, fine, his mind repeated, over and over, after he had replaced the receiver. What, he wondered, was he doing? Apart from shivering.

No illuminated sign, metal plaque, plastic-wrapped visiting card or any word or symbol anywhere identified Jacko's Club. There was only the street number on the locked door, the bell Taylor pressed, and the eye through which he knew he was being observed. He found the unfamiliar villain who opened the door more readily identifiable: filmmakers' mafioso, 1970's-style. He was young, polite, hair black and probably dyed, and immaculately dressed in a pinstripe. The accent strived to be as credibly mid-Atlantic as Alistair Cooke's but was in fact borne struggling, clinging to a spar, closer to the Isle of Dogs than to Manhattan.

"Mr. Taylor, sure, Jacko mentioned you. C'mon in."

The word's out, the Rubicon's crossed, Taylor thought, following Pinstripe through a lobby toward a green baize door. *Heard who was at Jacko's place? Charlie Taylor. Straight up. Taylor. What d'yer make of that?* The whisper would be circulating already round the swankier underworld ghettos. Soon, when the first eavesdropping snout caught wind of it, it would reach the Yard.

Taylor followed into a lounge dominated by a bar upholstered in maroon leather. His expression was impassive, his excitement intense. Whether or not he had been spotted with Slicker, now for certain, for the first time in a dozen years, there were going to be stirrings at Scotland Yard. The file would be summoned, dusted, brooded over. Old sweats like Poole would urge that calls go out to Heathrow, to the banks, the post office. Calls urging that railway police and security guards be alerted to—to what? To be alert. To check and double-check and switch schedules and quadruple all guard patrols. To be on their toes.

"Drink?" Pinstripe said.

"I'll wait for Jacko."

"'Ave a seat, I'll find out if he can see you," said Pinstripe, as though merely by seeing the visitor, Jacko would be conferring a favor.

Jacko would confer a favor, but for cash, and not by the fact of seeing him, Taylor reflected. It was he, Taylor, who would confer status on Jacko by being seen here. Anyone older than thirty would be aware of that. Only to pipsqueaks such as this pinstriped tearaway, jaunting now through a distant door, would the name Charles Taylor be unknown.

Taylor took out cigarettes and lighter. To this same coming generation Sears Crossing itself must have been as remote as Waterloo; such names as Goody, Reynolds, and Edwards as historic as Dick Turpin.

Of the dozen members in the lounge all but two stood or sat at the leather bar. Taylor sat alone at a glass coffee table and met their glances directly, still without expression, whereupon they looked away. Johnny Morrissey he recognized, and Dicer Samson, bald as an egg now and a case if ever he'd met one. Surprising Jacko even allowed him through the door, unless the violence had left him along with his hair. The two who were elongated in the easy chairs were virtual juveniles and unknown to Taylor. They might have been, probably were, junior capitalists in the motor trade, or in building, or professional soccer players on comfortable bonuses. The club was as snug and male as were the clubs of St. James's, the members as well-tailored and prosperous, and in two or three instances manifestly more so. The voices, larded with meaningless oaths, were the giveaway. To the eye the difference was that here at Jacko's the furnishings were contemporary, but the atmosphere indefinably temporary. The framed reproductions of trampling jumbos, seascapes, and the Queen and Prince Philip, had been assembled and hung with a haphazard what-the-hell air as though in expectation of having to be unhung and moved on, if not tomorrow, then the day after. A shelf of desultory books reached across an alcove, magazines lay on the glass tables, but the members were talking, not reading. Rooms at the back would be reserved for billiards, cards, and a gourmet dining room, but there'd be no library. Taylor made a circle of his lips and blew a smoke ring. These people were not readers, except of the sports pages and their horoscopes.

He was home again.

"Charlie," Jacko whispered, and held out his hand, grinning.

"You look well, Jacko."

"Can't complain. It's you I'm worried about." Jacko chuckled, and creaked his bulk into the chair beside Taylor's. "We've mostly 'Spurs supporters these days, this young lot. A few Arsenal, right bleedin' enthusiasts they are. They're not mad about some of the opposition."

"Way Chelsea have been playing I'm not too wild myself."

"We 'ad this Leeds geezer come visitin', month ago."

Jacko interrupted himself to raise an arm and snap thumb and finger in the direction of the bar. His hair was white, his round face pitted and cratered. He had boxed both Jack Doyle and Walter Neusel in his youth, going the distance with the Irishman but being knocked out by the German. Then he had turned wrestler and lost his voice when a Bulgarian elbow had cracked his larynx. Next, muscleman in a blagging gang and seven years in Parkhurst. But he had made money in the early days of betting shops and had opened a club where he did his own blackballing and admitted no riffraff. Members included show business celebrities, sportsmen, and only those underworld figures who were honest, established, and dependable.

"This is going to be a sad story," Taylor said.

" 'Is own fault, cocky sod," Jacko whispered. "The bogies found 'im in 'is Bentley at four in the morning; across the back seat 'e was, stoned blind. Outside Kings Cross. Not a stitch of clothin' and across 'is arse, Leeds Are Poofs. Gloss paint, white, the Leeds color. Must've been a 'ospital job gettin' it off."

"I'll keep my mouth shut."

"You always did that, Charlie. Like to go somewhere quieter? There's the office."

"This is fine."

"Like the old days?"

"You could say that."

"I'm not forcin' yer, but 'ave a Bacardi."

Taylor laughed. "Don't tell me. You've got a cellar of hot Bacardi."

"Nothin' to laugh at. Where am I supposed to put three 'undred cases of Bacardi? Two bob a tot I charge, two bleedin' bob, it's givin' it away. Still I lose money."

Taylor doubted it. He waived Jacko's offer of a cigar and said, "I'll have a Bacardi."

"Don't be soft, Charlie." To the hovering barman he whispered, "Two large scotch, lad."

Taylor returned the stares of the members at the bar. They looked away, then moved their heads together, talking about him.

"So what brings you slumming, Charlie?"

"That's not kind. If you weren't so damn exclusive, I'd try for membership."

"Course you would. Scout's honor." Jacko chuckled. "You could buy this place with the change in your pocket."

"Didn't know it was for sale."

"It's not," Jacko wheezed, and his chuckle became a cough.

Taylor unwrapped a handkerchief and offered the contents: an envelope with a Gower Street address. When the coughing had died down, he said, "For a friend." He knew and Jacko knew that this was the cliché opening. But no impertinent questions would be asked. "Key's inside. All he asks is caution. Four suitcases and a knapsack."

"Sale or disposal?" Jacko whispered, putting the envelope in his pocket.

"Sale."

"He want a reserve on it?"

"Reserve? For God's sake it's not an auction."

"All you know. Fencing's 'ard graft the last few years, Charlie. What they're sayin' anyway. They come expensive. Sixty percent commission. Some of the patrons are puttin' on a reserve."

"No reserve, Jacko. Just discretion. Probably only worth a couple of grand."

"What else, Charlie?"

Meaning, thought Taylor, I'm not here to help a friend flog four suitcases and a knapsack.

He said, "Information, Jacko, and at the risk of disappointing you it's legal. It's also pretty trivial."

He waited while two tumblers of scotch, a soda siphon, water, and ice were set down on the table.

"It's for my wife's niece. If that sounds like cobblers, that's because you have a suspicious nature."

"Never said a word, Charlie."

"She's American, a child, trying to get a start in magazines. Wants to write." He spooned ice into his tumbler. "There's always a market for royalty, she says. Below Stairs at Buckingham Palace. She wants to meet a chambermaid."

Taylor sipped and watched Jacko. They regarded each other wordlessly, Taylor with calculated lack of expression, Jacko with a frown, as though on the stool in the corner of the ring again, waiting for the bell, trying to size up the opponent in the opposite corner.

Jacko took a swallow from his tumbler. "One as works like at Buckingham Palace."

"Yes."

"Sounds ambitious. Same old Charlie, aimin' high."

"Same old Jacko, jumping to conclusions."

"Saw you won yourself a medal. Congratulations."

"If you've no ideas, forget it. I said it's trivial." Taylor buttoned his jacket. "She can always write about London clubs. That's something I could give her a line on. A broad spectrum of London clubs."

"Don't be that way. I 'ave to think, don't I?" Jacko sipped and thought, though his thoughts were not yet of chambermaids. "Would this information be in the course of friendship or business?"

"Friendship, Jacko. But I'll make out a check. Help you rent a cellar for that Bacardi."

"You must think a lot of your niece."

"She's full of promise. The article would bring her, say, five centuries. Sterling."

"Worth a grand."

"It'd have to have facts."

"What else? And no offense, Charlie, but don't drop in again." Jacko started to cough. He made no attempt to stand when Taylor stood. "Phone me tomorrow. And do me a favor, when you phone don't call yourself Taylor. Call yourself—Gawd, I dunno. Windsor. Phil Windsor."

Before Taylor reached the green baize door, the pinstriped mafioso loomed and opened it for him. Smiling, the mafioso showed the older man with courtesy through the lobby and out into the street.

twelve

Taylor left the Jolyon carrying his briefcase in one hand, paper bag in the other and crossed the road to the island in Sloane Square. Punctual by inclination, he observed that Inspector Moore was more punctual, bearded and overcoated on a wooden bench, pretending to light a pipe. Taylor had to observe carefully before identifying him. There had been no beard when last they had met, more than a decade ago.

All coppers are bastards, and some are bent bastards, Taylor reflected.

He sat on the bench and said, "Believe it or not I've a famous journalist niece, but you being a copper wouldn't have heard of her. Phyllis Windsor. She's doing an in-depth feature on Buckingham Palace but the press office aren't giving away anything on the alarm system for the royal suites. That's all."

Moore struck a match and put it to his pipe, but the wind blew out the flame. Pigeons strutted, questing and pecking.

"They'd have to put in a new system if she published that," Moore said. "If there is one. I've a funny feeling there isn't."

"I'm not interested in your funny feelings. I'd just like to have the facts."

"Fifty?"

"All right. If you cleared off now, I could feed the pigeons. They'll not have much appetite with you here."

Taylor took a bread roll from the paper bag. Even as he broke it in two, the air became filled with flapping wings. One pigeon, then a second, alighted on his knee, another on his arm. Their beaks darted at the bread. He did not say good-bye or even turn his head when Moore got up and walked away.

Phil Windsor telephoned the unlisted number of Jacko's Club the next evening and was put through to Jacko.

He received from Jacko a whispered name, Tania Beccles, and an address in Chigwell. The address was her parents. Tania Beccles shared a room at Buckingham Palace with three other housemaids. Tuesday was her day off, and normally Saturday and Sunday afternoons were free. She was free most evenings. If she didn't go home to Chigwell in her free time, she shopped in Oxford Street or went to bed with her boyfriend. The boyfriend's name was Colin Jukes. He lived in Mitcham and was a chef. When the Queen stayed at Balmoral or Sandringham, Tania Beccles went there too. Not always but sometimes. There was a rota.

That's a fair amount of detail for a free-lance niece who merely wants to meet a chambermaid, Taylor thought.

"There's a snapshot if you're keen, but you'll 'ave to

collect, and the bloke wants a cockle for it," Jacko whispered.

Cockle, cock and hen—ten. Good for Jacko, keeping his whispering mouth shut. Whoever had the snapshot, if he'd known who might be interested in it, he'd have added another naught to the ten.

"I'll have it," Taylor said, but Jacko had hung up.

He put a Rudy Vallee record on the turntable, raised the volume, then went into the kitchen and emptied teabags from their Brooke Bond carton. He brought the carton back into the drawing room, placed in it four blue wads of banknotes, each of fifty five-pound notes, then tracked across the cucumber-green, through the hall, back into the kitchen for brown paper and string. He locked the parcel in the safe for Martin to deliver to the club in Shepherd Street.

"Cheer, cheer for old Notre Dame," sang Rudy Vallee, urgent above the college choral society.

It was shaping up, Taylor thought. He parted the curtains and looked down on the windy evening in Grosvenor Square. Tania Beccles. Slicker and Montgomery. Soon he'd be in a position to focus on the detail. But until the invitation arrived, there was no particular point. If the invitation failed to arrive, some other approach would have to be found.

The one worrying aspect would be Slicker. Probably Montgomery too. What to do about them, after the job.

"Old Notre Dame will win over all."

The job itself, no problem, given the care he'd give it, the meticulousness. Smooth as a shopgirl's tit, to borrow from Slicker's book of jailhouse similes.

It was afterward that the big capers sprang leaks, when the team ponced about the decks with money spilling from their fingers, and sloppiness set in, and the whole bloody boat foundered because of chat and idleness and forgetfulness and jazzy birds and booze. The train tickle had been one hundred percent proof, the laurel crown with stars, ribbons, and crossed forks, until Leatherslade and the carve-up. The pity was that there had to be a team, people. If only the thing could be done without people but on paper, wholly from the brain; symbols as in a mathematical problem, or words as in a sonnet, to be handed over to a board of examiners for the A-plus grading plus scroll of honor plus check.

Slicker and Montgomery vanishing off to Tasmania or wherever was no answer. Half the train team had vanished, and where'd it got them? He alone had had the steel to sit it out and let the Yard come calling. He alone, though this time he'd not be at home but in the heart of it, would have the impregnable alibi, and the authority to suggest to Chief Inspector Poole or whoever that unless he call off his dogs, the Home Office might have ways of hastening his retirement. For Slicker and Montgomery there could be no such solution. On a caper this size they were almost certain to be nicked, sooner or later. They might as well board a jet and try to enjoy a couple of years of big spending.

Maybe Slicker would pull out when the job was put to him. He'd recognize his short-term chances would be slight and his long-term chances zero, though he'd not talk about it and might not admit it even to himself.

But Slicker would not, Taylor was certain, pull out. Pride, glory, self-delusion. The naïve delight, should he be nicked, in the books that would inevitably be written about him. The acceptance, the shrugging fatalism of ninety-nine villains out of every hundred that somewhere he would be nicked, and nicked again.

Taylor, the unaccepting hundredth, switched off Rudy Vallee. He toured the flat, checking lights, taps, the kettle, smoldering ashtrays.

He walked up North Audley Street, then west toward Marble Arch, resolving to walk more often, and use his gymnasium more often. He quickened his stride so as to be in time for the nine o'clock showing of the new Julie Christie.

In the next few days Taylor occupied himself exclusively at Charles Taylor Ltd. with board meetings, accountants, the Eastbourne precinct scheme, and Howard's tantrums over the Porte de Vanves development. "Ees bon," Taylor reassured his brother. "I read ze figures, ees magnifique. Himmel, but you are ze worrier, 'Oward." On two evenings he played bridge at Crockford's; on two others he went alone to the cinema. The weekend he passed with his mother in Brighton.

In the following week, having telephoned Slicker and canceled the Long Pond rendezvous, he took a leisurely trip north for the Newcastle-Chelsea cup tie, driven in the Corniche by Martin and accompanied by a fellow director. On his return to London he passed a heated, even torrid afternoon with Suzy. Subsequent mornings he spent at Charles Taylor Ltd., dictating to Miss Widdicombe, deciding, signing his name. Boardroom sessions in these weeks were a little fraught, Howard and three other directors being chary of further expansion into Europe, but Taylor enthusiastic. Howard was unenthusiastic, he suspected, because he was such a failure at the frog language; terrified by it.

He visited Kew and, in fulfillment of a promise, collected Ann one afternoon from school and took her to a film of her choice, which to his dismay was a three-hour rock musical.

April became May. Taylor piloted Ann and two

schoolfriends in the Crestliner to Woolwich and would have enjoyed piloting on to Purfleet and beyond had the girls not grown bored with water and started complaining of the cold. One afternoon he bumped into Lord Moreton in Berkeley Street, where the exchange of pleasantries were sufficiently strained to shunt Taylor forward to the very rim of laughter.

He sought through his bookcases and found a handbook which had stood there for years, unconsidered, certain to be out of date: *Manual of Infantry Training for Non-Commissioned Officers. No. 4, Tactics & Strategy. Restricted. HMSO.* He ran his finger down the index. "Tactics, diversionary."

In front of the mirror in the slate bathroom he practiced sneezing into a handkerchief. When he took the handkerchief away a mustache adorned his upper lip. The mustache was full and gray and sometimes looked genuine but at other times was tilted or partially unstuck. "Mafeking," he told the apparition in the mirror in a slow, senile voice, "is relieved. Long live the Queen." If they thought he was old, fine, he'd play it old. The disguise would be no disguise to anyone who knew him, only foolery as for a fancy-dress dance at the Hurlingham Club. But for ushers and doormen in the corridors of Buckingham Palace it would add ten or twenty years to his age, and confusion to the question-and-answer sessions which would follow the tickle.

Daily for a week, at a different time each day, he strolled with bowler and furled umbrella around the brick, spike-topped walls of Buckingham Palace: Queen's Gardens, Constitution Hill, Grosvenor Place, Lower Grosvenor Place, Buckingham Gate, and back to Queen's Gardens. A tourist among tourists, paying his fifteenpence admission, he visited the Royal Mews and the Queen's

Picture Gallery. He rode along Grosvenor Place on the upper deck of buses 2, 2B, 16, 25, 26, 36, 36B, 38 and 52, looking over the wall onto unhelpful trees and gardeners' sheds at this western extremity of the palace gardens. There were inner walls, and early summer foliage so dense that he could not see even so far as the tennis courts and lake, let alone to the lawns that lay beyond the lake or to the palace.

Only after a meeting with the board of the Panco Group, however, following which John Pollard mentioned to him that it would be all right about the garden party, that an invitation would be arriving, did Taylor try to dial Slicker. He was impatient to meet Slicker right away, that evening, but at seven he had the bloody opera. The familiar mangled vowels sounded through the earpiece.

"Thought you'd changed yer mind, Charlie boy. I was just off to the Zambezi."

"Make it tomorrow evening at D, nine o'clock."

After a pause Slicker said, "Okay."

"What's wrong?"

"Nuffink. Tonight would've been better. I was goin' down the White City tomorrow. Bought a share in a dog. Just for the giggle."

The dogs had never riveted Taylor. He tried to think of anyone he now knew, or knew him, who might frequent the dogs. Jacko possibly, but not on Saturday nights. Watching for faces that might recognize his would balance the tedium of the dogs.

"Far as I remember there's a bit of an enclosure near the traps," he said. "Geraniums or something."

"There's usually a couple of bogies down there," Slicker said.

"I wasn't going to say down there. Opposite, up in the stand. Nine o'clock."

"I'll be there 'alf seven. Wearin' me geranium."

* * *

"*Ridi Pagliacco, sul tuo amore infranto-o-o,*" slobbered the clown.

It meant nothing to Taylor. He sat in evening dress in a passably comfortable orchestra stall amid the dripping gilt and plush of Covent Garden. On his right, openmouthed with emotion, the Lady Rose; on his left, Mrs. Hartley-Rumbold, rouged and scented; further along the row, Lord and Lady Oakham, Phoebe, Sir Arthur Jacob. In the royal box sat royalty, British and Norwegian, the bemedaled Norwegian ambassador, and chosen diplomats and wives. Public relations, Taylor supposed; politics and North Sea oil; next week an agreement would be signed. His eyelids were heavy; his mouth was arid for want of tobacco. If his mouth fell open, it would not be from emotion.

He remembered the last time he had attended Covent Garden, too brief a time ago. He remembered little about the opera, though it had been Mozart, frothy and incomprehensible, and more agreeable by a mile than this weeping and wailing tonight. But he remembered that evening because his private gloom had contrasted almost to the point of pain with the bounce and frivolity of the orchestra, and had deepened in inverse ratio to the mounting, flouncing nonsense on stage. The entire performance he'd spent in a reverie, convinced that so far as happiness went, he had missed the boat; that if he could have chosen again his time since the train robbery, he would have chosen not to climb, but to cement himself in gangland and take his chances with the Pooles of the world. The higher he'd swung, gibbonlike, toward the plushy peaks of society, the closer the coronets had glittered, the more he'd been breathed on by bloodshot lordships, the emptier the years had become. Never had he been more solitary than in the last decade. A zero within a zero.

But now things were moving. All he needed at this moment was a cigarette and to be out of sight and earshot of the wailing pantaloon on stage. Preferably in an aisle seat at the Odeon, Leicester Square. Or even the dogs.

At least it wasn't ballet. Ballet was sexy, all those limber gymnastic maidens pirouetting in their skin-tights. But it was dangerous. In ten minutes it could send him to sleep, with the dread possibility of snoring through mind-boggling entrechats like a pensioner in a public library.

The curtain came down; the houselights went up. Hands clapped and eyes swiveled toward the royal box. Taylor clapped with vigor. "Splendid, splendid," he said, beaming approval, turning first to Lady Rose, next to Mrs. Hartley-Rumbold.

thirteen

They were tulips, not geraniums, and the two constables in helmets and raincoats strolled by them oblivious, their eyes on the traps.

Taylor turned his back on the policemen and mounted toward where Slicker sat in a pocket of empty seats. Slicker held a race card and field glasses. He was oblivious of tulips, the law, everything but the traps. The lights had gone out, a bell sounded, and glancing back, Taylor saw the furry hare humming through the grass. Except for the illuminated oval of green turf, and high in the night the electric board of runners, odds and dividends, the stadium was in darkness. Now that the greyhounds were out of the traps, hurtling in futile pursuit, the crowd was shouting. Slicker was on his feet, watching through the field glasses. He wore the same cocoa-colored mackintosh, but a new cockily Tyrolean hat.

In thirty seconds it was over. The crowd roar expired. "First, number four, Pot the Black," announced the loudspeakers. Taylor trod through a litter of betting slips.

"There's too much company, we'll move to the end."

They walked past a squad of bookies: Manny King, Ted Craze, E. Pogson (Victoria Club), Pat Maloney. The loudspeakers were announcing the forecast dividend, then the consolation combination.

"Cheer me up, Charlie boy. Tell me about mail trains." Slicker kept glancing down at his race card and up toward the changing odds on the tote board. "I always picks the one 'as been nobbled, did yer know that? Last one 'ad been fed on sultana puddin'. Ran like a sultana puddin' too. It's a knack I 'ave."

"I feel for you."

"Not important. I'm 'ere to be briefed, ain't I?" He fell silent until they had passed three punters communing together over the *Greyhound Express.* "Two months since that light luncheon in Wapping, and what's 'appened since then? Bleedin' Silver Stick, which a schoolgirl could've done."

"It's going to be another two months before we make the front page."

"Bleedin' 'ell. I'm takin' me 'olidays while we're waitin'."

The bulk of the crowd was gathered in the stand overlooking the traps, and in the cheaper stand on the opposite side of the track. Both ends of the oval, under the tote boards, were empty. Taylor and Slicker walked past clients with folded newspapers and race cards. Many were West Indians. The gray faces of the Londoners were those of plumbers' mates in smart sweaters and bus inspectors who had stood all day at bus stops noting the times and numbers of buses on official paper. Now they noted odds and prices.

"Have you heard of the Cullinan?"

"Cullinan Express?" Slicker sniggered and eased the Tyrolean hat upward on his head. "Can't say I 'ave. One of 'Er Majesty's royal cash-carryin' trains?"

"One of Her Majesty's royal diamonds, in fact. In fact, to be exact, and from now on we're going to be exact in everything, two of them. They're a brooch. A square-cut diamond two inches square, and the pendant's pear-shaped, three inches across, about four lengthways."

For his own benefit rather than Slicker's, Taylor looked down at his hand, measuring: an approximate four inches of air between thumb and middle finger. They had paused at an unoccupied stretch of perimeter wall. To right, left and behind were twenty yards of vacant space. In front, beyond the wall, was a fence of barbed wire. Through the wire lay the track, an exaggerated incandescent green under the sodium lamps.

"We're going to have them" Taylor said.

When Slicker failed to comment, Taylor looked at him. The lotion-tanned face, mustached and contemptuous under the Tyrolean hat, was regarding him with a sneer: a compound of disbelief and frustration that threatened to spill over into sarcasm or to give up and shamble away, conned, the defeated victim of a practical joke.

"I see," Slicker said. "Nice. We're goin' to nick the crown jewels."

"No one mentioned the crown jewels. These are the Queen's jewels. You'd need an army for the crown jewels. We've got you, me, and Montgomery."

"So we 'ave. Me, you, and Monty. That's all right then, because you 'ad me worried for a minute. Monty, me, and Mr. Big. I suppose we'll be nickin' the Queen while we're about it! And we could throw in Philip. And a small prince or two. Mean to say, might as well make a clean sweep."

"Do you want to listen or are you going to be amusing?"

"I'll be honest, Charlie boy, I think I'll be amusin'. Like you've been amusin' so now it's my turn. Got to admit, them royals 'd fetch a quid in ransom. And Windsor Castle, we could lift that. Flog it to the Yanks."

"It's not Windsor Castle we'll be visiting. It's Buckingham Palace."

"Where else? You've the entry there, 'aven't you? You was there the day I got out. Tea at the palace lately, old boy?"

"Not lately. July. There'll be a garden party. I've an invitation."

"Funny, I 'aven't 'ad mine yet."

"It'll be arranged."

A grin sliced Slicker's face as light dawned, or pretended to dawn. "Thought yer meant the real Buckin'ham Palace, like where Christopher Robin went down with Alice. This one's a pub. There's a boozer, the Buckin'ham Palace."

"Here's what you do," Taylor said. "You piss off and have a drink. Because you're getting to be boring. Then come back and I'll tell you about the Cullinan."

"You think I'll come back and listen to this swill about 'Er Majesty's jewels and Buckin'ham Palace?"

"You'll come back. The Cullinan's worth rather more than your piddling about with dogs." Taylor dipped into a pocket and passed Slicker an envelope. "That's the two I owe for Montgomery. There's a bar back through the stand."

Slicker peered into the envelope, then pocketed it.

"I'm listenin', aren't I?"

"I'd hate to interrupt your racing. What about this dog you've bought—did it win?"

"Seventh race, after the next." Slicker's voice was sulky. "The Cullinan then, it's two diamonds and they're at Buck 'Ouse. And we knock 'em off at a garden party, right?"

"In a nutshell" Taylor said, walking.

"Thought so. It's just that when you go for a big one,

well, like I say." Slicker kept pace. "You don't think you're bein' just a bit ambitious?"

"Which is why I could buy this stadium while other people buy half a dog."

"Wrong 'alf too, knowin' my luck."

"The Cullinan's the biggest gem diamond crystal ever mined, anywhere," Taylor said. "Three thousand and twenty-five carats. That's about one and a half pounds. From South Africa. Dug out of a mine run by a Sir Thomas Cullinan, near Kimberley."

"Turn right at the Zambezi."

"That was 1905. The Transvaal government bought it and gave it to Edward the Seventh. He gave it to Queen Alexandra. There was a flaw in it, so it had to be cut into more than one gem."

"What a cryin' shame."

They climbed a deserted terrace at the north end of the stadium and sat in the gloom of an empty block of seats. A fanfare like coronation trumpets blared through the loudspeakers, and a file of men in bowler hats and white doctor's coats started walking six greyhounds around the track.

"It was cut by Asscher's in Amsterdam. Asscher, the top man, put the cleaver on the diamond, tapped it with a rod, and the cleaver broke. He tried again with a new cleaver, cut the diamond in two, then fainted."

"That's the Dutch. Weak hearts. It's all them spuds and lager."

Taylor lit a cigarette. The greyhounds were passing below, stringy muzzled beasts with coats of different colors across their backs.

"The stone was cut into nine main gems, ninety-six brilliants, and some odds and sods of fragments. The biggest is Cullinan One, the Great Star of Africa. That's one of the crown jewels in the Tower."

Taylor paused for the next Slicker flippancy, but there

was none. Eyes on the walking greyhounds, Slicker picked at his mustache.

"Cullinan One's the biggest diamond in the world," Taylor said. "Cullinan Two's the second biggest, and that's in the Tower as well, in the imperial state crown. The rest, the other seven, they're all private property. Asscher's took them as their fee and most of them were bought by South Africa and given to Queen Mary. Cullinan Five's heart-shaped and in one of the Queen's brooches—that's this Queen, Elizabeth. Six is a pendant to one of her necklaces. Seven, Eight, and Nine are all in brooches and rings."

"Leavin' Cullinan Three and Four."

"Granny's Chips."

"Granny's what?"

"Granny's Chips. It's a nickname, what the royal family calls them."

"Stone me," Slicker said. "Granny's Chips."

Taylor dropped and trod on his half-smoked cigarette. From his wallet he brought out a recent folded newspaper photo of the Queen and a folded glossy color plate of Queen Mary, cut from a book.

"There. Cullinan Three and Four. Inherited by and currently in the possession of Elizabeth the Second, Queen of England and Her Majesty's Commonwealth overseas, Defender of the Faith, great-great-great-whatever- grand-daughter of William the Conqueror by the Grace of God. The square one's sixty-three carats, the pendant's ninety-four."

"'Queen Mary wearin' Cullinan Three and Cullinan Four as a pendant to 'er necklace,'" Slicker read aloud, twisting his head and the color plate in search of light, holding the caption to his eyes. "'She is also wearin' Cullinan Five, Cullinan Seven, and Cullinan Eight.' What's she done with Six then, and Nine? 'Avin' 'em polished?"

His eyes moved from the caption upward to the gems. He brought the photo within inches of his eyes. The eyes squinted, screwed themselves up in an attempt to focus. They regarded the gems for fully a minute, until a bell rang.

The lights over the terraces died, and Slicker passed the pictures back to Taylor. The hare hummed. From the traps bounded the greyhounds. Slicker's field glasses remained on his lap. He eased the Tyrolean hat forward, seeming to have trouble with it, as though the shop had been without his size but he had been unable to resist the cut and dash and had bought the closest fit they had. The crowd's shouting mounted.

Slicker said, "The big one."

"The big one," agreed Taylor.

They watched the greyhounds.

"Think I'll 'ave that drink," Slicker said, but he stayed seated.

Hare and dogs streaked past the post. Lights came on; the loudspeakers announced results. Distantly in the dispersing mob by the tulips the two police helmets could be seen.

"Does she carry 'em in 'er 'andbag, or do we creep up, like during the strawberries and cream, and grab 'em off 'er neck?"

"They'll be in her safe, which I hope won't cause you too much trouble."

"In the palace?"

"In the palace."

"I see."

The loudspeakers requested that the owner of a black Austin van registration UYM 551, parked at Gate F and interfering with access, would remove it.

"And you've got it all planned out?" Slicker's voice was more worried than thrilled.

"You'll know exactly what to do. Like before."

Slicker brooded, then said, " 'Ow much is a carat then?"

"Depends," Taylor said. "Let's see the card. Which is yours?"

"Jampot. Number Two."

"Jampot." Taylor slid a finger down the runners for the seventh race. The finger halted and started moving horizontally. "Ran sixth last time out, beaten by nineteen lengths. Messrs. J. Anstruther and T. Beauchamp." He grinned. "Which are you, Anstruther or Beauchamp?"

"Anstruther."

"Who's Beauchamp?"

"A mate."

"Nineteen lengths must be a record." Taylor started to laugh. "Where'd you find her? Battersea Dogs' Home?"

"Very jocular."

"You wouldn't exactly describe nineteenth lengths as a hairbreadth defeat, would you?"

"She's young. Practically a puppy. She's got to find 'er way."

"Couldn't you give her a hand? In a taxi perhaps? Back to the home?"

"Ho-ho-ho."

"Where's your partner anyway, the solid Mr. Beauchamp? Couldn't face the excitement?"

"Lay off."

"So how much have you got on her? Fiftypence?" Taylor was laughing. "A tosheroon?"

"With respect, Charlie boy, that's my business, and serve yer bloody right if she won."

"Half a dollar each way?" Taylor's merriment increased. "Don't tell me. For God's sake don't tell anyone. It'll play havoc with the odds. 'Owner Backs Jampot for Half a Dollar.' "

"Might I 'ave my card back if you're finished?"

"Christ, Slicker, you never told me you were one of the nation's leading greyhound owners." He started to laugh again, then stopped. "Wait. There's one here called Queen's Bargain."

"She's all yours."

"Thanks anyway, but I'm not a gambling man." Chuckling, subsiding, Taylor handed back the card and stood up. "Not for the next couple of months."

They walked down the steps of the empty terrace and continued around the stadium, past the switching figures on the tote board, through open unmanned gates and toward the crowd in the thirtypence stands. Here stood a score of bookies. Around them milled Jamaicans, gray bus inspectors, confident young men from council estates, watching the chalked odds on the blackboards and drinking from cans of beer. At the tote an old woman in bedroom slippers was arguing through a grille; behind her the queue grew restive.

"Approximately then," said Slicker, "because I'll be honest, I 'adn't been reckonin' on a frolic like this, with royals and all. So 'ow much?"

"A carat?"

"I wasn't offerin' a share in Jampot."

"Cullinan Three and Four are flawless. Five grand at least. At the very least."

"That's per carat?"

"That's per carat."

"'Ow many carats was Three?"

"Ninety-four point forty."

"And Four?"

"Sixty-three point sixty."

Under the mustache Slicker's lips started silently working. They had found a blank space at the perimeter wall. The dogs for the seventh race were being walked round the track by six girls in anoraks and riding hats.

"Don't you want to be round the other side for the finish?" Taylor said.

"Shh," Slicker shushed, lips working, eyes aimed upward into the night.

"The round figure," Taylor said, "is three-quarters of a million."

Slicker's lips pursed as if to kiss the night, or whistle, though no whistle came from them.

"Which is Jampot?" Taylor said.

"What?"

"The blue and white, Number Two, that her?"

"C'mon, darlin', you teach 'em."

"She looks trim enough."

On one of the bookmaker's crates a tictac man was semaphoring across the stadium, his white-gloved hands stabbing and clawing the air as though in pursuit of a wasp. Behind Taylor and Slicker walked a group of superior bloods and girlfriends, one of the girls proclaiming in a quality whine for all White City to hear, "We're on Number Four in a big way." Taylor turned his head to watch the receding group, wondering whether Ann too, in ten years' time, would be slumming it at the dogs with world-weary Chelsea friends and announcing that it was a bore but they were on Number Four in a big way.

He said, "There's a girl I'd like you to meet. A chambermaid at Buckingham Palace. An unparalleled opportunity for the Slicker charm."

He passed a snapshot to Slicker, who glanced at it and said, "This the one dusts the peter then?"

The bell, the doused lights, the humming hare, the greyhounds leaping from the traps. Slicker, shouting, took off his Tyrolean hat and beat it against his hip. Queen's Bargain won by two lengths from Cozy Girl. Jampot ran fifth.

"She's improving," Taylor said. "She flagged a bit on the straight. I thought she was going to stop."

"Lazy bitch," said Slicker.

He put on his hat and walked with Taylor beside the perimeter wall, slowly, away from the crowd. The lights came on, allowing him to study the snapshot.

"She ain't Candice Bergen, but I've seen worse. What's 'er name?"

"Tania Beccles."

"Tania Beccles," echoed Slicker with distaste. He eased his hat, poking it upward and rubbing the pink indentation left behind on his forehead. "Sounds like a bleedin' ballet dancer. Maybe she'll be strong on the acrobatics."

fourteen

The sun burst like cymbals over London, melting the tarred repairs to the street surfaces, filling the parks with raw pink torsos, and throwing professional and amateur weather forecasters alike into fits of defensive double-talk.

E. Montgomery, consultant, Eupora Sports Cars, bought himself a cotton denim suit and before lunch took a down payment on an Alfa and sold a Jensen Interceptor to the wife of an executive at Australia House.

Slicker rented from the friend of an acquaintance in Soho, for thirty pounds, a Webley .32 pocket revolver, hammerless, with a three-inch barrel and six rounds of ammunition. Sooner than return to the nick he would shoot his way out if need be, for which he could get life. Life wouldn't mean more than twenty years, and if he was a good boy, behaved himself, he might get away with eight or nine. For nicking Granny's bleedin' Chips, he'd likely get thirty. He'd never tell Charlie boy. He liked nothing about his hired shooter and couldn't decide whether he was sweating because of the sun or because there was a gun in his pocket.

Taylor discarded topcoat and umbrella, skeptically, and wore with his bowler and briefcase a gray cotton suit. He had drunk copious tea in his mother's postage-stamp garden, bothered by bees from the hydrangea and ants that had crawled undetected until reaching his shin, but after kissing her good-bye and walking through visible heat to the New Kings Road, breathing tar and diesel fumes, thirst had returned and he had veered toward the lounge bar of an old neglected haunt, the Duke of Cumberland. Wedged sideways at the counter he recognized that probably he was the only citizen in southwest London to have been neglectful. The lunch-hour rush was in its beginning minutes, winding itself up for the controlled pandemonium of one o'clock. As he passed the girl a coin in return for a pint of chilled lager, a voice said in his ear, "Charlie Taylor, talk of the town, hitting the cold stuff."

It was Pinstripe from Jacko's Club, wearing not pinstripes but a silk tunic shirt with patches of damp under the arms. His chinking glass held something colorless with frost around the rim and a slice of lemon trapped among the ice.

"You can't drink that fizz, Charlie," he said. "I'll get you a real drink."

"I'm happy." Taylor took a swallow of lager. "What brings you this way? Collecting the protection?"

For an instant, Pinstripe's smile slipped. It remodeled itself. "Protection, Charlie, is Stone Age. Went out with 'ighwaymen." The tone was hurt, deprecating. "This 'appens to be one of my favorite 'ostelries, and I'd like you to meet a dear friend of mine."

Taylor wondered how many of the real drinks with frost and ice Pinstripe had already drunk. They had done nothing for the intercontinental accent, Manhattan being almost obliterated beneath a blanket of cockney fog. He followed with his eyes Pinstripe's pointing finger, leaning sideways, twisting his head to find a gap through the scrimmage, and glimpsing the profile of a blond girl seated with a glass of frost and ice. She wore immaculately faded blue jeans and a matching faded top with metal studs. Her profile was stonily aware of itself. Though alone for the moment, the profile let it be known that this was because her man was off acquiring for her the finest of whatever.

"Thanks, but I'm just leaving."

"Five minutes, Charlie."

"No, really." Resenting the reiterated Christian name from this pipsqueak gangster whose name he neither knew nor wanted to know, Taylor smiled and swallowed lager. "Why 'talk of the town'?"

"What's that?"

"You said 'talk of the town.' I wondered why." Taylor raised his voice to compete with the noise level. At least the noise was other voices. There was no jukebox among the Victorian stained glass.

Pinstripe grinned and leaned close. "You know why, and the way I figure it, you and your mob's the only one's goin' to know why until it comes through loud and clear on the nine o'clock news, so amen till then." The upper lip lifted in contempt. "But there's the usual loudmouths claim they know."

"Oh?"

"Whitey Page, 'e's one of the team, so 'e says. There's a laugh."

His eyes flickered to Taylor's but won no response. "Eddie Mackay says 'e was asked and turned it down."

"Turned down what?"

"Like I say, you know, I don't know, and I admit I don't know, though I'm free if you're wanting a spare pair of 'ands. Whittaker says it's the post office cage."

"Is that so?"

"There's one rumor it's bullion for the Gulf, you've bought a BOAC crew, pilots, 'ostesses, the works. It's also the Tate."

Tate, ruminated Taylor. Tait. His back squared against the bar, he looked ahead, away from Pinstripe, and swallowed lager.

"The Expressionists or whatever it is, next year. Five million quid. Though 'ow you flog a truckload of catalogued paintings, that I would like to know."

And that I could tell you, with names and addresses, Taylor reflected.

"Unless they flog 'em to the insurance for a bit less than the insurance value," Pinstripe said, fishing.

"What did you say my name was?"

"What?"

"My name, what is it?"

"Charles Taylor." Pinstripe was puzzled. The grin reappeared but with no conviction. He lifted to his mouth the frost and ice, revealing rising damp beneath the arm.

"I think you have the wrong Charles Taylor. I don't know what you're talking about." Taylor drained his glass, put it on the bar, and picked up his briefcase. "Not an uncommon name. There was a Charles Taylor who was a Tory MP; I'm not him either." He placed his bowler on his head. "Go and look after your girl, Sunshine. She's got her eyes on that cat with the beard and her knee up his crotch. I think he's a musician. One of the flutes with the London Symphony."

He walked out of the pub into the heat and the smells of asphalt and petrol fumes and crossed the road toward Parson's Green, where Martin waited in the Corniche.

He might have excused the damp under his own arms and the throbbing behind his eyes as the effects of sun and a surfeit of liquids, but there was no one to excuse it to except himself, and he looked for no excuses, knowing the sensation to be straightforward fear. Not crippling fear, because he also knew he was stronger than the fear, but the fear that excited.

So the word was out. Rumor was popping. How far his own name was linked with rumors of the simmering of something big he could only guess, and his guess was that his name was being mentioned hardly at all, beyond this Pinstripe and a handful in Jacko's Club. Jacko himself would stay dumb, as dumb as Slicker, and beyond the handful, in the reaching swamps of the underworld, other names would be rumored: fashionable, younger names. Only in certain cells in the security wings at Durham, the Scrubs, and the Moor might the guessing be inspired.

Had word seeped through yet to the Yard? Taylor wiped his palms on his handkerchief. He told Martin, "Kew," and settled into the back of the Corniche.

Faded carpet, unnecessary biscuits, painted sketches of hansom cabs and ladies in crinolines. Suzy had never looked in at lunchtime before. The bar was elegantly busy. Most of this lot wouldn't have to be back at their offices before four, she imagined. Something should turn up. She sat on a sofa with white wine on the glass-topped table in front of her, a society girl awaiting her escort, flipping the pages of *Country Life.*

"This seat taken?"

He towered, carrying what looked like a Bloody Mary in one hand, a folded newspaper in the other. Suzy smiled and shook her head.

"Dusty weather," he said, sitting.

"Too warm for you?"

"Take it as it comes. Business good?"

"Meaning what?"

"Meaning it shouldn't be too bad, pub like this."

Suzy reached for her wine, sipped. "I'm waiting for a friend," she said. "You're in his seat."

"Charlie Taylor?"

"Who?"

"No, of course, I believe you. Fifty. Six feet or so, keeping his waistline, reasonable head of hair."

Could be anyone, Suzy thought. Could be the government minister the other evening. He'd called himself Mr. Hooper, but she'd seen him on telly only the night before and he'd not been Mr. Hooper then.

"Bowler hat," the man said. "He's in property, one or two other things. Charles Taylor Limited."

"I've no idea, and I'm not interested."

The man named a Park Lane hotel. Leo the Lion, Suzy thought.

She said, "I tell you I've never heard of him. I don't have to talk to you. If you're not leaving, I am."

"I could be troublesome, Suzy. Or one day, you never know, I might even be able to help. Girl in your line of business. What's he talk to you about?"

"What's he supposed to have done?"

"No one said he's done anything. Last time you were with him, f'rinstance, what was he talking about? Anything at all. Any names he mentioned, or places. Try and remember."

"You're a copper, aren't you? I don't have to listen to this. If you'll mind your feet, please, I'm leaving."

"I'll go with you. We'll go along to the station. You realize at this moment you're committing two offenses?"

"You'll never make soliciting stick. So what's the other supposed to be?"

"Obstructing the police."

"Why can't you leave me alone? I mind my own business."

"Everyone minds their own business while London goes down, down, down."

"It's not going down for me. Would you mind your legs, please?"

"Think about it." He took out his wallet and passed Suzy a business card. He drained his plain tomato juice. "I'll be expecting to hear from you."

He stood up, a long, pale, stooping policeman, turned, and walked out of the bar.

"B. Poole. Detective Chief Inspector, C Department, New Scotland Yard." Suzy tore the card in two, then in four.

But if she mentioned B. Poole to Leo? That could be the end of it with Leo because he'd not be exactly breathless for a girl who was chatted up by coppers, mean to say, nobody would, would they? And she wasn't eager for Leo to end.

Suzy realized she was shivering. It wasn't fair. She hadn't done anything. B. Poole had no right. If she said nothing to anyone, anyone at all, it might all go away.

fifteen

His wife she out all right okay, said Greta, and tripped away to make tea.

Taylor went upstairs to change. He was sure the girl's English, far from improving, had deteriorated in the six months she had been with them. Why so? Hardly Phoebe's influence, or Ann's? The disc jockeys on Radio Two possibly, or that announcer woman on London Broadcasting? She needed professional tuition.

Turning on the shower, humming, he thought of his speech teacher, the aged vowel-mouthing actress of an age ago. He began to laugh but stopped in order to articulate, loudly and roundly above the clatter of water from the shower:

> She left the web, she left the loom,
> She made three paces through the room.

The sweat of fear had gone, leaving behind only the excitement. He showered, dressed in a cream silk shirt, tie, and lightweight suit, and came downstairs to tea and Phoebe.

She was depositing her handbag on the hall table and turned her head away as he kissed her.

"Too hot," she said, and started toward the drawing room. "I walked from the church. I need a drink."

"Greta's made tea."

"Help yourself." She paused to lift her head and call out, "Greta-a-a!" The effort left her breathless.

"Okay here!" Greta sang back from somewhere: the rigging or crow's nest or some subterranean closet.

"Bring some ice, will you?"

Taylor followed his wife into the drawing room, where she poured gin. "I'm honorary secretary of the Mother Theresa Appeals Committee, I think," Phoebe said.

"What d'you mean, you think?"

"Father Cotter's chairman, natch, and Jack Hutt was elected treasurer *in absentia,* natch, then Father Cotter wanted me as secretary, so I had to remind him I already had the fete and the Ethiopia Relief. Richard mumbled and burbled, I don't think he hears a word these days, whereupon the good Father changed the subject and it was left at that. We hadn't a quorum, but I don't think he bothers much about quorums, or quora. I think I'm secretary." She swallowed iceless gin and tonic. "He's very sweet."

"Who?"

"Father Cotter."

"Is there any mail?"

"In the desk. Top drawer."

Taylor sifted through a half dozen letters addressed to himself, but none bore the royal coat of arms. He put the letters in an inside pocket.

"You had a visitor," Phoebe said. "Your friendly neighborhood bobby. Chief Inspector Thing. What's-is-name. The one who used to be a sergeant."

Taylor waited for her to say Poole.

"Poole," Phoebe said as Greta sailed through the door with ice.

Taylor waited, and when Greta had left, he said, "When?"

"Yesterday. I called you, but you were out. What're you up to?" She fed ice into her glass and topped it up with gin. "He said it was social."

"He'd be after some favor."

"Have a drink."

"Did he come in?"

"Greta let him in. Don't sack her."

"What did he say?"

"*Rien, chéri.* He was just passing. He said."

"And he'd look in again?"

"Wouldn't be surprised. If you're doing nothing this afternoon, why don't you collect Ann, take her somewhere?"

Taylor set down his empty cup. "I can't today. Tell her the weekend sometime, will you?"

"You don't want lunch?"

"I'm on the shrimp vindaloo diet this week, and I'm trying not to imagine Greta's shrimp vindaloo. If Poole comes back, tell him—"

He hesitated, and instead of finishing the sentence, he kissed his wife.

"Tell him what?" Phoebe said.

"Nothing."

He was fairly sure Poole would not come back. Poole's next visit would not be to Kew but to Grosvenor Square, if he'd not been there already.

At the door he said, "Poole interests me as much as a nit on a cat's back."

* * *

For someone with so little interest in Detective Chief Inspector Poole, Taylor gave to that policeman a considerable degree of thought during the journey through south London.

His only other subject for contemplation was his appointment with Slicker. The last appointment, for Tuesday, in Kensington Gardens, had aborted. After fifteen minutes and no Slicker, Taylor had left. Reconstructing in his mind the subsequent telephone conversation, he was aware that to try to draw encouragement from that conversation would have been to deceive himself. Slicker had been evasive, no two ways about it. Evasive and overcheerful.

From Slicker neither attitude was out of character, but the evasiveness in particular nagged. He'd not been evasive about last Tuesday but blunt, bluntly stating he'd explain at the next meeting. And the acquaintance of Miss B. had been made, which promised well. But if Slicker had gleaned from Miss B., so far, anything of value, he'd not hinted at it.

That promised less well. That was what nagged. Slicker liked to hint, to drop innuendoes and private code words which as often as not were unintelligible to the listener. But he'd not been cryptic, he'd been noncommittal, stubbornly so, and with each of them in a telephone booth there'd been no need.

"Straight ahead," Taylor said, leaning forward and pointing, guiding Martin.

The Lewisham traffic peeled off to the right. The Corniche kept left, then swung into the outer lane and glided past a volcanic rattling juggernaut lorry, a rectangular mass of green tarpaulin and pounding tires emitting fumes and din like a battlefield. A brick clock tower went by, and behind it on Royal Hill a glimpse of blue lamp and the neon blue of a police sign. After the church, Taylor said, "Keep right," and minutes later, the car creeping as though lamed amid the jam of traffic: "Left here and park where you can."

The lunchtime executive cars had for the most part departed from outside the Trafalgar Tavern, but a regency-bronze Rolls was there, and a Mercedes, and Martin slid the Corniche in behind them, one luxury item among others.

"Probably be half an hour or so," Taylor said.

He was early. Hatless in the sunshine, carrying only the evening paper, he walked along the stone-flagged path in front of the Royal Naval College. On his right the railings were a freshly painted black. The tide below slapped at the river wall. Trippers, couples, foreigners with cameras, passed him along the path. Most of the score of wooden benches in front of the lawn were occupied, but Taylor quickened his pace toward one being relinquished by two matrons holding parcels. The bench lay a pace or two beyond a granite obelisk.

TO THE INTREPID YOUNG
BELLOT
OF THE FRENCH NAVY
WHO IN THE ENDEAVOR TO RESCUE
FRANKLIN
SHARED THE FATE AND THE GLORY
OF THAT ILLUSTRIOUS NAVIGATOR

FROM HIS BRITISH ADMIRERS
1853

Taylor sat, lit a cigarette, and unfolded the newspaper. He looked ahead to where, somewhere on the north bank, lay Slicker's choice, Island Gardens. In train days Island Gardens had been rendezvous Eleven, and on the telephone Slicker had suggested it. The West End was beginning to give him claustrophobia, he'd said, prompting in Taylor disbelief and the prickings of uneasiness. Taylor had no objection to a foray beyond the West End but instinctively had rejected a venue not selected by himself and rationalized the veto by finding practical difficulties: no tube in or out of the Isle of Dogs, bringing the Corniche or even the Rover would have been an invitation to gawpers and urchins, and the Crestliner was out of the question. Now the whisper was out and toe-rag Poole would be shooting off memoranda, every patrol boat and Port of London snooper on the river would have on its list one Crestliner Crusader 23, twin 120 Mercs, cream and orange, property of Charles Taylor, movements to be kept under observation.

Island Gardens would be the clump of trees, Taylor supposed. The trees were flanked by cranes and wharves, and immediately to the left stood a red-brick rotunda, glass domed and capped by a cupola. Beyond the warehouses and blackened chimneys towered the council blocks of the Isle of Dogs, a corner of the East End he had never known well. He watched two swans on the black water in front of him. The air from the river was fetid, smelling less of the sea than of docks and tankers. A Hovercraft swarmed toward the pier, causing the Thames to rock and thrash against the wall below the railings and lifting the unperturbed swans upon its swell.

"Saw your car, if it is your car," Slicker said, sliding into the space beside Taylor. "Outside that posh boozer."

He wore a new hat, a raffish tartan fedora which gave him a dated air, as though he were on his way to the racetrack to meet Harry the Horse and Liver Lips Louie or about to bounce onstage as light comedian at a St. Anne's-on-Sea pierrot show.

"It's mine," Taylor said, and inconsequentially, "I spy coppers."

"Where?"

"There." Taylor flicked the cigarette end over the railings. "What's wrong? You're jumpy."

Slicker followed the direction of Taylor's gaze and relaxed at the sight of a twin-diesel police launch cruising upstream in the sun. The sergeant in the wheelhouse wore shirt sleeves. The windshield wipers licked from side to side, washing the spray from the ports.

"I'm jumpy all right," Slicker said. "Before you say anything else, there's one of 'em been followin' me, and about five seconds from now I'd say it'd be a good idea to split."

Taylor kept his eyes on the launch; bows lifted, spray spurting, the craft receded at full ahead toward the bend in the river and Millwall Outer Dock.

"You're sure?"

"'Alf an hour ago I gets out of the cab at that pub on the corner, Spanish somethin', and this bloke gets out of a cab behind. Not too close behind. Remember that copper at Oxford Circus, the thin one we said was watchin' the dips? It was 'im. I seen 'im Tuesday, Bayswater Road. Sorry about Tuesday."

"Where is he now?"

"I 'ad a saunter past the Spanish whatsit and into the Admiral 'Ardy. Lounge bar. Straight through into the four-ale bar, count up to ten, and out. I'm callin' it a day, Charlie boy. And quick."

"Stay still. That's him."

Again Slicker looked in the direction Taylor was looking, along the path, but identified no one among the strolling sightseers. A woman in inappropriate jodhpurs was focusing a camera across the river. There were two

Americans in bright seersucker, holidaying air force colonels or professors on sabbatical. A robust girl with polished country cheeks was walking a Labrador dog. On the adjacent bench, separated from Slicker by the iron armrests, a youth with an Afro haircut was reading a textbook. Slicker leaned forward to look past the youth, along the benches.

"Gawd," he said, then swore, causing the youth to glance up from his book.

Four benches away, seated by a dozing ancient with his hands on the crook of a walking stick, a man as thin as the walking stick and with sideburns down to his jaw was peeling a banana.

"That's it then. He's seen yer, must 'ave. You scarper first. I'll lose 'im somehow."

"I've not come halfway across London to say good-bye." Taylor, thinking hard, groped for cigarettes. "That Tait job, I suppose you didn't by any chance leave one of those filthy hats on the safe? Or a visiting card?"

"Get stuffed."

"Cool down, he's not going to nick you, and what if he does? What's he got? You're not carrying a bomb on you."

Slicker tilted back his head and inhaled through his mouth, but he said nothing. A pigeon scavenged past, head thrusting from side to side. When Taylor spoke again his voice was like a cracking ice floe.

"Are you?"

"Got that snap of Tania Beccles."

Taylor blew cigarette smoke. He smiled, a pink and ominous crevasse in the ice floe. "Cretin," he said, smiling.

"Watch it," Slicker muttered.

"Ignorant, incompetent, idiot cretin. God. Come on then."

sixteen

Stepping briskly around the idlers with cameras, Taylor a pace in advance, Slicker struggling into his jacket, they walked without looking back.

"That 'overcraft should be leavin'," said Slicker, catching up. "We could chance it."

"A cruise to Westminster with tea and biscuits. You chance it."

"All right, maybe I will."

"And if your friend hops aboard too and clips the bracelets on you, remind me to give evidence for the prosecution."

"Could be 'e's your friend too, now."

"Could be. Could very well be. Thanks for everything."

"Hell, sod it." Slicker, muttering, pushed through and out of a gaggle of schoolboys in striped blazers. " 'Ow was I to know? What's 'e think 'e's got on me anyway? Bleedin' buggerin' cock-up."

They emerged from the path onto concrete acres that purred and clicked with cameras. The voices, as though language school were out and the disgorged clients were practicing, were German, Dutch, polyglot Scandinavian, Spanish, Italian, French, Japanese, American. There may have been Swahili and Yoruba, for several of the visitors were black. The middle-aged held cameras and maps while the very young and very old bent their faces into ice creams.

Taylor, looking back, said, "D'you see him?"

"He's there, somewhere. We'll split. I'm getting a cab."

"You're staying with me. I've time and sweat and money invested in this frolic and it's going to happen. What goes with the Miss Beccles?"

"Nuffink," said Slicker, aggressive.

"You can do better than that."

They walked past the pier. A queue of customers was filing aboard the Hovercraft. Inland, distantly beyond parked coaches and the rising street, hung a green scrap of horizon that was Greenwich Park. Immediately in front, overhead, loomed the black hull of the *Cutty Sark.*

"Nuffink so far." Now he was sulky. "She's friggin' cold as a potato, and she's sayin' damn all."

"So you're going to have to coax a little. How many times 've you seen her?"

"Twice if you count the first time. That lasted 'alf a minute. Followed 'er from the flunky's gate out of the palace right to Victoria. She fetched up in a Wimpy place and I said 'ullo, but there's this boyfriend waitin'."

"Colin Jukes."

"All I know is 'e fries the wimpies. Stinks of onion. Just finished 'is shift because they caught a bus, a Two."

They navigated around a committee of schoolgirls poring over a single guidebook.

"Second time?" Taylor said.

"Saturday afternoon in the Kings Road. Followed 'er up and down, tryin' to get a clue what might turn 'er on, but all she did was look in the windows. So in the end it was the old 'ullo again, and I got 'er into the Jolyon for tea and buns."

"The full gourmet treatment."

"There 'e is, poxy bastard."

The thin man with sideburns was standing looking up at the *Cutty Sark,* munching.

"We're all right, we're going to lose him, all in good time," Taylor said, weaving through tourists in the direction of a smaller, newer nautical exhibit. "So what progress over the tea and buns?"

"Told yer. Sod all. She puts on the posh. 'Ho, dear, we never discuss hintimate palace matters, ho, dear, no.' Pain in the rectum, no jokin'."

"When d'you see her next?"

Slicker shrugged. The mustache seemed to droop; his eyes were unhappy. "When's your garden party?"

"For God's sake, get her into bed. We need to know everything about the Queen's apartments—everything. Doors, windows, furniture, staircases, lifts, make of the safe, exact location, size, I even want to know the color scheme and curtains and what the flowers are, and is there a kitchen or does she have a gas ring, and is the telly twenty-two inch or twenty-seven, and where's Philip, and are the royal slippers on the left side of the bed or the right? There's not a lot of time. Slicker, listen. We need to know."

"It's all very well. I've met 'er type." Slicker, aggressive again, glanced back toward the thin policeman. "Hermetically sealed to all except her beefburger boy. Faithful and true."

"Become a beefburger. What's the matter with you? You're supposed to be all round, a pro. You can crack a safe and lay a woman, and right now you're to lay that Beccles bint. Take her to Claridge's. If she's not interested, get her drunk. If she won't drink, take her to a bank, wave the folding stuff at her, and if she's incorruptible, you'll have to get her to name a mate, another maid. But I'm telling you she's not incorruptible, no one is, and you're going to corrupt her. God, man, she probably doesn't need corrupting, if only you found the way, she's probably aching to show off her inside knowledge. Do it how you like, but do it."

"Why don't you do it? Anyway, why the Queen? I don't like it. What's the Queen ever done?"

Taylor opened his mouth to speak, then closed it.

They joined the schoolboys and Sunday yachtsmen milling around *Gipsy Moth IV* and studied it with feigned interest. When they walked around it and paused near the stern, backs to the river, they were able to watch the lanky policeman without turning their heads. He never appeared to be watching them, but he had moved again and stood twenty yards away beside a concrete platform between *Gipsy Moth IV* and the *Cutty Sark*. From somewhere he had conjured a second banana and was peeling it methodically. Segments of yellow skin drooped over his hand. He regarded, as he bit, not Slicker and Taylor in the throng by the yacht, but the banana.

Taylor sauntered away from the yacht in the direction of the red-brick rotunda, a replica of the one on the north bank. The sun glinted on the gold and white cupola atop the glass dome.

"Don't quite understand you," Taylor said. "What's the

Queen done? I don't know what she's done. I'm not with you. What's she supposed to have done?"

"Why've we got to do the Queen is what I'm sayin'. Sixty bleedin' million population, and we 'ave to 'it the Queen. What's she ever done to you?"

"Amazing." Taylor halted near the rotunda entrance and lit a cigarette. "What did Silver Stick ever do to you? Or the post office train, or the firms paying the wages you snatched, or the scores of houses you've looted?"

"They was different."

"Why?"

"Well." Slicker, inarticulate, eyes on the munching, unregarding plainclothesman, stroked the brim of his tartan hat. "Mean to say. The Queen."

"The Queen. I'll tell you the difference. She may be upset for a day or two, but she's not going to go short. That's the difference. She's got more jewelry than any woman in the world, and we're helping ourselves to one brooch with pendant."

"So why don't we clean out the peter while we're about it?" Slicker spoke in triumph, a debater scoring a point. He followed Taylor on a tour around the rotunda, talking into his ear. "She can collect on the insurance, can't she? Don't tell me she 'as this peter and inside's just these Granny's Chips surrounded by nothin'. You've got it in for 'er, 'aven't yer? Like you'd gone bloody Communist or somethin'. You just want to nick somethin's that's 'ers—anythin'!"

"You talk a lot of swill, Slicker. If you want out, say so now. You can always go back to blagging and the nick."

"The nick's where we're both goin' to fetch up, Charlie boy. The moment we're in spittin' distance of that peter, if we ever get that far, there's goin' to be bells clangin' in every copshop in London."

"Not a tinkle, would you believe? It's all checked out. The alarm system's the guardsmen at the gates, plus faith in the loyalty of Her Majesty's subjects."

"They'll turn the loyal army out after this one, mate. It'll be worse than shootin' a copper."

"It's going to go smooth as silk. Once you've done your homework with our Miss Beccles. Just trust me."

"I do. That's what scares me. You were lucky with the train tickle, so now you think you're God."

"There was no luck," Taylor said, angry, but holding his voice level. Having completed the tour, he paused near the rotunda's entrance. "I'm beginning to think my one mistake is you. You've got the vision of a fourth-rate footpad. Old women with handbags walking back from bingo. Green Shield stamps and pension books."

"For Chrissake." Slicker took a step to the side to peer past a knot of polite camera-slung Germans. "You do as you like, but that copper gets on my wick. I'm off."

"We both are. Here's the lift."

Slicker looked into the rotunda. Wide iron steps spiraled downward around a cylindrical shaft of wire mesh. Upward, electrically sibilant, rose the roof of the lift, then its walls.

"About flamin' time," murmured Slicker, stepping toward the open doors of the rotunda.

"Wait," Taylor said. "Unless you want him joining us."

They waited, backs to the entrance into the rotunda, and heard the lift hiss to a halt. Then silence. Then the clanking open of its doors.

Slicker looked over his shoulder, through the entrance, but the doors into the lift were on the far side of the shaft, out of sight. Four or five people straggled into view around the shaft and emerged from the rotunda into sunlight.

"Look front and take a cigarette," Taylor said, offering his pack of cigarettes.

"I don't bloody smoke."

"Take one and shut up."

They both took a cigarette. The group of polite Germans had started walking toward *Gipsy Moth IV*, leaving the policeman exposed beyond the spot where they had stood. He had assumed a leaning posture against the concrete observation platform and was watching the two men by the rotunda. When their eyes met, he looked away and put his hands in his jacket pockets, as if hunting for bananas. At the moment Taylor lit his lighter the lift doors clanked.

He didn't have to run from this copper, but he was going to. For the simple perversity and challenge of it. And he was going to win.

"Okay," he said, and swiveled like a discus thrower.

Slicker was even faster off the mark. Sidestepping past a woman with a loaded shopping basket, he careered around the shaft and wedged foot and shoulder into the gap between the closing door and the lift wall.

"Tryin' to kill yerself?" demanded the operator.

"Thanks, Dad."

Slicker, Taylor on his heels, squeezed into the lift.

"Take 'er away, Dad."

The lift was antique and spacious, licensed to carry sixty persons and occupied by four women and a teen-age girl with an infant in her arms. Taylor turned his face to the wall and lit his cigarette. He listened to the sound of running footsteps. The aged operator heaved the door shut and pushed the starting lever.

"Some people." The operator's gaze roved to each of his passengers in turn, seeking confirmation. He wore a sour expression and a donkey jacket with leather patches on the shoulders. "Some people," he grumbled. He would have been the last to admit that the least trivial incident, even a gallop from late passengers, lightened his day. "Some people 'd rather be twenty years early in the next world than twenty minutes late in this."

Taylor counted, trying to estimate the depth of the shaft. The deeper, the better because the copper would have farther to go and he'd be slower than the lift. Though maybe not much farther and not much slower.

In fact, possibly quicker.

He had counted only to nine when the lift stopped.

"You'd think twenty years early in the next world," pronounced the operator, pulling at the door, "twenty years early oughter make some people—"

"Gawd bless yer, Dad," said Slicker, first out of the lift.

Taylor was second, sliding in front of the girl with the infant, dropping his cigarette, and sprinting after Slicker.

" 'Ere!" the operator called, and continued to call out to sprinting Slicker and Taylor, his day lightened beyond his dreams, his shouts a diminuendo of futile echoes through the tunnel, unintelligible and unheeded.

" 'Ere!" he shouted with renewed, vibrant enthusiasm as a third man hurtled down the stairway and ran in the wake of the first two.

For a hundred yards the tunnel slanted down. In the pauses between the liftman's fading shouts, Taylor could hear slapping footsteps behind, as well as his own and Slicker's. They had the tunnel almost to themselves: a cold, brightly lit cylinder beneath the river, the floor of paving stones, walls faced with chipped white tiles, and no visible end. Exhilarated, anxious, surprised by Slicker's speed and excited that the younger man should be able to keep ahead, pacing him, Taylor sprinted. He lifted his legs and pumped with his arms, gripping his rolled newspaper like a relay runner's baton. A splash of sweat entered one eye.

The copper's footsteps were so hard to hear above his own that the gap must have been wide, and the smell of achievement made Taylor lengthen his stride to a point where his legs were almost beyond his control, and the stride would lengthen no more.

Slapping, reverberating footsteps were the only sound. If I fall, that's it, Taylor thought.

He drew abreast of Slicker but could not overtake him. Slicker ran with his hat in his hand. A woman in a head scarf, round-eyed, clung to a small child and to the concave lavatory-tiled wall, letting the race pass.

The stone floor slanted up. Running down on a collision course came a squad of adolescents in white shorts and vests. They made way for the men, backing against the wall and jeering, uncertainly at first, then in a unison of lifted voices as the pair dashed by.

"Milwall!"

"You're offside!"

"Got taken short, John?"

"Up the Lions!"

"Nice one, Cyril!"

The voices, treble, alto, and newly bass, cannoned off the tunnel walls. Ahead was a lift shaft, and inside its encircling mesh, emptiness. Two Asian women awaiting the lift stared and moved close to each other. Slicker drew fractionally ahead, veered for the stairs, and hit the third step with a smack of crepe-soled shoe.

There were some eighty or ninety steps. To Taylor they seemed like a hundred and ninety. The lift descended past Slicker and Taylor before they had reached halfway. They bounded up the steps three and four at a time, meeting no one, Slicker drawing ahead, their shoes on the iron steps filling the echoing well with a clamor which submerged any sounds of feet that might have been ascending behind them. Taylor, flagging, a slow, scalding sensation beginning to invade his legs and chest, doubted whether he could run much farther.

They surfaced by the closed lift gates, Slicker ahead, and raced from the rotunda into sunlight and an empty lane. A high wall to the left, to the right a hedge. Trees and space which might well have been, Taylor found himself wondering, probably was, Island Gardens.

"Slicker!" he called.

The lane ended in a T junction of corrugated iron fences, and Slicker had vanished around the corner. Before turning the same corner, Taylor glanced back. He saw no one.

"The snapshot, if you don't mind," he panted.

They ran in tandem between vertical sheets of corrugated iron, past a staring quartet of West Indian boys, and onto a road. A solitary car drove past. The landscape was exposed and dreary: forsaken acres of cleared bomb sites, unattended building sites, random rows of houses. Slowing to a rapid walk, Taylor took from Slicker the photo of Tania Beccles.

"Saturday noon. Putney Bridge."

"Yer don't do bad, Charlie boy," Slicker panted. "Considerin'."

Taylor was already running across the road, aiming for an opening between blocks of houses from where he would be out of view of anyone coming from the direction of the footway tunnel and rotunda. He skirted a builders' shed. Looking back, he saw no Slicker, no thin copper with sideburns. There were narrow streets of houses with television aerials. On a green rag of grass some youths were playing unseasonal soccer with a beach ball; two were bare-chested, another wore soccer boots, shorts, and a striped football jersey.

Heading toward a wide road, he ran from the housing blocks, past a rubbish dump, desultory thistles, a water-filled crater into which someone had rolled a car tire. The nearest taxi would be miles away, the nearest bus or underground half a mile at least. He walked, steadying a corner of the photograph in the flame from the lighter. Tania Beccles smoldered grudgingly, then became a whirling flame which he let float to the ground. He sprinted for the road. One lorry was the only vehicle in sight, an aimless five-tonner trundling along the road's center. Taylor ran into the road and held up both arms in front of the advancing lorry. Aloft, like traffic control on an airport runway, the rolled newspaper wagged and commanded. The lorry braked, squealed, stopped.

Behind the wheel the driver wore glasses and a beret. Taylor reached up and wrenched open the passenger door.

"Wife's having a baby! Twenty-five to take me through the Blackwall Tunnel!"

" 'Op in, mate. Make it thirty, I'll take you to Scotland."

The lorry strained into gear and rumbled north on Manchester Road. On the backless horsehair cushion that was the passenger seat Taylor wanted to close his eyes. But he watched the road and pavements. His chest throbbed; his ankles smarted as if sprayed with boiling water. He lit a cigarette, brought out his wallet, and passed two ten-pound notes and a five to the driver. The driver made no attempt to talk. The din of engine and clattering chassis filled the cabin.

Cats on a scrap of wasteland. A mother wheeling a pushchair. No copper with sideburns. No Slicker.

In both directions through the Blackwall Tunnel early traffic was struggling to beat the rush hour. South of the river, rattling past gas works, Taylor leaned toward the driver and shouted.

"Keep on. Greenwich. I'll tell you where."

In Trafalgar Road, a block from the Royal Naval

College, he told him. The driver, grinning, drew in at the curb.

"If your missus is 'aving a baby, so's mine," the driver shouted above the engine roar. "And mine's been dead six years."

Taylor jumped down and slammed the door. He crossed the road. Martin, waiting, would be bored out of his mind, but that was something he was paid to be.

seventeen

"Yes, speaking," Mr. Batley said into the telephone. "Yes. . . . Yes, sir. . . . Certainly we do, sir, and in the very strictest confidence, naturally. I might say, perhaps I say it who shouldn't, but we have not yet suffered an unsatisfied client, sir, not to my knowledge. I might add—"

Interrupted before he was able to add, Mr. Batley listened instead, simultaneously baring his teeth at Mrs. Batley, grimacing, rolling his eyes and shaking his free arm at the television set. Mrs. Batley leaped forward and turned the volume low. On cushions in front of the screen the twins, Donna and Dawn, set up an exasperated whispering.

"Yes, sir, perfectly in order I'd say, sir. . . . Of course, yes. . . . What I say, like the advertisement says, 'We try harder.' Round the clock, I might say. In fact I would probably consider myself undertaking—"

Interrupted again, Mr. Batley rotated his jaw at Mrs. Batley and agitated his free arm. Wrist, hand, and fingers shook with exaggerated scribbling movements like an ignored diner demanding the bill. Mrs. Batley scuttled to the mantelpiece for pen and paper. She found a pencil and pink dry cleaner's ticket.

"Of course, quite so. . . . Yes. . . . Yes, sir. If I might have the name, sir?" Mr. Batley listened and wrote. "And address? I see. . . . Tomorrow would be in order. . . . Perfectly convenient, sir. . . . Yes, sir. . . . Yes, I will. . . . Good-bye, sir. Thank you."

He put the telephone down. Donna and Dawn fell upon the television set and turned the volume up.

"We're in business." Mr. Batley made no attempt to subdue the triumph in his voice. "Lady, we are in the money."

"Who—what? How much?"

"The Batley Detective Agency, madam, at your service. Strictest Confidence, Moderate Terms. For a couple of days work, only about what I got in three months in uniform, that's all."

"Who? Why?"

In spite of the smattering of scars and bruises, after seven years of marriage they remained much in love. They moved to the table by the window, away from the television.

"Straightforward observation of a bloke who's done time. To phone in midday and twenty hundred hours plus a written report daily to Scofield at the Star Street post office. Till further notice." He studied the scribbled names and numbers on the dry cleaner's docket. "The phone-in will be taped, bet you. Bet you I never see our Mr. Scofield. And whatever his name is, I bet you it's not Scofield. Tell you something else."

"What?"

"I don't care. We've two fifty arriving in the post tomorrow." He paused to relish the opening and closing of his wife's mouth. "And two fifty when he calls it a day."

"Five hundred!"

"Plus expenses." Mr. Batley began to talk airily, playacting. "And with the possibility of another small job later."

Dawn and Donna, practiced at grasping the relevance to joy and misery of things financial, were swarming around their parents' legs, tugging at skirts and trousers.

"Can we have a colortelly?"

"Mum, Dad, can we have a colortelly?"

Taylor locked the safe and carried the money to the desk. He placed the banknotes in an envelope which he stamped, sealed, and addressed. Batley had sounded pretty typical. A frustrated ex-copper probably, with ambitions, and a headful of anxieties, and mortgage repayments gnawing into every incoming check, if there were any incoming checks. For five hundred, cash, he'd work himself silly.

The empty mug and teapot he carried back to the kitchen; then he returned to the slate bathroom to make sure the taps were off, the cap back on the toothpaste tube. In the drawing room he chose a record for the stereo, maneuvered the armchair to a side-on position against the window, parked in front of it a coffee table for two worn, shoeless feet, and sat. The sun was inching down behind the eagle on the American Embassy. Problem was, whether to put on shoes and go out to catch the last post or to telephone down to Harry, ask him to do it.

Odd how the difficult decisions derived from the no-account problems. Yet not odd. Being of no account, that made them difficult.

Was it imagination or was the strolling uniformed law on the pavement below looking up at his window? The schoolboy Burt Lancaster, cream-complexioned with a squirt of peach from the sun. Shoulders like a wall. Head thick as a wall, no doubt.

It was not imagination. The lad had been looking, now was strolling on. Taylor leaned closer to the window and gazed down. He could have opened the window and dropped his cigarette pack, or the marble ashtray, onto the blue helmet.

Foliage, thick as a copper's skull, hid Roosevelt, the greater part of the gardens, the whole of the south of the square.

Walter, Walt-e-er
Lead me to the altar

The second problem to which there was no solution was the four walls of the drawing room.

Loneliness was not the word. There was no way a man could be lonely when he had family, friends, girlfriends, brains, power, work and every kind of resource, emotional, material, you name it. But he'd no great yen to watch Phoebe pouring gin; and Ann, by the time he reached Kew, would be in bed. He did not feel bright enough for Suzy or bridge at Crockford's or John Pollard's enthusiasms. He did not want to read or move or eat or be with anyone or with himself. If the word was not loneliness, he did not know what the word was, but there was a lack, a sense of letdown, a lassitude almost, that would pass, as on previous occasions it had passed.

The closest to a solution, ready-made as a TV dinner, would be a movie, anodyne of his generation. Both the *Times* and the *Guardian* had wet their knickers over the new Chabrol, but then they would. There was the recent Ken Russell, which sooner or later he supposed he'd see.

Some Mafia stuff which had missed the band wagon: blood in close-up and mobsters embracing one another. Not a Western in months apart from geriatric John Wayne. *Ryan's Daughter* somewhere, wheedling back for the twenty-seventh time but still avoidable to men of resolution. Jane Fonda in something bitter and comic; she might be the best value, if she didn't make him angry. In Hampstead there'd be either the Bergman season or the Marx Brothers season. If he'd lived in Hampstead, he'd have had to sell up and move to Grosvenor Square to escape Bergman and the Marx Brothers.

Sally, Sall-e-e-e
Pride of our alley

Thick young Burt was returning, proceeding along the pavement in a westerly direction, your honor, and with company. Taylor, allowing cigarette smoke to curl from his mouth and up into his nostrils, sat in the armchair and pressed his forehead against the window, looking down. The company was as big as Burt but without the green and youthful spring. He carried a raincoat over one shoulder, and the hair on top of his head was wispy and undernourished. The main contrast with Burt was the sandy, sallow complexion, becoming visible when both men stepped toward the curb and turned their faces up to the penthouse flat. Taylor swayed away from the window.

He could put on shoes, walk down the back steps, through the garden, and take in the last showing of the Jane Fonda. Or he could telephone Harry to let him know he was at home to no one. After which, if Poole still hoped to get past Harry, he'd have to go away and come back with a search warrant.

Taylor stubbed out his cigarette. He padded in stockinged feet to the telephone, dialed, waited.

"Harry? Charles Taylor. There could be someone to see

me, any moment. Bring him up, would you? I've a letter I'd like you to post if you wouldn't mind."

He switched off the stereo and walked along the corridor to the dressing room. In white canvas espadrilles he trod back to the drawing room and swung the armchair, then the coffee table, away from the window. When the doorbell rang, he returned to the dressing room and brushed, needlessly, his hair.

The bell rang again. Taylor walked into the hall and opened the door. He let Poole speak first. Prepared for an obscenity, sarcasm, something, but receiving nothing, Poole hesitated.

"Ask me in, Charlie. I've always wanted to see how the cream live."

Taylor moved aside to allow the policeman past. "Hold on, Harry," and leaving Poole standing in the hall, he went to the drawing room and brought the envelope. "Thanks. I'd like it to catch the post."

"Right away, Mr. Taylor."

The door closed. Poole followed Taylor into the drawing room and dropped his raincoat over the back of a rattan chair. He stood on the green carpet and turned through three hundred and sixty degrees, regarding the Sheraton secretaire bookcase, the unplayed piano, the sofa in green leather, the mingled contemporary and antique, the picture-hung walls.

He said, "I was never much on the visual arts, but they're not Van Gogh, that I know."

Taylor poured himself a whisky.

"Nice view," said Poole, moving to a window. "Prefer the country myself. Half an acre of vegetable garden, runner beans, strawberries fat as your fist, smell of silage across the fields. Roll on."

Taylor carried his drink and an ashtray to the armchair farthest from the window. He sat back, crossed his legs, put the whisky down untasted, and found cigarettes.

"Lucky to find you in," Poole was saying, picking up a jade Buddha from a table, testing its weight, putting it down again. "I called before, but you're not easy to catch." He wandered past the piano and scrutinized a William Roberts street scene, eyes inches from the pale blocks of brown and orange. "Hear you've been running about a bit. In bad company."

Taylor shut his eyes and blew smoke toward the ceiling. Detective Chief Inspector Poole took a pace to one side and studied the adjacent picture.

"Thought you'd hung up your running shoes after the train robbery, Charlie. I honestly thought that." He sat on the piano stool, lifted the lid of the piano and struck a high solitary note. "Not saying anything without your lawyer, that it? Who is he these days—the Lord Chancellor?"

"'When you say something worth listening to, like good-bye, you'll have my rapt attention."

"Do you play?" Poole struck a lower note. "No, course you don't. One thing, though, Charlie, I admire your style. You've improved yourself, and it must've taken some doing. You make me vomit, but that's the professional thing, being a copper and knowing what you are. You've clawed your way up all right." He lowered the piano lid. "Not as far as Booker's Club because it takes a gentleman to sit down with gentlemen, and you'll never be that. But you've fooled quite a few. Make the most of it because Slicker will pull you down. He's going to trip up, Charlie, and so are you."

I shall not be provoked, Taylor resolved, deeply inhaling smoke. His palms were damp. If you stepped back into the game, you had to suffer the Pooles of the world. They were inevitable, like weather. He had forgotten the whisky on the carpet by his chair.

"What beats me is why you don't give it up. Retire. I'll be honest, I thought you had. God knows you can afford to. Me, I've got a down payment on a place near Cirencester, and I've another four years." Poole might have been talking with an old friend. "Three up and three down, and a bit of a field. Needs a lot of doing up. The wife's going along next weekend to sort out a builder."

Inconsequential bastard, Taylor thought, and reached for his glass. Typical inconsequential bastard copper. It was the technique. Inconsequence, crap, the disconnected hopping from one crap topic to another. Then the knee in the groin.

"Revenging yourself on the real gentlemen, are you, Charlie? Blokes like that whosit, the Booker's Club man, few weeks ago? Tait. You'd have to be really vindictive to do a soft thing like that." Poole's chat dripped on, offhand and equable. "But if it wasn't malice, it couldn't have been fund raising either because people like Tait don't have funds. More of a practice run? Talking about running, I'm told it was like you were rehearsing for the Olympics this afternoon. Both of you. Gather you left our sergeant looking pretty sick."

"He was sick before he started. He was full of bananas."

"Bananas? Well, he could do with fattening. Challenge time, was it? Show the fuzz who takes the gold medal? And if he'd won, you're still laughing. 'How was I to know, m'lud? Believed he was a bandit, m'lud. Name's Taylor, OBE, m'lud. Unaccustomed to being breathed on by the busies, m'lud.'"

Taylor regarded the ceiling. So many questions, none expecting or waiting for an answer. He sipped from his glass and watched Poole walking away from him, hands in pockets, halting at a painting and pushing his nose toward it.

Poole was potentially a threat but only potentially, because he knew nothing. Taylor was sure of it. Coppers gave little away, ever, but Poole had nothing to give away. He was groping, copper's mind suppurating with suspicion, but he knew only two things: that Charles Taylor and the villain Slicker were meeting and that today they'd raced a detective sergeant into the ground.

Probably, too, that Taylor had called at Jacko's Club. All of which intelligence could only have been fuel to the bastard's frustrations. As evidence, even as a basis for theorizing, it added up to a fat round zero.

Still he was a threat, not to be predicted. You underestimated disappointed, hard men like Poole and you fetched up at the Bailey with defense counsel looking ill and the judge sharpening his slide rule. If Poole were now to drop the name Tania Beccles, for instance, the job would be off. Forever.

Taylor wrapped his damp palm around the whisky glass and sipped. What kind of tricky copper was Poole anyway? Would his aim be to prevent crime, to forestall it? Or in the case of Charlie Taylor to let it happen, then move in, and preen and smirk and play with himself while His Honor droned regretfully about the tragic misuse of talent and handed down thirty years?

"Quite like this one," Poole said, peering. "Is it English?"

"William Roberts. Vorticism. You'll find him in the Tate."

Where shortly the Expressionist exhibition was to open. Let the bastard copper grope. The art critics had brought out their notes on Marc and Kandinsky; the gossip columnists had disinterred widows of Expressionists and publicized Expressionism in terms of cash, security measures, and insurance cover. Tate. Tait. Let the bastard worry and patrol the exhibition with a score of Heavy Mob coppers, tried and true.

"I've given Slicker money if that's all right with you," Taylor said. "I may give him more. I used to know him, and he's just finished eight years of nothing. Nothing. Okay?"

"Blackmailing you, is he?"

"Poole, you are a bag of pus."

"All ready to burst over your balding nut, Charlie. Who else is in this new team then? Eddie Mackay? Dicer? We know there's already one besides Slicker."

But we haven't a clue who, could even be someone with no record, Poole thought. His stomach hurt, and it was pill time, but he could not allow Taylor the satisfaction of seeing him reach for pills. The chat was going as badly as he'd feared. He'd wind up giving away more than Taylor if he wasn't careful, and Taylor was giving away nothing.

Plus the total nothing from Slicker's photo being touted around the Gordon Square area and a hundred square miles of Hampshire. Nothing everywhere, only blind, deaf Englishmen.

He sauntered to the window and gazed out. "The new generation, is that who? All wide-eyed and a-tremble to be given a start by Mr. Big with his OBE? Don't tell me. I almost feel sorry for them. Some of your train mob still rotting in the nick, and now you're going to land a fresh lot there. Just to massage your ego, because it can't be loot you're after. I ought to laugh. They'll land there anyway, sooner or later. It's the big boys like you save us a fair amount of trouble."

"The big boys these days are teen-agers, brats of nineteen with spots and a gun. They read the business pages. Thought everyone knew that."

"I know you, Charlie. One day I'm going to put you away."

"Time to piss off, Poole. You're so boring you give me cramp. I can't even understand you anymore."

"Wanted to tell you about my memoirs." Poole turned from the window. He sat in Taylor's favorite armchair, beside the coffee table, hands still in trousers pockets, slumped and sallow. "See, it's unusual for a mere chief inspector to write his memoirs. It's the chief supers and commanders and commissioners who're into the memoirs lark, and I'll never rise to those eminences because, well, just like you say, I'm too boring."

"Send me a copy of your boring memoirs; I'll find a use for them. Just for now, would you clear out? I don't have to take anymore."

"See, I bored them all stupid at the Yard arguing that you were our Mr. Mastermind behind the Great Train Robbery. Some agreed, still do I wouldn't wonder, but they don't say it out loud, not anymore. They haven't for years. Bad for the image to suggest we missed out and there's somewhere a Mr. Mail Train puffing cigars and having his toenails trimmed by topless virgins. Fatal for promotion. And I'm left as the bore with the Charlie Taylor fixation. You know how some of these memoirs by the top brass have sounded off? You should, they must be your happiest bedtime reading." Poole, slumped in the armchair, assumed a top brass voice: measured, unequivocal, with the merest trace of a London accent surfacing through the committee-room vowels. "'I am in a position to state, and do so most categorically, that there was no Mr. Mastermind behind the Great Train Robbery, repeat no Mr. Mastermind, but that this dastardly crime was planned and perpetrated by a group of criminals who were subsequently brought to book by the devoted efforts of our police and who, as is well known, are now enjoying their just deserts behind bars, their names being Douglas Gordon Goody, Buster Ronald Edwards, Bruce Reynolds—'"

"I'm having a drink; then I'm leaving," Taylor said, carrying his glass to the tray of bottles on the Adam commode. "If you've got to stay, fine. I'll have the porter up to watch that nothing gets nicked."

"My memoirs are going to say, 'As a member of Scotland

Yard's Flying Squad for the better part of my working life, I knew Charlie Taylor for many years before we finally nailed him for his role as Mr. Mastermind behind the Great Train Robbery and for those subsequent crimes which resulted in this apparent pillar of respectability, this arse-creeping thug, this con man with the posh suits and the smile of a dockland whore, being sentenced to that term of mailbag stitching which will keep him out of circulation until he is a hundred and ten."

Poole permitted himself the ghost of a smile. He said, "Should make a quid or two, wouldn't you think? Pay for the bedding plants? They're still sewing mailbags in the Scrubs and on the Island, far as I know. If it's the Island, you'll likely have a couple of the IRA for company. Watch out they don't slip a stick of gelly in your soup."

At the commode, pouring whisky, back squarely to the policeman, Taylor made no reply.

"The intimate touch, that's what sells," said Poole, "like this room, and you there with your pants messed, accepting you're going to have to forget this next tickle because we know too much about it, and it doesn't have a prayer and never did." Sprawled, the policeman brought a hand from his pocket and rubbed the skin above the bridge of his nose. "You'll be able to read it on the Island, Charlie. *Progress of a Mug. Charles Taylor. Mail Train to Mailbags.* Try to get a job in the library because the book's going to be in demand."

"Get out your notebook. I'll give you a quote." Taylor remained standing, holding glass and cigarette, elbows resting on the commode, eyes on the chief inspector. " 'Taylor was the most patient man I ever met. He did not at this moment telephone his friend Dickie Buxton at the Home Office or Commander Wilson at the Yard or Assistant Commissioner Perceval, with whom the previous week he'd shared a bottle of Bollinger at Sandown. He did not offer me refreshment or money either, because although fully aware that I was bent as a pig's tail, like most of us in the Heavy Mob, and that for half a dollar I'd have kissed his backside, he saw no reason why I should refresh myself or reap financial benefit merely as a result of my being a poor bent floundering copper and a turd.' " Taylor raised his glass to Poole and sipped. "How's that? Any use?"

The windows were crepuscular oblongs through which the tops of the chestnut trees had become silhouettes. The only sounds were the gear changings and occasional burp of a horn from the traffic in the square. Poole gathered up his raincoat.

"You look sixty, Charlie. I've yet to meet the villain who didn't age fast. Watch your heart. That dance through the tunnel can't have helped."

"Good-bye."

Taylor saw the policeman out of the flat and closed the door. He walked back into the drawing room, turned on the table lamp by the telephone, and drew the curtains. A movie was no longer adequate for salvaging the evening. He needed company, release, silence, the impossible combination of irrelevances which no one but a wife, Phoebe, even Phoebe if she were halfway cut, could provide.

Only when he lifted the phone to dial a radio cab did he dare look at his damp hands to regard the tremor.

eighteen

"Howdy, stranger. Park your horse, draw up a chair. So what brings you to these parts? The Big Noise from Winnetka. Pour yourself a slug, Big Noise, take your hat off. You don't have a hat. Take your pants off. Been a long winter, pardner. Suit yourself. Whassa weather like out thar on the trail, Big Noise?"

Her voice was disheveled, her chin propped up by her fist. She sat in a corner of the sofa which faced the television.

Taylor kissed her cheek and poured a taste of whisky. The gin bottle at her elbow was almost full, and he caught himself glancing among the bottles on the cabinet and into a wastebasket for the one that must be empty. He sat at the other end of the sofa and helped himself to a French cigarette from the box. They watched on the screen a magnified sequence of a throstle feeding its young.

"Ann?"

"Ann is alive, well, and living at home. She knows about"—and Phoebe, pausing, enunciated with care—"isosceles triangles."

Taylor looked at the pearl earring in his wife's ear. She sat in profile, and he could not be certain but he was almost certain there had been no earring in the other ear. As though in sympathy with this lopsidedness, one slipper dangled from her upturned toes. The other protruded from under the sofa.

"Any mail?"

"Bills. All for you."

"That all?"

"Card from Daddy, he's into acupuncture for his rheumatism. Circulars. Invitation to a garden party at Buckingham Palace."

"Where?"

"That shack with the flag, Big Noise. Buckingham Palace. Don't be coy."

"I'm not being coy. I'm asking where's the invitation?"

"I'll be in the States. You said you'd had your bellyful of pedigrees and royalty. You said that. I threw it away."

Taylor trod down the steps to the basement and knocked on Greta's door.

"Get in," Greta sang.

She had a friend with her, a sprig in National Health glasses and a sad brown suit that reminded Taylor of his demob suit thirty years ago. He was seated on a hard chair at the table, holding a cup of instant coffee. Greta was snug in an armchair. In place of throstles the television showed people. "I can't go back, Jenny, don't ask me to go back," a man was saying to a woman.

"Hullo, sorry to interrupt," Taylor said. Was he interrupting romance or an English lesson? Or might the sprig be taking lessons in—in what? Taylor frowned, unable to remember whether Greta was Dane, Finn, Swede, or Norwegian. "I just wondered, could you tell me what happens to the garbage? Has it been collected?"

Greta stared blankly. Taylor realized that his hands held a whisky glass and a cigarette. The sprig in the brown suit, blinking from Taylor to Greta and back again to Taylor, had half risen from his chair and seemed as though stuck in a crouch, an arthritic victim in a game of charades, neither sitting nor standing.

"There's a letter may have been thrown away by mistake. The bins at the back door are empty." Taylor smiled with patience into the blankness. "Gar-bage bins."

"Hey, good," Greta said. "You find in broom closet for tomorrow. Tomorrow she collects outside in front okay."

"Broom clo-set," Taylor mouthed, grasping at what he believed to be a major clue and closely watching Greta for reaction to the encored broom closet, if any.

"Okay, yes."

"Thanks, good. There's no more? I mean, what there is is there, in the broom clo-set?"

"Hey, yes."

Behind the round spectacles the eyes of the stooping sprig wore a pleading air. He was swaying slightly, supporting himself with one hand on the table but retaining in principle the coiled posture, as though ready to bolt. Taylor nodded gratitude and farewell and retreated, closing the door after him. He hoped that after the television, and the lesson, if that was what it was, the pair would get together, if that was what they wanted.

There was a broom cupboard, he believed, in the passage off the front hall. Maybe garbage went there before being put outside for the dustmen. He switched on lights. In the cupboard among vacuum cleaners and mops stood two bulging black plastic bags, tied at the neck. He carried them, cigarette in mouth, to the kitchen. He spread newspaper on the floor, untied the first bag, and gently tilted it.

Weeks, seasons seemed to have passed since ants had nipped his shin in his mother's garden and in the Duke of Cumberland the pipsqueak Pinstripe had offered a spare pair of hands, that morning.

A crushed cornflakes carton. An empty jar of Maxwell House. An empty tin of Heinz mushroom soup. Newspapers, tissues, a blackened toothbrush, a dead bottle of Mouton Cadet, a white meatbone like a cudgel, speckled with tea leaves. A squashed tetrapack of chocolate milk that must have been Ann's. Or Greta's. A crumpled envelope.

From its color the envelope was unpromising but Taylor straightened it. "Barclaycard. Private & Personal." Private and personal to whom? There was no name and address, only a staring window.

Bastard Poole, Taylor thought, sifting and probing and cursing Poole to keep from dwelling on keener anxieties. Poole suspected but didn't know what to suspect. For months before Sears Crossing there'd been suspicion at the Yard and in gangland. Suspicion and rumor and talk. It had meant nothing. None of the talk had come even close to the mark. Neither would it do so now. The more talk, the better. Let them circle their squad cars around the Tate.

Taylor ground out his cigarette on the meat bone and suffocated it with a cold sodden teabag. His head ached. He looked around for his whisky, but he had left it somewhere.

The lost invitation was a bitch, but that was not the end either. An apologetic note would bring another. Invitations would have gone astray before and been replaced. He started shoveling the debris back into the bag.

Slicker was the snag.

Maybe Slicker would fetch up all right, too. He had

before. Maybe Saturday noon, Putney Bridge, he'd show with a stapled twelve-page folder of drawings in scale plan and cross section of the Queen's private suite at Buckingham Palace.

If he didn't? It'd-be-all-right-on-the-night might be fine for the amateurs doing *HMS Pinafore* in the church hall. But for Sears Crossing and for Granny's Chips that despairing platitude was a signed confession of incompetence. Worse, it was a plea of guilty. The mad cry of the already defeated. A ticket of admission into the nick and deservedly so.

Taylor tied up the first bag, untied and tilted the second. The contents spilled with a rush. Refuse squelched and clanked onto the newspapers. Assorted no-refund tonic and bitter lemon and lemonade bottles rolled across the newspapers and over the floor.

Taylor swore, recovered the bottles, and knelt. He swore again, lifting his leg to discover the trousers knee wet with the smear of an unidentifiable mess.

Two dead gin bottles and a vermouth bottle. Potato peelings, orange skins, avocado skins, a shoebox, a two-pound chocolate box, cooked fish, congealed rice on everything, brown and yellow scrapings of plates, a pair of sandals, a *Vogue,* a clutch of rice-spattered *Diana* comics, ruined flowers, squashed cartons.

> FRESH Medium-Strength PORK CURRY. Sell by 18 June. 68p. This product is FRESH not FROZEN. Keep Cool. Eat within 1 day of purchase or within 3 days if kept in a refrigerator.

He knew who paid for all this junk, but who in hell ate it? He shifted forward on his knees, delving among crumpled paper. There was an odor of rancid fish and his head throbbed.

Damn Slicker. Lost and frightened as a child in the night at the idea of the Queen. From the moment she'd been mentioned, at the dogtrack, he's been less than enthusiastic. "'Adn't been reckonin' on a frolic like this with royals and all." What was the matter with him? He wasn't a child in the night; he was a grown, skeptical, twentieth-century Londoner. Intelligent enough and by profession a thief. "Sixty million population and we 'ave to hit the Queen." Anyone else in the world, Taylor brooded, there'd have been no problem, Slicker would have laughed. But the Queen. Diamonds belonging to the Queen. Queenship was myth and magic and taboo and patriotism and laying down your cloak in the mud and fear of burning hellfire in the hereafter. *Close as from me to you she was, I could've reached out and touched her, really I could.* For Slicker the Queen was different. As ghosts would be different, and hobgoblins and the curse of the one-eyed yellow idol to the north of Katmandu and voices in the dark.

Slicker had not said no. Did he intend to say no or know what he intended? Was his failure with the Beccles woman his subconscious saying no?

"Christ," cursed Taylor, grubbing through crushed paper. If Slicker wanted out, the job had to be off. There could be no replacement, not now, not in the four weeks before July 8.

He held in his hand half of a white card torn vertically through the center. Under a truncated gold squiggle and the gold capital letter *R* was black print and his own longhand name, or the better part of it, written in ink.

erlain is commanded
jesty to invite
harles Taylor
e garden of Buckingham Palace on July 8
orm or lounge suit

He snatched a portion of blue card of identical size, identically torn, and the gummy left-hand half of a car windshield sticker for entry through the palace gates. Shuffling on his knees through garbage he picked and searched.

"Daddy," Ann said.

Taylor turned his head. She stood in the doorway in a striped nightdress which reached to the floor, her face contorting in delighted grimaces.

"Yuk." Advancing, Ann held her nose, released it, giggled. "Thought you were saying your prayers."

"It's a bill, got thrown away, nothing important." He slid the recovered halves of invitation under his leg. "You should be asleep."

"I'm thirsty. I've just finished *Black Beauty.*"

"Good, good. Have your drink and get to bed. It's nearly eleven."

"I've read it before. I'm going to read it every year." She positioned bare toes on the pork curry wrapper and steered it like a snow plow through shriveled white carnations. "How long are you staying?"

"I don't know. We'll try and do something together at the weekend. Now, off to bed."

"Bring me cocoa?"

"I'll see. If I can find it. I'll bring you something."

"And three of the biscuits with the bits of chocolate stuff. No, four."

"Go on, quickly, don't let Mummy find you here."

At the door Ann turned to grimace and hold her nose. "Yuk," she announced. "Poor *you.*"

She went, and Taylor grubbed and found the right-hand portion of car sticker, and next, one with the other, the left-hand halves of the blue and white invitations. The blue was headed "Personal Card." This was not an invitation, he deduced, but a card of admission. It carried the date, July 8; the designation, Her Majesty's Afternoon Party, Buckingham Palace; the names Mr. and Mrs. Charles Taylor; and instructions to the effect that this personal card must be handed in. He brushed rice from the four halves and put them in his pocket.

The garbage he stowed back in the bag. He cleaned up, carried the bags to the broom cupboard, washed his hands in the kitchen sink, and made cocoa. He could not find biscuits, so he put an apple on a plate. Ann was asleep when he brought the apple and cocoa into her room. He left them with *Black Beauty* beside her bed.

The drawing-room lights were on, but the television was off. Phoebe had gone presumably to bed. Taylor sat at the desk and pieced together the two cards. Grease had stained both. The blue personal card which had to be given up seemed the more necessary of the two, but he'd have to have replicas of both. There'd be a long hard look at Charles Taylor, OBE, if he arrived at Buckingham Palace with an admission card torn in two and daubed with curry.

For several minutes he stared down at the cards. Under the gold crown and initials ER on the white invitation, the Lord Chamberlain was commanded by Her Majesty to invite Mr. and Mrs. Charles Taylor to an Afternoon Party in the garden of Buckingham Palace on July 8. Morning dress or uniform or lounge suit.

There was no RSVP, which was a pity because he was in a mood for writing a loyal acceptance. Presumably everyone commanded to attend attended, and if a few hundred did not, they'd hardly be missed.

nineteen

"So what's Mr. Bighead up to tonight? Seat in the stalls and a bag of cashews?"

"Domestic."

"Wife or tart?"

"He took a radio cab to Kew," Sergeant Fothergill said. "Far-flung Kew."

Poole, pensive, rotated his cylinder of pills between thumb and forefinger. The pills chinked rhythmically. His chair was tilted back; his legs were stretched out across the papers and dossiers on the desk. The air smelled of metal. Everywhere in this well-lit Scotland Yard smelled of metal: metal filing-cabinets, metal chairs and tables, frames, fittings, and everything of aluminum and steel. When he looked back a dozen years to the old Scotland Yard warren by the embankment, smelling of floor polish and disinfectant, he did so with profitless nostalgia. This new warren at Victoria was identikit office box, the same, he supposed, as a million other identikit office boxes across the world.

"So now's the time," he said, "for a quiet break-in in Grosvenor Square."

"Without a search warrant?"

"Why—d'you have one?"

"I never know when you're serious."

"I'm never anything else." Poole reached forward and scratched a patch of exposed white calf. "But we'd want a bomb for his safe. And a pontoon bridge and horses to get past that porter."

"Harry."

"Very likely. A God-awful bollocks we'd make of it all. His door's got a Chubb castle deadlock, that'd take five hours for a start. Easier to bring artillery. He'll have one alarm that goes off in the Home Office and another under the commissioner's mattress."

"The Heavies'd be round in a flash," Fothergill said cheerfully. He had feared, briefly, that the chief inspector was serious.

"His office might throw up something. Sometime. Leadenhall Street." Poole spoke without conviction. Why couldn't he just jack it in, let Bighead go ahead with whatever he was going ahead with? The top brass would carry the can, as they deserved to. "No need for artillery there. Do we have an ambitious female in C Department who can keep her mouth shut and looks like a cleaning woman?"

"They all look like cleaning women."

"Save a lot of agony if I had a few quick photos of his appointments' book for the next month or two." Year or two? The cylinder rotated and chinked. "Hullo, Watergate."

"Watergate was a cock-up."

"Don't lecture me, Sergeant. Would you describe yourself as ambitious?"

"I don't get the time to think about it."

"Think about cleaning women. Window cleaners and decorators, that kind of thing. You might even earn yourself a little quiet promotion."

"Or a little quiet jail sentence."

"Don't be a clown. You don't go near Bighead's office yourself, ever. You're a marked man. In certain circles you're now known as Bananas Fothergill."

Flaming June, the following day, showed no inclination to heft up its caldron and tote it to a more probable situation like Morocco or Pernambuco. Traffic drove with windows lowered to let in the breeze, then with windows raised to shut out the dust and heat. On cue, the air conditioning failed at Charles Taylor Ltd. Its decibel level mounted, but no air circulated, and Miss Widdicombe addressed the engineers on the telephone with style and vituperation. An ill-tempered board meeting and a working lunch at Wheeler's with Howard, Lord Pollard, and a Panco Group accountant filled Taylor's time until midafternoon. At three o'clock, from a telephone booth in the Green Park underground, he talked with Ronnie Robb. Could Mr. Robb make himself available, with transport, on July 8? Mr. Robb believed he could. Without haggling, terms were agreed.

Robb was a detail, one among threescore details, and he'd not be needed any more than he'd been needed on August 8, 1963. Then Captain Robb, British Skylines pilot, had stood by with a Piper Comanche in a field in Kent for a fee of a thousand pounds. Now for five thousand pounds in advance, plus fifty thousand pounds in the event of his having to fly his client from the country, Mr. Robb, former British Skylines pilot, would stand by once more.

Watching through the glass of the telephone booth, vaguely prepared to spy Detective Chief Inspector Poole regarding his boots by the far wall, but seeing only scurrying strangers, Taylor dialed the Batley number and learned nothing of interest from a taped recording timed two fifteen, if Slicker's failure to be with Tania Beccles could be described as nothing of interest.

The person under surveillance had left his flat in Wardour Street at ten twenty and passed the subsequent seventy minutes in the Joe Coral spieler in Poland Street, correction, in the Joe Coral betting shop in Poland Street, revealed the recorded voice of Mr. Batley. From eleven forty until one ten the person had drunk beer in the Three Greyhounds at Greek Street and Old Compton Street in the company of a bald, wiry man of middle years, name and occupation unknown. The person had returned to his flat in Wardour Street at approximately one fifteen, on the way purchasing newspapers and confectionery. End of message.

Three Greyhounds? Bald, wiry man? Taylor, replacing the receiver, gave a laugh which was the first he had uttered that day. Mr. Beauchamp, could he possibly be, this bald and wiry companion in, of all places, the Three Greyhounds? Baldy Beauchamp, Slicker's business colleague, Terror of the Tote, part owner of the illustrious Jampot?

Taylor walked to the Ritz and telephoned a number in Amsterdam. From the Ritz he took a taxi to the Hilton, where after a delay of one hour he was connected with a number in Singapore. Mr. Kuan Lee of the Kuan Lee Diamond House agreed that he had been asleep but please not to apologize, was not sleep a death, a thief of time, and had he not known one day they might talk again?

From the Hilton, tense and dusty, Taylor trekked toward Audley Street and Grosvenor Square. He kept alert, and found satisfaction in his certainty that he was not watched or followed. There was less satisfaction in the knowledge that the rate offered in Amsterdam was seventeen percent less than would be forthcoming from Kuan Lee.

He had enjoyed the irony of the thought that Cullinan Three and Four might be disposed of in Amsterdam, where once they had been cleaved from their three-thousand-carat parent crystal. But it was as though Mijnheer Dietermayer had been made aware of the irony, too, and intended to make his client pay for it. Mijnheer Dietermayer, Taylor had already decided, could go swing on a windmill. The guess of bastard Poole had been accurate; the game was not money, not primarily. At the same time, seventeen was too high a percentage for indulging an irony. Seventeen percent came out at around a hundred and twenty thousand pounds sterling. Seventy-two thousand deutschmarks. Three hundred thousand Yankee dollars.

Taylor was exhausted now, but later, after dealing with the garden party invitations, he would try Hong Kong. If their price matched Kuan Lee's, he could auction Granny's Chips between them.

So much detail, so much preparation. The bulk of the detail would turn out to have been unnecessary as well as costly, but there was no helping that. Where jobs failed, they failed almost invariably in the afterward. Not in the execution but in the hours, days, or months following.

The courier was fixed, tremulous Mrs. Jacobson with her fluttering ringed fingers and heart like a flake of Welsh slate; and the standby courier in case Mrs. Jacobson fell under a bus. The handover was fixed too, in the mezzanine cafeteria at the British Airways terminal,

Victoria. Buckingham Palace to the terminal was a nine-minute walk. He had walked it, twice, with a stopwatch. Walking through rush-hour London with Granny's Chips was going to be hairy; even for a mere nine minutes, he'd be sweating like a stale Cheddar by the end of that little stroll. Still, rather that than another middleman, or middlewoman. Mrs. J.'s reservation for the evening of July 8 ought to be made soon, but that couldn't be done until the route was settled. Singapore or Hong Kong?

That evening there'd be an airline strike, of course. Or a hijack scare and Heathrow would be closed. But no one, not even Chas. Taylor, OBE, could plan for every possibility and stay sane. At least there'd not be fog, not in July.

Walking, he realized he was too weary to face the bath he needed, and the invitations, and the pointlessness of his empty flat. He turned into Mount Street and headed in the direction of Berkeley Square and the Curzon cinema.

With a razor blade Taylor cut the longhand names "Mr. and Mrs. Charles Taylor" from the scotch-taped invitation card. The printer who would reproduce the card did not have to reproduce the name or know it. Taylor razored the names "Mr. and Mrs. Charles Taylor" from the blue admission card. The two mutilated, anonymous cards he placed in an envelope with two hundred and fifty pounds in ten-pound notes. He sealed, addressed and stamped the envelope.

The slivers of card with his handwritten name he placed between pages 50 and 51 of *An Encyclopedia of London* and returned the book to the shelf. They'd be needed for forging his name on the duplicate cards. Forgery was not his line, but he'd practice the handwriting and take pains, and it would work. It was not as though the coppers who'd be collecting the invitations at the gates into Buckingham Palace would know how to read, let alone be able to tell one handwriting from another. Simpler and cheaper to have left the invitations in the Kew trash and telephoned Buckingham Palace humbly for replacements, Taylor reflected, not for the first time. But he had a bad feeling about telephoning the palace. Bad vibes, Ann would have said. Perhaps they'd ask for the request in writing. Even if they didn't, his name would be noted. Filed away somewhere. Anonymity did not lie along that road, and success was anonymity.

A little over eleven grand, he estimated, the Cullinan job had cost so far. By the evening of July 8 the two gems airborne out of Heathrow and the bulk of expenses paid, the figure would be close on nineteen. His original rough reckoning had been around the twenty mark. It was cheap enough, and all was advancing smoothly. With the exception of Slicker and Miss Beccles.

He switched off the stereo, carried pajamas into the bathroom, turned on the taps, then walked back to the bedroom to dial a last call to the Batley number.

The person under observation, according to the recorded voice of Mr. Batley, had passed the latter part of the evening at Chung Fu's in Gerrard Street, alone, eating steak and chips. He had then spent ninety minutes at the Savoy Turkish and Sauna Baths in Jermyn Street before returning to his flat at twenty-three fifty hours.

Taylor, yawning, glanced at his watch. Nearly two o'clock.

Shortly after midnight, observed Mr. Batley (boring but conscientious, I've picked the right man, Taylor thought), a man in his early twenties, six feet two or three, long brown hair, smart suede jacket, had entered the lobby and, according to information subsequently elicited from the night porter in return for the sum of ten pounds, had entered the flat of the subject under surveillance. Observation would continue. Message timed one thirty hours.

Taylor ran into the bathroom and turned off the taps. He grabbed his jacket and left the flat.

twenty

"That'll be all right, sir. You didn't mind my asking, I'm sure. Easy to see you're a gentleman. Some we get are a funny lot though. You'd be surprised. As much as my job's worth, you might say. Canada, you said?"

"Vancouver. It'll be a great surprise to him."

"We've had Canadians here, sir, Australians, all sorts. South Africans. What I say is, where'd we have been in two wars without the colonies? They can say what they like."

The night porter was an etiolated gnome who plainly had not seen the sun for years. He handed the middle-aged man a Yale key. The two ten-pound notes had vanished from his other hand like a conjuring trick, into the shine of the uniform.

"Number Four, sir, first landing. You could take the lift. Like I say, I could tell you some stories."

Taylor mounted the stairs. The carpet silenced the soles of his shoes; the building was as quiet as a church. A feeble light gave an impression of yellow emulsioned walls and chrome banisters.

He had failed to find a taxi, and his walk due east from Grosvenor Square had brought him to the north of Soho and the wrong end, as it turned out, of Wardour Street. Now his feet ached. He was worried, and his temper was short. Twice in Wardour Street yobs had called to him from uninviting doorways of strip clubs. When a third doorman had said, "Free membership, mate," Taylor had suggested to him, striding past, that he piss off, mate.

He put his ear to the door of Number Four, hearing nothing. With such slow care that no sound disturbed the silence, he eased the key into the lock. The figure 4 was in chrome, fixed by unmatched screws, one of brass, one of steel.

Taylor took a step into an unlit, uninhabited room. He opened the door farther so that the glow from the passage settled on an outline of chairs, table, sofa, television. To the left was a curtained window, and beyond it the muffled crescendo of a speeding car. To the right, two darkened doors: to kitchen and bathroom, he supposed. There was a fitted carpet and an aroma of cigar. Beyond the table in the center of the room, beneath the door directly ahead, shone a ribbon of light.

He closed the door with both hands. Arms outstretched like a somnambulist, he felt his way around the table, toward the light under the door. At the door he paused and held his breath, listening. He could leave now, and wanted to, as noiselessly as he had come, delivering up the key to the gnome, intently nodding at a farewell story, and out into the night and the neon streets. From the other side of the door came no sound. He caressed his fingertips down the flanks of the door, searching for the handle.

The handle was a horizontal bar like a lever. Taylor pushed it down and the door open.

The bedroom was hot, brightly lit, and hazy with cigar smoke. Taylor blinked into the dazzle of light. The bedclothes had been rolled back from the double bed and lay in a mound on the carpet. Propped on pillows, prison-white and staring, Slicker was combing his hair. Montgomery, similarly propped and naked, looked at Taylor from over the top of *Classic Car*.

Taylor pulled the door shut. On his course to the door out of the flat he exclaimed aloud as he banged into the table.

The forecast for cooler weather with rain had been half accurate, for though the night was balmy enough for cotton dresses and antics in the Serpentine and the fountains in Trafalgar Square, rain had started to fall. Fat drops detonated on Taylor's head and hands and knees as he walked fast out of Soho and across Piccadilly Circus.

In spite of aching feet he would have liked to walk and walk and lose himself, but losing himself in these familiar streets was impossible. He'd have liked to have walked with a mind as thoughtless as first love's because he was aware that anger and fright and fatigue left his thoughts totally without profit. But the thoughts swirled like an insomniac's. He had a feeling of being very young again in the worst way: solitary, with the cinemas and pubs shut, but too awake to go home to nothing, and with nowhere else to go or want to go.

The one place he could have gone to and been content, he felt, so long as no one spoke to him, not even whispering Jacko, was Jacko's Club. Back into the womb. He had frequented one such club in the tearaway days in Fulham, a basement off the Broadway, and been at home there, but only for as long as he'd taken to discover that birds of a feather flocking together get winged, sooner of later, and carted away, one by one. Had things turned out differently, had his IQ been only average or his judgment and ambition less, he might now have been an habitué of Jacko's, between spells in prison. But things had turned out the way they had turned out, and to have returned to Jacko's would have been to seek out trouble.

Assuming, that was to say, the Cullinan job was still on.

Damn those two to hell. It was unbelievable. What price teamwork now? Tonight lovers, tomorrow probably scratching each other's eyes out. What kind of team was that?

They had increased the risk one hundredfold. The job had to be off, for this year anyway, with this team. What if next week they were on spitting terms, each plotting to shop the other?

Taylor stepped round a puddle of vomit on the pavement. A youth lay in a doorway, another man standing close by, moving his hand in the air as though conducting. Taylor strode past bleak faces, fixtures in this sleaziest hub of empire the world could ever have known. There was dinginess and menace, but though he quickened his pace past the all-night Boots, he could not refrain from glancing through the open doors. The customary queue of youths and girls waited at the prescriptions counter. One boy was leaning on a mate like a soldier in a frieze on a war memorial. Two girls in ankle-length skirts and a man with a guitar in a canvas cover stood apart from the queue and in silence.

He remembered the one occasion when he had queued there, for of all things cough medicine for Ann. In front of him had queued a man of his own age, a stooped unshaved derelict with a shuffling step and string for bootlaces, looking about him and every now and then making a loud, unintelligible statement. Taylor had supposed him to be on meths rather than drugs and in the chemist's for the warmth and company. Just before his turn at the counter the derelict stepped out of the queue, muttering and performing a jigging retreat and pulling from his pockets scraps of string and paper. When Taylor had left with wrapped medicine, the man was in line near the rear of the queue, shuffling and looking about him.

The fat drops splattered upon Taylor: the persistent beginning to a downpour which refused to arrive. He walked down York Street and across St. James's Square. If he turned left, he'd be a minute from Crockford's, where there should be no difficulty in making up a rubber of bridge. If he turned right he'd reach St. James's Street and Booker's, where he could—what? Ring the bell and run away? Throw a bomb?

Plead for membership?

He walked along Pall Mall, ignoring clubs. A panda car cruised by, two peak-capped uniforms in front, a lounging plainclothesman in the back.

Whether or not the palace job would now take place, he knew he'd carry on as though it would, at least until Slicker and Montgomery were able to show they were more interested in its success than in each other, and a bomb was the diversionary tactic he needed. More than ever he was convinced of it. A harmless bomb with a big bang. A terrifying bomb that would tip askew the hats of the grand ladies and have the generals and bishops scuttling for cover. Only sophisticated idiots and losers dismissed an idea because it was cut from a child's comic, with "Pow!" shrieking across it in multicolored print.

An unlit taxi returning home to the suburbs. A Mini. No late-night buses, not in this quarter. No pedestrians.

Might a firework do it? Or would it have to be a thunderflash with a bang like the end of the world. Who in the army did he know with access to thunderflashes? Where did you buy a fifty-quid Roman candle? Where did you buy any kind of firework five months before Guy Fawkes Night?

He had arrived in the Mall and was walking along the pavement in the direction of Buckingham Palace. At forty and fifty miles an hour the desultory traffic speeded along the thoroughfare as though to break the law in such proximity to its source and chief defender was an achievement with a rare specialist pleasure of its own. The rain had ceased. Taylor met no one.

Poole had planted the idea of a bomb. "You'll likely have a couple of the IRA for company. Watch out they don't slip a stick of gelly in your soup." Taylor relished the irony of the Yard's coming forward with ideas for the big one. Not that he'd not have thought of it for himself; and another twenty ideas more.

The frustration, the pleasure forgone in never being able to thank Poole for his part in the big one, was minor. A dozen years ago the telling would have been hard to resist, though it would have been resisted. But it was something you grew out of, like lemonade or long hair.

How much warning did the IRA give? Five minutes, half an hour? But any warning at all would wreck the whole exercise because the garden would be cleared and within seconds the Queen and her detective and entourage would be out of it and into the palace and presumably up to her private apartments, opening doors and "Who are you? What're you doing with Granny's Chips?" On the other hand, the IRA was too useful a scapegoat to lose. The situation was always volatile enough for no one to know what might happen, and royalty was always a possible target.

If there was no IRA warning, how to ensure that the heat in the first hours after the ban would be on the Irish?

If there was a warning, there might be no party. And no party, no tickle.

If, and assuming, which now was the assumption of the year, the tickle was on.

Damn damn damn those two. Already they'd be at each other's throats, each blaming the other.

The team that lays together stays together. The team that shacks up cracks up, more likely.

Was he making too much of it? Damn them. Damn everything.

The Victoria Memorial glowed gold and marble in the reflection of the lamps in Queen's Gardens. Beyond the memorial shone lights from a handful of the sixty windows in the east front of the palace. Policemen would be patrolling the gates and railings. There'd be a parked squad car and a couple of motorcyclists in white helmets and fascist gloves. There always were.

In no mood for bidding a passing good-night to Her Majesty's upholders of the peace of the realm, Taylor turned onto a path leading into Green Park and headed across the park for Piccadilly and Grosvenor Square.

He awoke late and frightened, certain the Cullinan job must fail, if he were harebrained enough to go ahead with it.

At least once in the night the telephone had rung, and he had ignored it. Sunshine from the cracks between the curtains washed the white wall by the window and projected into the bedroom shafts of light which fell across the foot of the bed, the scarlet carpet, the ivory handles of drawers. His forehead was cold with sweat. Poole was too close and ambitious. Montgomery and Slicker were flops. He had nothing, totally nothing, not the least scrap of information on the Queen's apartments. And though never before had he known it, he had known in the night that Slicker had been on the mark when he'd said he, Charlie boy, had been lucky with the train robbery.

Luck, like lightning, never struck twice in the same place.

Taylor lit a cigarette. He drew the curtains back, then telephoned the Batley number. The latest message was timed three o'clock that morning.

At two twenty-three, informed the recorded voice, a middle-aged man, possibly Canadian, well-built, graying hair, lightweight suit and tie, had entered the building and tipped the night porter twenty pounds for the key to the flat of the subject under surveillance. Aforesaid middle-aged person had left the flat at approximately two twenty-six and the building at two twenty-seven. At two forty-four the person in the suede jacket who had entered the flat earlier departed also, proceeding in a northerly direction along Wardour Street.

Sorry, thought Taylor, if I dampened the sport, sport.

Batley? There at least was a worker. Where'd he been lurking? Taylor recalled seeing no one near Slicker's Wardour Street pad. Only strip club doormen.

He had opened the door onto the resin and leather smells of the gymnasium when the telephone rang. He picked up the wall telephone by the parallel bars.

"Before you 'ang up—"

"Wasn't there a little decision about you not telephoning here?" Taylor said. "Two things, since you seem determined to play the part of wrecker. Don't bother about Putney Bridge because I'll not be there. And stay away from Tania Beccles. Stay right away. It shouldn't be too difficult. I may be in touch later, and I may not."

He hung up.

Caring for his body without loving it, alert to signs of strain and stiffness, Taylor labored for twenty minutes:

tedious slow press-ups, chin-ups, calf machine, dumbbells. In the shower he soaped himself until his hair stood up like horns and the lather streamed down his skin onto the drumming tiles and accumulated over the drain in a blossom of white bubbles. He shaved. Slicker, he had to admit, might be none too enthusiastic about humping the Miss Beccles if his eight years in the nick had inclined his tastes into other, so to speak, channels.

Couldn't Slicker have said so at the start? A month had been wasted, and time pressed.

What was unforgivable was picking Montgomery. From the squadrons of willing queers he'd had to have Montgomery. Like some sort of puerile and calculated act of cheek. Thumb to nose. Self-assertion in the sound of a raspberry blown at Big Charlie.

And yet. If there was no longer any future in Slicker seducing from Tania Beccles the scale cross section and safemaker's name, better he should be gay than a raving royalist. If Slicker's lack of drive had been due to a distaste for gamboling with chambermaids, well, all right. The jumbo-size problem would have been if he'd had a horror of poaching from Her Britannic Majesty.

If he'd been a Queen lover rather than a queen lover.

Taylor dressed in a gray mohair suit, white shirt and Chelsea FC tie. In the kitchen only two teabags remained. He would have to leave a note for Mrs. Barnett. He plugged in the kettle for tea.

Details of the palace apartments could still be got. The bitch factor was time.

Waiting for the kettle to boil, he hurried to the study for his address book and Suzy's telephone number.

"It's mad. Why me? This niece, she's the journalist. For heaven's sake, I wouldn't know where to start. Anyway, it all sounds very foot-in-the-door. Why can't they just do a piece on her corgis?"

"They've done the corgis. They've done everything except this tour of the private apartments."

"The final invasion of privacy, to the sound of trumpets."

"How do you stop it? Anyway it was only a thought. Forget it."

Taylor guessed she would not. She was game and bright, the smartest tart in years. Her fingers twisted in the hair on his chest; the nails scraped against the skin.

"I mean I don't even have shorthand or anything."

"If you produced a notebook, she'd probably run a mile. Really, forget it."

"Why all the rush? I don't understand the deadline. It's hardly wildly topical."

"Maybe the *Ladies' Home Journal* is after the same story. Vicki's got most of the stuff. The Beccles girl is simply cross-checking. Just to be sure the facts are right."

"I could trade in the Renault, buy something really flash."

"They'll sell the rights round the world. Vicki gets two thousand, would you believe? You'd give Tania Beccles fifty. Everyone wins."

To forestall the picking of holes in this last argument, he stopped Suzy's mouth with his own. She tasted of the champagne. Eyes open, gazing beyond the rumpled head to the windows and the blue sky over Hyde Park, Taylor embraced the white bamboo-thin body. She was in the net, as good as.

" Leo?"

"'Suzy?"

"I mean, supposing she does chatter. Girl to girl, as you say. There we are with the wimpies sizzling all round—"

"Not in the Wimpy House. Here."

"Here?"

"Much simpler. All you have to do is be sure she keeps to the subject." Now that he had her he wanted her to leave. "Furnishings, flowers, the safe—where the baubles go when they're not being worn, that's important, all the trivial details these magazines love. You know the sort of thing."

"I'd never remember it."

"Doesn't matter. It's only for checking, Vicki says. You'd be doing Vicki and one million readers a big favor. And a new car for Suzy. You wouldn't give Tania Beccles your right name, of course."

Bet your life I wouldn't, thought Suzy. No one gives anyone their right name round here. But it sounded all right. Jokey. And the new car. Not a whisper of that nosey copper at the Ritz. What was his name?

A wheeling speck that was a bird entered the blue framed by the window, then disappeared.

Taylor winced at the recollection that earlier, fleetingly, he should even have considered the proposition that luck had entered into the Great Train Robbery. Charlie Taylor's Great Train Robbery. Luck had been no more an element at Sears Crossing than it was going to be at Buckingham Palace.

"You're a very strange man, Leo Scofield."

"You're a very skinny Suzy."

twenty-one

" . . . Yes, Mr. Scofield, quite so. . . . In point of fact, sir, he went into the Green Man about, let's see. I've only this moment got in. Half an hour ago at most. . . . Across from Great Portland Street tube. . . . On this other matter, I wonder if I might think about it. . . . Yes, understood. . . . In which case the answer's affirmative. . . . That's very flattering. Most grateful, sir. As I say, I think I do try harder. . . . Goodbye, Mr. Scofield."

"Well?" Mrs. Batley said when after several moments her husband had said nothing, but stood with his hand like a pink plaster cast on the telephone, looking down at the hand and replaced receiver. "Does he want you to carry on?"

"What?"

They had no need to retreat to the other end of the

room to talk. Donna and Dawn were in bed, and Mrs. Batley had turned down the sound on the nine o'clock news. They had the money now, cash, for a color set, but were wavering. A new kitchen table was needed, slipcovers for the lounge suite, clothes for the girls, a wedding present for Mrs. Batley's sister; there was no end. But if the color television was not bought now, probably it never would be.

"The surveillance is finished," said Mr. Batley. "He's very satisfied. Congratulated me."

"Oh." She watched her husband. "That's hopeful, isn't it? He might want you again sometime?"

"He does."

"He does? There you are then! When? What's the job?"

"He didn't say when. I think soon, in a day or two."

"What's the matter then? What's he want?"

"He wants me to bug a room at the Dorchester for five hundred quid."

Mr. Batley turned up the volume on the television and sat in his chair, eyes on the screen. A railwaymen's leader was denying that his men were holding the nation for ransom. They were asking only a fair wage for the job. If the Prime Minister and Whitehall and all that lot thought the present rates fair, they could drive the bloody trains themselves.

"You said when you started on your own," Mrs. Batley said, "I remember it like yesterday, you said you'd never take on anyone without seeing them first. The personal touch, you said. Nothing dodgy. I said this Scofield sounded funny. I told you."

"It'll be nothing. The usual domestic. His wife's probably getting it on the side."

"That'll be what they told those Watergate people." She watched the railwaymen's leader staying cool under fire. "You've said you'll do it, haven't you?"

"It's five hundred quid."

"It's five hundred quid that'll put you in prison if you're found out."

"Don't nag me, woman. I'm trying to think."

Taylor looked behind him as he walked out of the Great Portland Street underground into the night. The character in the hacking jacket who had boarded the tube in front of him and at Great Portland Street had stepped off behind had so plainly been a copper that he could not have been following him. Even the Yard was not so obvious as that.

Even so.

On a wall in words four feet high a zealot had painted GAY IS GOOD. Taylor crossed the street and outside the door into the public bar of the Green Man glanced back once more. Problem with the Yard was that though the majority were thick as soup, there was always the bright boy or two capable of double and triple bluffs. And no point pretending Poole would not have dared. Poole would have had half the Heavy Mob watching him around the clock if he'd believed it might produce results.

Anyway, no hacking jacket.

Slicker was not a public bar man, not the liberated ex-nick Slicker of the crackling tiepins and lionskin hats, and certainly not if he'd got a rendezvous with Montgomery; but Taylor peered in. A quartet with pint glasses performing the ritual slow-motion dance in front of the dart board: throw move drink, throw move drink. Alone at a table with Guinness, like a posed model for an album of London scenes, a lined crone in bedroom slippers.

Taylor opened the door into the Disco Bar. If Slicker had an eye on the door, as Slicker would have, he'd see Charlie boy before he'd be seen. Which would be a pity because he'd have liked to watch Slicker for a while. Ninety-five percent sure of Slicker, even the new queer Slicker, still he needed the other five percent. Whether watching an off-guard Slicker would confirm the final five percent, Taylor was unsure. Without trying he'd never know. There were people who betrayed a great deal, off-guard. Phoebe was one.

No Slicker. No Montgomery. Or even Beauchamp, of Baldy Beauchamp and Anstruther, proprietors of the peerless Jampot.

The counter had a right-angle turn beyond which the faces of customers were hidden. Taylor walked by the counter and made the turn, scanning faces. Still no Slicker. Slicker had come and gone.

At the bar Taylor positioned himself where he could see the door. No hacking jacket. Not his night for company. He brought out cigarettes and ordered a scotch.

The jukebox gushed pop music. A woman at a table behind him was lecturing on weight control in a cultured voice that penetrated like a road drill. Taylor looked around and saw chest and arms of a scales-breaking amplitude. The woman's escort was a cartoonist's stereotype of the sober bank cashier.

At a farther table a bearded boy in a black gaucho hat held the hand of a girl whose wrist and forearm were looped about with a thousand bangles.

"Suppose you haven't by any chance got an evening paper?"

The inquiry was from a tall youth in a blazer who had materialized with his glass by Taylor's elbow.

"Sorry."

"Last race at York. I'd a fiver on."

"Afraid I can't help you."

"It can wait. My name's John."

"Well, John, I'm having this one drink, then I'm leaving."

"Bully for you," John sneered, and removed himself round the angle of the bar.

Taylor held the whisky in his mouth before swallowing. He might find Slicker at the Wardour Street flat, but he lacked the ardor for a second excursion into those premises. He'd let Slicker sweat another day or two. Let him crack his knuckles over whether the big one was still on or killed dead by his impertinence with Montgomery.

"Hampstead," announced one of a male threesome to Taylor's left, "diminishes me."

But for reassurance he badly wanted a word with Slicker. One minute would do. A couple of sentences. Reassurance, for God's sake? It was self-preservation.

Damn and damn Slicker. There was enough to be done without those two acting like a couple of half-cut clerks up from the provinces.

"Personally," a silk jersey in the threesome was saying, "I only function in the stews of Chelsea."

"And doesn't Chelsea know it, dear? We all remember your nice Irish stew from the guards' depot. A private, wasn't he?"

"Not especially."

There came a madrigal of giggles. Sipping, Taylor watched the door open, an aged unshaven head peer in and withdraw. Hacking jacket had been imagination, or he'd been called away to reinforce the parking-ticket patrol. What in hell am I doing in this place? Taylor wondered.

On the other hand, all he needed to know about Slicker's level of enthusiasm he could learn from Montgomery. Couldn't he? A hundred and fifty things to do. But tomorrow he would fit in Montgomery.

Taylor's thoughts moved on. It was going to be all right. Slicker would be able to dig up a contact for the gelly. If he had no contacts, if they were retired or inside, there'd be Jacko.

He swallowed the last of his whisky and nodded good-night to the barman.

"Sharp work," said Poole. He perused the barely dry photostats. "Pity, great pity, but that's the way of it, because someone really deserves promotion. To deputy commissioner at least."

"Thank you, sir."

"Not you, Bananas. Since when were you a cleaning woman?"

"She wasn't a cleaning woman. She was—"

"I don't want to know." Poole spread the photostats. They wore a shiny, bleached look in the block of sunlight which fell through the window and upon the desk. "I see he's off to the preview of the Expressionists at the Tate. Which doesn't mean a bloody thing."

Any more than Mr. Big Boy accepting the invitation to the Federation of British Industries dinner meant anything. And all the others. Royal Lifeboat Society dinner. St. Dunstan's lunch and interim meeting. Eastbourne council buffet lunch and press conference. Royal Festival Ballet (supper with director). Garden party, Buckingham Palace. Sherry, Monday Club, House of Commons. United Charities Board AGM. Westminster Conservative Association dinner (vote of thanks). In August began the Chelsea FC fixtures, home and away. Birthdays were noted. A weekend in Brighton with his mother. The handwriting was the secretary's: precise but with a trace of devil-may-care. Poole wondered again if he might profit from a visit to Miss Widdicombe. But why would he? There'd been no profit in visits to anyone else. Not even to Charlie Big himself. Mr. Bighead stayed cool under fire, or seemed to. On the other hand the alternative to jacking it in was to keep going. Keep visiting, keep digging, keep trying. You did one or the other.

His stomach hurt. One day, at one go, he was going to shoot the whole shower of pills down his throat. A pill cascade. Kill or cure.

A uniformed constable had knocked and carried in a carbon of a typed sheet of foolscap. He had placed it on the desk and departed wordlessly. Fothergill, leaning, read the carbon upside down.

"Like they say in the laboratories of science research," he said, "this could be a breakthrough."

Poole picked up the foolscap sheet. It was from Inspector Peter Church, Hampshire Constabulary, and timed 11:08. A Mrs. Mary Shears, licensee of the Dog and Pot, Alton, Hampshire, had identified the photograph of Slicker as that of a man who had lunched and drunk beer in the lounge bar on Sunday, April 17. He had been in the company of a taller, younger man with long hair and an expensive jacket, possibly leather or suede. She thought both men had London accents. They had moved into the saloon bar, where they played the pinball machine until approximately 12:45, when they left. They returned after about half an hour and played darts until closing time. She was positive about the identification. Business during the last hour of Sunday lunchtime was normally slow and by 2:30 the two men were the only customers. She remembered the day because she was arthritic and the following day, April 18, was admitted to Alton General Hospital for a plastic replacement to her hip. She had returned to the Dog and Pot last weekend after nine weeks in hospital.

"I could go down and have a word with her; they've a nice drop of beer in that part," the sergeant said.

Poole did not hear. The sensation in his stomach was not pain but a peculiar, prickling hunger. Suddenly, he felt, he was drawing close. But close to what?

Slicker's crony, the taller, younger man in suede or leather, wasn't Charlie Taylor. So who was he?

"If I bring in Slicker," he said, "that could be finish to their caper, whatever the hell it is, and I lose Taylor. If I don't bring in Slicker, and they pull off their bloody caper—"

"Yes?" Fothergill prompted, awaiting the end of the sentence.

Poole brought from his pocket the cylinder of pills. It was a bitch. What was politely known as a dilemma. But the kind of dilemma he'd been short of for far too long. The kind that might put the lining back on his stomach.

"That plastic hip sounds nasty," Fothergill said.

twenty-two

The older, ill-looking salesman with warts on his hands said, "Good afternoon, sir. Can I help you?"

"Thanks, I'll wait for Mr. Montgomery, he saw me before."

From the glass office advanced E. Montgomery, Consultant. He was succeeding in seeming unconcerned. The glossy locks lapped the collars of open-neck shirt and hand-stitched jacket. He wasted few words in skirmishing.

"The Ferrari Boxer, wasn't it, sir?" He smelled of Brut after-shave. "Or was it something else?"

"Anything else. Not too obtrusive. Just for ten minutes."

"I've an Opel outside. Got your license?"

"You're the driver, sonny, not me."

The consultant eyes flickered about the showroom and toward the secretary in the glass office. "If it's all the same to you, we ought at least to look as though we're buying and selling."

Montgomery returned to the office and came back carrying leaflets, which he handed to Taylor. The ill-looking salesman had a customer, an Asian shopkeeper who moved from Skoda to Simca to Datsun Cherry, opening the trunk of each as though looking for a relative.

"Opel Rekord, one-point-nine liters, naught to fifty in ten seconds, roomy, excellent family car. Sir." Montgomery pointed at print on a leaflet he had put into Taylor's hand. "You'd like to be sure I can drive. Right?"

"I'd like to be sure you can drive without showing off. And one or two other things."

At a meter in a street behind the salesroom Montgomery unlocked a white Opel. The two men sat and fastened their safety belts. Before switching on, Montgomery lit a cigar.

"So we're pressing on," he said.

"Pressing on where?"

"The eighth. Buckingham Palace."

"Why not?"

"Just wanted to know. One of us seemed to have doubts after the other night."

"Have you?"

"How would I know? It's not my party."

"Can we drive then, or do I get out and crank?"

Montgomery switched on, put the gear into first. "Buckingham Palace?"

"We'll save Buckingham Palace."

The car slid forward.

"Try west up City Road," Taylor said. "King's Cross, Great Portland Street. That'll bring us to the Green Man."

Montgomery stayed silent.

"Heard of the Green Man?"

"Round the corner from Warren Street. Warren Street where the stoppo drivers hang out." Montgomery slowed at a Give Way sign. "That's the word, isn't it—stoppo?"

"Sounds like a certain someone's been trying to educate you."

Montgomery insinuated the car into the Hackney Road traffic. Cigar smoke smothered the aroma of upholstery and after-shave.

"My advice is forget Warren Street," Taylor said. "They're bad company. You don't need them."

"Well, don't worry. I've never been in Warren Street, and I know who I need." The car spurted then slowed, prematurely obedient to an orange light. "After the eighth of next month I'm not going to need you two either. Or anyone."

"Amen," Taylor said, tearing foil from a pack of cigarettes. He approved of his driver's attitude: cold, self-regarding, ambitious. "So what else has Slicker told you?"

"A round figure of three-quarters of a million."

"How about my name?"

"No."

"I don't believe you."

"Your privilege." The Opel halted at a zebra crossing. Jamaican schoolgirls with satchels chattered across. The car drove on. "If you're really interested, I did ask but he wouldn't say. After you'd looked in on us at his place, he called you a creeping toe-rag. He was in a state. Can't say I blame him. In deference, no offense, sir, but where I come from gentlemen knock before entering other gentlemen's bedrooms. Car to your liking, sir?"

"Take the next left."

"Roundabout way to the Green Man."

"Sod the Green Man. To coin a phrase."

South along the shabby length of City Road Montgomery held the outer lane at a patient thirty miles an hour. Where lights loomed he made no attempt to beat them.

"Truth is," Montgomery said, "your pal Slicker hasn't come to terms with his true nature. As they say. Shame, guilt, all that."

"Unlike you."

"Unlike me."

Montgomery slowed the car behind a bus, ignoring a chance to steal through on the near side. In a stretch of fifty open yards the Opel, queue leader, declined to accelerate but maintained its lawful thirty. Cars and lorries behind, honking and light-flashing, streamed through on the left.

"You're showing off," Taylor said.

"Can't win, can I?"

"We're all going to win," said Taylor. Cigarette-smoking, he wound his window down, letting tobacco smoke out and dust and diesel fumes in. "The name Tania Beccles mean anything to you?"

"That your name?"

He makes jokes too, Taylor thought, he's balanced, it's going to be all right. He said, "You said Slicker had doubts. What sort of doubts?"

"Why don't you ask him?"

"I'm asking you."

"Told you, he was in a state about you. Being discovered with his big secret uncovered, so to speak. Thinks you might call it all off. He's tried to phone you."

"What about the royalty bit?"

"What royalty bit?"

"For God's sake, the sacrilege, the diamonds being the Queen's. The blasphemy of ferreting around her apartments."

"So that's what we're doing?"

Taylor looked sideways at his driver. Evidently it was

news to him. Professional Slicker, Taylor thought. Silent, dependable, professional Slicker. Even between the sheets.

He said, "It's Buckingham Palace, isn't it? What did you think we were doing?"

"Didn't think anything. Don't want to know. All I know from Slicker is I dump a bag over the wall and clear out. Then I wait with some speed and a full tank. And I get rich." The Opel stood becalmed amid bleating traffic. "Knew it was a garden party. The quality. There might've been some loose cash about. The odd tiara."

"Some loose cash and the odd tiara. Fantastic. What about the band's wages? And four hundredweight of cucumber sandwiches?"

Taylor exhaled: a mixture of sigh and smoke. The professional, he thought, and the unprofessional. He had them both. Though for what Montgomery had to do he'd be professional enough. The car inched forward escorted by taxis and red double-decker buses.

"Slicker never mentioned the Queen?"

"No. I did, couple of times, because I didn't much like the sound of it. Don't get excited, though. I'll be there. Outside. Just don't blind me with details."

"What did he say about you not liking it?"

"Colorful stuff. I'd the vision of a fourth-rate footpad and this wasn't the minor league, nicking Green Shield stamps from old ladies' handbags."

"He said that?"

"Green Shield stamps and pension books."

The traffic was moving again. Taylor tossed three inches of cigarette out of the window. He had his final five percent of reassurance and wanted to laugh. Slicker the Nicker, By Appointment to Her Majesty. Crown Thief Imperturbable. Peterman of the Year. Lock up your gewgaws, lady, here comes Slicker with the oxyacetylene. Slicker for President.

Sunshine warmed the window frame. Alongside, keeping pace, an adolescent ruffian piloted a dented delivery van: Freezameat (Sales), Hidalgo J. Gazzi, The Broadwalk, Wembley. Taylor wanted to reach through the window and shake the youth by the hand.

"Left at Cheapside and keep going," he told Montgomery. "Drop me in Leadenhall Street."

"Not the Bank of England?"

"I'd like you to get back to your customers. You'll be losing sales."

"Not going to matter, is it? Not after next month."

"Depends."

"Oh? Meaning what?"

"Meaning it depends how smart you are because I'm not going to hold your hand. You're about to become a moderately wealthy man. It's a time people are going to get curious about you. All kinds of people. Hope you've thought about it."

"I've thought about it. I've had all this from Slicker."

"A shining example."

Gutter Lane. Milk Street. Bread Street. Ironmonger Lane. Old Jewry. Poultry. The Opel waited at lights. Taylor looked for blue helmets outside the Bank of England but saw none. They're there all the same, somewhere, he thought.

Montgomery said, "Exactly how much does this three-quarters of a million split into?"

"For you two hundred thousand. It'll be in six separate bank accounts. I'll let you know."

"And the car I'm to use, who's going to let me know about that? Slicker says I don't get it till the eighth. I don't even know what it's going to be. He says leave it to him."

"What's the problem?"

"No problem. I just want to know."

"You'll be having a Westminster Council van for dumping the bag over the wall. You can't know the car you'll be picking up Slicker in because no one does. It doesn't exist until the eighth. Nervous?"

"Course not."

"You should be. I've been nervous for three months."

"All I'm saying is I want to check it over. Cars are different. You have to know them. They need handling."

"You'll handle it. Don't go into Leadenhall—turn left and drop me."

"The Ferrari would be perfect. I've spare plates. I can do the spraying myself"

"Forget it. Trust Slicker. You trust us both, don't you?"

"Of course."

"Because we trust you. My name's Taylor." The Opel turned left into Bishopsgate and slowed. Taylor released his safety belt, took hold of the briefcase on his lap. "I ought to tell you no racing at Silverstone on Saturday, but if you're a racing driver, you'd better go and race. Just don't kill yourself."

"I was going to tell you about Silverstone. I'll scratch if you want."

"Certainly you will. But it's your decision. Keep in trim." Taylor stood on the pavement and closed the door. He stooped to speak through the open window. "It's all going to go like a song."

He crossed the road in the direction of Leadenhall Street and the offices of Charles Taylor Ltd. at the distant end. "Charlie," called a voice.

Howard fell into step beside him. His brother was identically kitted out with bowler hat and briefcase, but he wore a hand-knitted tie with a knot as big as a lemon, and lacking only an embroidered insignia, Trendsville.

"I know that bloke," Howard said. "Racing motorist, isn't he? He chased us for a loan. About a year ago. Montague? Mitchell?"

"I don't know what you're talking about."

"The fellow who just dropped you. I didn't know he was still—"

"He's a footballer. Bertie Smith. One of the Chelsea reserves. We just signed him."

"No, no. I remember the face. Not Smith. Morecambe? Hell, I'll look it up. He wanted the lease—"

"His name's Smith, he's a footballer." Taylor was pale. He made no attempt to keep the anger from his voice. "You've never seen him before. You're always getting everything wrong."

Taylor quickened his pace. He strode ahead, away from his brother.

If Montgomery should kill himself at Silverstone or fall dead this night from choking on a cigar, a substitute could be found. Even at this late date a wheelman would be easy enough to recruit, though not, and here was the swine of it, not a wheelman with Montgomery's clean bill of health.

Howard? Damn and stuff Howard. Of all the luck. One minute sooner, one minute later, it would have been okay. No one needed cruddy luck like that.

Taylor, alone at the end of an empty row, six empty rows from the screen, elongated his legs into the aisle. He tried to concentrate on the film, a bucolic summery comedy without nudity or blood which had won a prize at San Sebastian and praise from the critics of the ritzy papers. The dialogue was Czechoslovakian, the subtitles against bright exteriors of grass and river were invisible, and the audience was sparse. The film had not been at the top of Taylor's list. His mind wandered partly because the film was so remorselessly gentle, partly because of preoccupations elsewhere.

Howard would have checked his files and found the name E. Montgomery, Consultant, Europa Sports Cars Ltd. Then what would Howard do?

The main danger, Taylor warned himself, was not overconfidence, or a weakness in planning, or lack of foresight or judgment or contacts. The main danger was sheer bad luck.

Howard would do nothing. What could he do? He would brood and sulk. He'd be baffled and hurt at not being in his brother's confidence. Poor old Howard. Rot him.

Allowing Montgomery to choose whether or not to race on Saturday, that was a calculated risk. His guess was that Montgomery would scratch. Not because Montgomery thought he would go up in flames—sooner or later most racing motorists did exactly that—but because he'd want to prove his seriousness to the boss.

On the screen a bacchanalian character with rumbling belly and trousers held up by a tie brewed tea in a field. Two men and a matron with a parasol sat on the grass around the paraffin stove, regarding the brewing. Yellow sunshine melted over the figures, landscape, and subtitles.

Taylor slid lower in his seat and propped one bent knee against the empty seat in front. He had his team: peterman and wheelman. Slicker had caused a passing anxiety, but not anymore. Loyalty to loot was taking precedence over loyalty to royalty and over myth and taboo. For Slicker and Montgomery, both. And their bed games, hopefully, were an irrelevance. Unexpectedly irrelevant.

He had the invitation for July 8. White and blue cards as crisp as originals.

The gelly would be easy, Slicker's department, because even after eight years out of circulation, if Slicker couldn't lay his hands on it, no one could. The car and the van, Slicker's department again, though he'd be needing half a grand to pay the heist.

Taylor made a mental note for the morning: Martin to the bank.

He mused on Montgomery's anxiety over the car, the car he'd wanted to handle in advance. He'd not be able to because it wouldn't be stolen until the morning of the eighth. But the anxiety was a bonus. Basically a serious man, the team's wheelman. Seriousness plus the coolness on the Tait job as reported by Slicker. Ideal.

In the field a portable record player was playing a waltz and the matron with the parasol was waltzing through the long grass with the man in the boater.

Mr. Kuan Lee's offer had been accepted. At fifty-two hundred and fifty pounds per carat the offer topped Hong Kong's by four percent. As for Mijnheer Dietermayer, up his Dutch nostrils with his florins. Payment in Singapore and Australian dollars, rounding out at eight hundred thirty thousand pounds gross for 158 carats of Granny's Chips. Less twelve percent wastage from cutting and reshaping in the workshop of the Kuan Lee Diamond House, leaving seven hundred thirty thousand pounds net. Tax free. Not quite three-quarters of a million. Only a fourth of the train haul. But substantial for a carve-up among a team of three.

The air ticket of Mrs. Jacobson, courier, was bought: Flight 738 to Sydney by Qantas Kangaroo Route through Rome, Bahrain, Bangkok, and Singapore. Her passport and international certificate of vaccination, she had flutteringly assured him, were in order.

What if the Qantas flight was chosen for a spot security check and the mobile detection device wheeled out? From calculatedly idle telephone chat with sources which had the answer to such matters Taylor had learned there was no certain answer, the detection device might or might not pick out diamonds, but if it did, diamonds were not what the security check was interested in. This minor poser had not been worth mentioning to Mrs. J. No sense unnerving her. Though God knew it was not her nerves that fluttered, only the hands and eyelids. She was so looking forward, she had enthused, to the trip.

Mr. Robb, pilot, though not of the Qantas or any other scheduled flight, would be making no trip anywhere. But he had received his five thousand pounds for a guarantee to stand by with transport in the field in Kent.

The field on the screen had been replaced by a different field beside a riverbank. The man in the boater, the bacchanalian man, the third man, and the matron with the parasol were seated on the bank doing nothing.

Taylor lit a cigarette from the butt of the last. Details such as Robb fell into the category "contingency planning." They were costly and would prove unnecessary, but in just such details lay the difference between success and failure. The trifling extra capital for a double check on Leatherslade Farm, and the fingerprints would have been wiped clean, the team would have stayed free. And for anyone who hadn't stayed free the fool fault would have been his own.

This Cullinan job had coasted along more smoothly than Sears Crossing, and the main reason was money. Money, the simplicity of the job, the tightness of a team of three. But chiefly the money. These days he had it. What the hell if he didn't even possess the blue and white invitations when he could slip a bundle to the copper checking invitations at the gate and slip him a second bundle if he so much as hesitated?

Some aspects of the planning had coasted along more smoothly than others, but all from the start had been so much simpler than the train tickle. The train job had worked in spite of its numberless complexities—until the end. Granny's Chips by comparison promised to be as uncomplicated as the ace of trumps.

Promised to be, brooded Taylor. He lowered and straightened his knee from the back of the seat in front, lifted and bent the other knee. The job still was a matter of promise, not performance. A little under three weeks to go and he'd have flung fifteen thousand pounds in bribes and down payments through the window unless Suzy came through with the Beccles girl.

But if he were honest, even with enough cash to spread like manure, the job was not really coasting as it should. Bastard Poole, Banana-boy with his yellow eyes on Slicker, they were part of the game, integral to it. But no one deserved the debacles of Howard spotting him with his wheelman. Or of wheelman and peterman bedding down together.

In the end these would be laughs. Afterward, always, it was the bad moments which bombarded you with giggles.

There'd be no afterward because there'd be no nothing until Tania Beccles talked her heart out.

The bacchanalian man, now wearing swimming trunks, teetered on the riverbank. He fell backward into the river with an inevitability and rustic charm that failed to raise a smile from Taylor or more than a murmur from the sparse audience.

twenty-three

"Reelly I don't think I ought to say," said the voice, wincingly genteel. "I mean, like, well, I know it's different but they've their rights the same as you and me, I always say." Spasmodically the honest vowels of Chigwell warred with the gentility. "Anyway, it's locked, innit?"

"How d'you go through then?" Suzy said.

"Get the keys from Mrs. Bellows, don't we?"

Pause, and chinking, as of a cup or ashtray being moved. Taylor reached forward, drew his own ashtray closer and dripped into it a gray grub of cigarette ash.

"That's the underhousekeeper, Mrs. Bellows. Windy Bellows we call her, but there's plenty worse, she's fair, whatever some of them might say."

"How many of you are there?"

"Forty, round about. Fifty there was once, but His Royal

Highness did the time and motion. After the coronation that was. Before my time."

"Not forty all for the private suites?"

"You're joking. Two for Her Majesty's, that's me and Jean, and two for His Royal Highness', that's Maeve and Linda." Pause. Chink. "Course we swap about, and we never touches the windows, not ever. That's important. Nearly had a strike when Linda started on the windows, but she was new so she didn't know. I usually do the bed and vacuuming, Jean does all the surrounds and polishing, then every second week we swap."

"Swap jobs or swap with Maeve and Belinda?"

"Linda. Linda Wesley. Both."

"Why?"

"Keeps it more interesting, doesn't it?" A faint squeaking as from the wheels of a waiter's trolley. Suzy deciding that now was champagne time? "Variety's the spice of life, you might say. Mrs. Bellows doesn't care, not if it's done right. I'm not saying it's like looking after ordinary people, don't think I'm saying that, but when you come down to it, what the public outside doesn't understand is, we're all people deep down. That's what you ought to write. I mean they're just the same as us reelly, only they've more rooms and things, and the castles, I've done Balmoral four times, and they go off on royal tours. But they can't just go off like that, when they feel like it. I mean they haven't our freedom, whatever you say. What I'm saying is it's only accident, innit, being royal. I mean it could have happened—"

Taylor pressed the stop button, ran the tape forward, pressed the play button.

"—staff area to the private apartments?"

"Don't be daft, it'd take half a day, and Mondays, Wednesdays, and Fridays there's the buckets too, they weigh a ton. It's all on the ground floor by the linen cupboards, and we've got our own room there for tidying up in, just in case. All we do is bring it up to the first floor in the service lift. Except of course for clean water, then one of us has to go down again. When the lift wasn't working—"

Stop button. Forward. Play button.

"—right little madam, ask anyone you like. But of course that was before."

"I'm sure. So there's this sort of hallway area off the landing, then the reception room where the dog baskets are, then the large sitting room with the photographs and TV, then the bedroom. Can you get from the landing to the bedroom, is there a door from the landing or do you have to go through the sitting room?"

"Through the sitting room because it's further back. Or from the dressing room the other way. The dressing room's my favorite, Jean thinks I'm barmy, but reelly it's lovely. I mean it's as big as the sitting room but like cozier, I think so anyway, with lovely furniture, reelly old, antique, but comfortable, you know, and these high ceilings. You have to stand on a chair to get in the corners even with the feathers. We've got a stool for that, but it's such a weight dragging it around we use one of the white chairs. Put a duster on it first. Here, don't you write that."

"No, no, of course not. But the dressing room connects onto the landing and also through into the bathroom?"

Attagirl, Suzy, Taylor thought.

"That's right," Tania Beccles said. "I mean it's personal taste, but the bathroom isn't what I'd have chosen, I don't mind saying it. There's this—"

"—quite ordinary bath," Taylor and Tania Beccles said in unison, "like of course it must be Harrods or somewhere, but it isn't sunken or round or gold like in Hollywood and the pictures. I mean it's just a bath. The shower's sort of set back. . . ."

Taylor reached for the mug of navvy's tea and drank, leaving Miss Beccles to prattle on alone. He knew the tape by heart. He knew every word, every background and foreground clink and clatter, the point where the champagne cork would pop, and the previous evening he had finally guessed, accurately he was sure, the unenlightening words drowned by the popping cork and ensuing shrill enthusiasm. Since Sunday he must have run the tape fifty, sixty times: slow, fast, loud, soft, forward, backward, sideways, crossways, uninterrupted, interrupted occasionally, and during the early playings interrupted at each phrase while he had scribbled down the words. No technician, he had suffered when first bringing the tapes to the machine a sick sensation at the possibility of erasing his palace housemaid and losing everything. He had put the tapes on one side, plugged in a second recorder, set up the microphone, and made dummy runs with Vera Lynn and Al Boley. "Goodnight, sweetheart" Al Boley had crooned from the first machine into the second, successfully. Damp-handed and dry-mouthed, finally Taylor had taped the Beccles tapes.

The reserve tapes he had not needed. They lay now on the coffee table against which he propped his back. He sat in shirt sleeves and bare feet on the green carpet, marooned amid paraphernalia: tea and cigarettes, impeccably labeled tapes, Hitachi stereo recorder, pens, notebook, a plate with remnants of cheese and salami, thumbed but uninformative histories of and pictorial guides to Buckingham Palace, a drawing board with clipped papers, and elsewhere, here neat, there strewn, papers, papers, papers, papers.

The Suzy-Beccles conversation ran for sixty-eight minutes and the transcription to twenty-seven typed stapled pages. He had transcribed the tapes laboriously, word for word in longhand bursts, yearning for just one, any one of the yacking mob of secretaries at Charles Taylor Ltd., driving himself by the drudgery of it to whisky, and from whisky to reviving champagne, which resulted in his pressing the stop button when he wanted play, and play when he wanted rewind. From champagne to bed, with the transcribing abandoned and as hung-over as himself until the next day. The final pages, checked and double-checked against the tapes, were far from Charles Taylor Ltd. secretaries' standards. There were erasures, smudges, inked insertions, deletions. But they were exact.

They were also almost wholly irrelevant. The dry bones of the conversation—topography and twenty words on the subject of a safe—he had abstracted into one and a half typed pages and two drawings.

Outside peeped a car on its travels into or out of the square: a muffled sociable sound. Through the windows the evening sky was tangerine tinged with mauve, like a gas fire. Shepherd's delight, mused Taylor. Or sailor's delight. Whichever. Flaming June was going out as it had come in. Garden party weather. Diamond thief's delight.

He thought of his brother. Howard had been almost invisible since being walked away from in Leadenhall Street. Poor mistreated Howard. He'd have examined his requests-for-loans files and turned up E. Montgomery, Europa Sports Cars Ltd. Perhaps he was wondering whether he did after all forget faces, whether the man in the Opel might not have been some unknown footballer. Howard had no real confidence in himself.

"—never there because usually we go up at nine thirty, but if she's there Windy Bellows makes us wait, like she doesn't want us traipsing around while she's choosing a gown or studying documents of state, I mean any more than we would, would we? I mean it's only us and her page is ever allowed in the private suites at all, ever. You ought to write that."

"Do you ever see her?"

"Oh, yes, seen her at Balmoral twice, it's different there, more relaxed. Well, all right, you could top it up, why not?" Titter and pause. Chink. "Cheerie-ho. Yes, as near as you are to me she was once, with Prince Charles and Bobo MacDonald, that's Her Majesty's dresser, they're very close, been with her since she was a baby. Anyway, such a smile she gave me, and 'Good afternoon,' she said. Honestly, she was so natural. Me, I was rooted to the spot, literally, I started to curtsy, but she'd gone by. Prince Charles, he's very natural too, he smiled. He'd stop and chat with anyone."

"I'm sure he would. At the palace—"

"When she'd gone by, there was this stick, we were at the back where the lawn starts, she picked it up and threw it, like this." Silence. Taylor silently counted: one, two, three, four, five, six, seven—go. "'Chase it,' she said, and the dog scampered after it and picked it up and brought it back, but he wouldn't give it up."

"And you still curtsying?"

"What?"

"You're so lucky, Tania, it's all fascinating. It must be almost like being part of the family."

"It is, it is. That's exactly what it is. And Prince Charles tried to make him give it up, but he wouldn't at all. He didn't want to know. He stood there shaking his head and growling, you know how they are, but he wouldn't drop it."

"But at Buckingham Palace—"

"There was this terrific struggle with Prince Charles getting hold of one end of the stick—"

Stop button. Forward. Play button.

"—ever so. His Royal Highness' suite at the near end,

see, off the same landing, like it's all one big flat but with two of everything, and Her Majesty is the far end, over the swimming pool. Prince Andrew and Prince Edward, they're up on the second floor, but me and Jean don't do for them. I'll tell you—"

"So the farthest room of all in Her Majesty's suite, this sort of combined office-study by the dressing room, does that look out over Green Park or over the gardens at the back?"

"Over the park, love. Just the one window, but we don't touch the windows. Oh, I couldn't, reelly."

"Come on, I've had more than you. It's got to be finished."

"Have we drunk all that?" Titter. Chink. "It'll only go flat if it's left, won't it? Still, if the magazine's paying."

"Bottoms up. So outside this office room is the corridor and the doors out of the private bit, but the lifts are at the near end—"

Taylor turned to page sixteen of the transcript. He followed the dialogue.

"—your back to the door there's this reelly lovely table, like antique, that's on the left, with bits of pattern round the edges, all in colored squares, ever such tiny squares, all different colors," said Tania Beccles, the words starting to slur, Chigwell in a runaway victory over gentility. "Then under the window's a table with flowers. Windy Bellows does the flowers, changes 'em every day. What else? Chairs. And this sofa with like struts at the back, proper devil it is to dust, all knobby. A desk with green on the top, very grand, shines up a treat, but the chair isn't old, it's one of those black swiveling ones. Dirty great pelmets with tassels, we're supposed to dust on top, but I ask you, every day; I mean if Windy Bellows climbs up to look once a month, it's like they ought to sound trumpets. Go on then, love, slop it in. That the end?"

Taylor turned the page. He was laughing, not for the first time, at a particular fancy. Miss Beccles couldn't repeat herself word for word every time, could she? She couldn't be word perfect? Sooner or later, surely, she'd say something different, omit a table, mention a hitherto unmentioned carpet?

Mention where the key to the safe was kept?

"—like the pelmets, I mean we're supposed to dust every book, but honestly. Dozens of horses and show-jumping there are, there's this one on the Derby weighs ten tons, Agatha Christie, a lovely row of Charles Dickens, *Oliver Twist* and all that—"

Here it came now. Unsmiling, following the typed words, Taylor moved his head closer to the recorder.

"—there's a radio, that's on the cabinet, I suppose if I could tell you the make, they'd sell a million sets tomorrow, but honestly they're all the same to me. Oh, and on the right of the door there's a fitted cupboard with a safe. Dirty great monster it is, big as me, greeny color with a handle and round top, far as I remember, and legs. Course we don't open cupboards or drawers, not ever, I can promise you that, but this one 'ad been left open. Bathroom cupboard was open once, but no joking, Jean shut it without even looking. I would of too. There's such a thing as respect. I mean, whatever they say, it's not the same. 'Ow would you like it—"

A stickler for her lines, Miss Beccles. Like an old-school actress. Never deviated.

Stop button. Forward. Play.

"—even what you might call a steady job, like he calls 'imself a chef, but a road mender could do what he's doing, and now this Pakky bloke's buying it up he'll be bringing in all 'is aunts and cousins, doing curried wimpies I wouldn't wonder—"

Leaving Miss Beccles and Suzy to meditate with the

verve of the inebriated on domestic matters, Taylor hoisted himself to his feet, stepped over the recorder, and drew the curtains across the window. He carried the mug and plate of remnants to the kitchen and plugged in the kettle.

It was not much. Whether or not it was better than nothing, only Slicker would be able to say. *Dirty great monster, big as me, greeny color with a handle and round top and legs.* Sounded as though it had flown down from Loch Ness.

Still, it was in a fitted cupboard to the right of a door into the office-study room. Presumably the door from the landing but possibly the door through from the dressing room; it wasn't clear, but wouldn't matter because there was only one fitted cupboard. Or only one mentioned by the Beccles girl. The room was the last of the suite, on the first floor of the northwest corner of the palace. Window looking over Green Park to the north.

Waiting for the kettle to sing, Taylor left the kitchen, hurried down the passage, stepped around papers and recorder, and gathered up the drawing board.

"—at all mind being a journalist," tiddly Miss Beccles was saying, "on a posh magazine like yours, though I'd be more interested in the photography side myself—"

Stairs led up the northwest corner to the far end, the greeny round-topped monster end, of the Queen's apartment; presumably from the administration complex on the ground floor, behind the swimming pool.

He looked up from the map. Returning along the passage to the kitchen, he could no longer make out the detail in the dark, and he was not about to switch on the passage light. In the kitchen he placed the drawing board on the work space beside the kettle.

A second flight of stairs surfaced at the near end of the landing, Philip's end, where also stood the lift. The service lift seemed to be back another fifteen or twenty yards, in the corridor on this side of the landing. A fifth approach was the first-floor corridor along the west front. This corridor stretched from the state dining room, past the Queen's audience room, and at the northwest corner became the landing off which lay the private suites.

Five approaches, two question marks. Two red-ink squiggles which stared up at him from his map like warning lights. But one squiggle queried whether the fitted cupboard stood by the door to the landing or the door to the dressing room and was trivial. The other questioned the service lift, which was not exclusively for Windy Bellows and her housemaids. Buckingham Palace had a staff of two hundred. The pastry chefs and postillions and hairy-armed blacksmiths from the Royal Mews might not be interested in this particular service lift but others would be. There'd be no profit in encountering butlers or stewards or gartered footmen on the way up or down.

No profit for himself. Okay for Slicker who was going to be a gartered footman anyway, a new boy late of Clarence House and service for the Queen Mum, now starting at the palace. Inside the palace gates they would split. Never any question of Slicker with his lag's shifting eyes and cockney chat swanning about the lawn with the guests and mingling security cops.

The tea brewed. Taylor gazed hard at the plan on the drawing board. Two question marks were two too many, but they were considerably fewer than those which had disfigured the maps both for the Heathrow job and Sears Crossing. There were bound to be question marks, imponderables. When there were none, that would be time to leave well alone, to get out of the game. The art was in recognizing where the question marks lay.

Taylor's finger slid across the map from the ruled

square of the service lift to the serried oblongs that were stairs. Five approaches were riches.

Call it four because the service lift was out for himself. Call it two when the stairs and lift at the near end of the north wing were eliminated, because there was no way of arriving at the palace, a guest among eight thousand guests, and blithely making a right-hand turn through the barricade of flunkies who'd be ushering honored guests through the palace and into the garden. How would such a right-hand turn into the north wing, toward the private apartments, be made? With doffed topper and "Excuse me just a moment"?

Which left the two approaches from the west, garden wing. Stairs and the royal lift.

Taylor carried tea and drawing board to the drawing room. He switched off the recorder and sat, drawing board on his lap, in his chair by the curtained window, the chair where three weeks ago Poole had sat. He lifted the top sheet which was the plan, the second sheet which was the elevation, the third sheet which was foolery, artistic foolery showing the throne room, the state guest suite, the diplomats' entrance, the cinema, surgery, police and post offices, kitchens and stores, and let them hang from the board so that he might study again, on the fourth sheet, the reconstruction of the Queen's suite.

The tea cooled; ash from the cigarette between his fingers spilled to the carpet. Taylor frowned and thought, motionless, teeth biting against lower lip.

When he returned to his surroundings, picking up the mug, the tea was cold. He nursed the cold mug.

The royal lift would be foolproof. The stairs would be near foolproof so long as no staff lurked on them, stealing a quick smoke. Yet lifts played tricks. They stuck. Other people pressed the button.

It was all academic. Until Slicker could tell him,

tomorrow, whether a greeny monster with handle and round top and legs would need two sets of hands or whether he could crack it alone, academic it would remain. If Slicker could cope by himself, Charlie boy would be out of it, partaking of tea and an eclair on the lawn, discoursing with a prince or two, and sending up a silent blessing to the office-study on the first floor. If Slicker could not cope on his own. . . .

Taylor yawned, but not from tiredness.

Ten days to go. The preparations were done, the payments made, and on the eighth, at Buckingham Palace, four fifteen in the afternoon, it would be solely a matter of nerve. Tomorrow, at the rendezvous with Slicker, the last details would be made clear. Already, with the clarity of a color film, Taylor saw in his mind the probable procedure. He suspected there was going to be one major difference from Sears Crossing, where Mr. Big had stayed coyly absent from the action.

Well, he'd gone into this one because he'd wanted to, and he'd chosen to keep the team small.

Slicker would have to be smuggled in, as staff, and hide until the Queen and her retinue had descended to the lawn. The obvious foxhole would be the lavatory, the one in the ground-floor cloakroom for the office of the Comptroller of Supply. Then the service lift up. He himself, once the Queen was on the lawn and no eyes were for anyone else, would slip back into the Bow Room and ask to use the nearest lavatory, which was adjacent to the household dining room off the ground-floor corridor.

Lavatories for the upper classes; toilets for the lower. Whichever you were, they always succeeded. The irrefutable password, the unfailing escape hatch, learned by every schoolboy and schoolgirl.

Routes and timing. It was all in the routes and timing. The Queen made her appearance usually at ten past four and took fifty minutes walking along the lane of guests to her tea tent. Slicker would move in at four fifteen. The bomb would need to bang, ideally, the moment the safe was open and the Cullinan pocketed. Smoke and consternation, and staff and security rozzers surveying the hole, allowing Slicker to toddle out of the palace unbothered, and himself too if he was going to be in there polishing the oxyacetylene. The moment after the bang the Queen and her lot would be herded back into the palace, no doubt about that. Probably up to her suite. So there could be no hanging around after the bang.

How long would the Queen's lot take from her tea tent, through the crush, up to her suite?

Bastard Poole, Taylor thought without malice. He was musing about defeated, benighted Poole when the telephone rang.

twenty-four

The double rings had mounted to eleven before Taylor had disentangled himself from mug, drawing board and chair.

"Yes?"

"Charles? Howard. Listen, I don't want to talk on the phone. Will you be coming in tomorrow?"

"Of course I'll be coming in. What is it?"

"I want a word with you about Bertie Smith. I don't know what you're—"

"Who?"

"Who what?"

"Bertie Smith?"

"You call him Bertie Smith; I call him Montgomery. You'll be in the office in the morning?"

"I might call on Mum first. Howard, I told you, we happened to have signed up—"

"See you then."

After the click Taylor continued to hold the handset to his ear. Being hung up on was a novel experience. Phoebe had done it, but Howard never.

He walked to the whisky on the Adam commode, and the telephone rang. He turned back. The handset was still warm.

"Hullo."

"Moore here. That you?"

Taylor scraped in his memory. Bertie Smith had been bad enough. Moore? The moments passed in which he was unable to place the name Moore. All coppers are bastards, and some are bent bastards, he thought.

"What is it?" Taylor said.

"Slicker's going to be brought in. Don't know whether you're interested. There were a couple of houses done in April, one in Gordon Square, the other—"

"Where is he?"

"Couldn't tell you, but there's a car on its way to Wardour Street. They—"

Taylor killed the connection and opened his address book. In the four seconds he took finding the Wardour Street number the telephone rang again.

"Yes!"

Phoebe said, "That's a helluva greeting for a li'l ladykin who sits home—"

"I'll call you back."

He mashed down the button, released it, and dialed Slicker. So long did the *brr-brr brr-brr* persist that he became ready to concede he might be too late. Except that the Heavies did not scream up to a villain's pad, pounce, and the next moment scream away again, the villain kicking and clawing on the back seat. They turned the pad over, poking their noses, questioning, taunting or superficially amiable, but always taking their time. The first thing they did was answer a ringing telephone. Or see that the villain answered.

The ringing tone ceased.

"Who's that?" Slicker said.

"You alone?"

"Yes."

"A squad car's coming for you, so don't ask questions, just get out. Phone me in fifteen minutes."

Taylor replaced the receiver. For four days, since visiting the Green Man, he had not had a drink. Twice each day he had worked out in his gymnasium. The day's second session in the gymnasium was still to come, and he would go through with it, later. But now was deferred scotch time.

This time Taylor made it to the commode. He carried half a tumbler of whisky to his chair and sat with it, sipping.

Outside in Grosvenor Square the evening was quiet as a prayer.

Howard. Slicker. A great man, Howard, for minding other people's business. If Howard was onto something, or if he thought he was, he might have to be told something, just a very little, to boost his punctured pride and shut him up. Younger brother clearly didn't care for mysteries and being excluded.

And big brother would be damned if he'd tell him anything. There had to be another way. A new Paris office with Howard in charge, permanently resident?

One way or another Howard was going to have to be made to shut up about E. Montgomery, Europa Sports Cars Ltd.

"It's plain the train's a gravy train," Taylor mouthed aloud, soberly, but detonating the consonants and molding tongue and lips to the vowels like a first-year drama student. "The bread is baked with grain aboard the train."

And later, lowering the whisky glass, lifting his head, vibrant as Gielgud:

> Keep your head down, Slicker,
> Button up your lips,
> Let cops come thick and thicker,
> We'll still have Granny's Chips.

He carried his glass to the telephone and dialed Howard's Surrey home. One of the children answered. Daddy wasn't home yet. Mummy was out. Would Uncle Charlie like to talk to the baby-sitter?

Uncle Charlie resisted the offer and said good-bye. He dialed Kew.

"I'm sorry. It was exactly the wrong moment. Howard—the Paris thing, one of his traumas. How's everything? How's Ann?"

"How's everything and Ann, she watches in the bowels, the box, with Gorgeous Greta. An' your li'l ladykin, she sits and spins, tapestries, got the treadle going, spinning—"

"You've been to the club."

"If the club won't come to li'l ladykin, so li'l ladykin, why don' they just put the club on wheels? Wheel it over. You fix it, why don't you? You're the big cheese."

"D'you want me to come over?"

"Not 'less you come on wheels." Laughter swamped the earpiece, then died. "Something 'bout you in the public prints. Something you have got to know. Wait."

Taylor waited. Yesterday's *Financial Times* had carried a paragraph about the loan for the Paris development, but he had seen nothing else. Earpiece between chin and shoulder, he felt for cigarettes.

"Here now, get this, an' I quote," said his wife. "'Others present included Lord 'n' Lady Dinford, the Honorable Robert Oswald, Philippa Countess of Hemsley, Miss Jane Lyon of Kinloch—'"

"Is this what I've got to know?"

"Shut up, cheese. 'Mr. and Mrs. Bertie Lestrange, Lootenant Colonel Peter Vere Pratt and Mrs. Pratt.' A grisly sight she was too. Where in hell are we?' Sir Hubert and Lady St. Aldgate over from Capetown, the Spanish ambassador and—ah, here." The voice assumed a honeyed, though sloshed, sweetness. "'Mr. and Mrs. Charles Taylor.' Thought you should know these things. Want me to read it again? 'Mr. and Mrs. Charles Taylor.'"

"Ascot," Taylor said. "Where's all this rubbish? Jennifer's Diary?"

"Wait. Two more columns of also-rans. 'Mrs. Hortense Masham, Major and Mrs.—"

"I'll come over if you like. Give me an hour."

"I'll do the cookin', baby, I'll pay the rent, You know I've done you wro-o-ong—" She sang the last phrase but switched off as though interrupted by a thought. "Why I called. Come in, C for cheese, come in, C for cheese. You receiving me? Ann says you promised her lunch and will you meet her and Maggie at Biba's tomorrow at twelve?"

"Who's Maggie and I promised what?"

"Best Friend of the Week, and fact is you promised 'bout six weeks ago. Correction. Years ago. Suit yourself, Bill Bailey."

"Tell her I'll be there. Where?"

"Lolita, she said, second floor, somewhere. Who knows? Come home and cuddle me, Bill Bailey."

"I'd like to do that. I'm waiting for a call. No more visits from Poole?"

"Who's Poole? If he's not in Jennifer's Diary, I don' wanna know. What ol' ladykin wants is a drink, just a small one, so here's good-bye. Good-bye-e-e," Phoebe sang.

"What time's your flight?"

"Sa'day. The gin girls' jet."

"I know it's Saturday, I'm taking you. What time?"

"Closing time in the gin palaces of the West, Bill Bailey. Curfew at Kew, ol' Bailey, ol' cheese." Phoebe started to sing. "For it's clo-o-osing—"

Singing, she hung up. Taylor put down the receiver. Next year he'd go with her, perhaps, if her old man were still kicking. He looked at his watch. By the time he reached Kew she'd be asleep, stretched out like a cadaver or comatose in front of the television screen.

Ol' Bailey, Old Bailey. There was a wordplay he could have done without.

He was tidying the papers from the carpet, stacking them on the recorder, when Slicker telephoned back.

"Thanks anyway," Slicker said. "Nice to know we've all got friends in 'igh places."

"Nice to know you made it."

"Easy. All of thirty seconds to spare. Recognized the thin one. You know, with the bananas?"

"Poole there?"

"Dunno. Wouldn't wonder. I'm givin' up wonderin' for medical reasons. When's the next flight to the Zambezi?"

"July the eighth, early evening. Don't worry about it, it's all going to work. Where are you?"

"Leicester Square, and I've 'ad this thought. You've got a place in Sussex—"

"Not a chance. Go to the Hyde Park Hotel. Now. Your name's John Pratt, they'll be expecting you. You'll have to get a suitcase—"

"Bit grand, innit, pub like that?"

"Just keep your head down. Tomorrow you'll have a flat. Make it ten o'clock—"

"Seein' a fellow at ten. Like it's for the mutual benefit and furtherance of our, ah, business. Could manage twelve."

"No. One. Ground floor of Biba."

"Who?"

"Thought you'd kept in touch. Down the road from your hotel. Ask a policeman."

Taylor telephoned the Hyde Park Hotel. Later, from the gymnasium, wearing shorts and sneakers, he telephoned Martin, ordering the Rover for eight thirty next morning.

The early clouds offered no clue to whether the day would flame or be a shepherd's disaster. Taylor folded the *Times*, leaned forward in the back seat and told Martin there was an afternoon garden party at Buckingham Palace, Thursday next, and the Corniche might as well be kept under wraps till then. The car drew up at Parson's Green.

Carrying bowler and briefcase, Taylor walked through leafy streets of Victorian villas and at eight forty-five reached his mother's. She was frying a breakfast of bacon, kidney, and tomato. There was no sign of fried onion, but its smell lay in the kitchen like an almost tangible pall, which was a change from the smell of cat.

"Should of told me you was coming. Go on round the Co-op, get some of the Sweetcure. Unsmoked I always 'ave. Purse is in the top drawer."

"I've eaten, thanks. How's the leg?"

"Still there. What've you eaten then? Bet you 'aven't. Old man like you needs some fat on 'im, keep 'is strength up. Looks to me like you 'aven't eaten since Christmas."

"Eat like a horse, Mum. So what's the doctor say?"

"What 'e always says. I've stopped listenin'. Sit down then; at least 'ave a cuppa tea."

Taylor put a wrapped bottle of Campari on the dresser and sat at the table. Calling at this hour, he had not had time to buy sherry and Turkish delight, and the Campari had come from his wine cupboard. She'd not like the look of it, but she'd enjoy herself trying to exchange it at the store in the Wandsworth Bridge Road.

"Weekend after next, Mum—Brighton. Bring your swimsuit."

"Well, I don't know. It's a bit short notice."

"Or Eastbourne. Take your pick."

"I like Brighton." She poured tea. "What you up to then, Charlie?"

"Up to?" He glanced at her. "I've four million pounds sunk in the new shopping precinct at Eastbourne, that's one thing I'm up to." He looked down again, cooling his tea with milk. "Has Howard been round?"

"Only bloke who's been round is a copper. Poole. The one as used to visit years ago. 'E's a chief inspector now." Mrs. Taylor sat down opposite her son and spooned salt onto the edge of her plate. "Just passing, 'e said 'e was. For old times' sake, 'e said. Coppers don't fool me."

"He wasn't fooling; coppers are sentimental." But Taylor's fingers had tightened around the cup, and he returned it to the saucer in fear that he might snap off the handle. "Did he come in?"

"Only for a minute. Sort of invited 'imself. I didn't offer 'im anything, cheeky devil. Catch me." Mrs. Taylor chewed kidney. "Said 'e read in the papers sometimes about my sons in property and 'adn't they done well."

"What else?"

"Nothing. Said to tell you 'e was starting writing 'is memoirs. 'I'll borrow them from the library,' I said, 'because if I don't, likely no one else will.'" She began to laugh, her shoulders shuddering up and down. "Tee-hee-hee," laughed Mrs. Taylor, and a green thread of tomato pips slid down her chin. Teeth and wrinkled lips clamped over a rectangle of Sweetcure bacon. "Goin' regular to mass, I 'ope?"

"Pretty regular." He returned both hands to his cup.

Why, he wondered, did he lie more to his mother than to anyone else? "Phoebe keeps me up to the mark."

"So when's she off?"

"Saturday."

"You looking after Ann?"

"She's staying with a friend. Can't wait. She's packed already. Probably a cabin trunk."

"Tell 'er to come say 'ullo to 'er Gran. If she gets off at Parson's Green, I'll meet 'er. Couldn't do with 'er overnight, wish I could, I mean if anythin' 'appened."

Bastard Poole, crawling everywhere, leaving his slime, trying to put the wind up. The book would be unique. *Memoirs of a Total Loser: The Wasted Years.*

"Mum, I ought to be off, I'll telephone tomorrow. We'll drive down Friday evening, the ninth. You say where. We'll have the sea view, and we'll go to mass together."

twenty-five

Howard Taylor's early-warning system was so oiled and serviced that his elder brother had hardly received from Miss Widdicombe the tray of mail than he knocked and was in: the breathless messenger from a Greek drama, doom-laden, overworked, overfed, anxious, puffy.

And out on your neck, dear Howard, Taylor reflected; out and away to Paris forever, *adieu,* if you're going to be tiresome about my wheelman.

"Charles, thank God. There's every kind of crisis. Pollard's being impossible. He's having second thoughts."

"Or he'd like us to think he's having second thoughts. We'll talk to him."

"I have, but I get the impression he wants to deal with you, and he can only manage this morning."

"Then we'll meet this morning."

"Are you available?"

"Until half eleven. What about this other matter?"

Like a headwaiter who knows when to be neither seen nor heard, Miss Widdicombe had vanished. She would reappear in the instant before Taylor realized he needed her.

"We must have a meeting with the accountants," Howard said. "The whisper is that bank rate's going up again."

"I heard. Three o'clock suit you?"

"I don't know it's as urgent as that. Can you manage it?"

"Howard, you keep giving me this guilty feeling I'm on half time."

"Well, you were away Tuesday morning and two days last week."

"I always let you know."

"It's just that things keep coming up."

"Been a little hectic. Phoebe's off to the States. One thing and another. So, next crisis. You telephoned about Bertie Smith. Alias, you tell me, someone named Montgomery."

Careful, Howard, he wanted to add, because we don't want to lose you. Losing you won't exactly be the end of the world, not for me, but think of yourself. Exiled among the frogs' legs and those snooty cafés up the Champs-Élysées, you of all people, with your crummy French.

"I'm sorry, Charles. I checked with Chelsea, and there's no Bertie Smith. It's just that I have to know where I stand. If I'm to take responsibility, then it must be full responsibility. I turned Montgomery down. If next thing he's getting to you and you're playing it all close to your chest, where does that leave me? Either I make the decisions or I don't."

"You make them, Howard. It's for me to apologize. This Montgomery pitched me a tale about a new racing engine, and I admit I was curious. But I told him no. I told him your decision was final."

"You said that?"

"Of course I did."

"I see." Howard fingered the knot of his tie; it was lilac-colored, fluffy angora wool. "I'm sorry, Charles. When you insisted it wasn't Montgomery, I mean, I never forget faces. I didn't know what was going on."

"I'm sorry. I should have told you. But he sought me out, and even though I said no, I was embarrassed you might have thought I was going behind your back, seeing us together. It seemed simpler to make out it wasn't Montgomery and forget it. It was stupid, and I'm sorry."

"No, no, I'm sorry. I should have realized."

"Nonsense."

"Yes, I should have."

"Hang on a minute, there'll be coffee. No other crises?"

So. All clear on Montgomery. And all clear on Poole, because if Poole had visited, that would have been the first thunderbolt of grievous news.

"I'll have the accountants here for three," Taylor said. "We'll try and get John Pollard and his bruisers over right away. I saw Mum earlier. She's in good shape."

He extended a finger toward a button on the intercom, but already Miss Widdicombe was gliding in with shorthand notebook and coffee.

A musical braw laddie, unkilted and unsporraned but presumably a Scot, stood at attention on the pavement near High Street Kensington tube, playing the bagpipes. He wore glasses and a track suit, and his hair was the texture of Brillo pads. Curious, Taylor thought, walking by, weaving through the crowds, how the wailing persisted even when the laddie, gulping air, removed his mouth from the mouthpiece. Taylor weaved with agility, encumbering briefcase and bowler having been left at Charles Taylor Ltd. in deference to Ann, who'd made known to him on more than one occasion how his City gear embarrassed her. The anguished pipes, diminishing now, only patchily audible through the rumble of buses and cars, played him as far as the entrance to the store, where he paused to light a cigarette, look back, around, and across the street. Farther along, lights halted the traffic. The pipes welled and keened above a temporary calm. At least they were "Tramping O'er the Trossachs" or "Gathering the Clans" and not pumping out the "Amazing Grace" which had headed the charts when Ann had been six or so and resolved to discover the tune on her toy xylophone, daily, morning and afternoon, month after month.

Out of place in his somber suit, but less so than if it had been embellished with bowler and briefcase, he strode across the ground floor in search of stairs or lift. And less out of place, he thought, than the stereophonic pop music, the compulsory contemporary sound, heaving and booming through this emporium of twenties and thirties gimmickry. If the corners and counters piled with painted feathers and stuffed lions and woolen typewriters and football-sized artificial fruit could have been shipped out, and Paul Whiteman shipped in, the experience might have been closer to that of a walk through the foyer of the Roxy, 1928, if the customers could have been heaped onto the decks of the counters and shipped out too. Taylor progressed through the acres of waste space with his gaze fixed as unwaveringly ahead as a marching guardsman's. From an earlier visit with joyous Ann he knew that if he looked to right or left, he would see only himself reflected in full-length mirrors. Everywhere were mirrors, glass, glitter, gloom, and towering potted jungle plants. Nothing was real. Least real was the clientele. He was a City freak among Jesus freaks, schoolgirls, au pair girls, shopgirls, shoplifters from home and abroad, and here and there a bewildered tourist.

Outside the lifts waited a crush of youth, most of them standing, some sitting on the floor. Taylor headed for the stairs, risking a sideways glance into the unpopulated book department of art and movie books. A solitary teen-age salesgirl sat enthroned at a desk, not reading one of the books or looking at the pictures or even turning pages, but with her hands in her lap, staring into space. She wore black saucers of eye shadow which made her look like a badger.

Taylor avoided the first floor. On the second floor he hunted past cowboy-style façades emblazoned "Saloon" and "General Store," behind which the stock was not, so far as he could see, liquor or general stores, but clothing. On a gate he found the warning "Lolita 10–14 years." He ventured in and among coat stands, mirrors and Lolitas saw Ann wearing two hats and something in patent leather and fringes. She was bent double with laughter. She saw him.

"Daddy!"

She plunged into the coat stands, out of sight, and reappeared from the flank, hatless, free of the fringed leather, but modeling in front of her an irregular section of skinned yak.

"Daddy?" Beaming and shining, she struck a pose: leg forward, bottom backward, shoulder hoisted beneath her chin like a violinist. "What d'you think?"

"I honestly don't know."

He honestly didn't. The thought came to him that Ann was perhaps the only female in his life, perhaps the only person of either sex, to whom he never had to lie. Her questions were unanswerable, but they did not require from him a response of lies and evasions.

"Is it dead?" he said.

Ann staggered with laughter. "Charming!" she screeched, and when she had straightened up, brace glinting against white teeth: "Daddy, please? Will you? It's *reduced!* Please?"

He was sure that he would, in the end, unless the yak turned out to be only the first in a queue of items. His features became stern and doubting. "We'll have to see. I don't know. You should really save up your pocket money. Don't you think Mummy ought to see it first?"

"But it's *reduced!* And it really fits! Look!"

Yak and Ann struggled, Ann winning when her head emerged tousled through the shank of clotted gray wool.

"How much?"

"Only four pounds."

"Four!"

"Four thirty-five," murmured a renegade Lolita into Ann's ear, a sprite who had hopped out of coat stands wearing a spangled boot on her left foot, raging nail varnish on her right.

"Reduced from five thirty-five!" Ann countered.

"Are you Maggie?" Taylor inquired amiably.

The girls stared blankly at him, and at each other, then began to laugh and totter at the hilarity of the question, shrieking with laughter, stumbling backward and sideways and lurching together to cling to each other for support. The faces of other Lolitas and a quizzical Mum peered from behind coat stands.

"This is Cara, silly!" Ann said when she had subsided sufficiently to be coherent.

"Hullo, Cara. Listen, girls, before we do anything further, I have to mention lunch."

"Daddy?"

"What?"

"Would you mind terribly if me and Cara went to the place by the Odeon, they've got chips and hot dogs and stuff; then we're going to the Odeon. I mean, come if you like, we don't mind, but you don't *have* to."

Taylor assumed a thoughtful expression. "Well." Eyes and mouth registered at midpoint between regret and approval of the girls' ability in decision-making, he hoped. "I'm not sure about chips and hot dogs, I mean for me. What's the movie?"

He bought the yak and prevailed on Cara to let him pay for the boots. Cara, he observed, wore a Pola Negri button on her sleeve; Ann a Rudolf Valentino button on hers. He dealt out money for lunch. Then he dealt money for the cinema, for a snack in the cinema, and for the tube home. With half an hour in hand before the appointment with Slicker he offered Cokes and chocolate eggs at one of the toadstool tables in front of the fairy castle, but the girls were scornful, and anyway, if he really didn't mind, they ought to be rushing along. He had to wait while they picked like dealers through shelves of Mickey Mouse puppets, Dougal table mats, and Snoopy shoulder bags and dog bowls. Why, suddenly he wondered, were they not at school? Was there no school today? He asked, raising his voice above the throbbing pop, and his question threw the girls into such paroxysms of laughter that they turned red-cheeked and fell about. Taylor laughed too but did not persist with the question, suspecting the answer to be something he should have known, such as this being half-term or a one-day teachers' strike or the Pope's birthday. On the pavement outside the store he waved the girls good-bye. They skipped away, turning to wave back to him, bumping into people, grinning, waving, swinging their black and gold Biba bags filled with yak and spangles.

The bagpipes had departed. Taylor crossed the road

with the lunch-hour horde and found shoulder room at the bar of a pub in Church Street. At five minutes to one he was walking again toward the entrance into the store, glancing in at windows. Each window had two window seats facing each other, their wooden armrests descending in a series of bumps like the sides of theater organs. On one, easing their feet, perched two subfusc dames in black straw hats. Facing them sat a pair of shiny Hare Krishnas with shaved heads and saffron robes, eating grapes from a shared paper bag. From the next window, in a seat to himself, a duffle bag reserving the space at his side, Slicker looked back at him through dark glasses. He wore a chamois leather hat and had razored off the mustache.

Taylor walked by, stopping when he reached the entrance into the store. He regarded the faces of the passing show and placed a cigarette between his lips.

He was not sure whether the clean-shaven Slicker was a good idea or not. He had disliked, without being sure why, the duffle bag on which Slicker's arm had rested. One point on which he was sure, and had been since arranging this rendezvous: If he went into the store now and the Heavies were lurking and pulled Slicker in, they'd pull in himself as well, and good-bye, Granny's Chips.

Good-bye, knighthood, whether they released him after five minutes or not for forty-eight hours. Taylor lit the cigarette. Before his resolve turned to mush, he swiveled about and walked through the entrance.

twenty-six

"Dodgy," Slicker said. He cleared the space beside him by lifting the duffle bag onto the floor, between his feet. "Every bloody face goes by begins to look like a copper."

"I'm not staying," Taylor said. "Neither are you. Nineteen Cranley Mansions, off Abbey Road. Be there at three; it'll be open. Key in the kitchen dresser. And stay there. You've stocks enough for a siege."

"Worthington or Whitbread?"

"And no callers. Your only visitor's going to be me. No close friends."

They had not seen each other since an occasion in Slicker's Soho flat at half-past two in the morning with cigar smoke in the air and the bedclothes pushed back. They both were aware of it. On the brown upholstered theatre organ opposite sat a boy and a girl in cast-off gypsy clothing, possibly together, but unspeaking, each bowed over a book.

Slicker said, "They've nothing on me, not for the Tait job, they can't 'ave. The old bleedin' story, once you've done time they never let you alone. I've a mind to walk into the nearest nick and stick my finger up their nostrils."

"Not till after our garden party. Don't worry."

"All right for you, Charlie boy. You'll find this 'ard to believe, but somehow I never saw myself sittin' on the banks of the Zambezi for the next fifty years. Wearin' my Rolex Oyster and tellin' Jeeves to do the steak medium."

"It's not going to be like that." Taylor did not know what it was going to be like for Slicker, but the immediate exercise was to instill confidence. "After the party you can show yourself if you're happy about the Tait job. All you have to do is go easy on the spending. You need never leave the West End."

There was no risk of being overheard. Such was the bedlam of pop music they could hardly hear each other. The risk of being recognized in this window corner of never-never land was very little greater, and that there was risk at all would be another memory for the knighthood years. Above Taylor's head the fronds of a jungle fern, iron-sharp, spiked the air. Beyond the fern arose hills of lampshades and monstrous satin cushions like mattresses. Beyond these, behind counters, the art deco shopgirls sat with black vacant eyes, staring, smoking, animated only in bouts of conversation one with another. Taylor's stare shifted from the duffle bag between Slicker's feet, to the boy and girl with the books, to the faces promenading past the window, and back to the duffle bag.

"Told yer, didn't I? Spot of business with a bloke." Slicker, a note of teasing edging the nervousness out of his voice, watched Taylor through the dark glasses. "Couldn't 'ave made it any earlier, could I?"

Glasses trained on Taylor, watching for the response that would be a wince, Slicker lifted a crepe-soled foot and lowered it onto the duffle bag.

Taylor watched the foot but did not wince. He said, "A bloke or a boyo?"

"What else? Broth of a boyo. Name of Mick."

"Or Paddy."

"Wouldn't be surprised."

"How much?"

"Sterlin' or avoirdupois?"

"Weight."

"We're lucky, it's still in pounds, wait till we go metric and it's all kilos, there's going to be some right muddle among the lads." Having played for time and gained nothing, Slicker said, "Ten."

"Ten! Wouldn't you know it. I said two."

"I told 'im two. Ten or nothin', it was. It's like wholesale, round figures only, fresh off a North Sea rig."

"Enough to capsize a bloody North Sea rig." Taylor exhaled tobacco smoke through his nose. He watched the girl and boy opposite, bowed and oblivous over their reading.

"Want me to saw two off for you then?" Slicker said.

"What I don't want is you carrying it around."

"I'm in agreement with you there." The crepe sole lifted off the bag and lowered itself to the carpet. The voice teased again. "Like I was thinkin', lucky you're 'ere. Wouldn't 'ardly do for a wanted man to be roamin' around with this lot, would it?"

A goal to Slicker. Difficult to credit, Taylor reflected, that a few months ago he'd been welcoming the risk, reaching out for involvement. Not for twenty years had he been more at risk than now. Never had he been deeper in.

"So where is he? His showrooms?"

"The Wellington, Shepherd's Bush." Slicker looked

down at his watch. "Till three o'clock. I'd been looking forward to it. They've got wrestling."

"I'll give you the results. Could be tomorrow." With an effort Taylor shifted his gaze from the duffle bag. Through the window, across the street, stood the piled Victorian slabs of the Town Hall, the Midland and National Westminster Banks, the gaudy façades of the Big Company Store and Hamburger City. "There's nothing he needs to know about it?"

"He knows it if 'e was listenin'. It's all in the bag. Gelly, cap, clock, battery, tested and guaranteed. I 'ope. Watch out yer don't drop that fag in it."

Ducking under the spearheads of fern, Taylor reached behind him and dropped his cigarette into the fern's glass pedestal.

"Listen." He turned back to Slicker. "If I described something as a dirty great big monster, nearly as big as me, greeny color with a handle and round top and legs, would that mean anything to you?"

Slicker's eyes might have shown puzzlement had they been visible behind the dark glasses. His mouth was scowling. Then it grinned. Taylor had an impression that Slicker was about to laugh, perhaps to jump up and applaud.

"'Ow many guesses do I get?"

"None. No guessing. Just what it is."

"Well, it ain't near as big as you, they don't stand 'igher than five foot, but it's twice as 'eavy. You wouldn't by any chance be talkin' about a Wilcott peter?"

"Possibly."

"I'll tell yer, yer bloody are. We used to say the round top was to stop yer sittin' on it and 'aving a cuppa while yer blew it."

Now Taylor was frowning. Slicker spelled it out.

"You'd slide off. Spill yer cuppa. See?"

"So not too difficult to open?"

"Collector's item. Did one in Barnet with Blinky Johnson, I was 'is wireman. D'you remember the Edsel?"

"The car?"

"The Wilcott was like the Edsel. A flop. Couldn't sell it. They only sold a couple of thousand, posh publicity in the trade; then they took it off the market. I've seen a lot worse, but the relocking mechanism was ten years out of date, and it wasn't laminated except in front. Good as anything against fire." Slicker took out a nail file. "Well, fancy. The Queen."

"How long to blow it?'

"Wouldn't blow it, not unless it's in cement. I'd cut the back."

"How long for that?"

"Fifteen, twenty? But if it's against a wall, like they always are, might be another 'alf hour turning it round. They weigh a ton." Slicker, filing, looked up from his nails. "And in case you're wonderin' if I can shift 'er on me own, love to try, Charlie boy, but it'll take two."

"There'll be two."

So that was it. Decision made. Some decisions made themselves.

Taylor wanted to ask why the Wilcott couldn't be blown. Exactly how long to cut it from the front? How long to burn? If it was so heavy, was it certain that even between them they'd move it? But for the peter he was in Slicker's hands, and Slicker had said his piece.

His eyes lowered to the duffle bag. "Is it wrapped?"

"Like a birthday present," Slicker said.

"I'll take it. Not the bag."

"Safer in the bag, Charlie boy."

"What surprises me about that bag, Slicker boy, is that you haven't got 'Danger' stenciled over it."

The Hare Krishnas, grape-filled, glided past the hill of

cushions. "Goin' where I belong," whined amplified voices and full orchestra. Slicker was grinning, as well he might now he was rid of it, Taylor supposed, walking with the brown paper parcel through the store.

He did not look back toward the window seat. Slicker would have vanished. Cradling the parcel, Taylor slowed to allow two boisterous black girls in patched panchromatic trousers pass in front of him. At a counter he halted, fingered millinery, and picked out a fashionable hat which was identical, as far as he could see, to the round flat-brimmed hats of private girls' schools.

"If you could put it in one of the bags," he said, pointing.

The breastless girl-child behind the counter did so without a glance at him. Waiting for change, looking about him, he thought of Carnaby Street of a decade ago. Swinging Britain, the Liverpool scene, mods, rockers, long hair, and rosy-cheeked Beatles were an ineradicable part of his train coup memories. He wondered whether Biba, a decade hence, would be part of the Cullinan coup memories.

Alone and surreptitious in his metal-smelling office, Poole, like a secret drinker, unlocked the left-hand drawer of his desk and from under the wad of unfinished reports and memoranda and rubbish slid out the photostats of Taylor's appointments book. He felt furtive and weary. He placed the photostats on the desk in front of him, leaving the drawer open to swallow them up again at the first signal of an interruption. He spread the photostats, looking at them with unfocused eyes. He was merely trying to nail a villain, doing what any copper should do, and he was totally on his own. Church down in Hampshire had helped, but there was no more he could do. Fothergill was uncomplaining, up to a point, and okay for the donkey work, but his heart was not in it. Others, high and low, regarded him quizzically when they passed in the corridors. Now the commander had had him on the carpet. ". . . not telling you what to do or not to do. . . Taylor . . . experienced officer like yourself . . . decorated, credit to the Yard . . . only think of your future . . . support you to the hilt if you offered the least shred of evidence . . . no future . . . deeply embarrassing . . . up to you."

All he needed was a lead, something new, a call from a snout, an inspiration, a sign, a burning bush. He was skeptical of the Expressionist exhibition at the Tate. Far too much in the public eye, and not Taylor's line anyway. Taylor bought paintings; he didn't nick them.

What then? *What?*

The telephone rang at this elbow, startling him. It was not a snout. It was Janet, who telephoned him at the factory rarely. Tony had fallen at school, in the gymnasium, he was all right, but a broken ankle, she was off to the hospital, taking the car. 'Bye.

Poor Tony. How long in plaster for a broken ankle? No cricket, poor lad. Get him that pop record, what was it called?

Poole stared at the photostats. "St. Dunstan's lunch and interim meeting, Eastbourne council buffet lunch and press conference. . . ."

The Biba bag bulged under the weight of the brown paper parcel. Taylor carried it not by the handles but beneath his arm, traveling by tube, changing at Earl's Court and ridding himself there of the schoolgirl's crumpled hat, unobserved into a litter bin. The receipt he tore into a dozen pieces and dropped into a bin at Shepherd's Bush. In the back bar of the Wellington he found Montgomery at a table with a glass of beer and sausage rolls.

The young man's shampooed locks rested on the collar of a jacket of maroon suede. Among the vocal off-the-peg clientele he looked, had anyone been interested enough to look, as out of place as Taylor himself.

"Thought I was expecting somebody else," Montgomery said. "Everything all right?"

"Everything's fine. Just nurse that, will you? And be very gentle with it." The Biba bag changed hands. "It's yours from the somebody else. If you grab me that chair, I'll get a drink."

Buying the drink took time. In places the long bar was two deep with men holding beer and stout, their backs to the counter, commenting aloud and breaking from time to time into ragged jeers and cheers. A scattering of girlfriends sat among the customers who had found tables and chairs. In the ring a sweating man in a swimsuit was kneeling on a prone adversary.

The uppermost man strained, grunted, and bared his teeth. Taylor watched from the bar. The prone man being motionless, Taylor could not understand what the effort was for, unless it was for the customers. He had never bought wrestlers as he had bought boxers. The sport held no interest for him. The referee, curly-headed and paunchy, crouching in his silk white shirt over the wrestlers, began to call out, "Let him breathe, Cassidy, let him breathe."

Taylor brought two large whiskies to Montgomery's table.

"I couldn't drink that," Montgomery said.

"It wasn't for you," said Taylor, pouring one whisky into

the other. He put down the empty glass and turned his eyes on Montgomery. "The Yard's after Slicker."

"What?"

Solid Slicker, Taylor thought. This was the first Montgomery had known of it. For silent, solid Slicker another bonus point. The job took priority over the lover, as already guessed. But reassuring nonetheless.

"It's not serious," Taylor said. "Routine. He's got a record; he has to live with it. He's gone to ground for a while."

"I should hope so. Where? This is all we needed. Is it off then?"

"It will be if you blow us all into a pudding with that bag. Why don't you put it on the floor? Nice and easy. And I don't know how reliable your memory is, but try not to forget it."

"Nothing personal, but I might do just that. This is the part that fails to have me in ecstasies."

"What part?"

"You know what."

"No one's going to be hurt," Taylor said patiently. "The bang goes off in trees. Trees, brambles, nettles, and nothing. On the other side of the wall. You said yes and you're being paid a modest fortune. For virtually a walk-on part. Second sword bearer on the right."

"Bomb bearer."

"After which you'll be able to put in a bid for Silverstone."

"If I'm alive."

"Oh, cock."

"I must've been demented."

"For God's sake, what about Slicker? Think. Is he demented?"

"Why? What's he got to do with it? Since you ask, yes, he's demented enough."

"He's also a pro; he was using this stuff before you were out of your cot. Seen any scars on him? Missing organs? You'd know better than me."

"Very amusing."

"He says it's all been explained to you."

Montgomery shrugged. Not pop music but shouts from the fans made hearing difficult. In the ring the prone wrestler was no longer prone but flinging his opponent first against one corner post, then against the opposite corner post. There was a balletic, monotonous rhythm to the flinging.

"Well?" Taylor said.

"I set the alarm for quarter to five, dump it over the wall, and get the hell out."

"Where over the wall?"

"Tenth lamppost from the bottom of Constitution Hill."

"When?"

"Five to five. As near reveille as I can manage."

"How?"

"Van, ladder, sodding tree-pruning outfit."

"And you get the hell out where?"

"The getaway car, Halkin Street, key in the ignition. Look, it's all right, I know what to do."

"So what's your difficulty?"

"I just wish it was over."

Good, thought Taylor. Because that is a normal, healthy wish, friend, and there were the moments I wondered if you weren't just a little too cool.

"Listen, an amendment," said Taylor. "The safe's heavy, and it's got to be shifted out from the wall, so it may take a little longer. You set the alarm for five fifteen. All right?"

"Whatever you say."

"Because if our diversion goes off too soon, we're going to be left with a half-sawn safe and a palace running with royalty and coppers. Say it."

"Say what?"

"Your timing please."

"Five fifteen," Montgomery muttered. "Sight simpler if I left it on the pavement or in the van up on the curb. I mean if there's no one about."

"We do it my way," Taylor said.

Like the song. Silky smooth and peaceful. Not a scratch on anyone. Not like Sears Crossing, with the bludgeoned driver, the stupid messy mistake that buggered the image of a wholesome and roistering band of Robin Hoods.

The bout between the sweating wrestler and the prone wrestler who had leaped to life had ended. Taylor had not noticed how or why. In the ring a youth dressed up in velvet like a dance-band leader was introducing Black Jack Friday the Dropkick Kid from Barbados at two hundred and ninety-eight pounds and Hopalong Man Matterhorn from Salford, Lancashire, at three hundred and seventy pounds. One more area for muddle, thought Taylor, when the nation goes metric.

"Sit on 'im, 'Opalong," a fan shouted.

"Squelch 'im, cowboy!"

"Stick a pin in 'im, Black Jack! It's all gas and rubber!"

"So's your cock-a-doodle, mate!"

Laughter. A bell sounded. The giants circled, gripped each other's hands, and Black Jack was forced to his knees. He writhed onto his back. Man Matterhorn sat on Black Jack's chest, reached out, and began twisting a black ankle. Back and forth he twisted, grimacing, as though attempting to loosen a rusted piece of machinery. Taylor swallowed scotch.

"Do you," he said, "come here often?"

"Wasn't my choice," said Montgomery. "Took me an hour. So where's he shacked up?"

"As well if you don't know. And in case he gets in touch with you, I'm sure he won't, but if he does, don't bother. Not till after the eighth. All right?"

"Right."

"Saturday evening, ten o'clock, we'll meet for a chat, the three of us. And that should do it." The whisky warmed. A man in dungarees carrying six bottles of Guinness pushed past the table. "It's all going to be all right. Smoothly, simply, no snags. You believe that?"

"I believe anything."

Like money is what you believe, money and cars, you grasping bastard, Taylor thought, and if you didn't, I'd not have looked twice at you.

The wrestlers were more or less upright. Hopalong Man Matterhorn was holding Black Jack by the neck with a tattooed forearm, squeezing the life out of him. The men at the bar bayed. When the curly-headed referee intervened, wrenching at Man Matterhorn's hair, Man Matterhorn released Black Jack and dealt the referee a slow backhanded swipe. The referee skated across the ring through the ropes, and onto the barroom floor.

He clambered back into the ring. Black Jack had scuttled on all fours through the open legs of Man Matterhorn and executed upon the back of Man Matterhorn's head an acrobatic two-footed kick which had no effect. The crowd crowed and hooted. From outside the ring, through his microphone, the bandleader was announcing that the referee had issued a public warning to Hopalong Man Matterhorn.

"Fixed," Montgomery said. "Black is beautiful. Whitey's going to lose."

"How?" Taylor said.

"How?" Montgomery took a bite of sausage roll. "With a missile launcher. Don't you think it's fixed?"

"May have been at the start. It isn't now. It's nasty." Taylor finished his whisky and told Montgomery he'd telephone with the rendezvous for Saturday night. "And take good care of that bag."

Man Matterhorn was holding the bewildered Barbadian

bodily and horizontally aloft above his head like a weight lifter and starting to rotate in a circle. Taylor shouldered through the crush toward the door. He had an appointment at three with accountants and Howard. Though he knew what was about to happen in the ring, he did not turn his head even when Hopalong Man Matterhorn threw Black Jack Friday the Dropkick Kid, and Black Jack floated high through the smoke-heavy air with his muscled black tangled limbs trailing cord and popping light bulbs from the overhead fixtures. If Black Jack floated far enough, he might come to ground upon the Biba bag, but the odds against it were long, and it was now too late to do anything about it. All future bets, if fate had in fact chosen the long shot, would have to be placed with the Big Bookmaker in the Sky, and he'd know in a moment or two whether this was to be the case or not.

Or rather he wouldn't know about it, any more than would Black Jack and Man Matterhorn, or Montgomery or the referee or anyone in the back bar of the Wellington or within an acre around.

Taylor strode from the back bar into the corridor and out into the dingy Shepherd's Bush sunlight.

twenty-seven

Following a fish fingers, crisps, and ketchup lunch from Greta, Ann and two suitcases left Kew Green in the Rover for ten days with mate Maggie and family at Richmond. Phoebe walked around the Green to St. Winefride's and Father Cotter's house, carrying a box of circulars for the Mother Theresa Appeal. Her husband made telephone calls. Then he sat on a public bench at the fringe of the Green and watched the Saturday afternoon cricket.

The sky was a creamy blue, decorated at intervals with jet planes bound for Heathrow. Taylor wore slacks and a cotton shirt and smoked a cigarette. He wondered whether Phoebe might like to be made love to when she returned, if she returned sufficiently quickly. Check-in time was seventeen hundred hours. She'd appreciate the gesture, he believed, even if she rejected it.

She might as easily accept. Never to be predicted.

A dim clattering of applause, brief and sarcastic, sounded around the Green for a boundary struck by the plumper of the two batsmen. The home team were batting execrably. Having lost their first three wickets for a paltry handful of runs, they were attempting a rearguard action which their supporters might have termed stubborn but to an objective eye was boring and more than likely doomed. The bowler doing the damage was a West Indian who at first had seemed a comic character but was comic no longer, particularly to the home team. He was the only player wearing not white but gray flannels, a dereliction which had not excluded him from the visiting side, and he bowled erratically but fast, intimidating the batsmen with a galloping run which culminated in a leap into the air and a whirling of both arms. The ball was likely to fly anywhere. Once it had flown backward and been caught by an astonished fielder. On the occasions it flew straight it destroyed the stumps.

Now the plump batsman who had survived for thirty minutes had hit a full toss to the boundary. The next ball smote him on the foot, causing him to jig and hop. Gamely he carried on. The next ball he snicked past the wicketkeeper. He started to run, changed his mind, and was run out.

O my Compton and Bill Edrich long ago, thought Taylor. His body was warm in the sun, and he sat enjoying the indifferent cricket. He watched Phoebe returning around the Green, chin slightly forward, hands freed of the box of circulars, striding with the long-legged American-girl legs that once, spangled and flashing, had high-kicked and cakewalked down Main Street and over college football fields while the college band blared Sousa and the tossed batons twirled and wheeled. An age ago that'd been, before train days, before he'd known her, or she'd set out on her European experience and met her limey crook. But she still had drum majorette's legs, breasts and bum like round ripe fruit. Taylor left the cricket and walked back across the road and into the house.

He made tea and heard Phoebe climb the stairs. Then the plunge of bathwater. When he went up, she was in her slip on the edge of the bed, peeling off stockings. Steam curled in through the open bathroom door. He sat beside her and traced a finger down her back.

"We've an hour before we leave."

"You're crazy," Phoebe said.

She stood up, and he watched her reach down, arms crossed, and draw the slip over her head. She shed bra and bikini pants, lifted her hands to the back of her neck, and performed a prodigious grind and bump. Father Cotter would have been disturbed. Taylor followed her into the bathroom.

Manipulating taps, she called out above the gushing water, "If you love me, if you're really passionate, a drink would be the ultimate, the sheerest blissikins, dahling, no crap."

"I've made tea."

"Good-bye, dahlin' blissikins crapikins."

He brought her a gin and tonic, then returned to the cricket. By the time they had to leave for Heathrow and Martin was hefting suitcases into the Rover's trunk, Phoebe had refreshed herself with several gins more. She wore a denim safari suit, ebony bangles, heady scent. On the Great West Road, passing the Gillette factory, she took his hand.

"Be a good prot—" She made a second attempt. "Property devel'per. While I'm gone."

"You give my love to your dad if the right moment arises."

"No snaking off with hotshot señoras to the land of the setting sun, you snake."

"No gropes behind those New Jersey Petroleum pumps with hairy Yankee mechanics."

"Fly out next weekend. Surprise us."

"We'll see. I'll telephone."

He would telephone every day, but there would be no flying out or traveling anywhere, not next week of all weeks. After Thursday, when the heat would be on, the one place to be would be home, anchored to the spot. Home and the office, blithely available, blank as tomorrow.

"Remember," Phoebe said, "Dr. Johnson. Sam-u-el Johnson of goo' ol' London town. 'When a man's tired of goo' 'ol London town, there's always Apaculco.' "

"Apaculco?"

"What the man said."

"You said Apaculco. What—"

"Don' hang aroun' at the airport, big boy. Shan't be waving back. Once on the silver bird, it's down with the shades, Mrs. Taylor. Till cocktail time."

At the terminal he watched from the viewing platform, but her Boeing 707 was so distant across the tarmac that he could not make out the boarding passengers. He was not even certain he was looking at the correct aircraft.

He motioned Martin back into the Rover and climbed into the front passenger seat.

"Take the motorway, would you?"

With speed and amenable traffic he'd be in Leicester Square in thirty minutes and in time for the new Michael Caine. There was nothing else he wanted to do to fill in the hours before the session with Slicker and Montgomery. Grosvenor Square would be too solitary, Suzy too demanding. They had reached the Martini Clock before he spoke again.

"How's your unpatriotic Peugeot going these days?"

It was a fairly old joke between them, and his chauffeur played along. "Best on the road, sir. I wouldn't trade her."

"How old is it?"

"Three years and better than ever."

"Like to trade her in for a new one better than better? Give me the bill?"

"That's very generous, sir."

"Thursday, for Buckingham Palace, we'll be having a passenger. We'll be going in from the Mall, you'll have a sticker, and I'd like you to back tight against the wall beyond the Privy Purse entrance, I'll show you exactly where. The passenger's in the nature of a practical joke. Strictly between us, all right?"

"Naturally, sir."

"Wanted to let you know. If you'd like to make any plans, the rest of the day'll be yours. I won't want you to wait."

"Thank you, sir."

Slicker's furnished hidey-hole off Abbey Road had been named as meeting place, as convenient and secure a spot as anywhere for so long as the briefing session remained a briefing session and restrained itself from developing, under the benefit of alcohol, into an orgy of horseplay and broken glass, bringing to the door the residents of adjoining flats with complaints and bleary faces and threats of summoning the police. Slicker had set up two dozen bottles of beer on the bar in front of the empty bookcase. Montgomery, like an impoverished guest at a bottle party, had brought a bottle of red Egyptian Omar Khayyam, forty-five pence from Maison Oddbins.

"Think he'll turn up?" Montgomery said.

"In my time, man and boy," said Slicker, "I've 'eard some ignorant questions. That 'appens to be the most balls-achin' ignorant of all. And while on the subject of ignorance, put those soddin' gloves back on. What the 'ell d'you think you're playin' at?"

"Cops and robbers, since you ask. Like school kids. That's what it feels like. Like playing games." Montgomery drew the gloves back on. "I wish it was over."

"Tell 'im, not me. Perhaps 'e'll bring the date forward for yer."

"You think he's some kind of ideal. Big man of action, brains like a miracle worker, poncing around with all the top brass. Rags to riches. Abracadabra, let's all tug our forelocks. The complete man."

"Jealous." Slicker wagged a finger. Pouring beer, he became contemplative. "Never thought about it, but now you ask, yes. 'E is, isn't 'e?"

"How naïve can you get. He's—"

"Oh, sod off."

The living room had an expensive but piecemeal air as though the landlord were in the habit of buying from the best stores during the January sales, taking anything reduced to half price, and distributing the results haphazardly through his various properties. There was an air cushion, some reproduction Chippendale dining chairs, a desk-chair in steel and black leather, a glass coffee table, a coffee table that was a gnarled and varnished section of tree, and a third coffee table that was an oval of slate. But there was no table for eating a meal off or writing on. So when Taylor arrived and wanted to draw a plan of Buckingham Palace, he had to sit on the carpet at the glass coffee table.

He had brought cartridge paper, colored felt-tip pens, and two bottles of Moët et Chandon in a plastic bag. He wore doeskin gloves, and when he moved from one spot to another, he carried with him the same ashtray. There being neither fire nor fireplace, he examined the kitchen for a site for burning before beginning to sketch his map of the palace.

"Five possible approaches," Taylor said, and with his pen tapped the paper at five different points. The map was rapid and accurate. Slicker and Montgomery bent over Taylor, listening, studying the map. "Service lift, could be empty and could be jumping with slaves. Lift and stairs here at the northwest end, out, because there'll be troops of ushers guiding guests straight through to the garden. Anyone wanting to head off in a fancy direction is going to need visas and a signed photo of the Queen."

"Or yer actual disguise," Slicker said.

"This is the overall picture so we know exactly where we all are, okay?"

"Keep going, Charlie boy," Slicker said cheerfully.

"Which leaves the private lift here on the north front and the stairs either here or here in the angle, and I'm taking the stairs here."

Slicker's route he marked in blue. When Montgomery straightened up and moved with his glass to the bar, Taylor called him back.

"No more of that until this is all clear, d'you mind? May take an hour, may take until breakfast. Depends on you."

He sounded to himself like army days inside drafty lecture theaters, but they listened while he talked, explained, and after explaining fired questions.

If they were worried that this was a job where there could be no dress rehearsal, they were right, there could be no dress rehearsal, he said. But they'd be wrong to worry because basically it was simple as a game of snap.

He talked, explained. Detail upon detail, possibility upon possibility. The hour moved beyond midnight, on to one o'clock.

In the event of an encounter in a corridor and no way back, the excuse was to be vague and pat; for Slicker, uniformed and carrying cases, that the cases were being returned for His Royal Highness. No more than that. And no violence on dogs if dogs appeared, any more than on any other breed of nosey parker.

Anything in fact sooner than violence on dogs, the British public being what they were, and a quick hara-kari, friends, before violence on royal dogs.

Slicker grinned nervously.

But for Slicker and himself, Taylor said, ninety-nine point nine of the tickle was going to be a matter of routes and timing, both up to and out from the private apartments.

For Monty too it would be routes and timing. The map showed Constitution Hill in geographer's detail. A leafy thoroughfare dividing Green Park from the north wall of the palace grounds, eighteen Victorian lampposts, twenty-five sycamores at ten-yard intervals, the brick wall eight feet high and topped by spikes, and barbed wire behind the spikes. Monty in overalls would drive the Westminster Council van into Constitution Hill, where he'd park on the pavement—where?

"Little over halfway up, tenth lamppost, where the grass finishes," Montomery said. "Stepladder against the tree, gelly over the wall, into the van with the ladder, back to Halkin Street, quick change in the back of the van."

"And?"

"Fingers in ears and run like the clappers."

Taylor regarded his fingernails. "Joke?" he asked.

"Tell me seriously," Slicker said, his voice pleading, his palms spread out. "Would you buy a used car from this man?"

"Shut up," said Taylor, and to Montgomery: "We're in Halkin Street."

"Walk then, to the stoppo car. Same street. And wait."

"How long?"

"Till Slicker comes."

"Right. About half five, twenty to six. Tell me the timing."

Singsong, Montgomery said, "Queen arrives around four, bit after. You go in at four fifteen. Gives you an hour to crack the safe. Five, the Queen gets to her tea tent, everyone starts noshing. Five five, I dump the bag. Five fifteen—bang. Your cue to get the hell out because Queenie'll be coming up. Five thirty or soon as maybe, pick up Slicker in Halkin Street."

"When you get into Constitution Hill with the van, you'll be in a pretty heavy traffic flow both ways," Taylor said. "There may be pandas, there may be coppers on horses, but most of the security will be at the gates, particularly after that nut tried to snatch Anne in the Mall. Unless it's pouring, there'll be people in Green Park. But there's hardly anyone on the pavement, ever. You keep your eyes open and time it. If there's a copper anywhere in sight, you keep going, right round the palace, and you try again. I'm ready for a drink."

Slicker moved like a sprinter. At the bar he poured champagne. He tasted from one of the three glasses and screwed up his eyes. He tasted again, copiously. "Useful vintage," he muttered offhandedly, refilling his glass. The room was misty with cigarette and cigar smoke, like the top deck of a bus after a Saturday football game.

"Once a day from tomorrow until Thursday you'll be doing what?" Taylor asked Montgomery.

"Drive the route. And walk it."

"So 'ere's to Granny," Slicker said, bringing the champagne, "and 'er beautiful Chips."

"Land of loot and glory." Montgomery raised his glass. "Mother of the free."

"Slicker, you bring meat for those damn dogs, okay?" Taylor had taken his drink to the window. He tucked the curtain back and looked out onto the black empty street. "Half a dozen chunks at least."

"Fillet of venison or the woodcock *flambé*?"

"No bloody fillets, chum. Bone. Bone, gristle, and flesh. I don't want them swallowing it whole and howling for more."

"Dog I knew once was a vegetarian," Montgomery said. He had taken up a regal position in the air cushion. Champagne in one fist, cigar in the other, he was the ex-minor public schoolboy making his way in the world and faintly surprised to find himself making it so satisfactorily. "Bread and eggs, nothing else. Sometimes a sprinkling of currants."

"If you think I'm fillin' me cases with bread and eggs and currants on top of soddin' meat," Slicker said, "yer can soddin' forget it."

"Dalmation, named Charity. Belonged to my aunt. Big breeder."

"I'm not sayin' a dickie-bird, matey. Nature's straight man, you are. I wouldn't take advantage."

"You'd take anything you could get your hands on."

"Anything except you, dearie."

"Well, next time remind me to keep these gloves on."

"Next time? Matey, let me—"

"Shut up, both of you. Like kids," Taylor said.

He carried his ashtray and the sketch of Buckingham Palace into the kitchen. Cartridge paper and cigarette paper burned in the sink.

He had vaguely anticipated, not without misgivings, party spirits taking over from the work session. After the briefing the boozing, commando camaraderie before going over the top. By bringing champagne, he'd even been prepared to give the proceedings a nudge, seeing himself mildly tight with the team, demonstrating thus that they were a team. He would let his hair down, jokey insults would ricochet, the scowling threesome, arms meshed, would circle in a sloshed, stamping Greek tavern dance.

But peterman and wheelman were now bickering like husband and wife across a card table, also as he had anticipated. Maybe, as the champagne worked, the bickering would give way to maudlin affection. Maybe not. Taylor returned to the living room, sick of both of them.

Montgomery was on his feet and heading for the door, his unopened Omar Khayyam in his gloved hand. Slicker sat with a transistor radio, twiddling for late-night inspiration.

"Leaving?" Taylor asked Montgomery.

"If that's all right."

"I am too. I'll give you a couple of minutes' start. All I've left to say is thanks, to both of you. Until Thursday."

twenty-eight

Slicker approached closest to boredom. In the flat off Abbey Road he watched television and read the newspapers.

"Best to spend as much time as possible away from home today," advised Lord Luck in the *Express,* while the next day Katina in the *Evening Standard* prophesied, "A day which favors those now launching advertising campaigns. Do your bit toward community welfare by rendering voluntary service toward a good cause." Slicker checked and checked again his gear: drill, sundry chisels, cloths, spare plugs, screwdriver, monkey wrench, hammer, and files. He changed into and out of, and ironed and brushed, the footman's uniform: black shoes, tie and trousers, white shirt and gloves, and scarlet jacket with gold trim. It'd have been a black jacket like a pallbearer's if he'd been a downstairs footman, but he was upstairs according to Mr. Big, who knew these things. One thing Mr. Big did not know was the .32 pistol.

Often enough Slicker thought of returning it, getting back his deposit, or dropping it in the Regents Park Canal, but it stayed in the biscuit tin in his suitcase until such time as it would be transferred to the footman's jacket. Anything sooner than the rest of his life in the nick.

Montgomery sold the Panther J72 to the Argentinian diplomat and a Honda Civic to the wife of a West Ham footballer. But enough remained at Europa Sports Cars Ltd. for him to choose a different car daily for the drive to and around Buckingham Palace. He parked wherever he found legal parking space, on two occasions in Halkin Street, then did the circuit on foot. The gelignite and appurtenances he slid under sweaters in his wardrobe, unexamined, wrapped in its brown paper and Biba bag as he had received it. Its proximity did not prevent him from sleeping, but it was not stuff to be taking out and unwrapping and playing catch with.

Taylor made substantial appearances at Charles Taylor Ltd., visited his mother with port and Fruitignac morello cherries, and treated Ann and her Maggie buddy to a box at *The Mousetrap*. He sweated in his gymnasium and telephoned New Jersey each evening before going to bed, sometimes making contact with Phoebe and sometimes not. He made no attempt to reach either Slicker or Montgomery. And Detective Chief Inspector Poole made no attempt to reach Charlie Taylor. No hint or suspicion of him, almost as though the poor cruddy toe-rag were off on his summer holidays, digging a damp course for the retirement shack at Cirencester. On the morning of the eighth Taylor attended briefly a reception at the Victoria and Albert for the opening of an exhibition of Mongolian treasures. Then he walked into the Brompton Oratory because it was there, a step away.

He was not certain whether this was the whole reason, but he did not pretend that he had entered to pray or confess or in the hope that godliness might brush off on him or even to rest his feet and find calm prior to the afternoon. He knelt, crossed himself, and sat in an empty pew near the towering carved-wood pulpit. No service was in progress. A half dozen people kneeled or sat; across the aisle a handsome middle-aged woman sat with folded hands, looking straight ahead toward the sanctuary, the seven-branched candlesticks and high altar. A priest in a soutane brought wine to the altar, genuflected, departed. In a side chapel a gray man in overalls moved chairs and swept beneath them. With an effort Taylor refrained from smiling and congratulating himself on the success of the Cullinan job, because they were not home yet. His eyes roved over Italianate domes, veined marble, mosaic, statuary.

In Brompton Road droned the traffic. The gray man moved with his broom from the Chapel of the Seven Dolors to the Chapel of St. Mary Magdalene, pausing to kneel as he crossed the central aisle.

The drops of malice and revenge of three months earlier had wholly evaporated, as he had known they would. As the details of the job had crowded in, the job itself had taken over. The exercise had become just that, an exercise, existing for its own sake, not for revenge or money or in proof to his vanity that he was still Mr. Big, but for itself, with nothing except the exercise being of consequence. An operation as cheeky as any the world had seen in peace or war, to be successfully executed and successfully concluded. No less or more than that. Far from hanging onto those initial proddings of malice he was aware that lately he'd not allowed his thoughts to dwell on the target, the Queen's Cullinan brooch, for fear of regrets that this should be the target. He had admiration and affection for the Queen, not animosity. He no longer felt animosity even toward lordships and aristocrats in general, or no more than toward the plebeian classes from which he had risen, or the middle classes. They were all people and fairly worthless. The job was all.

Except that at this moment something even more vital than the job was the need for a cigarette. The priest had reappeared in the sanctuary and was lighting candles from a candle in his hand. Taylor slipped from the church and strode out for Knightsbridge tube. He inhaled as though storing nicotine for the approaching affair in the royal suite when there would be no smoking. The palms of his hands were as damp as haddock on a slab. Like Montgomery, he wished it were over.

London's West End scuttled about its business, a harried populace, overdue for appointments. Though the day was warm, there was no sun. The sky was colorless, like a sick patient. Rain, thought Taylor, would be true to form. There was a comic tradition of rain at the Queen's summer garden parties.

He could not look at lunch. In Grosvenor Square he sat by the window smoking and looking down on foliage, the rooftops of cars, the streaked shoulders of President Roosevelt. He drank tea, bathed, changed into morning dress, brushed with his hand the gray topper. In front of the mirror in the slate bathroom he regarded himself. Should he wear his OBE? Decorations presumably were optional. He took the medal from the safe, opened the case. "For God and the Empire." Small profit in God and the Empire becoming unpinned and lost on the carpet of the Queen's private office. You never knew. He snapped the case shut upon the medal and returned it to the safe.

He looked again at his watch. Another five or ten minutes, and Harry would telephone from below to say the car had arrived. Taylor lit a new cigarette. He sat and stared down through the window. When it was over, first thing tomorrow, he'd buy that guidebook to British birds he'd always meant to buy, and the companion book on British trees. Teach himself exactly what these trees and birds were that he gazed at in the square.

The telephone rang. A humdrum everyday ringing which in this instance was critical, like the kickoff whistle at the start of a Cup final or blast-off at Cape Canaveral.

Martin's shortcut brought the car into St. James's Street, past Booker's Club. Along the lower reaches of the Mall streamed one-way traffic. There were routine diversions because of the garden party, and additional police had been brought into Queen's Gardens to keep the flow from damming up.

The Corniche, a late car in the queue, inched past the policeman on the chestnut mare and at quarter to four reached the open gates into the forecourt of Buckingham Palace. Martin put the gear into neutral. A policeman as patient as a shepherd held the knot of tourists back from the gates. The tourists retreated, bending low to peer in at the windows of taxis and the chauffeured cars with windshields decorated with X stickers. On the other side of the car stood an unconcerned police superintendent. A sergeant stepped up to the Corniche. Taylor, alone on the back seat, extended his arm through the window.

The sergeant took and glanced at the invitations, handed back the white, added the blue to the stack in his hand.

"Leave by the other gate, plenty of parking in the Mall," he told Martin.

Martin drove into the forecourt. He steered toward the area where the Corniche had waited four months earlier during the investiture.

"There, the gap to your right, reverse in," Taylor said, leaning forward. "Quickly."

Men in morning suits, women in considered hats and

clicking shoes, were moving through the forecourt toward the center arch of the east front. Cars turned and departed to park in reserved slots along the Mall. Before the Corniche had come to a halt, bumper closing against blank wall, Taylor was out of the car, stooping as he stepped to the trunk, looking to left, right and back toward the forecourt, feeling for the catch.

The lid of the trunk swung up.

Slicker, fetuslike, unwound and scrambled to the ground. He made off in a crouch between the wall and the empty cars. Then he straightened up and looked about him. He walked po-faced in the direction of the Privy Purse door: a red-jacketed footman, in each hand an attaché case embossed with the royal coat of arms.

Taylor saw none of this. Already he was among the morning suits and party dresses drifting across the forecourt toward the center arch, strolling with topper on head, hands clasped behind his back in the manner of Prince Philip himself.

All the women wore hats. Many of the morning-suited males carried their top hats in their hands as though worried that if worn they might not fit or fit only approximately. Some wore their top hats with a selfconscious air. Others neither wore nor carried a top hat, because they were not obligatory, and hired from Moss Bros. they added ninety pence to the six pounds for tails, trousers, and waistcoat. Taylor wore his unhired private topper squarely and unselfconsciously, suspecting that when the rain started others might do so too. The sky was sour. Under the echoing center arch, over the flagstones, the air was almost chilly.

He emerged into the quadrangle. There was no one among his fellow guests whom he recognized: a quartet of youngsters with officer and officer's wife voices, laughing too loudly, probably with a table reserved at Annabel's for the evening; a florid nervous alderman and his plump wife from Gateshead or Rotherham; an unappetizing character with a sunken mouth, stained shirt, and red nicks on his chin from shaving, probably a Nobel prizewinner in biology or engineering. Watching the guests file through the quadrangle stood household staff in dark suits. A page with gold lapels and cuffs and black knee breeches answered as best he could architectural questions from an elderly woman who was inside the palace for the first time. Taylor identified, without knowing their faces, a brace of metropolitan police detectives in blue suits. They stood a little apart from the household staff, talking to each other and watching the guests. One wore a white carnation in his buttonhole.

From the palace copshop, Taylor reflected, walking by. A Division based on Cannon Row. He had known they would be here. Elsewhere, mingling with eight thousand guests on the lawn, would be a couple of dozen more. But identifying them gave him no pleasure.

Between coupled columns and up the broad stone steps of the Grand Entrance. Up carpeted steps into the Marble Hall. Scarlet, gilt, velvet, cold marble, space, liveried stewards and pages, a red-jacketed footman who was not Slicker. This footman wore his hair short with a center parting, and under the hang of the red jacket bulged a beer belly. But Taylor's first glimpse of the uniform sent a tremor through him.

All well, Slicker was now in the Comptroller of Supply's lavatory, locked in, counting the minutes.

Taylor wanted to look at his own watch but refrained. Carrying his topper, he trod slowly but without lagging, an unremarkable guest with wandering eyes, considering the detail of marble columns, carpeted marble stairs, oil paintings of long-ago royalty, and the compass points of doors, doormen, windows. Into the Bow Room. Directly ahead, glimpsed past the heads of queuing guests, were open french windows onto the terrace, and beyond the terrace a green populated lawn.

To the right and left of the bow windows, past the recesses at each corner of the room, were doors. The door to the right would be his door, later, when the Queen was on the lawn. Beside the door stood a man in knee breeches, gold on his cuffs and lapels.

Taylor moved around the Nobel prizewinner and down the terrace steps. He lit a cigarette. From beyond the tent to the right, the tent where the Queen and selected guests would take tea, sounded "Hello, Dolly," martially played. The lawn being one of the largest in the world, eight thousand guests did not crowd it unduly. Several hundred of the company were forming themselves into two curving parallel rows, along the center of which the Queen would pass from the palace to her tea tent. Taylor recognized a Cabinet minister, an actress, a trade union leader. There were robed Africans and Asian women in saris. The first face he identified which he also knew personally was that of Lord Moreton, honking at an anonymous aristocrat and prodding the grass with a shooting stick as though temporarily sidetracked from his true destination, which must have been a point-to-point.

How, wondered Taylor, if I asked him now for my sixty-five grand? He looked away before his lordship should sight him and strolled across the lawn.

The first guards' band had fallen silent, and a second, on the opposite side of the lawn, now launched into Gilbert and Sullivan. Taylor tucked back his cuff, looked down at his watch. Three fifty-six. Guests drifted past him in the direction of the hundred yards of grass catwalk formed by tails and frocks for the royal family.

"A Wandering Minstrel, I" liltingly played the band.

Three fifty-eight.

Numberless faces. Furled umbrellas. Beefeaters ornamenting the fringes of the lawn. A sky that threatened but did not rain, waiting perhaps for the Queen to make her appearance.

He walked past the Archbishop of Canterbury, gaitered and beaming in a circle of top hats and flowered dresses. The Prime Minister crossed his path, pointing himself vaguely in the direction of the diplomats' tea tent and looking as though he would have preferred to have been at work.

Taylor could see the black shine of the lake now, and on its far side a silhouette of trees, sullen in the sunless afternoon. The path around the right of the lake would lead through the shrubbery, past the tennis courts, to the gate at the top of Constitution Hill, at Hyde Park Corner. Where he would be, Granny's Chips in his pocket, a little over an hour from now.

He raised his wrist, looked down, plucked back his cuff.

"Hullo, Charlie," a voice behind him said.

Poole was in tails and striped trousers.

"Four o'clock," the policeman said, studying his own watch. "Just after. She usually arrives about five or ten past."

"Really," said Taylor. His features were without expression. Coppers gave nothing away; there was no reason why he should either. "On duty, Poole, or making your way in society?"

"Never off duty, you know that, Charlie." Poole looked around toward the terrace where milled the greater density of guests. He had one hand in his trousers pocket, chinking coins. "Wouldn't call this society exactly, would you? Public figures. Saw a pop singer and his bird a minute ago. Anyway, you should know."

"Enjoy your tea," Taylor said. He nodded a brusque good-bye and started to walk away.

"Friend of yours was suspended from duty yesterday," Poole said. "Or perhaps you knew."

Taylor stopped, turned, looked at Poole.

"Rex Moore," Poole said. "Inspector, C-Eleven. Pal of yours, isn't he? Looked after the card index at the factory."

"Never heard of him."

"Thought you probably hadn't. Lucky for you. Likely he'll be upsetting a few applecarts at the inquiry."

"One more bent copper? Surprise me."

"I never said he was bent."

"Suspended for writing 'The commissioner's got VD' on the canteen wall? That it?"

"We'll have to see, won't we?"

"You see. You do just that. Would you excuse me? I'd like to enjoy the party."

"We're looking for another of your pals. Slicker. But no problem there. Likely he was tipped off. It'll buy him a day or two."

Taylor swung around and strode away from Poole, across the grass, toward the crush of guests at the north end of the terrace. Some of the frocks and tails were fluttering past him in the same direction, dignity tossed to the winds, hurrying for a vantage point lest they be too late, left to scrabble at the back of the scrum, and without a single sighting to report home with at the end of the afternoon. Several continued running, oblivious, after the band had begun playing the national anthem.

Taylor stood to attention, facing the distant garden gate at the terrace's north end.

His forehead felt hot, and he was silently swearing, eyes momentarily shut, then open again.

But no cause for panic, none, the job went ahead, because whatever had brought Poole to Buckingham Palace for the first garden party of July it would not have been Mr. Big or anything concerning him. It was the social thing. Had to be. Invitations to the recent bemedaled must have been common enough. The last move by any copper keeping an eye on any villain was to make himself known, as Poole had made himself known. Poole was irrelevant. Moore's being suspended was irrelevant. The hunt for Slicker was irrelevant, so long as Slicker was a footman, invisible in the Supply Comptroller's john. There never had been one iota of evidence against Charles Taylor, evidence of anything at all, and there was none now. And there would be none one hour from now if he stayed cool, followed the procedure.

He could see the motionless head and shoulders of the Queen in a beige hat. Prince Philip. Prince Charles. Not Anne and Mark. Not the Queen Mum. Princess Margaret and Lord Snowdon. The Duchess of Kent. The Lord Chamberlain. Ushers.

The national anthem concluded. After the briefest hiatus the band flung itself into "Get Me to the Church on Time."

Eleven minutes past four.

Taylor hurried forward and joined the mass of people flanking the grassy thoroughfare along which the Queen had started to walk. He moved down the line toward where the melee was thickest, edged in front of a woman who made the mistake of stepping back to speak to her husband, found a gap to his left, took off his top hat. Looking around, he saw no sign of Poole.

He passed along the rear of the row, paused, glanced around again. He looked over his other shoulder. The press of guests was four and five deep, and on either side of him the frocks and tails hopped up and down for a sight of the Queen. Smiling, handshaking, talking, advancing barely at all along the lane, she was the sole focus of interest. Taylor stood on tiptoe, then bent forward in a silent sneeze, handkerchief to nose. He straightened up, tucking the handkerchief away and taking from an inner pocket the executive glasses. He moved further along the row, peeking over the clustered heads and hats, putting on the glasses. Enthusiastic, distracted, mustached, he combed his hair forward with his fingers.

Not maneuvering to see the Queen but walking and talking on the lawn from lake to terrace were guests who had given up the attempt or who had seen it all before or were biding their time until the crush might thin out. As he neared the steps up to the Bow Room, Taylor paused and again looked back. A raindrop splashed on his hand. He identified Poole among the guests flanking the royal walk, his long copper's back stretching high, head bobbing and craning as it angled for a better view.

Fodder for the memoirs, Taylor supposed. Hunching his shoulders, he hastened up the terrace steps.

twenty-nine

"Rain stopped play, what?" he said to the two liveried staff inside the french windows, and hurried past.

He might have been an early leaver, fleeing the downpour to come.

Immediately Taylor veered left. Fifteen paces would bring him to the door into the garden-front corridor. There were people at the far end of the Bow Room but he disregarded them. Behind him the liveried characters at the french windows would be watching, wondering, perhaps starting after him. He could not look back. He passed a jardiniere on a pedestal, a marble bust of a prince, a marble pillar, a recess displaying dishes and tureens from the Mecklenburg-Strelitz table service. The doorman was in his twenties and darkly suntanned, as though all his free time were spent recumbent and seminude at the Serpentine lido.

"Have to spend a penny. Know the way. Back in a tick, eh?"

Taylor's voice was conspiratorial and doddery. Also it was ineffably superior. The bronzed doorman hesitated. But the ancient fool with the mustache and topper was reaching for the door handle, leaving the doorman only two alternatives: to restrain him or let him through.

"Lord Chipstead. Knew the king well. Before your time, young fella, what, hm?"

Chipstead was the Fulham street along which Taylor frequently walked when visiting his mother. The door in front of him opened, and he passed through.

"Might go out by the garden gate. Pity about the rain, eh?"

Hunched, he scurried along the corridor. Again he did not look back. Was the doorman watching his progress, joined perhaps by the two from the french windows? The corridor was wide and opulent, hung with paintings, furnished with antique tables, chairs, porcelain. He dropped his top hat and bent down to retrieve it. The door into the Bow Room had closed. Taylor hurried forward, drawing gloves onto his hands. He wanted to sprint, to cover as much ground as possible while the corridor remained empty. Windows to his left looked out onto the terrace and lawn. Wherever the bog was, he must have passed it. He came to mirror-glass doors reflecting the corridor behind and barring his way. He opened the right-hand door sufficiently to peep through. There was a different color scheme of carpets and walls but a continuing glaze and polish of antique treasures. The corridor extended interminably.

Taylor closed the door behind him. For a dozen paces he ran. He resumed walking.

"Stupid," he breathed. He walked stooping, in a Lord Chipstead shuffle.

Ahead, to his right, stretched a branch corridor. If he continued straight on, he would finish up—where? The swimming pool? He turned right, into the corridor, and almost collided with a crimson and gilt butler carrying a pair of shoes.

"Steady, old boy, what?"

Taylor was astonished to identify the voice as his own, but quavering with years and class and empire. He scuttled on, topper swinging from his gloved hand. There was no looking back. He waited for the butler's call, but none came. His hands were so hot and moist that soon the palms of the gloves would be stained with damp. His mind remained as cold as a logician's. He was heading east toward the required stairs. The job was on.

Stooping, scuttling, he passed a lift, ignoring it, playing his role. Through a second set of double mirror-glass doors, into a hall with monotonous marble and curving staircase. The hall was empty. Taylor mounted the stairs, controlling the impulse to take them three at a time.

A landing, and open doors into an empty hall with candelabra and a throne. The Queen's audience chamber? There were more stairs and a choice of corridors. The vastness menaced and appalled. Momentarily Taylor hesitated, glancing about him, gaining his bearings. In his mind he saw his maps, burned to ashes three days ago in his Grosvenor Square flat and washed down the sink. He crossed the landing in the direction of the double doors with fan vaulting. The doors were painted in gold and ivory, and if locked, if Slicker had not unlocked them from inside, they would have to be forced, and too bad for gold, ivory, and fan vaulting. Halfway across the landing he heard voices from below and stopped dead, listening.

Male braying voices, somewhere below. Not far below. Coming closer?

No footfalls over the silent carpet, just the lifted,

unamused voices. Head cocked, breath held, Taylor was almost off-balance in the contorted stance into which he had frozen.

"—your second-in-command has it all his own way, there's very little you can do."

"Couldn't agree more, it's the plum job. Give 'em an inch—"

For a doddery off-limits guest, Taylor moved fast. He crossed the remaining yards of landing and gripped both door handles. Forehead against gold paneling, once more he held his breath. He pressed down on the handles, then forward. The left-hand door held; the right-hand door opened. He slipped through and with infinite caution, millimeter by millimeter, closed the door.

He tilted his head back against the door. Rich carpeting. Above, under the cornice, a molded frieze of whorls and curlicues. A crisp scent of polish and flowers. No male voices.

Neither would there be voices of any kind unless they too were bound for these private royal apartments. Taylor trod soundlessly to the first door on his left. He placed his ear to the cream panel and listened. When he opened the door, he believed he heard, or felt, a movement, but he saw in the room only office furniture and a pelmeted Georgian window in the wall opposite. He stepped inside, sympathizing with the disinclination of Tania Beccles and her chum Jean to bring stepladders and dust on top of the pelmets.

"Jesus," hissed Slicker, sliding behind Taylor and shutting the door. "What the 'ell kept yer?"

Slicker had removed his red jacket; folded, it sat beside a radio on a cabinet. He had rolled up the sleeves of his white footman's shirt, wore gloves, and over his head, down to his neck, twenty inches of mesh cut from a leg of a pair of women's tights. In one hand he held an electric drill swathed in a cloth, in the other a hammer, raised as if he had been about to use it.

On the inside of the door was a key which Taylor turned. He put the half-moon glasses away in a pocket. From the same inside pocket he drew out a silk stocking and unfurled it. Slicker lowered the hammer.

"Where'd yer get that 'orrible mustache? You look like the night watchman."

"That it?" Taylor said, moving in front of the open doors of a fitted cupboard.

"It's not a friggin' fridge, mate."

"Thought you said you couldn't move it by yourself."

"Couple of inches. I ain't bloody 'Ercules. 'Ere, give us a 'and."

The dirty great monster, greeny color with a handle and round top, stood askew, partly in and partly out of the cupboard. Slicker had already started work. Ignoring the lock, he had moved one end of the safe sufficiently clear of the wall to squeeze himself behind. Three rivets along the top seam were exposed and he had begun drilling down the near side. Steel shavings sprinkled the carpet. Taylor realized that Slicker had lied. If Slicker had managed on his own to shift the safe so far, he could have shifted it far enough to clear wall and cupboard. Had Slicker merely wanted Mr. Big on the spot, going fifty-fifty with the risk? Later, Taylor told himself, he could deal with Slicker. Not now.

Gripping the safe's underside, inside the legs, Slicker and Taylor heaved. There was no denying the weight. The steel lip cut into Taylor's gloved fingers, the sweat rose on his forehead. He heard Slicker's grunts from the other side of the safe. The legs of the safe rucked the carpet. Taylor sweated and heaved until from the other side of the safe he heard Slicker pant, "Okay."

Slicker collected putty and a can of oil from his open

attaché case of tools and kneeled behind the safe. He tipped the can so that it leaked oil into a channel in the putty. The window was open, and the music in the room murmured not from the radio but from the guards' band on the lawn outside.

Taylor was breathing heavily. The inside of his fingers burned, the muscles in his arms ached. "No dogs?" he said.

"Not so far," said Slicker. "I'm leavin 'em to you. Meat's in the other case."

"That room okay?" Taylor nodded toward the closed door on the other side of the office-study.

"Empty."

They spoke in low voices, barely above a whisper. Whispers would have been inaudible in competition with "The Lincolnshire Poacher."

"Monty's car?"

"In Halkin Street," Slicker said. He was tightening the cloth around the bandage of felt which swathed the drill's motor. "Jag, E-type. Black. No problem."

"Van okay?"

"Van okay."

"We've got forty minutes," Taylor said. "Will you do it all right?"

"You're in the light."

With each spoken word the area of stocking over their lips sucked in and swelled out. Their faces under the stockings were formless like melting wax. Taylor felt spare. He trod across the Queen's office, opened the door, looked into the empty dressing room. He closed the door.

"Send us victorious," Slicker murmured from behind the safe.

"How long—"

The muffled vibrato of the drill interrupted the question and endured for moments which seemed to Taylor like forever. An instant of silence, then again the vibrato. Then silence while Slicker dripped more oil into the putty. Taylor stood chilled, trying to gather his thoughts. The vibrato sounded again. And again. Sharp bursts punctuating the calm. Anyone from here to Hammersmith and halfway across the Atlantic must be asking what the hell, Taylor thought.

No use protesting. Not Slicker's fault. The putty and cloth must help. Maybe it couldn't in fact be heard beyond the corridor. He returned across the carpet and pressed himself against the door to the corridor, listening.

A renewed burst from the drill, and Slicker said, "Should do it."

He placed drill, oil and putty tidily in the attaché case and began chiseling around the rivet heads. He worked with the swift, economical movements of a craftsman. The chisel gave out a metallic sound, rhythmic and ringing. But nothing like the drill.

Taylor turned the key, the door handle, and looked into the corridor.

No one.

He shut and locked the door. "Good Old Sussex by the Sea" played the guardsmen. Taylor wanted to halve the length of the business by aiding Slicker. But any help he might give, Slicker would let him know. Slicker hammered. Hammer, chisel, hands, and hooded head seemed to be an entity, a collage of moving parts framed by the steel square of the safe's back. The chisel cut into and through the steel.

"You're in the light," Slicker said.

Taylor moved away. Lest he forget his top hat, putting it down, leaving it on the desk like a visiting card, he placed it on his head, over the silk. He stood against the wall by the window and looked out. The garden party was closer to him than he had anticipated, though he could see only a corner of it. The spitting of rain had done nothing so far to quench its spirit. Only occasional umbrellas had gone up. The Queen, without umbrella, he immediately identified. She had progressed perhaps to halfway between the two rows of guests. Lesser royalty followed after.

Mechanically Taylor's hand groped in his tails pocket for cigarettes and withdrew without them.

Four fifty-two.

The panorama was green under a grubby sky. In Green Park the foliage obliterated even the slenderest view of Piccadilly. Immediately below and ahead, and beyond the crawling lawn to the left, were trees in full leaf and glimpses of the spiked wall beyond the trees. The first-floor suite was not high enough for a sight of Constitution Hill, cut off by the trees and wall, but he picked out the milky glass of Victorian lampposts and in the band's breathing spaces heard the hum of traffic.

The hum of Montgomery's van? Taylor wondered, and looked again at his watch. Four fifty-eight.

Queen and family were surely well beyond halfway along the walk to the tea tent.

"Psst!"

Taylor looked around.

" 'Ere a moment, 'old this."

The peterman was boss, as the captain of a ship or aircraft was boss, and in these peter-cracking moments you obeyed the peterman. Taylor did so with alacrity, holding in both hands a screwdriver inserted between the backing steel and the frame, while farther up Slicker cut and prized at the seam. They kneeled side by side as though at prayer. Through the gap between backing steel and frame Taylor could see blue oblongs which had to be, he was certain, drawers. Drawers and shelves holding the Queen's jewelry. Thousand upon thousands of grands of jewelry.

Cullinan Three and Four.

He did not ask about the oblongs. Neither did he ask the question to which he most wanted an answer: how much longer?

"Other side," Slicker said.

Slicker shifted on his knees. Taylor squirmed behind him to the other side of the safe. The screwdriver changed hands. Slicker prized it in and up and returned it to Taylor. Taylor's gloves clung to his hands like Monday's wash leather. The fingers of Slicker's white gloves were black and snagged from the steel. The chisel grated and dug. Taylor strained for sounds from the corridor; for sounds from behind the door to the dressing room; for any sounds other than the chisel, the band's roistering muffled music, and their own breathing.

"Ta," murmured Slicker through the mesh tights, and dropped the chisel into the case.

He removed from the back of the safe a square sheet of steel, which he propped beside him against the wall of the fitted cupboard. He took the screwdriver from Taylor and tried to insinuate its tip into the division between two blue drawers, to no effect. He returned the screwdriver to the attaché case, sorted through the contents of the case, and brought out wire and a penknife.

Taylor waited, sick with impatience.

Five minutes past five. Ten until the bang.

Slicker eased wire and knife home like a surgeon. The drawer moved. Taylor heard Slicker exhale, watched him drop the wire and penknife back into the case. He had to clasp his sodden hands together to prevent them from reaching for the protruding drawer. First look through the contents of any safe was traditionally and exclusively the prerogative of the peterman. It's got to be kept professional, all of it, it's the only way, Taylor told himself, but resentfully. Both knew what was being sought, and he'd identify it more readily than Slicker.

Slicker slid the drawer out of the safe and placed it on

the carpet between them. The drawer was nine inches deep; its collection of cases and boxes were neatly stacked in ascending order of size, as if in some rough reference system. Slicker flicked up the lid of one of the larger boxes and squinted through mesh tights at a solitary diamond ring on a pad of velvet.

Taylor put his hand up to the safe and said, "Okay if I go ahead? We've eight minutes. You've probably got all rings there."

"Help yerself," said Slicker, and started opening box after box, casting them to the carpet when he had seen inside.

With the first drawer removed the rest gave no trouble. Taylor pulled out a second and third, shuffled backward to make room on the carpet in front of him, and tipped out the contents. The necklace of emeralds and sapphires which chinked into his wet glove he swore at and threw aside. He snatched up a second pouch, wrenched it open. A second necklace. The entire contents of the drawer he shoved away. He grabbed from the second pile, pressed the catch of a carved ebony box, and looked at a bracelet.

Five ten.

Easy, he told himself. Cool and easy. No panic. For the first time he felt himself on the rim of panic, teetering. He slid from the safe a broad shallow drawer like a shelf, opened a mahogany box substantial enough to have held Cullinan Three and Four, and flung box and diamond cluster across the room.

He glanced up and met the gaze of Slicker, watching him. Briefly, as through gauze, they eyed each other. Slicker flipped aside a case containing a gold wristwatch and pulled from the safe another drawer. Taylor discovered earrings.

Five eleven.

Taylor found and discarded pearls; Slicker a second exiguous gold watch.

The bang from the direction of Constitution Hill came three minutes too soon, rattling the Georgian window. The band music became unruly, then silent. For several seconds in the first floor office of the Queen's apartments the only sound was a barely audible tinging, as of unrequired stone or gold or crystal dropped upon the discard pile.

thirty

Slicker swung around to close his attaché case. Taylor reached across him, snatched up the drill and held the spiraling point against the side of Slicker's head.

"We keep looking," Taylor said. "I'll tell you when."

Slicker did not move or speak. He had been caught off-balance, and his posture was squatting and twisted, his weight on one hand. Taylor returned the drill to the case and moved away, jerking from the safe another drawer.

"Two minutes." He opened a lid to reveal a gold filigree hairpin, flicked the box aside and grabbed another. "Then you can fill your case and we quit. Okay?"

Slicker opened a box, saw a pendant of colored jewels, threw them down.

Through the open window wafted a distant muddle of shouts, a police whistle, the brusque *pam-pom* of a police car or ambulance or fire appliance. The band would be hastily unscrewing trombones, thrusting horns and pipes into boxes.

The Queen and her entourage would be—where? Not yet at the terrace, Taylor believed. There'd be a confusion of guests she'd have to negotiate first.

Pendants, necklaces, rings, an enameled tiara, a cruciform brooch in gold and garnet. Taylor glanced at the safe. Only two or three drawers remained. Had they missed it? Buried somewhere in the heap? He wanted to weep. Already he saw only blearily through the sweat in his eyes. When he tried to wipe them, sodden glove smeared against soaking stocking and he had to rub his eyes through the silk, and blink and rub them again.

Bracelets, pearl spray. Did it have to be Cullinan Three and Four? Why not this fancy clip? These earrings? There had been a reason why it had to be the Cullinan, but he could not remember it.

Cullinan. The word had no meaning. His hands trembled, unable to raise the clasp on a leather case, and the seconds were flying. Something glittered through the air, struck his hip, and dropped into the jeweled debris at his knees.

"'Ow about that?" Slicker said.

Taylor recovered the offering and blinked at it in his wet wash leather palm. A brooch of two diamonds: one square-cut, two inches square, the other a pear-shaped pendant, three inches by four.

Granny's Chips, heavy as a jugful of sand.

Slicker was on his feet, putting on his red jacket and scanning the carpet for mislaid tools, though he knew cloths, putty, oil, and every last tool, everything, were back in the attaché case. Taylor wrapped the brooch in his handkerchief and put it in his trousers pocket. His hand went to his head to check the top hat. In front of him, encumbered by attaché cases, Slicker was unlocking the door. Taylor touched Slicker's arm. The two looked at each other through silk and mesh, Taylor grinning.

"We've done it," he said.

Slicker grinned back. He looked down at the hand. "Fancy me then?"

He opened the door. They stepped out into the corridor and almost down the throat of a woman in a blue suit and starched white collar.

The word Bellows swam into Taylor's mind. Windy Bellows, he wondered. She stood two paces away, a tall, terrified woman gulping air for a scream, mouth and eyes equally wide open. Her head tipped back so that the pink of an upper denture plate came on display in the stretched mouth. Slicker swung an attaché case at the instant the scream started and an edge cracked against the woman's face. She went down like a ship, her scream a paltry squawk.

Taylor grabbed at Slicker's jacket. He tugged him toward the fan-vaulted doors leading from the suite as though not to have done so must have meant more thuggery. He was shaking. It was the train robbery all over again. One pitiful, futile moment of violence, and gone for all time the Robin Hood image. Flung to the winds the dreams and plans that were to have culminated in a clean, glamorous job.

Slicker wrenched himself free. Neither spoke, though Taylor's breathing was hoarse, almost bronchial. Inch by inch he opened the doors, peering out. They sidled through to the landing and closed the doors. Taylor took off his top hat. Slicker rested the attaché cases on the carpet. As they dragged their masks off their heads, voices sounded up the stairwell. Even before the masks were folded and pocketed, the voices had doubled in volume.

The voices were excited and close, male and female, a

staccato well-bred gabble drifting up the curving stairway and across the landing into the hall. In the next moment the voices were no longer drifting but almost on the landing, mere yards away. There was no time for replacing masks. Taylor believed his mustache was askew. He reached back for the handles of the fan-vaulted doors, but Slicker had picked up the attaché cases and was running across the hall toward the closest alternative, a corridor to their right. Taylor ran after.

"Footman?" called a voice. "Hullo, you there!"

Slicker and Taylor dashed along the corridor. Mirrors, marble, tapestries.

"You there, stop! Hey!"

They stopped at closed doors across the corridor.

"Footman!" The shouting was fainter. "You two men! Stop!"

Slicker was through the doors first. Taylor was on his heels, slamming the doors shut, extinguishing the shouts. He raced after Slicker along a corridor like a picture gallery. A stout man in a decorated coat, knee breeches and buckle shoes appeared in front of Slicker, who swung his arm and ran harder. He kept hold of the attaché case, but it had snapped open on striking the stout man's skull and now the lid flapped. Meat and wrapping paper strewed the carpet. The stout man lay on his side, bending and unbending his knees, and Taylor had to jump over him. He swerved into a side corridor in Slicker's wake, one hand flat on top of the uncertain topper.

"The stairs!" he called out, though there was no other place to go except down the stairs.

Three, four stairs at a time, past paintings, statuary in alcoves. A landing, and more stairs. At the foot of the stairs an empty lobby with Persian carpets on marble paving. Doors. Two corridors.

Which way? Where? Taylor's sense of direction had left

him. He pursued Slicker down the nearest corridor, past alternating paintings and windows, reaching him at the closed door at the corridor's end. Slicker had dropped his cases and was tugging and rattling the handle of the door. He was uttering sighing sounds and knocking his forehead against the door's cream paneling.

"Locked," he whimpered.

Taylor recognized through the window the north corner of the terrace and a wedge of lawn. Guests and staff stood in animated groups. Two uniformed policemen with outstretched arms were trying to marshal people toward the terrace, away from the tents and trees in the Constitution Hill area.

"Quick!" Taylor looked along the corridor, the way they had come. "This way!"

"You buggered it!" Slicker wheeled around. His face was savage and white, a sorry advertisement for the bottled suntan. "Your chat about timing! Timing and routes! Planning! You buggered it!"

Taylor's hands circled Slicker's throat and squeezed.

"It's all right," Taylor whispered. "You're staff, and it's all right. You're leaving by the top gate, at Hyde Park Corner, no one's going to bother you, and when you're there, you take that jacket off. Your sweetheart's waiting. In a black Jag."

He released his hands. Slicker started to choke. Taylor picked up the cases and forced them into Slicker's arms.

"It is all right," he whispered, monosyllabic, savage as Slicker.

He flattened his hand against Slicker's back and gave him a starting shove. They ran back along the corridor. Slicker jerked his head up and down, gasping, working to recover his breath. The lobby remained deserted. Outside in place of music a voice was crackling incomprehensibly through loudspeakers. Ignoring the second corridor,

Taylor tried the door beyond the stairs. It opened onto rain and a view of grass.

". . . to the terrace please. You will best help the police by please staying away from the north side of the garden. Please stay clear of the north side of the garden. Thank you."

Twenty yards to the left was the corner of the terrace. Then the lawn, tents, thinning guests, and distantly through the rain, the lake and an outline of trees. From Constitution Hill sounded a renewed *pam-pom* of ambulance or squad car. From the same direction came and went the greatest concentration of people: officialdom and the merely curious, milling beneath the trees and in and out of the gaps in the herbaceous borders. One matron was treading through the border, skirts delicately hoisted above the soil and flowers. Taylor could see no royalty. He stripped the mustache from his lip.

"I'll give you five seconds' start. You're staff. Walk like staff. Get going."

Slicker walked into the rain. Taylor turned his head, glancing over his shoulder into the empty lobby. He touched the knot of his gray silk tie, straightened the topper on his head. He was a guest again. He was Charles Taylor, OBE, property developer and philanthropist. Slicker was walking purposefully past the corner of the terrace, into the groups of guests.

Taylor put a hand in his trousers pocket and touched the swaddled brooch. He watched Slicker very slightly changing course, veering ten degrees to avoid a Beefeater and a uniformed copper disputing together. The two policemen shepherding guests were gone from sight, probably closer to the front wall of the terrace. If a copper recognizes him, thought Taylor. He left the thought suspended. No copper would recognize Slicker. The bomb was the sensation, as planned. They'd be watching for bombers. Not for trivial Slicker, one wanted forgotten man among the hundred or more on the Yard's wanted list.

The rain was frail but steady. Lighting a cigarette, Taylor strode across the lawn. To a limited but British extent the show, he noted, went on. In spite of loudspeaker requests and shepherding police there was an absence of flap. Several robes and saris were departing hastily up the terrace steps and into the Bow Room, but many score of frocks and tails were in the tea tents, sheltering from the rain, surmising, considering bombs and the Irish, and taking the tea for which they had been invited. He'd join them only if he could not otherwise, elsewhere, establish his presence. Now was alibi time. He was ready to leave, tealess, the moment he knew he had been recognized, Charles Taylor, here on the lawn where he'd been for the past ninety minutes.

In defiance of loudspeakers he gravitated toward herbaceous borders and the wall dividing the palace from Constitution Hill. If he could find Lord Moreton, exchange with him a brief unforgettable word.

The attempted police cordon was ramshackle for want of police, though to Taylor's watching eyes their numbers were increasing minute by minute. He slipped through the cordon behind a perfumed debutante and her escort and into long grass between trees.

". . . bloody madmen," a top-hatted aristocrat was saying, "maniacs, I'd truly shoot the lot of 'em, line 'em up. . . ."

There was a smell of burning and on all sides talk and bustle. Here at the wall the cordon was unorganized but owing to sheer weight of numbers impenetrable. Police uniforms, frocks, top hats darkening in the rain, occasional gilt and knee breeches.

"Please keep moving, sir, there's nothing to see," a

constable told him, and Taylor moved on, parallel with the wall.

He trod over trampled nettles and stopped where in place of eight feet of brick wall there yawned a hole big enough for a gate. Above the hole was a contorted hump of iron spikes. Such was the crush of people that over their heads, beyond the hole, Taylor could see only the shattered top of a lamppost and the white roof of an ambulance on the road. Even as he craned for a better view the ambulance accelerated away.

Pam-pom pam-pom pam-pom.

"Keep clear, sir, would you please? It's not making our job any easier. There's tea on the lawn."

This one was a superintendent with a crown on his epaulettes and trimmed gray sideburns below the peaked cap. He carried a two-way radio.

"More from the IRA?" Taylor said, craning.

"Your guess is as good as mine."

"No one hurt, was there?"

"Only the driver."

"Badly?"

"Badly enough. They're still looking for the pieces. Now, sir, if you'd just pass through to the lawn."

Over the top hats, floral hats, police helmets, and firemen's helmets, toward the farther side of Constitution Hill, a group of police with notebooks and tape measures started to walk down the road. Their departure exposed to Taylor's gaze the wreckage of a Westminster Council van, upturned and smoldering. He turned away. He found himself treading like the delicate matron through the wet soil and flowers of the herbaceous border.

It's going to be all right, he told himself mechanically. It's time to go. I'll go the way I came, through the palace.

Several household staff were running from the garden gate at the north end of the terrace. A lone policeman was running toward him, and then past. Two more policemen were running toward the terrace. Something's up, Taylor thought. He was trembling and hot as if from a fever.

"Charlie?"

Poole was approaching across the grass, beckoning.

thirty-one

Taylor chose not to hear or see. He increased his stride. Don't run, he warned himself. It's all right.

If Poole wanted to talk, might he reasonably reply in sign language? Because there was bile in his throat, and if he opened his mouth, he would be sick on the royal lawn. A mark against him in the knighthood stakes.

Poole had increased his stride too.

"Where've you been, Charlie?"

"I don't have to talk to you."

But he had to stop walking, and he had to look up to meet Poole's eyes because the policeman stood like a pillar in front of him.

"Suit yourself, but for the record I'm going to caution you that anything you say may be used in evidence."

"For the record you're going to be sorry."

"Where've you been?"

"Eating strawberries and cream, copper, with a few thousand witnesses to it."

"Your few thousand witnesses are going to have to perjure themselves because there've been no strawberries and cream at these parties for years, and there are none today. When did you last see Slicker?"

A car backfired, if it was a car. Two very young constables who had been running toward the palace stopped and looked around. Poole's stare left Taylor and directed itself past him toward the lake and trees. He looked at the constables and pointed at them.

"You two, over here!"

The constables hesitated. They were too new and rosy to be able to identify behind the camouflage of morning suit a detective chief inspector.

"Taylor, I'm arresting you—"

Poole turned back to Taylor, but Taylor was gone, sidestepping a lordship holding an opened umbrella and sprinting across the grass.

"Taylor!"

For the guests the garden party would be one for detailed description in diaries and telephone calls and at future dinner tables. There had been a bomb. There were mobs of police. Now one of their own, a guest, and not an especially youthful guest, was racing like a lunatic through the rain. His top hat had left his head and was bouncing over the lawn. Before the larger, sandy-haired guest had got into his stride, or the sundry bobbies who were also starting to give chase, the guest had skirted the lake and was lost in the trees.

Coughing and sobbing, Taylor lurched between chestnuts and sycamores. The light was gloomy, and he seemed to be alone. But almost immediately he was out of the trees and on a path, dashing past tennis courts and a huddle of guests who scrambled aside to let him pass. He ran off the path, back into the trees, struggling to force his wash leather hand down into the trousers pocket. To succeed in reaching the gems, he had to slow to a walk, then to halt. But he grasped the swathed Cullinan with his fingertips and plucked it out and the pocket lining with it. He glanced around before unraveling the brooch from the handkerchief and flinging it: a glinting arc between the trees and invisibly into undergrowth where it would be found, sooner or later, but not in his pocket.

Arrest me now, copper, wept his mind, and try to make it stick.

He ran hard through long grass, patting his pockets in quest of the half-moon glasses. They too would have to go.

And the mustache, which pocket was the mustache in?

He was on the path again, sprinting on failing, watery legs. A second backfire scarcely registered in his mind, which was shocked and self-pitying. A third backfire, and a fourth, rowdier than before. A police whistle shrilled and was echoed by another.

In front, the open gates out to the north end of Constitution Hill and Hyde Park Corner were alive with tails, frocks and passersby. But not, so far as Taylor could see, with coppers, and with not one person looking his way. He did not reason why. He was weeping and beyond reasoning. He barged through the throng at the gates, and looking the way they were looking he saw the reason why.

Across the road, on the treelined walk bordering Green Park, Slicker in his footman's red jacket stood with his back to a tree, pointing a gun. He had acquired an audience, not only here at the gate but under the lampposts of Constitution Hill and on the grass in the park. A schoolboy in a cap had found a vantage point on the lawn below Constitution Arch. There were policemen dodging between the muddled taxis and buses and cars which labored to negotiate Hyde Park Corner but which at several points had come to a stop, five and six abreast. Taylor, puzzled, wondered what his second-in-command had done with the two attaché cases. Yet more puzzling was the smile on Slicker's face. It seemed to be a smile. Slicker was holding the gun in both hands, arms outstretched, smiling as he fired it.

From somewhere banged an answering backfire. Taylor's wet eyes had to search before they spotted two plainclothes rozzers with guns crouching beside parked cars at the curb. A third policeman, kneeling, resting his pistol hand on his forearm as he fired, wore uniform and a tidy, nautical beard. Slicker, he saw, had sat down and was leaning crookedly against the tree. Matching red flowed from his head and over the footman's jacket.

No one, reflected Taylor, not Mr. Big himself in his green drawing room, could have devised a happier diversion. He ran across Grosvenor Place and into Halkin Street. A black Jaguar E V-12 stood at the curb. He heard a tedious police whistle but no backfiring.

The door was unlocked, the key in the ignition. The gears grated, and Taylor grated them persistently, almost willfully, as he drove out of Halkin Street and through Belgrave Square. Through Victoria, heading for Vauxhall Bridge. He found the windshield wipers. One-handed, he manipulated a cigarette out of his tails pocket.

Stopping at stoplights, indicating left and right, he drove like a candidate for the driving test. But he had become unaccustomed to driving and to London routes, and discovering himself in a wrong lane, he was swept away from Vauxhall Bridge before he could reach it and along the embankment. Eventually he was circling Parliament Square and crossing the river by Westminster Bridge. But again he was in a wrong lane, borne along in the gehenna of rush-hour traffic toward the Elephant and Castle.

The fever which caused him to sweat and shake and refused to subside was shock, he supposed. He concentrated on road directions, gears, and the clanging traffic, striking south through the brick deserts of Kennington and Camberwell, seeking signposts to the A23, Redhill and Brighton, and finding them. Redhill, where Ronnie Biggs came from, long ago, he recalled.

The traffic grew less horrifying; the gears functioned more smoothly. He passed an accident, broken glass and flashing blue lights, and felt pity. At Croydon he turned left off the A23. Twenty minutes, half an hour, he'd be through Biggin Hill.

He preferred not to think. Later perhaps. One day. The only words intruding upon thoughtlessness were "It'll be all right." He knew it would not be all right ever again. Never, ever. That was not to be thought about.

Past Biggin Hill the black Jaguar and Taylor were alone in high countryside. The secondary road became a tertiary road of muddy craters and puddles.

If I started to think, he thought, I'd only worry. Worry and questions. Is this the road? Will Robb have cigarettes?

And anyway it was the road because there in the field was the Beechcraft turboprop or whatever Robb had said it was going to be, its nose elevated, tailfin only yards from a bedraggled hedge. Taylor switched off the engine and climbed from the car. Would Robb have aspirin or codeine? What destination would he give him? Brazil? The Zambezi? A man in a flying jacket stood watching him from under the near wing, sheltering from the drizzle. Taylor walked, ran, and walked across the field.

"Didn't expect to see you," Robb said. "Where've you come from? A wedding?"

"Come on, please, let's get off," said Taylor.

Robb had no aspirin, and he had given up smoking. Taylor sat buckled into the first seat behind the pilot's, shivering and weeping, as the Beechcraft roared through the green field and lifted up into the sky.